We didn't know that eighteen months of fighting lay ahead . . . the last month being the worst.

The Trail Through Hell

A Novel of the Army's Pacific Victory

J. Scott Payne

Published in The United States of America
By Argon Press

This is a work of fiction. Other than obvious historical characters and events, the names, characters and most incidents described herein are products of the author's imagination. Any resemblance to actual persons living or dead, events or locales is purely coincidental.

Cover design by
Deanna Compton

Published in the United States of America by Argon Press.
ISBN: 978-1-944815-40-0

Library of Congress Control Number:
2018907354

Other books by the Author –

The Green Hell
A Novel of the Army's Pacific war

Brought To Battle
A Novel of World War II

A Corporal No More
A Novel of the Civil War

One, Two, Three Strikes You're Dead
A Brad Powers Mystery

Dedication

To my nephews Chris and Matt, Army sergeants and the fifth generation of our family to serve in the military. With earnest prayer for the safety and happy return of all American warriors.

Chapter 1
VJ Day -- August 15, 1945

Nothing was going right and I was grinding my teeth. Snipers wounded two of my men and killed a third. Rain and fog frustrated me in trying to see whether movements in the hills above us might presage another attack.

So when the Pfc. said, "Hey, guess what, Sarge?" I snapped at him.

"Pipe down, dammit!"

Voice rising, he said, "For Christ's sake, Sarge! The war's over!"

"Bullshit!"

He held out his walkie-talkie to me. "Listen to it for yourself, Sarge! Headquarters just said Japan surrendered. We're to cease offensive action. The war's over."

I pointed up toward the stony crags and razorback ridges. "Yeah? Did anybody bother to tell those bastards shooting at us?"

"Jeeze, Sarge, don't yell at *me*! I'm only telling you what …"

Somebody behind us yelled, "*Down*!"

As I dived into the muddy slop at the bottom of my foxhole, the faint metallic chatter from the walkie-talkie continued. Four mortar shells exploded around us. The Pfc. screamed. Four more mortar rounds silenced him. Four more landed and then I lost count.

By the time it ended, pieces of the Pfc. and his walkie-talkie were strewn all over me and two other guys.

Maybe Japan had surrendered.

But World War II sure as hell didn't seem to be over.

# # #

I'm Jim Mays, U.S. Army master sergeant and the temporary reconnaissance leader for the 32nd Infantry Division. Our boss is a mustang captain, Dan Irish. Right now Fourth General Hospital is sifting him for Japanese shrapnel and the troop is down to little more than a squad, so that's why I'm leading

Yeah, I'm just a kid, age twenty-three. But I know this business. I've got two of my own Purple Hearts and I've been in this stinking Southwest Pacific meat grinder thirty-three months with the captain and my buddy, Sergeant Charlie Riegle – plus a lot of other guys who are dead or also in the hospital.

They should call us First Division instead of the 32nd.

See, we were the first National Guard division that Congress activated for World War II. In fact, they activated us before Pearl Harbor. We also were the first division the War Department sent overseas.

And we were the first division -- courtesy of His Nibs, General Douglas MacArthur -- to attack the ground forces of an Axis power, Japan. For my money, the Japs are the toughest, meanest warriors on earth. And we attacked them in New Guinea, the nastiest real estate on earth.

There's more.

Headquarters claims we're first among all American infantry divisions – including Europe where the war really *is* over -- in the number of days spent in actual combat, six hundred and seventy some. I forget. We also were the first troops the Army Air Corps flew to a combat zone.

But though Japan supposedly surrendered today, we're still – how do they put it? – mopping up.

That means clawing uphill against General Yamashita's Fourteenth Area Army. The Japs still have plenty of ammo. That *rat-tat-tat* and *boom, whomp, thud*? They're still pouring it to us.

Weekend passes to Paris? Forget it. The Southwest Pacific Theater of Operations has no Paris. If one of the men persuades a Jap to surrender he gets a three-day pass, a break from combat. That's it.

# # #

With the mortar barrage ended, I crawled from my foxhole and started flicking bloody chunks of Pfc. off my muddy fatigues. I didn't know his name so I hoped to be able to find his dog tags. As I searched, I wondered if we might end up being The Last, the last division to go home … if any of us survives.

Our adversary looking down on us in Luzon's Cagayan Valley is Tomoyuki Yamashita, probably Japan's most adept general. (By the way, you pronounce it *Yah-MAHSH-da* not *Yah-muh-SHEETA*. I know. Before Pearl Harbor I took conversational Japanese as part of my major in East Asian studies at Washington University.)

The Japs call him The Tiger of Malaya, honoring his 1942 conquest of British Singapore. Now in August of '45 we just call him The Gopher of Luzon.

See, he and his troops burrowed deep into the stony ridges, jungle flanks and grassy ravines of the Philippines' Caraballo Mountains. They're making their last stand. And the 32nd couldn't sustain its attack against them without using the Villa Verde Trail, a tortuous, serpentine cart path with dozens of hairpin turns featuring overhanging ridges and other excellent sites for Jap machine guns.

Every bullet we fired had to travel The Trail to the front. Every wounded man had to be carried back down it.

At first glance, the Caraballos don't look like real mountains. Compared to the snow-capped Cascades near my home in Washington, or, say, the Colorado Rockies, they're mere foothills.

Believe me, though, they're damned mountainous when you're fighting your way up arroyos and boulder-strewn slopes. Our troops face plunging fire from machine guns and mortars in caves and bunkers above us, many interconnected by tunnels. Manning them are tough little devils willing to die for Emperor Hirohito.

I don't care what headquarters said about Japan surrendering. Maybe one in a hundred Jap soldiers surrenders. The rest apparently prefer death. And it doesn't help when half your own men keep falling on their faces with malaria relapses.

We were issued quinine tablets in November 1942. That's when I was a corporal in the first patrol toward Buna on New Guinea's north coast. But we had to live and fight in tropical downpours and wade up in swamps, so those tablets dissolved in our pockets.

That's why, almost like clockwork, lots of us still go down with malaria attacks every three weeks or so. Now they give us Atabrine, a synthetic for quinine. It mellows malaria's 105-degree fevers, but also causes jaundice, giving our tropic tans their yellowish tint.

Some of our dopey draftees refused to take Atabrine because Tokyo Rose giggled over the radio that it causes impotence. One medical unit tried countering Rose's propaganda. They set up two posts topped with grinning skulls – real ones. And between the posts they hung a big sign with bold-face lettering: *They Didn't Take Their Atabrine*.

Just for the record, I think I might have killed the first Jap, a Nambu gunner, in the opening of our three-month campaign to capture Buna, ten miserable square miles of stinking New Guinea swamp, rotting, steamy jungle, coconut plantation and hundreds of sturdy Jap bunkers.

I was flat lucky. None of us knew much about combat. And MacArthur threw us into the swamps without ten seconds of jungle training. For six solid weeks he couldn't let us have our own artillery, either. He just gave orders: Capture Buna! Regardless of cost! Now!

I'm quoting him with fine accuracy.

Well, Japs and New Guinea ate up most of the 32nd Division.

But now, after damned near three years of the most realistic training – combat itself -- we know exactly what we're doing and we're damned good at it. The boys flatten themselves below the line of fire – butts down, feet flat. They recognize any slight fold in the earth as Blessed Cover.

Now we have artillery, lots of it, plus on-call support from the Air Corps. Of course, even half-ton bombs and 155 howitzer shells don't do much to people deep inside bunkers or tunnels.

So we either have to shoot them, immolate them with flame-throwers, blast them out with explosives or seal off their cave entrances with bulldozers. Every step is a cast-iron bitch when you're negotiating a hair-pin turn along a ridge that features a drop-off on your left and a cliff above your right.

The Japs still are very, very tough. They won't surrender so we have to kill them. A process in which they wound, maim or kill a hell of a lot of us.

So most of our companies are down to platoon size.

Reinforcements? Forget it.

The Army is running on Empty.

Before I get on with this story, I'll take you back to early 1943 in Australia where they hospitalized so many of us.

Our wounds were from Japanese lead or scrap iron or the *Anopholese latens* mosquito, or all three, plus hookworm, Blackwater fever, scrub typhus and dengue fever.

And nightmares. Sometimes the horrors come on even when you're wide awake in broad daylight having a beer or coffee.

Chapter 2
Thirty-one months earlier -- February 1943

As I limped beside a weathered picket fence on a breezy Melbourne morning, rusty gate hinges gave a squeal. A tow-headed little Aussie girl was opening the gate to me.

She was crying and begging for help. “Can you reach my kitty, please? Look how she climbed way up in this tree and now she won’t come down! Can’t you see her up there?”

I grinned doubtfully. “Well, Missy, I don’t know, but I’ll see what I can do.”

“Oh, thanks heaps. You’re a sergeant, aren’t you?”

“Yep, I sure am.” I was in no shape to climb trees. But this particular tree, a half-grown acacia, actually was little more than a twelve-foot shrub. The kitten was wobbling on a narrow limb half an arm’s length higher than my overseas cap.

“She wants to come down ever so much,” the girl said. “She really does, but I think she’s frightened.”

“I bet you’re right.” Hooking my cane over one low branch, I quickly grabbed another to keep my balance and gingerly side-stepped, shouldering my way in among the limbs. “So, Miss, what’s your kitten’s name?”

“We named her Silky because she’s so soft. Auntie said we should have named her Velvet but I think she’s more smooth like silk.” The critter was tuxedo black with big yellow eyes and a heart-shaped white blaze on her chest. Reaching for the kitty required a stretch which hurt my half-healed left ribs.

“Come here, Silky. Come on, now. Don’t play hard to get.” She gave a squeaky little meow when I grabbed the scruff of her neck.

“Gotcha!”

Once I clutched her football-like to my chest, the kitten started purring. As I eased out from the shrub, she batted at the bars dangling from my expert marksman badge.

I fumbled for the cane and succeeded in dropping both it and my cap. Balancing awkwardly, I asked “Young lady, what is your name, please?”

“I’m Judith Stone.”

“And Judy, how old are you?”

"It's Judith, not Judy. And I'm eight years old."

"I'm sorry, Judith. I'll never call you Judy again. Now here's the deal. I'll give Silky to you if you would be so kind as to rescue my cane and hat for me."

"Ripper!" she said with a big grin. "And, please sir, what's your name?"

"I'm Jim Mays." I handed her the kitten.

"Pleased to meet you, I'm sure."

As she handed cap and cane to me, I said "It's entirely my pleasure." And it was. After hospital surroundings with lots of injured men, not to mention months in New Guinea's bloody filth and mire, she was a visual ice cream sundae and a fleeting sense of home.

She beckoned me to come up the stoop into the little brick bungalow. "Won't you come in to tea? Auntie's just this minute steeping the tea." She leaned toward me and lowered her voice to impart some confidential information. "Auntie lets me have tea, as long as I pour lots of milk in it."

"Oh, that's nice. Well, I'd love to have tea, Judith. But perhaps it would be a good idea for you to ask Auntie first. I'll just wait out here and rest my sore leg."

"Oh, you are wounded, aren't you?"

"Yeah, just a little bit."

This meeting occurred because the docs wanted me to walk. The surgeon who removed the shrapnel from my left thigh – a Christmas morning present from the Sons of Nippon -- told me he had to dig deep, deeper than he wanted. Later, on one of his rounds, he joked, "Sergeant, I think I can show your leg as proof that I got my medical degree from the Pennsylvania School of Mines."

I pretended to chuckle but didn't find it funny. The wound still hurt most of the time and my leg was weak. And, frankly, that was fine with me. I was in no rush to resume swamp-diving in some stinking jungle.

"I want you to start walking a bit three times each day," the doc said. "At first, walking will give you some grief, but you need to get started."

So, it was on my fifth day afoot that I rescued Silky. I had limped some five blocks from Fourth General Hospital and my left thigh was about to go on strike.

Carefully cuddling Silky, Judith popped up the steps and went indoors. As she disappeared inside I heard her call, “Auntie, there’s a nice Yank soldier outside!”

I pictured a prim little old lady like Auntie Em in *The Wizard of Oz*, mouth set in rigid disapproval. Judith was every bit as cute as Judy Garland so she made a pretty good Dorothy.

Musing, though, that Silky made a pretty poor Toto, I leaned against the fence to give my leg a break.

With a wimpy crack a whole section of the fence collapsed. It spilled pickets, cross pieces, posts and yours truly onto the curbing. I gave a good loud yelp of surprise and pain.

Chapter 3
Meeting The Natives

A door banged open and a second later Judith, still holding Silky, and Auntie leaned over me. Auntie, fingers to her mouth said, “Oh, my God, Yank, are you all right?”

I didn’t answer because I was staring. This was no wrinkled Auntie Em from some Kansas hog farm. She looked perhaps twenty and had gorgeous wide-set green eyes.

“Wow. I think I just fell into the Emerald City.”

She frowned. “What?” Maybe she thought I was a Section Eight. She turned, “Judith, run next door and get Mr. Eccles.”

As Judith took off I said, “Oh, please don’t bother. I’m fine -- just startled.” Because of the malaria onset I was shaky and sweaty, but I rolled over and got onto my knees. Using my cane, it took two tries to get back to my feet. I couldn’t help noticing that Auntie’s figure rated an emphatic *va va vooom.*

Looking at the ruins of the fence, I said, “I’m very, very sorry, Ma’am. It looks like I’ve destroyed your fence.”

“Fiddlesticks!” She shook her auburn head. “Rotten old thing.”

A deep voice behind me rumbled. “Right! Should have replaced it long ago, but with war austerity all the lumber is going to you Yanks right now.” I turned to see a mountain with a grim leathery face below a military haircut. Judith, dwarfed beside him, was holding his shovel-sized right hand. His left arm ended at the elbow. Giving me a look filled with suspicion, he asked the young lady, “Are you all right?”

“No worries, Mr. Eccles,” she said. “I was just afraid this Yank was hurt when the fence fell.”

On seeing my cane he seemed to relax. “Stopped one did you?” He glanced at his stump. “Got mine as a section leader in Palestine. Call me Herb.”

“I’m Jim. Section leader? So, a sergeant?”

“Right.”

“Just look how the fence seemed to crumble,” Auntie said. “Splinters and dust all over his uniform.”

I began brushing at my khaki shirt. “Yeah,” I said. “Dust to dust.”

She gasped, turned away and stifled a sob. Her head bowed and she brought her hands to her eyes. Herb's craggy face tightened in a dark frown. It suddenly hit me that she probably had lost an Aussie soldier recently.

Trying to make amends, I said, "Whoa! My lord, Ma'am, I'm sorry. Beg pardon. Should have kept my stupid yap shut." I reached to pat her shoulder, but with Herb looming behind me, I thought better of it. Pulling out my handkerchief, I touched it to the side of her arm.

She glanced, took it with a shaky nod, and applied it to her tears. Herb relaxed again, giving Judith a quick reassuring grin.

Soon, Auntie faced me, eyes and nose red but trying to smile with a wide mouth made for smiling. Still dabbing at her eyes, "No matter." She brushed at the dust and splinters along my left side.

"Yow!" I flinched away. "Easy there. Please, Ma'am, don't worry about the uniform."

With a sniff and wistful chuckle she said, "Oh, fancy that. Now I've gone and hurt you." She took a deep breath, drew herself up, wiped away a last tear and gave a real smile. "And it's Suzanne, not 'ma'am'."

Herb snorted "G'die" and turned back toward his house.

Watching him, I said, "Wow, I take it Herb is some kind of a guardian. Very impressive man."

"Yes, he and his wife have been wonderful to us. He lost his arm five years ago and he's a pensioner now."

Suzanne surprised me, glancing at my left leg and saying, "Damn it all, you're bleeding right through your daks."

"My what?"

"Aussie for 'trousers.' The left leg. Above the knee. You must have torn your sutures. Judith! Please run back and fetch Mr. Eccles again. We need him to drive the sergeant to hospital."

The "damn" surprised me, as did her matter-of-fact remarks. Not only was she no Auntie Em, but she also seemed tough; no squirms about a little blood – it was only some seepage -- meanwhile bracing up in the wake of somebody's death.

It took some argument, but I persuaded her to just call Fourth General for an ambulance. I said I could just wait outside. "I've done enough damage without messing up your sitting room or having your neighbor waste any of his gallon-a-week gas ration."

She went indoors and called the hospital. I could hear her describe the problem, and then sounding angry. She came back outdoors spitting mad. “They said they’d pick you up in an hour or so.”

“Christ, I can walk back there in fifteen minutes.”

“Oh, you Yanks! Well, sergeant … you are a sergeant, aren’t you? Right! Since you rescued our cat and they’re in no bloody rush, won’t you please come in for tea? We welcome you blokes, after all.”

The steps to the door had no railing, so I wasn’t sure I could climb them. “Thank you, Miss Suzanne, but I don’t want to get bloodstains on your chairs or carpet.”

Another faint grin. “No worries. No carpet or rugs. The floor’s wood and you can sit in the rocker. It’s rattan. We need some company and you need the rest before you do another stroll. Here, I’ll help you up the steps. Right, Judith! Hold the door open but mind you don’t let the cat loose again.”

Suzanne was a tall girl, coming to my eye level, and quite strong. My weight, a hundred ninety when I enlisted, was almost back up to a hundred sixty-five. But she had no difficulty giving me a boost up each of three concrete steps.

Judith opened the door for us, grinned and told her aunt, “His name is Jim.”

I introduced myself and learned she was Suzanne Bennett.

Chapter 4
The Walking Wounded

The ambulance never showed up, so we chatted, sipping tea from flowered china cups and nibbling triangular biscuit-like things they called scones.

As Suzanne poured tea, Judith asked how I liked Australia.

"Oh, it's much like home except that in the Pacific Northwest it rains a lot more. Annnnnd, let's see, in my town we have only two kangaroos which we keep in a zoo. Annnnd, what else? Oh yes! In the States we drive on the wrong side of the street."

That produced a chuckle from Suzanne. "Most Yanks say it the other way 'round – that *we* drive on the wrong side."

I pretended exasperation with my countrymen. "I know. I know. I've tried to help those dimwits understand. I explained that things work in reverse in the Southern Hemisphere – winter is summer, summer is winter, and the cars here have steering wheels on the right. But they just can't seem to grasp it."

They laughed politely and then looked at each other in ill-concealed astonishment when I refused sugar for my tea.

I loathe tea. It makes my teeth feel as if fur is sprouting on them. But knowing sugar was rationed I felt I should pretend to enjoy it without putting a strain on their ration coupons.

Judith took Silky to her room as Suzanne poured our second cup. I noticed one of her palms was bandaged as were three fingers of the other hand.

Catching my glance, she apologized. "I bend out and cut sheet metal at a machine shop – nacelles for fighter aircraft. And the edges are often quite sharp." She explained that Fifth Air Force was contracting with Australian companies to help keep tired fighter planes and worn bombers flying against the Japanese.

"At any rate, that *was* my job."

"I take it you've found other work, then?"

She stiffened. "Not for now."

I tried to break up the long awkward pause by saying that before the war I studied modern Asian history.

"Did that include Japan?"

When I nodded, she gave me a puzzled look. "I love Japanese art . . . their silk screens, their fans, their kimonos. But it astounds me how a people that creates such delicate beauty can be so beastly." Suddenly she was weeping. "Sorry," she said, through her tears.

"No need to apologize. I apologize for asking. Who was he?"

She took a deep breath, "Another Jim … James Burnsley. He was my fiancé. He flew Airacobras. He had two Zeroes to his credit. But then he plowed in at one of the Port Moresby airdromes. His squadron commander wrote that his aircraft was decrepit to begin with and was all shot up. He could have parachuted out, but he said Jim was trying to save the old crate."

I shook my head solemnly. "Damn! Very, very sorry to hear it."

She said that after her fiancé's death, work at the shop became a nightmare. "I'd push a piece of sheet steel into the press and suddenly see it all twisted and blackened. I had to leave it. I must do something to help. I will. We all must do our part … but not that again. Never that."

"Right," I said, mulling over my own bitter memory of helplessly watching Tony Popalovski cough out his life's blood two months ago. "I think I know a bit about how you feel."

"Yes, I'm sure you do. It's all so sickening and tragic."

We were silent for a moment. As I went to sip the last of my tea, I suddenly found it difficult to hold the cup. My hands were shaking and the cup rattled in its saucer as put it on the table.

"Sorry. I think I'm getting a relapse." I thanked her for tea and said I'd better get back.

"Jim, I don't think you're in any condition to walk right now. Here…" She helped me out of the rocker. "Just kip on the couch for a bit before you collapse."

When I awakened, I felt better but was surprised to find it dark outside. "Thank you Suzanne. Now I think I can make it back."

She called for Judith. "We'll walk to hospital with you, Jim, just in case. It can be a bit dicey in the blackout." We walked slowly. Suzanne held my left arm which benefitted my morale a lot more than my sore ribs.

Like the city, the hospital was darkened, all blinds being pulled. Suzanne asked. "Jim, if the nearest Japs are in New Guinea, why do we have black-outs a continent away here in Melbourne?"

"Just because I'm a soldier doesn't mean I understand the military mind."

"I think it's bloody drongo," she said.

"Translate, please."

Judith said, "She means 'stupid'."

"Agreed."

As we chatted I learned Suzanne wasn't actually Judith's aunt, but a close friend of her mother, a war widow and a nurse. Judith was living with Suzanne while Judith's mother worked temporarily in a hospital on New Guinea.

Suzanne sighed, "It's beginning to seem more and more permanent. The need is so great, you see. Of course Judith misses her mother terribly, don't you, dear?"

Suzanne and Judith called our destination RMH, for Royal Melbourne Hospital. But under Lend-Lease it was the U.S. Army Fourth General Hospital, treating Yank and Aussie wounded.

We stopped at the main entrance, the hospital's ten stories and central tower seeming to lean out over us.

"I'd invite you ladies in for a Coke," I said, "but this time of night, the recreation center can be a bit raucous."

"It's just as well," Suzanne said. "You should get to your bed and we should get back to Silky. Another time perhaps?"

"Absolutely. I can teach you dominos. Or, if you're in for some real wild diversion, USO gave us some of jigsaw puzzles with 300 tiny pieces. They'll to drive you straight to the funny farm."

"The what?"

"The loony bin."

"Again?"

I chuckled. "An asylum for the insane."

Suzanne smiled. "I think chatting is quite enough. Toodles, Yank."

"G'night, you Aussies. And thank you again."

I stayed leaning against the door watching them walk into the darkness.

Suzanne turned back.

We both waved.

Chapter 5
Back In The Army

As I walked into the lobby, my mood soured because Sergeant Gerald Gergen was peering at me beady-eyed over the top of a *Life Magazine*. A slob who loves to needle, hHe lowered the magazine and gave me his toothy grin.

"Hey, Mays, that looks like real nice gash you're screwing there. She got a sister?" He gave a delighted chuckle, indicating my face probably turned beet red.

"No. No sister. But if she had one, I'd damn well warn her away from you."

He tilted his head back and gave a big belly laugh. "Man, I just seem to rub you the wrong way, don't I?"

"Nope. You rub everybody the wrong way."

He laughed again. "Well, that's me. I just love to josh with folks. Nothin' wrong in that, now is there? Now looky here . . . when they discharge you to go back and fight the Japs, how about you introduce me to that lady?"

"Gergen, I wouldn't introduce you to a sick dog. Besides, you'll be fighting, too."

"Naaaah, not hardly. I've got myself assigned to that new officer candidate program in Brisbane. I'll wind up a second lieutenant in some rear echelon."

"I'd rather have you with us in line. The Japs need targets."

He tensed, but laughed again. "Awwww, Mays, that's plumb un-neighborly. Now why not introduce me to that girl?"

"You really want to know why? Other than the fact that you always disappear when shooting starts?"

Eyes suddenly like stones he said, "Yeah. Why?"

"Her life already is difficult enough without contamination by you."

He gave me a leer. "Well, shit, maybe after you've left I'll just introduce myself to her."

"You might want to be careful," I said. "She's got a guardian. He's about 6-5 and looks real short-tempered. You already showed you didn't have the guts to face Japs, so you sure as hell wouldn't have the sand to face Mr. Eccles."

Gergen snarled, "You might want to watch your mouth, boy."

"No," I replied, "with you around I think the best bet would be to watch my back."

He jumped up and said, "Fuck you, Mays," slapped the magazine down on his chair and started to leave.

"Hey, don't go away mad! And don't forget General Gill is visiting us tomorrow. As an officer-to-be, you'll want to be there to kiss his ass.

# # #

Ah, yes. Generals. Someday, if you have absolutely nothing at all to do, take a look at the mug shots of army generals.

From Patton to Pershing and Sherman to Winfield Scott, their portraits give the impression that the photographers insulted them so that they'd stare daggers at the camera.

Something of the sort probably went for the artists who painted Wellington and Napoleon, too. They just look foul-tempered.

I don't know, maybe it's the nature of a general's work. Not only do they have dozens of plates in the air at once plus all that lust for another star, but they also from time to time must order people into battle, therefore knowing some of their men will wind up dead or, worse, maimed.

At first I thought generals were indifferent about their dead and wounded.

But one nasty day in New Guinea I overheard General Eichelberger rap out a flinty "no" when a surgeon pleaded for him to visit the wounded in a field hospital. But I caught sight of the general minutes later when he thought he was alone. He was leaning against a tree and his shoulders were shaking with sobs.

Long after the Buna campaign he was reported as saying that generals crack up if they don't ration their emotions.

So when generals pose for photos, maybe it's standard operating procedure to just look mean as a snake. Except for General MacArthur. He always tilts his face upward with the serene look of communing with all the other Gods.

But I did spend some time with a definite departure from the norm, Bill Gill – sorry, Major General William H. Gill, the new commander of the 32nd Infantry Division.

When I first saw him, his face looked frozen in standard government-issue Mean. But somehow he couldn't quite pull off that bad-assed look. Sure, he kept his thin lips compressed and, if necessary, he could give an Olympic Class ass-chewing. Even so, he always seemed to be trying to stifle a smile. His mouth was puckered in kind of twist … one corner turned down, the other persisting in turning slightly upward.

He had that quirky grin when he dropped in at Fourth General to visit some of the division's wounded. He was en route to Camp Cable up near Brisbane where he'd officially assume command of the Division.

He was very tall, lean and ramrod straight when he marched into the recreation center. About a hundred of us recuperating NCOs were playing cards with half an ear tuned to our Philco radio.

Someone sounded off, "Tennnnn-HUT!" and snapped off the radio. The rest of us grabbed canes and crutches and started to get up.

He barked, "At ease! Just stay seated, men. Worry about bracing after you're returned to duty."

In his Virginia accent, he wanted to know how many of us were there and some wag said, "General, this is most of us from fifth floor of the hospital. Ever'body's present and accounted for except Corporal Mulder. He had kind of an accident." The comment produced laughter from six or eight people.

The rest of us, including General Gill, looked questioningly at the speaker.

Somebody said, "What accident?"

"Oh, I don't think this is the time…"

"Sure it is," the general said. "What's happened to him?"

"Well sir, Charlie went out on pass and got into the sack with one of them angels of the night and she gave him a case of crabs. Well, the jerk was too timid to tell the docs about it. So somebody recommended that he slather some of that 6-22 mosquito repellant around his crotch.

"And he did."

Everybody including the general roared with laughter and were saying things like, "Oh, no! That poor bastard!" When the laughter died to chuckle level, the general said, "Well, I assume the corporal went into the armadillo position. Have they tried morphine?"

After more laughter someone wondered whether the general would award the victim a purple heart. He grinned and shook his head no, explaining that a purple heart is awarded only when enemy action causes the casualty.

Somebody immediately said, “Well, gee, General that's kind of rough isn’t it? Them crabs ain’t exactly allies …” More laughter and which redoubled when another wag suggested the Purple Heart would be superfluous because Mulder now had two bright red balls.

For all of us, major general included, it was as funny as if Bob Hope were doing a stand-up routine. I know I was trying to stop because the laughter hurt my side. And it gave all of us a warm feeling about our new leader.

As we all calmed down, General Gill said, “Well, the main reason I dropped in was that I’d heard morale in the Division was real bad. But I can tell you men are recovering nicely.”

Talk about a wet blanket.

Our laughter died. After three months of swamp assaults to capture Buna, our morale *was* horrible. Many of us not only were wounded, but also were trying to deal with suppurating jungle ulcers that refused to heal. Most of us had malaria and among us were cases of dengue fever and – maybe the worst – scrub typhus, a killer.

None of us wanted any more to do with jungle fighting and swamp patrols. We didn’t want to return to it.

We didn’t even want to remember it .

Chapter 6
Meeting The Skipper

The recreation center was dead quiet after the general left. We felt depressed, but as ever, Army routine took over.

Fourth General Hospital's particular routine was based on the Army policy of keeping the troops busy, even the wounded.

If a Pfc. with an arm or leg wound can sit at a desk, answer a phone and take notes, they put him on the Charge of Quarters roster for his bay. The Army requires recuperating officers to censor the troops' out-going mail. Command also details wounded officers to give security lectures or to teach classes such as land navigation, demolitions, radio procedure or the care, feeding and aiming of 60 mm mortars.

My duty each morning was to inspect the wards and hold roll call on both wings of the fifth floor. I was to see that all ambulatory patients were up by 0630 with their racks made nice and tight and their personal areas cleaned up. If somebody was AWOL it was my duty to turn him in to HQ and the MPs.

As long as casts or arm slings permitted, we all were to wear the uniform of the day – undress khakis. Otherwise, all patients wore GI-issue pajamas, robes and slippers. If you got a pass to go out on the town, your khakis better be starched and pressed and your tie knotted correctly and inserted between the third and fourth shirt buttons. And your shoes better be gleaming.

Fortunately, the command at Fourth General originally were civilian doctors from Cleveland. They were overworked and more concerned with seducing nurses and healing wounded doughboys than with spit and polish. So they took it fairly easy on us so we, in turn, took it fairly easy on the boys. Besides, just about everybody at one time or another kept having malaria relapses. Then the drill was to lie in your sack having weird visions while shivering beneath blankets and afterwards sweating through your sheets.

In fact, 32nd Division's unofficial motto was "Sweatin' it out."

I was one of the lucky few who had regular visitors. Suzanne and Judith came to see me two or three evenings a week and often on Saturdays and Sundays. We usually went out for a stroll and then we'd come back to try some board games. I won't deny Suzanne was very attractive to me, but seeing Judith was wonderful, too. She was an engaging, chatty kid like my sisters back in Seattle.

Dominos bored both ladies, so I introduced them to cribbage. Judith caught on like lightning and regularly beat both of us hands down.

Suzanne, though, turned out to be an ace at checkers. Nearly every game ended with her having five or six kings on my side of the board and all my checkers in her POW cage.

I didn't care about losing because spending time with the two of them kept me from brooding over New Guinea memories. Our games seemed to have a similar benefit for Suzanne and even Judith whose father had died three years earlier in a London air raid.

Both gals began smiling more readily and showing occasional flashes of quick wit. I got the impression Suzanne was fond of me. We certainly talked easily together. Once I asked why she only had one dimple, she said the other would be issued when the war was over and rationing was suspended.

One afternoon Suzanne jumped six of my checkers in one move, entirely clearing my pieces from the board. That coup sent Judith into a giggle fit. "Auntie probably wins so easily because she's a real good chess player."

"What?"

"Didn't you know, Jim? Her dad taught her chess when she was eight. Auntie, you played in some tournaments, didn't you?"

I threw a pretend fit. "What! Man *alive!* All this time you've been sandbagging me?" I gave the table a resounding slap.

They both flinched, making me feel like a dirty dog. "Hey, girls! I don't mean it. I'm just teasing. The joke's on me."

Suzanne gave me a dubious look. I sighed. "Look Suzanne, I can honestly say I'd rather lose to you at checkers than beat anyone else."

The anxiety disappeared and her eyes turned soft. "Maybe I could teach you chess."

"I'll see if I can find a chess set," I said.

"Yes," a voice behind me said, "and I zink you will lose often."

We all looked up in surprise up at a captain, a little guy, standing by our table. I started to get to my feet.

In his thick German accent he said, "No! Please to be seated. Sorry for zis interruption. You are, I believe, Sergeant Mays, yes?"

"That's right, Cap'n. How can I help you?"

"Again," he nodded to Suzanne and Judith, "sorry to interrupt, ladies. I only wanted to ask if Sergeant Mays could meet me tomorrow at headquarters office. Perhaps at 1300 hours?"

"I'll be there, sir. Can you tell me what it's about?"

He smiled. "It's just an idea you may find interesting. Nothing more." He apologized again, snapped a quick little bow to Suzanne and limped away.

"Oh boy," I muttered.

Suzanne frowned. "Jim, what is it?"

"Well, that's Captain Bottcher. He's 32nd Division's genuine hero. He was just another infantry sergeant until he led a squad to break through the Jap defenses at Buna. They stood off attack after attack for days on end. I don't know the details except that everybody ended up wounded while they killed about two hundred Japs. General Eichelberger promoted him straight to captain and I hear he's up for a big decoration."

"Such a short little bloke. Not much taller than Judith. Well, what does he want with you?"

"I have no idea, but I'm not in the market for medals."

She turned her eyes on me. "Bloody right, Jim. Please don't put your number in for something stupid or heroic. Two men in this family already have carked it."

I gently took her hand in both of mine. "Suzanne?" She didn't try to pull away. "You think of me as family?"

She dimpled. "Well, yes of course we do, don't we, Judith?"

"Strewth!" Judith said. "You're our own Yank."

"Wow. Now that gives me something to live for."

"Us too, Jim."

Chapter 7
An Interesting Offer

I marched up to Captain Bottcher's desk, snapped to attention and saluted. "Master Sergeant James Mays reporting, sir."

He closed the file on his desk and thanked me for coming. "We go outside for a walk, yes?"

As he stood up, he grimaced, favoring several wounds of his own. Once we were outdoors, he sauntered instead of striding. And though we were out in public in Class A uniforms, he slouched, often shoving his hands deep into his pockets. Definitely not a parade-ground tin soldier.

"What do you feel about Japs?" he asked.

"That's a tough one, Cap'n."

"Jim, just forget rank. What do you mean?"

"Well, Sir, I've studied a bit of Japanese history and culture. Whatever they do, they work as hard at it as beavers. They're very . . . well, I guess you'd say *directed*. Through the ages their art has been incredible, but they've also raised assassination to an art. They seem to place no value on life and, if Buna's any indication, they don't seem to care about living. As a society, Japan is about as bloody and violent as England and France four hundred years ago. They tried democracy recently but their military buried that."

"So?"

"So, for now I guess we've got no choice but to kill every one of the bastards until they quit -- but I'm afraid they'll never quit. They just don't surrender. You corner one and he fights 'til he's dead, meanwhile taking six or eight of us with him."

"Do you hate Japs?"

"When we're fighting, hell yeah. But I'm curious about them. I had a chance to talk for a bit with a prisoner at the opening of the Buna fight. There was something that made me think we could have been friends."

He nodded, giving me a pensive look.

"Cap'n," I said. "You're confusing me. I'll tell you this much for sure, I'm prepared to shoot every damned one of them and plan for a better crop next time."

"Sorry, Jim. I'm kind what you call an odd duck, so bear with me. General Eichelberger told me that you and Lieutenant Irish did some valuable scouting for the division around Buna. Now I won't claim the general and I are buddies, but he's trying to get citizenship for me and …"

"Citizenship?"

"Jawohl." He grinned. "I'm born German and I'm a communist. I was a major with the American Lincoln Brigade in the Spanish Civil War, so the U.S. government turned me down at first when I applied to enter the States." He grinned. "But no problem in enlisting after Pearl Harbor."

"Small world," I said. "My boss, Lieutenant Irish, was a major for a time in the Chinese Nationalist Army."

"I know," he said. "But at any rate, during Buna, I offered General Eichelberger a deal. I said if I could get us into the Japs' lines would he support my application to become a citizen? He said, 'Deal.' Well, we broke the Japs' line … split them up. They assaulted us from both sides and we killed them by the dozens. So he commissioned me a captain and now, just as he promised, he's working on citizenship for me."

"Damn."

He said General Eichelberger also had recommended him to General Gill to head up a division-level reconnaissance unit.

"I don't know if it will pan out," he said, "but I'm checking about setting up a group of odd-balls like me. All volunteers, not so? We'd be lightly armed, live off the land carrying radios and those pedal generators. Would you be interested?"

"Sounds scary *and* interesting. I guess I'd want to talk to Lieutenant Irish about it."

"I already met with him up at Camp Cable. He's interested. He recommended that I talk with you. So did Corporal Riegle."

I rolled my eyes. "Oh, boy, that joker. What a team that would be. Well, sir, give me some idea of how long it will be before..."

"Oh, it's going to be a while before we're all healed or before the whole division is even back at Camp Cable. What's left of the 126th – about six hundred uninjured men, all told -- is resting there and so is one battalion of the 128th. The rest of the 128th and most of the 127th are still in New Guinea."

"What's the hold-up?"

"Not enough planes or ships. The Air Corps can only fly them back to Port Moresby in quite small batches and then they have to wait for a ship to return them here. Right now Port Moresby is crammed with ships waiting only to unload cargo. But at least the boys are getting some rest. What's also good, though, is that supplies from the states are finally starting to roll in, so at last we're getting some up-to-date gear plus replacements."

He studied the sky for a minute. "General Gill will have his hands full getting the division restored and trained. Morale is terrible and we still have a hell of a lot of malaria. I'd say you have another month for that nice Australian lady to teach you chess, yes? Anyway, please give it some thought."

I did, and one thing struck me. As I said, the captain was a little guy, probably no more than 5-5. I towered over him.

But he didn't have an ounce of that Napoleonic put-you-in-your-place attitude you often encounter in short men.

And even though he was German, he sure didn't act one bit like that Eric Von Stroheim character.

Chapter 8
Second Thoughts

As we strolled the next evening, Judith said, "Jim, you're a right wowser tonight."

Suzanned snapped, "*Judith!*"

"Well, Auntie, it's true! We've walked for ten minutes and he hasn't said two words."

"Okay," I said, "I'll bite. What's a wowser? A flying wombat?"

For the first time since I'd met her, Suzanne laughed aloud. Then she said, "I'd better translate. I think the Yank equivalent of 'wowser' is 'bore' or maybe 'sourpuss'."

"Oh, gee, so I'm bad company, am I? Well, I'll try to do better."

I desperately launched into all the farcical complaints about Australia that I could make up. The sky was blue instead of green as in the States. The leaves were green not purple. Clouds were white rather than orange, violets were red and roses were blue, Aussie children were brats who spent their free time stoning the crows, all the shielas were matilda williwahs, Aussie fences were bloody fragile, and my words were the absolute dinkum oil.

Each statement elicited more laughter, especially the bit about stoning crows.

As we passed the house on the way back to the hospital, Suzanne suggested pointedly that Judith scoot inside and get busy with her studies. Judith pouted and whined, "Auntie!"

Suzanne spoke a dangerous "Joo-*DITH*!"

I chimed in. "Now Sis, you don't want to get behind in your Latin, right? Have you got *Hic, Haec, Hoc* memorized?"

Judith whirled away, stomped up the steps and slammed the front door behind her.

We were smiling as we continued on together. Suzanne took my arm as we strolled. Finally she said, "Jim, what's the matter? Was it your talk with that captain?"

"Not really. He has an idea that might involve a lot of behind-the-lines work. But, you can guess," I added. "The matter is that I'm healing nicely and I hate it. Sometime soon the docs will discharge me from the hospital and I'll be heading back to Brisbane to report for duty."

"I suppose it had to come sometime."

I stopped and turned to her. "The *real* matter is that I'm going to miss the two of you. You especially." I held my arms out to her . . . I couldn't help it.

Reluctantly at first she moved into my hug, but then pressed against me and tilted her forehead to the side of my neck. She heaved a great sigh. "I'll miss you too, Jim."

I kissed her forehead and stepped away.

I said, "I'm sorry, kiddo."

"I'm not. You've given me diversion and affection and no damned slap and tickle demands. And you've practically been a second father to Judith."

We walked a few paces when she stopped and turned to nail me with her eyes. "You'll write?"

"Damn tootin'. I don't know that I'll be able to write every day, but I'll try to inflict a lot of American English on you."

"You'd bloody well better, Yank, because I'm going to send you all the Aussie lingo I can."

"Do I need to get a dictionary?"

"No, I'll translate with footnotes."

After a pause, she said, "It's a bloody beaut that you'll be behind the lines."

"Right."

I didn't tell her we'd be behind the Japs' lines.

Chapter 9
The Aussie Iron Horse

Every damned minute took me another half mile or so from Suzanne, and I was in a foul mood about it. The greater the distance the more I missed her, far more than I would have imagined.

And in addition to that deep inner ache, my butt hurt.

Now I don't know what Australian railways are like today. In 1943, however, they seemed like the equivalent of the Iron Horse on the American prairies, just without bison and hostile Indians.

Or seat cushions.

Here we were, damn near mid-way through the twentieth century, rattling along at maybe thirty miles per hour, when headed downhill that is. Going upgrade seemed to slow our engine to a wheezy twenty. And the Imperial Transport Authority obviously had just pulled our passenger cars out of retirement . . . long overdue retirement at that.

They must have been modeled after British railway cars, because we rode in compartments seating groups of eight, four each on facing benches. But the fabric backs were worn, with batting pushing out here and there, and the seat cushions were long gone. Now our benches were weathered planks . . . splintery, too

They seemed to be second class carriages because the compartments were only partially enclosed. But if they once were in decent shape, generations of passengers slinging their luggage about had scratched and abraded the finish on all the woodwork. The floor looked like the mice had been at it and sagged ominously underfoot. One window had no glass, so the steam engine ventilated our compartment and our eyes with smoke and soot.

Guessing from the proliferation of spider webs and the remains of a bird nest overhead, I figured these cars sat on some deserted siding for years. Obviously the badly overloaded Australian railway system pressed its aged cars back into service to help handle floods of soldiers traveling north from Adelaide to Brisbane or Townsville or even Darwin.

But what made it almost unbearable were the kids in my compartment – seven alleged riflemen, eighteen and nineteen years old, fresh off some Liberty ship. And now they were riding a thousand miles north on this so-called troop train in which the Army had scattered some recovered wounded like me.

Don't get me wrong. I firmly support a soldier's need to gripe. It's an essential outlet.

But these kids acted like pansies. They complained about the food, about being cold, about how the shifting boards on which we sat pinched the backs of their tender thighs, how *foul* the car's lavatory was. (On that score, they were right. The water closet was a charnel house. Its nicest appointment was a rusted-through commode of, shall we say, the long-drop variety.)

Even so, this discomfort was nothing compared to what they eventually would face.

Finally one of the twits started grousing because he couldn't find Chesterfields so he was forced to smoke Lucky Strikes.

That's when my safety valve blew. I glared and bellowed, "WILL you whiny bastards shut your goddamn mouths! Jesus! You'd bitch if we hanged you with a brand-new rope! Either shut your hole or get the hell out of here!"

After a stunned silence, one said "Well hell, Sarge, you got to admit this is pretty unpleasant."

"Shit sonny, you ain't begun to see unpleasant. This is just slightly inconvenient. Where you're going is unpleasant . . . it's so godawful unpleasant you'll think this is luxury. You'll pray to return in this very car. In fact, you'll pray that you get to sleep in its crapper using that rusted-out stool for your pillow. And you'll *like* it."

They were quiet for a minute.

"Sarge, is it really that bad?"

All of a sudden I felt sorry for them. Babes headed for the woods.

"Look," I said, "when we get to camp you're going to receive some special training…"

"Jesus," the biggest one moaned. "More fucking training? I don't believe it."

I leaned across and stared him right in the peepers. "Look boy, that attitude will get you killed the instant you get up to the line.

"But," I added, "training *will* save your ass if you take it seriously and work at it … and I mean work! Hard. *Real hard*!"

My little sermon shut them up until 0300 when we reached the next little coaling stop on the line. Before the train completely halted they and every other GI spilled out of the compartment doors onto the loading platform. For the next hour, they'd try to find beer while pestering the volunteer ladies running the food counters.

Those Aussie women sometimes seemed amused, but were utterly dedicated to one thing – feeding supposedly starving Diggers and GIs.

# # #

Captain Bottcher told me I'd have about a month to learn chess from Suzanne. It turned out my orders gave me three weeks and four days.

She and I made the most of it.

It took only about ten minutes for me to learn the chess pieces' moves. But I was an utter dunce when it came to tactics. In two games, which seemed to take about the same number of minutes, my poor king was checked, mated, and perhaps assassinated or held in a dungeon for ransom.

Gravely, Suzanne told me, "You must be more patient, Jim. Before you move, you've got to study the board and look for threats . . . and my weaknesses."

Judith, kibitzing beside me in our third game, started glancing at me and jiggling her knee.

"What?"

She glanced pointedly toward Suzanne's side of the board.

"What?"

"Study the board, Jim."

It took me about ten minutes to trace out all the routes by which her pieces could start to decimate my line-up. *Let's see -- rook moves either right or left or up and back, knight up two and over one or vice versa, bishop diag...* Suddenly I started sweating. For a change, it wasn't a bout of malaria. What chilled me was the notion that chess bore an antiseptic but uncanny likeness to jungle fighting.

The first thing you'd damned well better do is ID all lines of approach. If you don't figure out all the unlikely places a Jap sniper might hide, you lose not a pawn or a rook but a buddy. Or maybe you get drilled and wind up flat on your back trying to scream about the bullets in your gut.

I never caught on to the French Defense in chess or most of the game's other nuances. For that matter, I never came close to winning. But by the end of the first week, chess was no longer a mere game to me. I was making Suzanne work a little bit for her victories.

One afternoon in my second week of chess instruction – Judith being in school – I proudly told Suzanne that a good many lessons I learned in New Guinea were valuable preparation for chess.

Suzanne turned pale. "Why Jim, whatever do you mean?"

"I mean you must instantly -- either by habit, or training, or practice or whatever – get to the point that you sense every possible way the enemy can attack you . . . every possible direction he can fire at you. I'm starting to see chess is like that."

She swallowed and asked that we quit.

"Why?"

With trembling fingers she began replacing the chess pieces in their box. Tears started rolling from her eyes. "Why? Because even in chess I don't want you seeing me as an enemy. And I don't like thinking about what you've been through, or where you're returning . . . or to know what you're doing when you get there."

I got up and came around to her side of the coffee table, bent over and reached for her hand. "Okay, Suzanne, I understand. How 'bout we just take a walk?"

She stood up, moved within kissing distance. "No. Please just give me a nice, long hug."

Holding her in my arms felt like heaven. It was something I wanted to do for a long time now.

But it was hell, too.

Now I knew she would worry constantly, shivering in hopes for the next letter, and praying that it would be a letter, not a telegram like the last time.

And now, half-way to Camp Cable, all I could so was just stand outside this damned empty passenger car and ache . . . ache oh so desperately – oh, so godawful deeply.

Chapter 10
Living Off The Land

"Jesus, they're ugly, Cap'n! You actually *eat* these things?"

"Of course. And believe me, they taste much better than C Rations, is that not so?"

"Wow, I don't know abou…" Captain Bottcher slashed with his machete and the sentence died in the kid's mouth.

Pulling the decapitated iguana from its perch on the tree trunk, the captain said, "There. You see? A single chop and you've got supper for three. This is part of what I mean when I say we'll live off the country."

Eight of us standing in a semicircle were listening to the captain's third behind-the-lines survival lecture. Holding the lizard's carcass against the tree, he used his K-bar to gut it.

"If you're lucky," the captain said, "it might be a female with some eggs in her. They're very nutritious and you don't even need to cook them."

The guy next to me said, "Oh, ugh!"

Captain Bottcher, who never put on a lordly officer act, gave the man a hard stare. "Mr. Robbins, if this is too much for your delicate taste, return to your unit. You can continue to feast on Spam and bully beef and need not worry about our missions.

"I mean it," he added, looking each of us in the eyes. "We'll spend days, perhaps even weeks, behind Jap lines. We must learn to live on food like this."

Robbins said, "Well, Sir, we'll have our weapons, won't we?"

"Of course. But our best weapons will be our eyes, yes? And our brains, ja? And radios, for example. Division won't send thirty of us out to fight five hundred Japs ten miles behind their own lines. They want us to find out *where* the Japs are. They need to know where they are, what they're doing, and where they're going and where their supplies and supply lines are.

"If we have to use our tommy guns or carbines, we're up . . . how do you say it? . . . we're up that Shit Creek with no paddles. If you don't want to do this, now is the time to walk away. Nobody will hold it against you and nothing will go on your records. Now, is that clear? "

Robbins let out a deep breath, "Yes, sir. Sorry."

Nobody left.

"Okay," the captain said. "Now pair off. Each pair take one of this iguana's limbs, peel away that skin and start cooking. And I don't recommend trying to eat the tail – it's very bony. Like a fish, yes?"

Soon we were roasting bits of iguana flesh on the tips of our bayonets.

"Unfortunately, there aren't too many iguanas in New Guinea's jungles," the captain said.

"But there are many snakes and occasional crocs, and they can be good eating, too. When you gut snakes, again, be sure to check for eggs. Very, very nutritious. And peel away the skin from snakes before you gut them. By the way, never overcook snake. That can make it almost as hard as a ceramic."

I was surprised that iguana had little flavor. As we ate, I said, "Well, sir, it needs some salt and pepper, but it sure beats hell out of bully beef."

Lieutenant Irish said, "Amen to that. The last can of bully beef I opened was pure mutton fat with a few little flakes of meat or maybe sawdust. Talk about gamey! It would make a dog gag. I spit out the first bite and gave the heave-ho to the rest."

"Damn right," Riegle said. "You either give it the heave-ho or you just plain heave. I don't see how the Aussies stand it. No wonder they're all so gaunt."

The captain gave a nod and a slight grin. "Right now boys, you're eating under ideal conditions. But I give you good counsel, fire often can be a problem in the jungle. You must use very dry wood. Otherwise, it smokes and that tips off any Japs to your presence. And the odor spreads even further than the smoke."

"Yeah," I added. "And finding dry wood in New Guinea often is a bit of a problem."

"Exactly, Sergeant. In fact, it's usually impossible. So what you must also learn is to recognize good vegetable food. The juice from the coconut – you call it coconut milk – is good and so is the coconut's flesh. The problem is that opening the nuts is noisy business. It takes chopping. So before chopping, you must have security out at least two hundred yards.

"But jungle streams sometimes supply us with fish. And in the jungle itself you can find squash, snails, taro roots, grubs, paw-

paw, bananas and sugar cane. They are not abundant – not enough to support a large group. But for a small group moving through the jungle, they are plentiful enough to keep you going."

After a few more remarks, he dismissed the class.

Lieutenant Irish and I lingered.

"So, Cap'n," the lieutenant asked, "is it set that you'll be running Division's intelligence and recon outfit?"

"Not yet. Right now I'm carried on the books as commander of Able Company of the 127th Infantry regiment. But not much of the 127th remains right now.

"The wounded and jungle rot cases are starting to come back from hospitals, but some of the serious malaria cases and people with dengue and typhus may never come back. We need a lot of replacements and we've got to teach them what we've learned about New Guinea and Japs. So meanwhile all I'm doing its trying to find a nucleus of recon people – odd balls, like I told you."

"I hope you'll count us in," I said.

"Well, that depends. Our job now will be much different from what they had you doing around Buna. I see much long-range scouting. As I understand it, General MacArthur says he wants no more Bunas. He wants to know where the Jap's numbers are so that we can seize land where they are few. He wants to use the jungle against them . . . to isolate them, to be imprisoned by the jungle, you might say."

"Makes sense," the lieutenant said. "Attacking them in their strongholds is like bashing your head against a brick wall. Better to cut them off from supplies and let them starve."

I agreed wholeheartedly. I never wanted to face another Jap bunker.

Chapter 11
Catching Up

Back in September '42 when they first shipped us from Camp Cable to New Guinea, the camp itself was raw and only half updated from World War I when Aussie troops trained there.

Before Buna, when we should have undergone jungle training, we'd done quite a bit of construction at the camp and taken out a lot of trees. We also had cut some rough single-lane streets through the woods.

I don't know who always comes up with these ideas, but we also had been required to find and carry a lot of head-sized rocks to line the walkways leading into the various headquarter tents. They had us paint the damn rocks white.

Made no sense to me. Seems like an engraved invitation to Jap fliers. "Hey, Tojo, those double white lines? They lead to the officers! They show where to drop your bombs."

Oh well, I guess by then everybody was pretty confident that the Japs couldn't send bombers this deep into Australia.

Anyway, last week when our rattletrap train finally pulled into Logan Station at the north end of Camp Cable, the Army did first what it always does first – it fed us.

It fed us good old meat and potatoes in brand-new honest-to-god mess halls. Along with the cooking, you could smell resin in the fresh-cut wood. We even had some actual tables and plus a few chairs. About half of us had to sit on wooden boxes. The windows had screens. One mess hall even had a concrete floor.

After chow I stepped outside for a smoke and noticed that while we had been fighting Japs in Buna, the engineers had given the camp a much more permanent look. Wooden barracks had replaced many of the big tents. The main streets around and through the camp now were graveled two-lane roads … and with posted speed limits, yet.

Some things hadn't changed, though. You still could see pairs of good-sized iguanas holding face-offs on tree limbs. They'd sit face-to-face a foot apart pumping their scaly mugs up and down, I guess trying to scare each other. Or maybe it was a mating ritual.

Others, solitary, seemed to do nothing but doze. I didn't see how, what with the piercing whistles of magpies and Mynah birds and the incessant yammer of the Kookaburra . . . not to mention the popcorn rattle of gunfire at the rifle range off to the south.

The engineers had configured the camp in three sections – three battalions of cannon-cockers nestled side-by-side along the east side of the camp.

The administrative offices, warehouses, PT areas and weapons ranges formed the west margins of the camp.

The three infantry regiments' cantonments extended along the rail spur that bisected the camp's center. Except that damn few infantrymen were in sight. Even now, the bulk of them still were swatting mosquitos in New Guinea and waiting for a lift back to us.

# # #

I was alone in our company dayroom, soaking in my own sweat and trying to write to Suzanne. And as Jerry Colonna used to say in his deepest bass, my morale was mighty lowwwww.

I mean, after all, I was here and Suzanne was not. And I was recuperating slowly from my fourth turn with malaria.

Lieutenant Irish leaned in and said, "There you are. I've been looking for you."

"Oh, hell," I said, "What now?"

He sprawled into a chair across from me. "Well, Jim, things are really starting to look up."

"Sir, you could have fooled me."

I also was depressed that, our home – the 128th Infantry Regiment – was barely half-full. We had roughly six hundred men … about all that was left of the original fifteen hundred in the pre-Buna outfit.

Rumor Central had it that soon we'd receive about three hundred green-as-grass replacements. With that kind of manpower, it was scary to contemplate the regiment's next operation. It gave me the feeling that if we had to go back into New Guinea's goddam jungles, nobody would make it back alive . . . me included.

But Lieutenant Irish, normally a sphinx, was practically fizzing.

"Two things, Jim. First, we'll be resting and refitting for at least three months, maybe more.

"Second, MacArthur still is saying, 'No more Bunas'."

I looked up from my letter. “Yeah, so I heard. And gee, it only took him eight thousand casualties to figure that one out?”

“Jim, don’t be such a hard-ass.”

“Well pardon me, sir, but after the way he stuck us out there on a limb with no supplies or artillery, I’m just a wee bit skeptical about the old bastard . . . especially with all that after-action publicity about how negligible our casualties were and how there never was a rush.”

He nodded grimly. “Yep, for sure that was Grade A bullshit from his public relations machine. But, Jim, generals are just like riflemen and squad leaders. They’ve got to learn. And from what I hear he really means it about no more Bunas. And he’s forcing his staff to make that idea the center of their plans.”

“So just what will we be doing?”

“Jim, the whole focus is going to be on leapfrogging and creating airfields. The Air Corps and the Navy have really started getting a twist on the Jap air forces. From what they told us at our briefing, we’re getting new planes and they’re better than Jap Zeros.”

“Well, sir, I’m real happy for the Brylcream boys, but I don’t see that it does a bit of good for us on the ground.”

“Wrong, sergeant. You remember how Jap planes sank our supply boats just as the Buna operation started? Left us with damn near nothing?”

“Oh, yeah. I remember it very, very clearly.”

“Well, the shoe now is definitely on the other foot.”

Chapter 12
Good News At Last

Lieutenant Irish told me how over a three-day period, the Air Corps – bombers and fighters -- virtually obliterated a big Jap troop convoy bound from Rabaul to Lae in New Guinea, a port and air base about a hundred fifty miles west of Buna.

"No shit? They sank 'em all?"

"Not quite," he said. "About a regiment of Jap troops got through. But the rest, several thousand, fed the sharks in the Bismarck Sea. And the Japs that did get through are starving because our bombers sank every blessed one of their supply freighters. So they've got no food, no canned fish, no medical supplies, no rice, no sake, no nothin'."

I stopped writing.

"So, are we still going back to New Guinea?"

"Yeah, eventually. Lae is one of several big Jap garrisons spotted along the north coast, each with its own airstrips. So what we're going to do is play hopscotch. Our bombers and fighter planes are going to hammer their airstrips while we go ashore a good distance away where our engineers will build new airstrips for our bombers. It's kind of a one-two punch.

"So instead of us attacking them in their bunkers, they'll have to attack us… but only after they first approach us by cutting through miles and miles of jungle. And, boy, you know that jungle. By the time they move two battalions through it to attack us, half of them already will be dead."

The beauties of the scheme began to dawn on me.

"So are we going to attack this Lae place?"

"Not us. That's the Aussies' problem. The air corps is bombing the crap out of Lae's airstrips and the Aussies are attacking it. For now, we'll keep resting and refitting. Remember, the big man is saying, 'No more Bunas' and it looks like he means it." He lit a cigarette. "I like it," he said. "The Japs' only choice will be to starve in place or cut through the jungle, starve while they do it, and then try to attack us."

He said he had some other good news.

"Compared to Europe, we're still sucking hind tit. Even so, supplies finally are flowing in. We'll have replacement foot gear for when this new set of boots disintegrates

"And we'll have carbines for jungle work, and a lot more Tommy Guns.

"And, again, the old man is telling his people to move us by air or boat, but never by foot again. We've got command of the air, and that gives us command of the sea."

"They said all this at your briefing?"

"Damned right. And, Jim, the *really* good news is that we won't have to count on any more dinky fishing boats for our supplies. Now we'll have LSTs."

"Okay, sir. What the hell is an LST?"

"Just saw a training film about them. It's a big-assed cargo boat designed by the Brits. It's longer than a football field and built to deliver stuff from tank size on down.

"Also it's got a real shallow draft so it can just push right up onto the beach. Then it opens those great big bow doors and you just walk or drive right out onto the beach."

"Yeah, so what, sir? Once you're on the beach, you're facing machine guns."

"Yeah, but instead of walking, you might ride in a buffalo."

"A buffalo?"

"Yeah, it's kind of an amphibious tank. An LST can deliver them to the beach, or they can swim on their own to the beach. And the other thing is that they can evacuate the wounded so they don't have to be carried on bamboo stretchers for ten miles."

"So where does our outfit come in?"

"Once our boys land, we'll patrol inland …"

"In the jungle?"

"Yep, in the jungle. We'll scout toward the Japs' bases and when we spot advancing Jap infantry, we'll call in air strikes and artillery. And this time around we'll have plenty of both. The Navy also will be able to support us with shelling from destroyers and cruisers . . . maybe even battleships."

I asked what he'd heard about replacements.

"We'll getting more and more recovering wounded. General Gill wants us to shape up the green kids coming from the States.

We'll hike them like crazy to sweat off that baby fat and run them through lots of jungle schools and night training."

"So you're going to run your old the-night-is-your-friend program again?"

"Damn right."

"Good. So what do you hear about Cap'n Bottcher's I&R group?"

"It's still kind of up in the air, but however it works out I think we'll be part of it."

"Well, that sounds more like it, especially if we can get them to attack our positions instead of us attacking them."

He said, "Damn tootin'." The phrase reminding me of what I promised Suzanne.

"I better finish this letter so you can censor it for me."

"Jim, are you writing anything about what I just told you?"

"Hell no!"

"Well, are you telling her where you are or what you're doing?"

"Only that I'm scratching my ass and writing letters to her."

"And are you conveying critical military information like which sock you put on first?"

"Hell, no, Lieutenant. That's top secret."

"Well, consider it censored. How's she doing, by the way?"

"She's started nurse's training. She thinks it will beat sheet metal work. She thinks it will be more fulfilling."

He pursed his lips. "Brother! After seeing what stretcher-bearers bring out of the jungle, I'd rather bend sheet metal any day. But what the hell? You get the right wound, she might end up taking care of you."

"Lieutenant, I really want to see her, but not that way."

# # #

Dear Suzanne --

I'd start by saying how much I miss you, but I've written those words so often that I should find some new way to express it. But believe me when I write those words <u>they</u> are the truth. I miss you terribly. Today at lunch ... would you call it high tea, maybe? ... they were playing some record or other by Vera Lynn. It suddenly hit me: I've never heard you sing. Having heard your voice so much and having seen so much of your eyes and face, I bet you sing *beautifully. Say, I have an idea: you could sing,* God Save The King *and I could sing* My Country 'Tis of Thee. *On second thought, that's a bad idea. I can't carry a tune in a coal scuttle. But it doesn't matter because talking with you is like listening to a symphony.*

Actually, that's not right. Merely being around you makes the world nice. I grant that this sounds pretty selfish, but when I'm with you I feel refreshed and I hope and pray that my company provides a like benefit to you. Letters have the same effect. My day is terrible until your letter arrives. And if none arrives, then I just dive into whatever work I can find so's I don't have to think about it.

You know, writing letters is a real chore because there is so much I can't say because of censorship. Somebody the other day said he heard of a new order that we can't even tell you whether I'm shoveling snow or mowing the lawn! Anyway, I save all your letters and read them so much I almost have them memorized.

Well, there's not a lot to report or rather that they would let me report. I'm feeling well and still putting on a little weight even though I'm very busy. And with your training, I bet – wait, would an Aussie write 'wager' instead of 'bet'? – that you have very little spare time on your hands. Please give Judith my best regards when you have a chance to see her.

All the best
Jim

Chapter 13
Getting Zeroed In

Each day, Corporal Riegle and I were assigned to help members of a newly-arrived squad zero in their M1 rifles. Figuring they knew nothing about what was going on, I explained this was how to be sure we'd hit where we aimed. "That way we can kill your Jap target with the first shot."

"Gee, Sarge, I don't know if I can do that." A husky young private nervously scrubbed his thumbnail at a blemish on the hand guard of his M1.

"Do what?"

"Shoot someone."

His statement stumped me. But only briefly.

We had discovered several boys arriving from the states with this same problem. In fact, it was a problem we also encountered among some draftees during the fight for Buna. Despite their training, despite Pearl Harbor and despite Jap butchery in China and Malaya, they were skittish about killing Japs.

Well, actually, they were skittish about killing. Period.

I get it. I mean, in the abstract, the idea of pulling the trigger on your M1 to turn a living, breathing human into a cooling slab of meat … well, to some people I guess it's horrifying for the first time or two. Killing goes against the upbringing of most American kids.

But combat is not abstract. It's real. Kill Tojo first or he kills you.

I tilted my helmet back and tried to sound friendly. "What's your name, son?"

"I'm Private John Ferraro."

"Well, Ferraro, when we fought around Buna we had some troops who felt that exact same way."

"They did?"

"Yep." I nodded. "For sure they did. They just couldn't make up their minds whether or not they could kill a Jap."

"Did they get punished … court-martialed or something?"

I rolled my eyes. "Man alive! Are you kidding? Of *course* not!"

He looked relieved.

Making lots of eye contact with him and his buddies, I went with a scornful laugh. “My God, Sonny, you can’t court martial a corpse!”

His eyes widened. “A corpse?”

“Sure! The guys who didn’t know if they could kill? The Japs killed them all in the first minute or two. And, believe me, it helped the other guys make up their minds real fast.”

He turned a bit pale.

I lightened up on him. “Now look, Ferraro, in the infantry we depend on each other. I mean we depend on each other a lot! Know what I mean? When we’re in a fight, I rely on my buddies to protect me and I do everything I can under the sun to protect them. And do you know how we protect each other?”

A stocky man beside Ferraro piped up. “Killing Japs?”

“Boy, you catch on real quick.” I slapped him on the shoulder. “What’s your name?”

“I’m Luis Mendez.”

“Well, Mendez, you go to the head of the class. Exactly right. It’s us or them.”

“Now look, Ferraro,” I added, “I want you to come through this war in one piece and with all your fingers and toes. I mean it. I want all of you to get through it alive. Me too. But here’s the deal. We’re a team … we back each other up. And my number one priority is to protect the men who protect me. First, last and always. Got it?”

Ferraro gave an uncertain nod while Mendez and the others exchanged glances.

I started to walk away, paused and turned back. “Look, nothing personal. I’m just not going to risk my sorry ass for somebody who won’t risk his by killing every Jap in sight. That’s just the way it is.”

I let them digest the notion for a few seconds.

“Okay, men, now to zero in your weapons, we’re going to work in pairs. Ferraro, you’re with me.” I turned to Corporal Riegle. “Charlie, I’ve got to zero my rifle, too, so take over firing line commands for me, okay?”

“You got it, Sarge.”

Riegle stood back. “Okay, men, now we got six targets and these here six rifle rests. So line up in pairs on the rifle rests and put in your ear plugs. The guy on the left is the first shooter. The guy on the right has a box of ball ammunition. We're going to fire single shots, so the guy on the right loads the rifle after the man on the left fires. Shooters! Assume the prone position! Open your rifle's breach by pulling the operating rod lever fully to the rear. Buddies, get down there beside them."

I flopped down and cradled the rifle to my shoulder. Ferraro lay down beside me.

"Okay, Shooters," Riegle called, "look through the peep sight on your M1 and put that front sight – that's the vertical blade between those two blade guards – put that front sight right on the target. Get comfortable with it."

After a pause he said, "Now the targets are set at a hundred yards. No wind at all today. So, buddies! Take out one round of ball ammunition and feed it into the chamber of the shooter's rifle. Shooters! Lock and load.

"So . . . Ready on the right? Ready on the left? Ready on the firing line?

"Fire at will!"

I shot as quickly as Ferraro could load my rifle. When the other five shooters finished, Riegle ordered the rifles cleared and double-checked. Then we went forward to view the targets. My shots were clustered two inches high – just right for a hundred yards – but three inches to the right.

I showed Ferraro how to adjust the windage nob on the rear sight. The group fired again and this time my shots were clustered directly above the bull.

Then it was Ferraro's turn.

He settled down and grouped his shots fairly well. I was happy to see that the recoil didn't seem to bother him. It took twelve shots to get his rifle zeroed.

Once we wrapped up and were having a smoke, he griped that his shot cluster was baseball-sized rather than half dollar-sized like mine. Riegle laughed. "Don't worry. If you can hit a baseball at a hundred yards, you'll be able to take out any Jap in the jungle."

"Okay," I said, "this is more important than shooting. Do you think you can kill, now? Because if you can't, Tojo will drill your ass first thing."

"Well if it's him or me, Sarge, I guess I can do it."

"You *guess*? It *is* you or him. So will you be looking out for your buddies?"

"I guess I don't have much choice."

"Damn right you don't. And if you're looking out for us, we'll be covering you, won't we, Mendez?"

"You got it, Sarge."

# # #

Dearest Jim --

I confess I am a coward. They took me and several other nurse training aspirants to Fourth General's receiving center. Patients were arriving from New Guinea. I don't know what I must have been thinking because I could not endure such concentrated misery amid limbs and faces so wretchedly torn.

I must have been white as a sheet. I will do my bit elsewhere. One thing led to another, and I now am with your Army's Signal Corps. They call me a DAC, for Department of the Army Civilian – identically pronounced but not to be confused with "dack," our slang for "trouser." Maybe it has something to do with chess, for I learned Morse Code very quickly. I am not at liberty to disclose anything further except that I work during the day so I still have Judith for evening company. She and Mr. Eccles have become great friends, but she misses Our Yank very dearly. As I believe you Americans say, "For me that goes double."

Concerning your suggestion about singing? I must emphatically say No. My warble makes dogs howl. I suggest that we buy a Victrola and just hum sotto voce. I do wish I could sing, however, because on the wireless yesterday I heard a beautiful ballad. I can't recall all the lyrics, but this part reminded me of your wonderful hug:

" … and when the night is new
I'll be looking at the moon
But I'll be seeing you."

I miss you so much, Jim.

Love, Suzanne

Chapter 14
An Amphibian's Life

We were taking ten late in our twenty-five-mile hike. Lieutenant Irish strolled up from the back of our little column. "Sergeant, how's your poor sore leg holding up?"

"Sore, sir, but still working. How 'bout you?"

He doffed his helmet and mopped the sweat from his face, "Well, you know what they used to say in the Old Army."

"No, sir, I'm afraid I don't. I'm not that old."

He laughed. "Oh, go to hell, you young pup."

"Yes, sir. Sorry, sir. Please tell me, what did they say in the Old Army?"

"They said that after the first thousand miles, your legs start to limber up."

"Yeah, well . . . you notice I'm not sitting down during this break. I might not be able to get back up."

"Right. Same here. Say, did you hear they sent Frank Benson back to CONUS?" Corporal Benson was my first boss a year ago in San Francisco when, right out of basic, I reported into the Division.

"Really? How did that lucky stiff rate, sir?"

"He ain't so lucky, Jim. Got the bug so bad that he's down to a hundred and ten pounds. He's just a shadow of hisself. Eyes all sunken in. Just pitiful."

I allowed myself one swallow from my canteen. "Malaria, right?"

"Well, supposedly. But maybe some bad intestinal problems too. Can't keep anything down. Can't put on weight. They might discharge him."

I said, "Shit, that'll break his heart. Being a National Guard paper-pusher meant everything to him."

"Yeah, well. Too bad. It was a nice peace time job for him. But he wasn't much of a soldier. A hell of a lot of other men have had lots worse luck. All told, Division's shipping a couple thousand men to guard duty in Australia thanks to malaria and all the other complications."

"Jesus, that many?"

"Yep, New Guinea took a hell of a toll. Now we're better prepared."

"That's for sure." I stubbed out my cigarette. "Okay, men! On your feet. We're moving out."

So far this hike had been a warm-up in wide-open country, but now we were headed downhill into the slime. Irish and I were leading our twenty-man group down a bluff to cross a bilibong, basically a slough formed by an oxbow left behind when a river changed course.

Dense jungle lay beyond it.

"Listen up, men! We're going down into a low-lying area. There'll be no wind, so roll your sleeves down! Make sure you have repellant on your ears, neck and faces. We don't want skeeters snacking on you."

The lieutenant and I named this particular bilibong Stink Lake. As you walk through it, your feet stir up the bottom muck. Large bubbles break open on the surface, releasing a stench like something that's been dead three days and lying in a ripe latrine.

"Hold your noses," Riegle yelled. "We're about to cross the skunks' secret burial ground."

But we also call it Sink Lake because, in places, it seems to have no bottom – just liquescent goo. Before you reach the far bank, you're practically chin deep and praying that nobody makes any waves.

Looking down on it from the crest of the bluff, the bilibong appears innocent enough – sun glinting off pretty patches of blue water between rafts of fresh bright-green lettuce.

Having been through it several times now, I figure the green stuff is some exotic algae. When you emerge, the 'lettuce' clings to you in dark, sodden strands, with a special pungent reek all their own.

At the bottom of the bluff, we formed the men in two lines. I led the first straight into the swamp and Lieutenant Irish followed with the second.

The complaints started in about two seconds as our boots churned the water into a sickly tan. "Awwww, phew! God what a smell! Sarge? What the hell? Why couldn't we hike around this shit?"

"Okay, halt right there! If you can't handle this, back out and find your way around. Then when we get you back to camp you're done! Otherwise, shut up and keep moving."

The lieutenant and I called this hike part of Operation Odd Ball. It's our way of finding men who will dare, and tolerate, the rigors of jungle scouting and, therefore, who might fit into Captain Bottcher's I&R Unit.

General Gill has yet to okay the detachment's formation, but he encouraged the captain to screen people for it. So the lieutenant, Riegle and I do the screening. The three of us are just kind of an appendix to Captain Bottcher's official command, Able Company of the 127th Infantry Regiment.

None of us has any idea when we – or the Division itself – will return to Satan's Shithole, our term for New Guinea. But we're sure it's our eventual destination because General Gill is really insistent about getting the division back into shape and ready for the jungle.

And, learning of Benson's return to the states, it hit me that we old-timers not only need to get ourselves back up to snuff, but we're also going to have to train a lot more green recruits.

We hear lots of fighting still is underway on New Guinea. Supposedly casualties are coming into Port Moresby and Milne Bay from the Aussie Eighth and Ninth Divisions.

Stories are circulating that one of the Aussie divisions is pushing the Japs out of the Huon Peninsula located almost two hundred miles west along the coast from Buna. Another is tackling a big Jap garrison inland from the peninsula.

None of it meant much to me until Lieutenant Irish got out a New Guinea map and drew a black circle around each Jap base spotted along the north coast of the island.

The island is shaped like a pregnant hump-backed dragon, and the enemy's garrisons are spaced out along the north coast, the backbone – sort of like widely separated vertebrae – Buna being the one we and the Aussies captured just after New Year's.

The others are scattered a hundred fifty to two hundred miles apart to the west: the Huon Peninsula, Saidor, Wewak, Hollandia and Wakde.

Right now, though, we're pushing through the slime and muck among a lot of brush and trees. It's not physically too demanding.

In fact, being chest-deep even in this thickened water is a welcome relief for weary legs. But many guys can't take the slime and stink coupled with heat, humidity, leeches and snakes. We're looking for hard cases who can take it days on end.

Several of the boys in my squad stumbled over sunken obstacles – logs, probably. Ferraro and Mendez both wound up fully submerged. They came up sputtering, each trying to rub the ripe gruel from his face.

"Oh, God," Ferraro sputtered, "I lost my rifle."

I smirked. "Yeah, you lost your helmet, too. You can retrieve it when you duck back under for your M1."

He stared at me aghast. Then he shuddered, closed his eyes, took a deep breath and went back under. Next to him, Mendez also ducked beneath the surface.

Both soon surfaced, Mendez holding Ferraro's helmet and Ferraro retrieving his rifle. As the coffee-colored water drained from their mugs, Ferraro said, "Couldn't find the helmet. Can somebody hold my rifle while I dive for it?"

Mendez said, "Already got it, man." As he handed it to Ferraro, he gave a sour grin. "Hey, John, notice something?"

"What?"

"This water or whatever it is … tastes kinda salty."

"Oh, shut *UP*!"

Mendez's comment had puckered the faces of the rest of the squad. I laughed aloud.

"Yeah, you're right," Ferraro said, draining his helmet. "It *is* salty." Then he added, "Luis, I owe you. Greater love hath no man than that he dive in shit for his brother's helmet. You're an okay guy."

I figured if the pair could make light of full immersion baptism in Stink Lake they might be solid candidates for Captain Bottcher's group.

Chapter 15
The Ultra VIP

Every now and then, I really wonder about the Army. I mean, just think for a minute about the 32nd Division. Even though it's only a shadow of itself thanks to casualties and diseases, it nonetheless is very, very powerful.

Its understrength rifle companies, supported by machine guns and mortars, could level a respectable town in less than a day. Throw in the division's tank destroyers, its antiaircraft weapons and three field artillery battalions – dozens of 105 and 155 howitzers plus some 155 guns – and you have a force that could pulverize downtown San Francisco.

But one middle-aged lady brought the division to its knees.

All we knew at first was that General Gill – who normally didn't seem to be the Nervous Nelly type -- suddenly was in a panic. Then The Word got out. General Eichelberger had called up to warn our commander that he was bringing a VIP, someone all the way from Washington, to inspect the division.

In fact, it wasn't just any old VIP but a VVVIP – a Very, Very, Very Important Person designated, for security reasons, as Flight 231 Pacific -- Eleanor Roosevelt.

The flap over her arrival showed us that a three-star general can terrorize a two-star general just as thoroughly as a buck sergeant can make a private cringe.

No, I didn't think Eichelberger would force Gill to do 50 pushups, peel a ton of potatoes or clean the parade ground with a toothbrush.

But it became obvious to us that generals apparently can inflict rarified levels of torture on their underlings – something like reassigning Major General Grumpsnarl to Fort Destitute as Director of P-38 Can-Opener Production.

What all the bustle meant for us was that General Gill's demands for training, training, training changed overnight to cleaning, cleaning, cleaning and painting, painting, painting.

His concerns about getting us ready for jungle combat vanished to the far rear burner. So, rather than training with carbines, it became our duty on pain of Grade Five Ass-Chewings to make sure that the First Lady not be offended by gum wrappers or cigarette butts fouling the pristine dust of Camp Cable's parade ground.

We troops had to apply a new coat of white paint to all rocks leading to our many headquarters. Under penalty of demotion, sergeants chivvied their squads to clean and reclean the latrines in case Mrs. Roosevelt wanted to see her reflection in the exquisitely polished surfaces of the brass urinal strainers.

And some genius also ordered us to find and pitch tents above the thoroughly scrubbed garbage cans ranked behind each company's mess hall.

We bitched furiously about this particularly gross example of garrison overreach. Tents? *Really?* So the flies and their maggots could feed in the shade?

Corporal Riegle helped us understand.

"Look men, the First Lady obviously is suffering homesickness," he said, "and the sight of tented garbage cans would be a warm reminder of home. See, everybody knows they have tents over the garbage cans out behind the White House kitchen."

Riegle, Lieutenant Irish and I were tickled to learn Mrs. Roosevelt was absolutely determined to meet our company commander, Captain Bottcher. She apparently was prepared to throw the weight of the White House, and its tented garbage cans, behind his application for citizenship.

It seems Captain Bottcher was every bit as popular in the states as in the division. His valor at Buna had made the papers. He also became a Democratic Party folk hero because, during the Spanish Civil War, he fought against Franco, fascist dictator and Nazi sympathizer.

Being a communist also made the captain popular because Uncle Joe Stalin now was our most staunch ally. Actually, Captain Bottcher told us he detested Stalin but that he greatly admired Lenin's writings.

We also guffawed at rumors that Mrs. R was equally determined *not* to meet General MacArthur, a determination which the general fully reciprocated. Rumor had it that he ordered General Eichelberger *not* to bring her to his Taj Mahal in Port Moresby. It seems FDR feared that the general one day might run for the presidency as a Republican. In later years, the general considered doing just that. Myself, I wouldn't have voted for Dugout Doug for dog-catcher.

We heard that Mrs. Roosevelt finally caught up with Captain Bottcher a thousand miles away when he was savoring an ice cream cone at Sydney's Red Cross Club.

Be that as it may, Mrs. Roosevelt's visit to Camp Cable hardly turned out to be an inspection. She and General Eichelberger may have stopped for coffee with General Gill, but all we caught was a glimpse of her in a gray Red Cross uniform as her car rumbled past our ranks on one of Camp Cable's gravel streets.

# # #

As the dust settled in the First Lady's wake, General Gill and 32nd Division took a deep breath and calmed down. The garbage can tents rapidly disappeared back into quartermasters' hands. We turned in our paint brushes and resumed training with M1 carbines.

Being light and short, the weapons seemed ideal for close-range combat, often what you need in dense jungle. An M1 rifle can nail somebody at three hundred to four hundred yards, but in jungle you often can't see the bad guys until they're twenty feet away or less.

Soon, however, complaints started surfacing. Corporal Riegle was at the head of that line. "Jim, I got my doubts about these carbines. Some of the guys think they kick too much."

"Oh, come on Charlie, the M1 carbine doesn't have near the kick of the M1 rifle. It's just a pistol with a long barrel."

"No, you sure don't feel it in your shoulder. But it's got a hell of a lot of blast and muzzle jump. You can't reacquire the target very quick."

"Charlie, it's like anything else. Just takes some familiarization and practice."

"Yeah, I can live with that," he said. "But watch this."

He pushed a magazine into his carbine. Then he took aim. When he pulled the trigger, the weapon fired and its magazine dropped to the ground at his feet.

"Boom! One shot and I'm disarmed. What am I supposed to do? Tape it in place? I mean, this is the third mag that did this."

"Charlie, quit bitching, okay? Take it to the armorer and have him look at it or draw some new magazines. Meanwhile, I'll approve you for a Tommy Gun."

"No thanks," he said. "The damn things weigh almost as much as me. And carrying that ammo would sink me into a swamp."

He returned an hour later saying the armorer believed the carbine magazines' detent needed some work. "Meanwhile we discovered something else."

"Good Lord, Charlie What now?"

"Well, we fired it at a target in the armory and, you know, it's dim in there?"

"Yeah? So what?"

"Well, you should see the muzzle blast. It lit up that place like a damn floodlight. I don't think that's very good for night fighting, do you?"

"Nope. What did the armorer say about the falling mag?"

"He's gonna get back to us."

Chapter 16
Fitting In The New Guys

"Lieutenant Irish, I wish to officially report that we have a problem."

"Sergeant Mays, we have more problems than mosquitos. What now? Carbines again?"

"No, this is something really special. I was hoping you could help me out."

"Spill it."

So I told him I was becoming discouraged. "We're getting ready to go back to New Guinea, right?"

"Right."

"So, sir, how are we supposed to get ready when the old hands aren't willing to work with the new guys? Our Buna veterans don't want anything to do with these recruits."

"Yeah, replacements always have that problem. So it's the officers' and NCOs' job to get them all to pull together. Let me think about it."

# # #

I was really concerned. It hit me earlier in the day when I was working with a platoon. Well, it was supposed to be a platoon – roughly fifty guys. Due to casualties, though, this outfit had only thirty-two men … nineteen seasoned veterans and thirteen green replacements.

Even though everybody in the platoon was in the same age range … eighteen to twenty-one … and was freshly shaved and showered and wearing brand-new fatigues, it was easy to tell New Guinea veterans from the kids just off the boat.

They appeared to be from entirely different generations.

The veterans' faces were slightly yellowed from Atabrine, of course. That aside, their belts were cinched way in because they still were way underweight. Their faces were grim, cheeks hollowed, deep lines either sides of their mouths. They almost looked middle-aged.

Most of all they were wary. If they had anything at all to say, they whispered it, but only to fellow veterans. They had the cynical look of waiting to see what chickenshit detail this particular sergeant would hand them.

The kids from the states acted like they still were on the high school pep squad. Their cheeks were full, rounded and unlined. They grinned and laughed constantly, sharing ship-board stories and they engaged in a lot of horseplay.

They were hard and strong, but dumb. One guy, defensive tackle size, proclaimed loudly he was tired of screwing around with all this training and hoped we'd see action soon.

A veteran spat near his feet. "You want action? For ten seconds, maybe."

The newbie bunched his fists and was ready to brawl, but I put a stop to it by shouting "Tennnn-HUT!" I walked over to the kid.

I'm a six-footer but I had to look up to meet his eyes.

"Name?"

"Private Alexander Krazinski."

"High school football player?"

"Yeah. What about it?"

"Varsity?"

"Yeah, I was a starter. So what?"

"You think you're pretty tough, right?"

"Yeah. I can handle any Jap that comes along."

"I bet. But, you know, most of the Japs carry an equalizer – either a 7.7 mm Arisaka rifle or a Nambu machine gun. Now, do you know anything, anything at all, about a 7.7 slug?"

"A what?"

"A slug, son. A bullet."

He sneered. "I think I can handle it."

"Really? Well, let's talk about that. What do you weigh? Maybe 235?"

"Give or take."

"And you've had line-backers, say 190-pounders, try to take you out of play. But they couldn't do it, right?"

He looked around at the rest of the men and grinned. "Not a prayer."

"Okay, now I want to try something." I stiffened my forefinger and poked him, hard, in his right shirt pocket. He looked surprised and rocked back slightly.

"Now, be honest. That stung, didn't it? Just a little bit."

He frowned. "Yeah, barely."

"Okay, now my finger poked you at a speed of about maybe one foot per second. And, look at it." I held my hand up and rotated the finger for his inspection. "My finger is blunt. And it's only made of skin and bone. But suppose I slipped a metal tip over the end of my finger, an arrow tip with a sharp point. That probably would hurt a bit more, wouldn't it?"

He suddenly looked concerned. "So what?"

"Might even draw a little blood, right?"

He gave a sneering nod. "A little. No big deal."

"Okay, now let's suppose that a copper-jacketed bullet with a lead core … about the weight of two fingers … hit this big, thick chest of yours at a speed of two thousand four hundred feet per second. Just in case you're slow at math, that's almost a half a mile per second. And if that's hard for you to get, then you can figure the bullet is traveling around sixteen hundred miles per hour. Still with me?"

He nodded.

"If you're lucky, that bullet will go right through you. It would leave a small hole here in front, say about the thickness of my finger, and maybe the size of my fist where it comes out in back."

He swallowed.

"But it's on the way through that the bullet does its damage. Now listen up. This ain't just a sergeant's bullshit. General Leonard Wood, he was an Army doctor, tested bullets on cattle and goats. And what he found was that a bullet is moving so fast that when it hits meat…meat like you…it creates a tunnel maybe three inches wide.

"That tunnel collapses instantly, a lot faster than you could blink. But drilling that tunnel ruptures all the little veins and capillaries and blood vessels around it. So you're instantly bleeding inside your chest. But before that even happens, all that back pressure on your veins and arteries might expand your heart's size about ten per cent or so. Just for an instant. Same for the pressure in all the blood vessels in your brain.

"Being as how you're young and in good shape, you might survive. Unless, once it hits you, the bullet keyholes through your heart. If that happens, you're dead.

"But all you'll know, if you're lucky, is that you'll wake up staring at the sky wondering where you are and what the hell just happened."

The veteran next to him nodded. "That's no shit, buddy. It's like a mule kick. At first, I just felt tingling. Then it started hurting . . . like someone just whacked my leg with a ball peen hammer."

I interrupted. "Of course, the bullet might just hit you between the eyes. So it will blow out the back of your skull and half your brains with it."

Other veterans joined the ragging.

"Okay!" I yelled. "Knock it off! You're at attention! We've made the point. This is a very serious, deadly business, Krazinski. Not like football. In football, the bigger you are, the better your chances of walking off the field after the game.

"In combat, the bigger you are, the better your chances Graves Registration will *carry* you off the field. So, young trooper, when we do fire and movement exercises, and cover and concealment, I advise you to pay goddamn close attention about how to stay low, inconspicuous and out of sight. There's nothing cowardly about concealment. It's just the smart thing to do."

I walked back in front of the platoon.

"You men who've been in combat, I know how you feel. You don't want new buddies because chances are the Japs will kill them. Well, before your first action you assholes were fat, dumb and happy, too. You didn't know crap about what was coming. Now you do. So you can damned well help your new buddies get ready for it.

"The sooner they get clued in, the better off we all are when we meet the Japs again."

I gave them "At ease!" and "Smoke 'em if you got 'em" and told them to stand by, because Captain Bottcher wanted to speak with them in a few minutes. As we all lit up, one of the veterans turned to Krazinski.

"Hey, Kraz, I'm Steve Miletich. Where'd you play football?"

I was happy to hear that question. A start, maybe.

Chapter 17
Scotch Comradery

Pfc. Jake Bellknap and an Aussie soldier were yarning and nursing their beers in a quiet downtown Brisbane pub. Near closing time, Bellknap stood up and said, "Bartender, it's my round, so please draw another beer for my buddy here, Lance Fucking Corporal Dawkins."

I was sort of chaperoning Bellknap and five other members of our prospective scout group on a weekend pass in Brisbane. Lieutenant Irish ordered me to keep the guys in line because he said Brisbane and Aussie soldiers could be dangerous.

So far, though, everything was calm. We'd been drinking beer, yacking and playing bar dice. The mood was mellow and nobody was even close to being drunk. Our Aussie soldier friends were, well, quite friendly, enjoying explaining the peculiarities of our accents and word meanings.

After ordering the beer, Bellknap stubbed out his cigarette, slapped Dawkins on the shoulder and said, "Mack, I'll be right back." Ten minutes later he returned to the pub and set a grocery bag on the bar.

"From one real fighting man to another, have a nip on us, courtesy of the US PX system."

The lance jack frowned as he lifted out a bottle tightly wrapped in another sack. Pulling away the paper, he revealed a fifth of Johnny Walker Red Label scotch. Dawkins gave a broad smile and said, "Jesus Christ, Jake, that's bloody generous of you." He held it up. "Hey, mates, look what this Yank gave us. Soon as the pub closes, we'll go out and have a real shivoo."

Dawkins' announcement produced dinkum cheers from four other Aussies. The noise doubled when Bellknap looked at us and winked. "Here's ours," he said, disclosing the top of a second bottle.

Bellknap explained he met Dawkins when GIs and Aussies worked so closely in the closing days of the battle for Buna. "We was like brothers taking out those Jap bastards."

"Struth!" Dawkins said. "When I got wounded, this fine Yank pulled me to safety and then he got pranged by the same Nambu what hit me. Flamin' brothers under fire, I tell you."

As the pub closed, we and the Aussies stepped out onto the sidewalk. Ferraro was chatting with a shiela and the rest of us were trying to decide where we could enjoy our scotch. A jeep pulled up beside us and we heard a truculent, "Show me your passes!"

An American MP hopped out of the jeep, giving a menacing wave with his nightstick.

As we fumbled in our shirt pockets, the second MP, the driver, pointed his nightstick at the grocery sack. "What's in there?"

"It's a fifth of Scotch," Bellknap said.

"Yeah. When you came out of the PX, you had two bottles. Where's the other one?"

Bellknap looked up angrily. "Well, fella, if you knew what's in the sack, why're you asking? What are you, some kind of Swiss Navy admiral?"

The MP flushed. Looking grave, Dawkins warned Bellknap, "Go easy, mate." He turned to the MP and pointed to his gas mask carrier. "The other bottle is in here."

The MP sneered, "Black market deal, eh? Turn that booze over to us. Now!"

"What?" Both soldiers goggled at the MP in amazement.

Putting in his oar, Mendez snorted, "Bull*shit*, man! Cops in Albuquerque used to pull this same crap. We buy a bottle and the harness bulls brace us and then impound the bottle. Then they take it back to the station and spend the night sucking on it."

The MP said, "Watch your mouth, you little spick."

"I'd be real careful about that kind of talk," Krazinski said, leaning his massive frame over the MP jeep. "Look, guys, the whiskey is a gift from one soldier to another. No money exchanged hands. And all of us – *all* ten of us – witnessed it."

Looking intimidated by Krazinski's sheer bulk, the MP leaned back in his seat. "Tell it to the Provost Marshal. Now, dammit, just hand over the booze." He dropped his hand to pick up the microphone for the jeep's radio.

Corporal Eddy Baker – the only professional soldier in our group – quickly reached into the back of the jeep. "Now, boys, no need for that." He gave a quick twirl to the radio's frequency knob then snatched the mike cord from its socket. The other MP reached for his holster but Connally, a lanky Australian Army sergeant with whom I had shared beers, grabbed his wrist. "I wouldn't mate. We don't need another fucking Battle of Brisbane now, do we?"

The first MP put the jeep into gear but Krazinksi reached past him and slapped the ignition toggle to Off. "Don't you go for that .45 either, friend." he said.

Baker came around to lean in on the jeep's passenger side. "Boys, what is it the officers say? Something like, 'This incident is closed.' Now I suggest we all just leave peacefully." He turned to me. "What do you think Master Sergeant Mays?"

"Men, I think that's an excellent suggestion. We're just here to relax with our Aussie buddies."

"Gentlemen, are you looking for a party?" It was Ferraro's shiela. "Why don't we toodle off to my flat. It's a scant three blocks from here."

One of the cops said, "Brenda, you could regret this."

She gave him a level look. "You whacker, I already regret ever meeting you."

I heard a sudden hiss as Pfc. Robbins suddenly stood up from the right rear corner of the jeep. "Hey fellas," he said. "It looks like you're getting a flat tire."

"Yeah, too bad," Kraz said. "We'd like to help you change it, but we've got party to go to. Can't be late."

# # #

Brenda and Ferraro took the lead and Sergeant Connally and I brought up the rear.

"Hey, Robbins? Did you stick a knife in their tire?"

He gave me a wide-eyed look. "I don't have a knife. That tire's in perfect shape and so is the inner tube."

"Well, how did you give them that flat?"

He grinned. "I just used the valve cap to unscrew the valve core."

I just shook my head and asked Sergeant Connally to explain the Battle of Brisbane. He outlined a two-day riot a year earlier between Australians, military and civilian, and U.S. Army troops.

"Brisbane was a right dinkum town," Connally said, "until about a month after Pearl Harbor. That's when you Yanks started rolling in. U.S. Army and Navy blokes and by the bloody thousands." Hastily, he added, "No offense."

I grinned. "None taken."

He said he heard that within a few months the Navy and Army swelled the population from two hundred thousand to nearly three hundred thousand.

Connally said most of the GIs and sailors were rear echelon types. "You know the sort," he said, "communications wallahs, transportation blokes, shipping, repairmen and dart-throwers … military Intelligence.

"They all was working a nice forty-hour week and spending the rest of their time courtin' shielas."

He said the American outfits occupied warehouses, took over vacated schools and many other establishments. MacArthur's Southwest Pacific Area headquarters occupied all nine stories of a downtown office building.

"Of course," Sergeant Connally said in dry tones, "they all were quite vital to the war effort. Quite vital, indeed. Like the colonel and driver who take General MacArthur's wife from their home at Lennon's Hotel on her shopping trips every bleedin' day."

He said problems arose mainly because, first, GI pay was far higher than Aussies' and, second, American troops could shop in American PXs in which Aussie soldiers were not permitted.

"So, in a nation that's enduring very stringent rationing," he said, "those PX goods are bloody luxuries. Our folk have a steady diet of mutton. Your rear echelon dingos here was eating steak, turkey, ham, chicken -- anything *but* mutton. And when it came to chasing shielas, a GI could buy ice cream, chocolates and even nylons.

"Now to an old farmer like me, long married, that's nought.

"But a 20-year-old digger just back from North Africa expects a welcome from the ladies. And when he finds Yanks hugging and kissing the gals right out in public . . . and there's none for him . . . well, the lads resented it.

"Mind you," he added, "we've no complaint with American fighting troops. You lot eat C-rations that ain't much better than bully beef. And there weren't no shielas to chase in New Guinea."

Connally said the riots sparked off with MacArthur's victory announcement that Americans captured Buna. "They made it sound like the Yanks did it all with diggers merely lending the odd hand now and then."

"Yeah, you're right" I said. "Those of us in New Guinea found the HQ announcements incredibly insulting to Aussies."

"Just so," he said.

"The fact is," I went on, "we'd probably be buried in Buna if your Brigadier Wooten hadn't found a way to bring in tanks to break the Japs' bunkers. And before that -- in fact, just as we were arriving -- Aussie infantry stopped two Jap offensives cold."

"Right," he said. "But the riots nearly ruined Brisbane for us all. Ever since the riots, the city crawls with American MPs."

"Aussie military police can be pretty damned starchy," he said. "But the bullet-headed bastards fought in Africa and the Middle East with us, the troops they were policing. They shared the same *esprit* like.

"We reckon the American MPs, on the other hand, ain't seen ten seconds of combat." Yet, he pointed out, they struck Aussies as surly, arrogant and over-eager in their petty authority to start bashing people with their hickory night sticks. "They seem to regard us infantry as fucking enemies."

# # #

On our run back to camp, I discovered my worries fading. The encounter with the MPs, along with some decent scotch, had narrowed the gulf between veterans and new guys. They were trading jokes and stories.

Corporal Baker roared, "Men, when we met those MPs, we were a MACHINE! Know what I mean? I jinx their radio and two seconds later old Kraz here flips off the jeep ignition. And with that Aussie sergeant cooling the one cop with the hog leg? Well, it was just perfect."

"Right!" Kraz said, "and Luis diverted them with that story about the cops in wherever."

Mendez said, "Right. Albuquerque."

"Yeah, that's it!"

"Well, I thank you boys for some fast thinking," Bellknap said. "I been saving up to buy scotch for a long time and I sure didn't want those bastards taking it."

"Say, Ferraro, what did Brenda mean by calling that MP a whacker? That really took the starch out of his drawers. Does that mean he's a pud-knocker?"

Ferraro laughed. "No, she told me it just meant he's a jerk, or maybe an idiot."

"Boys," I said, "you got to give credit to Ferraro, too. Far as I'm concerned, he was the key to the whole situation. He found the girl who knew the place where we could go for a nice quiet party."

"Yeah," Miletich said, "and here's a Czech who says that, for a fucking wop, Ferraro did real good. And, hey! Since he's a new guy, we can call him our new guinea, eh? Get it? Our brand-new guinea?"

"That's a terrible groaner," Corporal Baker said. "But we'll let it go if the new guinea will."

I didn't say it worked out perfectly, but it came close. A bit of discord with the MPs turned two groups of virtual strangers into buddies. When I reported in to Lieutenant Irish, I recommended he take the other half the team on pass.

He did and three of them had a run-in with the MPs and came back pretty bunged up, a tight brand of battered and bruised brothers.

They also had special advice to steer clear of MPs wearing gloves. The MPs had copied Seattle police who once upon a time wore sheet lead in the back of their gloves and if they back-handed you, lights out!

They had some fine stories with which to top our tales of Johnny Walker and the MPs.

At the court martial, Captain Bottcher fined each troublemaker five dollars…three dollars because they hospitalized two MPs and two dollars because they got caught.

Chapter 18
Learning To Love The Night

"Robbins, you're dead!"

That was Lieutenant Irish's voice growling out of the solid darkness.

The rest of the guys gave a collective sigh of exasperation.

"Yep," Kenton said, "the first flies will land on Robbins in a minute or two. By dawn he'll have a full working crew of maggots in his eyes and mouth."

"Yeah," Bellknap added, "and with this heat by noon he'll be swole up twice his size." Then, in a tuneless bellow he sang,

The worms crawl in,
the worms crawl out.
The worms play pinochle on your snout.

Lieutenant Irish said, "Robbins?"

"Yessir?"

"Do you know why you're dead?"

"Sir, because I sniffled?"

"That's exactly right. You had your brain in neutral and so your nose did what comes naturally. The Japs woulda heard you and killed your ass. Next time your nose is running, let the damn thing run. Clear?

"Okay, ever'body on your feet! Back to your original positions and start crawling again. Robbins, you lead this time."

We stood up, the dozen of us, and walked back to our start line. Seven of us were veterans and five were new-comers. This was the second session of Lieutenant Irish's the-night-is-your-friend training. The students were the people who, so far, seemed to qualify for Odd Ball duty with Captain Bottcher's behind-the-lines scouting outfit.

To hold down on noise, we taped our dog tags and armed ourselves only with knives and pistols in fabric holsters. Instead of helmets, we wore short-brimmed camouflage hats.

We all hit the deck again. I was prone beside Robbins, who was one of the newbies and a tough one. I whispered to him, "Don't get discouraged. This is how you learn."

"I think the old man has it in for me."

"Of course, he does! He wants you to survive. So pay attention! And when it's time to move, move quiet."

The idea was that you moved like a bit like a croc, slightly up on your hands and knees rather than dragging your belly along the earth. You lift your torso slightly from the ground, ease forward, then down, bringing hands and legs forward again, raising yourself off the ground again, and so forth.

God didn't create humans to move that way so it takes a lot of strength and hell of a lot of sweat to do it. It hurts, too. Say you're putting all your weight on a palm – or a kneecap – and it's on a sharp pebble. You can endure it or jerk the limb away and have the Japs butcher you.

It helps you appreciate the more forgiving qualities of mud.

The lieutenant sounded off from fifty yards away where he was hunkered beside one of those big sail-shaped termite mounds. "Okay, men, we're doing it a little different this time. So, start low-crawling toward me. Robbins, see if you can get past me without getting your whole squad shot up."

We crawled about ten feet when I heard *thonk*, a mortar being fired some distance behind us. Then came a sharp *pop* directly overhead … a flare bathing us in bright orange light.

The lieutenant shouted, "Freeze! Don't move! Not a muscle! Goddammit, Mendez, I said 'Don't move!' But you had to lower your head, didn't you? Congratulations, it made you stick out like a sore thumb and you and ever'body around you is getting slaughtered by Nambus right now."

We crawled the rest of the distance, two more flares putting us under their swaying light.

Lieutenant Irish lit a Coleman lantern and ordered us to gather around him.

"Okay, that was better with the second and third flare. Lots better. You froze. But my God, you guys make as much noise as a small herd of cattle, especially you, Kraz. You breathe like a damn steam engine."

He held up the lantern so he could see the whole group. "Now I know you men think I'm being awful tough. You're right. But believe me, I'm not near as brutal as Japs if you give them half a chance. Keep that in mind … *always!*

"Now I'm going to turn off this lamp and we'll let our eyes adjust to the dark. As we do, Sergeant Mays is going to slip off and try to show you how it's done right. You men spread out and keep your eyes peeled. The instant you see him, sing out. I got ten bucks says you won't see him. Spot him and you win."

I took nearly forty minutes, moving lizard-like obstacle to obstacle. I took the shallowest of breaths and froze the instant I heard the mortar cough. Once I damn near cussed aloud when some critters – I think they were little red ants -- began stinging my hands and arms. You want to swipe the little bastards off because *God* these stings hurt! But no fast movement allowed.

At least I could cheat.

Knowing roughly where the guys were, I maneuvered around their flank and came up behind them. The faint glow from the stars enabled me to pick out Lieutenant Irish's termite mound. From the ground right behind him, I whispered. "Say, Lieutenant, do I get the ten bucks? If I do, I'll stand you a free beer."

He chuckled. "Well, Jim, you ain't lost your touch. I'll give you that. But you're a cheap, ungrateful bastard if you'd only give me a single beer."

Then he called, "Okay, boys and girls! All the, all the, all the outs in free! Sergeant Mays is back and not one of you spotted him, not even with flares a'poppin'. You want to get back home to Momma alive, you better learn how to do what he does."

I briefed the group about how I had flanked them. Ferraro said he thought the tactic was unfair, especially since I already knew the terrain.

Lieutenant Irish said, "Jesus, son, you think the Japs *won't* know their terrain just as well or better than Sergeant Mays? Besides, there ain't no 'fair' . . . especially not in war. Forget about fair until you're a civilian again."

Robbins raised a hand. "Sir, I hear that on New Guinea, we'll be going into jungle and swamps, so why are we training like this on dry land?"

Lieutenant Irish said, "Good question, son. First of all, a lot of New Guinea's terrain alternates between jungle and swamp on one hand and areas like this … they call it savannah. Second, whatever kind of ground you're on, you need to know how to operate on it at night. Remember, the night is your friend."

The lieutenant assigned me to take them in pairs over the same course and to show them how to do it soundlessly. It took most of the rest of the night.

The following night they did better.

# # #

"Lieutenant, I've got to admit they're starting to learn." We were yawning and talking next day at lunch. Both of us were ready for a nap, but we still had paperwork to deal with.

"Yeah, Jim, they are. It won't be long before they get their diplomas. And from there we'll take them on to junior college."

"What do you mean, sir?"

"With the Navy's help, we're going to start learning amphibious landings. We'll practice on some nice sand beaches. Then we'll head to Milne Bay to learn how to land on New Guinea beaches, right where the jungle meets the sea. And after that we'll do some field problems on Goodenough Island."

"Goodenough Island?"

"Yeah, it's in the Coral Sea just around the corner from Milne Bay. It lies forty or fifty miles off New Guinea's north coast."

"The name actually is 'Goodenough'?"

"Yep, named in honor of some Limey admiral. If you say the name fast enough it almost sounds Russian – like 'Gudenov.'

"Anyway, the Aussies kicked a few Japs off the island a month or so ago. You could say it's ideal for advanced training. High humidity, lots of rain and heat, jungle, lots of swamp and some uplands, tons of mosquitos. And one of the landing points is called Mud Bay. Sounds just right for our purposes."

"So it's good enough for us? Get it, sir? 'Goodenough'?"

"Sergeant, are you trying to make a joke? Should I laugh now?""

"Sorry, Lieutenant Irish. Just a bad play on words."

"Right. Makes me wonder … d'you suppose after their wedding night the admiral's wife said 'Goodenough'?"

"That's very funny, sir. A real knee-slapper."

Chapter 19
Ropes And Boats

The term "amphibious landing" sounds simple. Get aboard ship. Get into boat. Boat takes you to beach. Jump onto beach. Attack Japs.

The last step sounds like the most difficult, right?

That's what I thought, too.

But that was before we spent damn near six weeks learning steps two, three and four – things the Marines started practicing back in the 30s. Lieutenant Irish summed it up: "There ain't no simple part."

"Okay, men," I yelled, "by the numbers. First, face the railing. Now do a left face. Great! You actually did it! So far so good.

"Next, grab the railing and swing your right leg over it. Place your foot on one of the cargo net's horizontal strands. Now the other foot on another strand. Now start your descent. Kraz! For God's sake grab only the vertical strands -- unless you want the guy right above you to stomp your fingers." It was exhausting, each step down caused the net to sag. Meanwhile, three other guys to your right and left are doing the same thing. You start to appreciate what life must be like on a spider's web.

After several practice runs from a tall timber framework, we tried it from the overhanging bow of an old freighter hulk. Now, instead of hanging against a wall, the net dangled free. So it writhed like a mad thing as each man took each step down it. And this time the boys were descending into an actual boat floating in real water. The boat crew did their best to keep the net taut while jamming their feet against the boat's bulkhead to keep it from drifting away.

But this still was easier than the real thing. None of us wore a pack or helmet or carried a rifle. And the water was flat calm so the boat wasn't rising and falling with the ocean swell.

"Okay, guys, that pretty much covers step Number Two, getting into the boat. We'll try it for real when we get to Milne Bay. But for now, we're gonna work on landing."

Things really become crazy once we practiced getting ashore. We who are first on the beach not only are supposed to assault the Japs, but we're also supposed to communicate with fighter pilots,

Naval gunnery forward observers, Army artillery forward observers, beach masters, engineers, mobile hospitals, you name it. Our first practice landing was chaotic, with a lot of people just standing around in the sand looking bewildered.

In our post-practice briefing, Lieutenant Irish seemed more stern than ever.

"Sergeant Mays, once you and your boys are out of the boat, you temporarily become the most important man on the beach. Yes, *you*. The CO still is in another boat or maybe he just landed say five hundred yards away, or maybe his boat sank and he went down with it. Either way, he doesn't know what you're facing. He doesn't know whether you need fire support from the ship, or aircraft support, or both. Maybe you're taking casualties. Maybe not. The point is, you're in charge."

"Well, what about our radios?"

"Sergeant, you hope for the best, but five'll get you ten that your radio either is in the drink or not working.

"And if it is working, maybe twenty other people are on that circuit – including some Japs who are trying to jam it -- all you hear is babble.

"Sergeant, you've got to take charge and make decisions before some enterprising Nip machine gunner does it for you. You've got to lead."

"How do you do that?"

"You say, 'Follow me!' and head inland."

Chapter 20
Practice And More Practice

Captain Bottcher and Lieutenant Irish held an informal seminar for NCOs after our third practice beach assault.

"So, gentlemen, now that you've been through these mock landings, what's your biggest worry?"

None of us could answer at first, but two items finally occurred to me. "My first worry is that I'll get my ass shot off when rolling over the side of that boat. Second, I'm afraid that once we're out on the ground I won't be able to control my men."

He gave me a smile. "Okay, once you land you won't worry about getting shot. You'll be too busy to think about it. And if you do get shot, your only worry is how soon the medics can evacuate you.

"Second worry? You've worked with these men for weeks. They'll be as worried as you and they'll look to your example. So you need to act calm and to give them very clear, simple orders. Believe me, they'll follow.

"Your real worries are that we who still are on the ships are getting ammo and water and then food to your troops ASAP. Ammo's the main concern at first. Water is just as important … otherwise they'll drink from the swamps and wind up within hours as amoebic dysentery casualties."

He paused. "Oh! One other thing. Maybe you won't have to roll over the side of your boat. The Aussies raised three landing craft that were sunk when the Japs tried to invade Milne Bay. Their boats have a big ramp that drops down onto the beach and you just walk off it.

"Well, the Army created an American version and they have arrived. It's called the LCP(R) for Landing Craft Personnel (Ramp) … instead of the LCP you've been rolling out of."

# # #

"Okay, men," I shouted over the engine noise, "keep your heads down! The coxswain and I will watch on the shoreline. Once we land, you'll get to see all you want."

It was our first ride in an LCP(R) and I couldn't tell if they heard me over the roar of the boat's diesel. But even if they did, I think most of them reveled in the sheer relief of having got down the net in one piece … and concentrated on trying not to vomit.

Thanks to the wash created by a passing destroyer, the landing craft that we climbed down into was rising and falling on the waves six or eight feet every ten seconds. First time for us. Moreover, also for the first time, we all were in full gear – helmet, rifle and musette bag, plus two full canteens. NCOs and officers also had a .45 pistol in a canvas holster attached to our cartridge belts.

If you timed your transfer from net to boat properly … just as the boat reached the top of its rise … it was easy as stepping onto an escalator.

But if you left the net just as the boat was starting to rise from its low point in a wave's trough, you fell six or eight feet and could break an ankle.

Which still was preferable to falling from the net between ship and boat. Then you'd sink like a stone unless, of course, boat and ship swung together and crushed you like a bug.

Thank God nobody fell, although several men dropped helmets and rifles as they clambered down the net.

Corporal Randy VanTuyl tried to step into the boat while getting one foot tangled in the net. So as the boat rose and sank, the panicked Dutchman alternately dangled head down or had the deck slam up against him.

If three of us hadn't succeeded in getting his leg out of the net and prying his fingers from the net's strands, I think he'd still be dangling there.

It took about thirty lurching minutes for the boat to get us to the beach.

The ramp dropped and we staggered ashore, immediately encountering the jungle stench. I got them in line and we headed inland which meant that in about a hundred feet we were off the sand and into the swamps of Milne Bay.

Riegle announced, "Hot DAMN men! This is the first time I've ever felt relieved to plunge into a goddam swamp."

It was about the only laugh we had that day.

Chapter 21
A New Pacific Cruise

Somewhere in the Southwest Pacific, maybe during practice landings in Australia, my immunity disappeared.

I mean, I never suffered seasickness as a kid when crewing aboard sailboats on Puget Sound. I could chomp down candy bars or hot dogs while going through some pretty rough weather.

As for ocean-going travel? No problem. From the Golden Gate to Adelaide in Australia, many of my comrades thought they'd expire from terminal nausea. But I never had so much as a qualm. Our ship at the time, the *S.S. Lurline*, was an ocean-going passenger liner that took the big Pacific swells with graceful dignity.

But now... now we were aboard an APD, a verrrry different world.

The initials APD stand for Auxiliary Personnel Destroyer. That's the U.S. Navy's designation for rattling, creaky, crapped-out old World War I destroyers transformed into small but fairly fast troop transports.

We infantrymen are the auxiliary personnel in question.

They shoehorn up to two hundred of us into these ships, company-size groups of riflemen for shoreline raids or acting as a point at the spear tip of an invasion.

It wasn't long before I came to believe the term Auxiliary Personnel Destroyer meant exactly what those words seem to say -- a vessel explicitly designed to destroy auxiliary personnel.

I've never been so wretchedly sick in my life.

Maybe that seems a little over the top. But put yourself in our place. We were voyaging inside a tube three hundred fourteen feet long. It behaved like a playground see-saw being used by very vigorous children.

But that was just the rocking.

Our stomachs also had to contend with rolling. Our seesaw was only thirty-one feet wide, and she constantly rolled with the waves. First she rolled hard to the left, then harder to the right, then even harder back to the left, all the while violently see-sawing.

The feeling brought to mind Conrad's novel *Lord Jim* depicting a mass of seasick Chinese coolies rolling back and forth in the hold of an old tramp freighter almost as if they were so much bilge water sloshing to and fro.

We didn't roll like *Lord Jim's* Chinese because each of us had a death grip on the stanchions to which his canvas rack was attached. But boy we did suffer … sweating, eyes shut, groaning in unison. Each vertical and horizontal oscillation of our little prison provoked a chorus of misery. Then the vessel would pause, swoop back, pause, and then swoop the opposite way.

We tried to keep it down. Actually, I don't believe anything remained inside our stomachs to be kept down.

But Mother Nature and Aunt Nausea always found a way.

Perhaps malaria gets the blame for wrecking my intestinal stability. But it could have been the ships' disparate sizes, too.

Looking all this up, I found that the beautiful liner *Lurline* displaced eighteen thousand tons and was more than seven hundred feet long.

But the amused crewmen of our APD rust bucket, the *USS Sands*, told me their ship weighs in at about a mere twelve hundred tons.

So she tosses about like a cork on a pond.

I think *USS Teeter-Totter* would be a better name for her.

The crew bitched constantly about how much they had to work to keep the *Sands'* ancient power plant steaming. But they also gave her the deck ape's highest compliment. They said she was a home and a feeder – and her galley served wonderful meals.

So who was eating?

Not me.

The fact is, I didn't like the *Sands* the instant I first saw her. She was ugly, mottled by camouflage paint of various shades of green which our complexions soon came to match. Aside from that, decades of slamming through stormy seas had dished her thin steel skin between the vessel's frames. Looking at her gave me the impression of an ocean-going checker board.

Sands had no gun turrets. Her main gun was a pedestal-mounted 3-incher shielded by nothing more than its canvas cover. She also had a few 20 mm and 40 mm anti-aircraft guns. It didn't seem impressive until we saw how potent those weapons could be against Jap positions on shore.

Her K guns and the depth charges they hurled were very potent against submarines, too, but we never saw them in use.

We troops lived – if you can call it that – in two compartments that originally were boiler rooms. It was humid, of course, blazing hot under tropic sunlight and merely hot as hell at night. And life aboard *Sands* was very, very noisy. Sergeant Riegle's rack was against the starboard skin of the ship. "I swear, Jim, the water tearing along outside that wall sounds like the damned Indy Five Hundred."

"It's not a wall, Charlie. It's a bulkhead."

"Oh, go blow it out, Jim."

"That's what I've done ever since we got aboard this tub."

When the two of us first started getting sick, we tried to go topside hoping fresh air would help us get over it.

No dice.

The crew explained that, being flush-decked, *Sands* had no guard rails. They were certain lubbers like us would wash right overboard.

"No kidding, sergeant," one of the petty officers said, "these Clemsen Class ships always are wet forrard. You don't want to be out on deck in any kind of seaway. I've seen kids swept off and then get sucked into the screws. Chopped them right into chum.

"See, in converting her to an APD they took two boilers out of this ship. So taking out all that heavy gear raised her center. And then they also hoisted these four landing craft up high on those big davits, so that raised it even more. Makes the ship real tender."

"Tender?"

"Yeah. It means she rolls a lot."

Riegle gulped. "No shit! We know."

The chief was sympathetic. "Don't worry, men, this trip won't last forever. The best thing you could do now is get some coffee."

Bastard!

The trip north from Brisbane to Townsville, a seven hundred-mile run, only took thirty-six hours even if it seemed like forever. And ominously, we weren't permitted to send mail before departing. "Yeah," Riegle said. "That's so when this ship sinks with all hands, nobody will know. It'll save all kinds of War Department telegrams.'

Once moored at Townsville, they let us topside to stretch and air out. One platoon of our GI passengers were disembarking there. But I won the Captain Bligh Award by first dragooning them to help the rest of us clean the now-nauseating troop compartments.

The *Sands'* crew were a big help. They lent us some buckets, mops and wringers. "And, gee, fellas, you'll make sure they're all rinsed and clean before you return them, right?"

The next leg of our trip was to escort a flotilla of LSTs on a six hundred-mile run from Townsville across the Coral Sea to Milne Bay at the eastern tip of New Guinea. Japanese submarines still appeared in the area from time to time and we'd heard that fearsome high-speed Jap destroyers came calling occasionally.

All of us could have cared less. What worried us was the weather and the length of time we'd be see-sawing the waves.

"The bad news," the chief said, "is that LSTs only go about fourteen knots, so it'll take us another day and a half. Try not eating until we get there."

"That will be real easy, chief."

If misery loves company, I discovered a sorry blessing of sorts.

While in harbor, I met a *Sands* sailor who suffered more, I believe, than all of us troops combined. His face seemed to mirror mine ... white as his sailor's cap, a pale green tinge about the cheeks and accented with a thin sheen of perspiration.

"I'm not just seasick now," he told me. "I'm seasick starting the minute we weigh anchor to get this bitch underway. And I stay sick until we tie up in some other port."

"Can't you transfer?"

"I've already put in a request. The exec and skipper both okayed it. We're just waiting for BuPers to process it."

"BuPers?"

"Yeah, the U.S. Navy Bureau of Personnel."

"Oh. Well how long ...?"

"Shit, who knows? It's been six months so far."

If I hadn't been so full of my own self-pity, I would have felt sorry for him.

Chapter 22
We Won't Be Home For Christmas

Perhaps I've dwelt too much on the misery we endured. We did, after all, have lighter moments. Many of them came from Pfc. Luis Mendez.

Mendez was a laughing, joking, black-eyed devil built like a tank, low and wide.

Though he was U.S. citizen, Luis was proud of his Mexican heritage. The only test of his invariable cheerfulness came when we mispronounced his first name as *Louis* rather than *Lou-eece*.

Naturally, we always pronounced it *Louis*.

During the Buna campaign, Mendez had suffered as much as the rest of us, taking a load of shrapnel. Malaria and jungle rot laid him low, too. Nonetheless, he always smiled if only to exhibit the gold canine crown that was his pride and joy. He extracted our promise that when the Japs killed him, he wanted one of us to pull the tooth and send it to his folks.

Yes, he always said "when," not "if," and quite cheerfully. "They'll get me one day, but I'll send lots of the little bastards ahead of me."

"Don't you want to survive, Luis?"

"Shit yes, man! But look at our odds."

The *Sands'* oceanic gyrations never troubled Mendez. He claimed his immunity came from years of working with his dad aboard their own fishing boat out of Los Angeles. As a youth, he at first suffered seasickness, but he claimed his Popi's perpetual banter and bullshit helped him overcome the problem.

So he favored us with unending chatter, apparently believing it would help the gringos survive *enfermedad del mar*.

One special event stands out.

We were moored in Milne Bay when a landing craft bearing supplies slammed alongside. The coxswain misjudged distances. I don't know, maybe he was drunk.

Or seasick.

At any rate, his boat struck the *Sands'* port side hard enough to punch a jagged six-inch hole into the aft troop compartment. Aside from the explosive "clank," the collision produced a brief deluge of seawater right onto the rack and the slumbering person of Pfc. Charles Jones.

Jones, thinking we had been torpedoed and were sinking, had a brief but intense bout of hysterics. Racing topside in his skivvies, he screamed things like "Take cover!" and "Man the life boats!" plus "Abandon ship!" and maybe even "Man overboard!" Accounts differ because several other men took up the chorus until the ship's crew calmed everybody down.

Up to this point, we simply called Jones "Charlie." But somewhere along the way Mendez noted that Charlie's middle name was Albert, so that he was listed on our roster a C. A. Jones.

Well, with the uproar over the accident, Mendez got revenge for our abuse of his first name by transforming "C.A. Jones" to the Spanish word *Cajones*.

He started it by congratulating the squad for so quickly overcoming its panic. Pointing to Jones, he'd say, "Hey, our squad has real *cajones* and that's him right there, *Senor Pfc. Cajones* himself. Them damn Nips better look out for us, you know."

From that day forth, all of us called him Cajones, giving his new nickname perfect pronunciation … *kuh-HO-nace* … thanks to Pfc. Mendez's very careful coaching.

But despite his very careful coaching, none of us ever pronounced Luis correctly.

# # #

Late the same day a machinist mate welded a patch over the hole beside Cajones' rack and we were off, this time for full-scale landing rehearsals on Goodenough Island.

The *Sands'* skipper announced that en route we'd celebrate Christmas – complete with caroling and a yuletide feast with turkey and dressing.

"Hey, Cajones? Can you say 'Feliz navidad'?"

"What's that, Louis?"

"Hey, *please* man, it's Luis! And 'Feliz navidad' means the same as 'Merry Christmas'."

We appreciated the crews' efforts to make merry. But trying to sing *Oh Holy Night* when you're nauseated and the humidity and temp are both 9 . . . well, it just ain't the same as caroling house-to-house with the choir on a snowy night in Oshkosh or Battle Creek

Perhaps it's just as well.

Our Goodenough Island training left no time for holiday depression. In fact, it proved to be perfect staging for an attack into New Guinea. Its geography and weather were identical to New Guinea's – inland mountain, coastal swamps and jungle with surging monsoon-fed streams, thanks to several inches of rain daily.

Despite almost constant downpours, engineers had cleared huge swaths of timber and filled swamps to create air strips. They also organized enormous supply dumps for everything from artillery ammo to rations to freezers containing bottles of frozen whole blood of all types.

After we arrived, Captain Bottcher told Lieutenant Irish that our oddballs now were a special scouting squad in Able Company.

The captain explained that we'd land soon somewhere on the north coast of New Guinea. "We're going to be part of Michaelmas Task Force – that's our regiment beefed up into a miniature division. We'll have our own howitzers, tank destroyers, hospital, supply unit, MPs and even malaria control units."

"Who the hell came up with 'Michaelmas'?"

"Beats me," Lieutenant Irish said. "Maybe the chaplain, 'cause it sounds like something to do with church. Who cares?

"So where are we landing, Cap'n?"

"I can't tell you until after we shove off."

"Do you know when?"

"Next year."

"Well, sir, since we just celebrated Christmas, that's kind of vague ain't it?"

"Yes. How about if I just say 'soon'?"

Chapter 23
Happy Damned New Year!

On New Year's Eve, Captain Bottcher gave Company A an hour-long break and two beers apiece. So much for celebration. Other than that, it was back to work for everyone, captain included. We spent the rest of that day humping supplies into ships through Goodenough Island's periodic downpours.

"I don't know," Riegle said, passing two boxes of .30 cal to Kraz. "Which is making me more wet, sweat or rain?"

"I think you've put your finger on it," Miletich said.

"On what? What do you mean?"

"What he means," Robbins said, "is 'Shut your yap and keep working'."

We loaded our machine guns, mortars, ammo, rations and other supplies into the *Sands*. As far as we could see in the rain and mist, the entire regiment, with sand and mud to the knees, was doing the same work at other ships.

After we wrapped up at *Sands*, they tagged us to manhandle two disassembled piper cubs aboard an LST. Then we formed a chain gang at the same vessel, passing construction timbers, cases of nails and screws plus extra cases of 105 mm howitzer ammo. The new guys bitched and moaned about the howitzer ammo.

We vets did not.

For six weeks at Buna last November we'd had no artillery support at all. Personally, I was delighted to invest some sweat equity in the big guns so they could cough out their thirty-three pound payloads when we needed them.

Other LSTs had pushed up onto the beach, towering clamshell doors open, with drivers revving motors as they backed tank destroyers and bulldozers up the ramps into the ships' interiors. Big exhaust vents jutted like black courthouse columns above the LSTs' decks.

They boated us back to *Sands* just after dark. It was one whipped company of doughboys who collapsed onto our racks. I was flat out scared. I knew we'd land somewhere soon, and probably in the teeth of the same impenetrable bunkers that the Japs constructed at Buna.

I was so whipped, though, that my fears, imaginings and Buna memories kept me awake only about two minutes.

At midnight, the ship's PA jarred us all back to consciousness when it announced that 1944 had arrived. Happy New Year, eh? I came awake just enough to turn over on my rack, to notice we were underway and then to sink into a sweet dream about snuggling with Suzanne.

At dawn I climbed the compartment ladder to take a look outside.

Despite the rain and wind and seas that were lashing the *Sands'* deck, I could see we were part of a fair-sized convoy, at least four LSTs, several modern destroyers and maybe six aging destroyer transports like *Sands*. Plus that there was a long, tossing column of big landing craft with spray breaking over their flat bows.

Despite the pitching and rolling, I actually was hungry for the first time in days. And the crew was right. The *Sands'* galley produced a great breakfast even though eating from a segmented steel tray took some practice.

As the ship rolled to port, you had to tilt your tray to starboard to keep it horizontal and then, seconds later, vice versa. I couldn't master pouring syrup on my pancakes while keeping my coffee mug *and* tray level. The flapjacks and scrambled eggs ended up sodden with maple-flavored coffee, but they still beat hell out of C rations.

At my table, two astute Naval strategic theorists assured me that the stormy weather was great for all of us. Between noisy slurps of coffee, a water tender stressed that the wind and rain would keep Jap planes on the ground. "And we got no worries about Jap subs, neither. They wouldn't dare take on a dozen destroyers."

"No way in hell," a torpedoman added as drops of egg yolk accented the front of his dungaree shirt. "Odds are we'll arrive in good shape. And you don't need to worry on the beach, neither, Sarge. We we'll back you guys up with pinpoint fire. We'll be real close in."

"Close in?"

"Oh, hell yeah. We'll anchor within five hundred yards of the beach. "All we'll have between us and Jap bullets will be the ship's skin, a measly quarter inch of steel."

"Wow," I said. "You guys really take some risks." He beamed with pride.

Then I added, "Of course, my boys and I will actually be *on* the beach. All we have between us and Jap bullets is a sixteenth-inch of cotton fatigue shirt."

# # #

Late that afternoon Captain Bottcher told us Task Force Michaelmas would land at dawn at a coastal village named Saidor. It had a small airstrip with a modest Jap garrison.

"Once the task force establishes a beachhead," the captain said, "its mission will be to block the Japs retreating west from Huon Peninsula where two Aussie divisions have been attacking them. They're trying to get to Madang. That's a very large Japanese base about seventy miles west of Saidor. Intelligence predicts that resistance at Saidor will be light."

Oh, yeah. Sure! Will the dart-throwers land with us?

"Company A's first objective," he continued, "will be the airstrip and the village. They're about a half-mile inland. In the next two days after that, the rest of the task force's three battalions will fan out and enlarge the beachhead.

"If the Japs attack us at Saidor, we'll have all the firepower we need, our own artillery plus naval gunnery, to defeat them. If they by-pass us to the south, they'll have to cover about a hundred fifty miles, *jungle* miles, boys, to get to Madang. And most of it over a mountain range. They'll be starving."

"Starving, sir? You said you can live off the jungle."

He grinned. "*You* can, yes. And a 10-man patrol can. But when three or four thousand men travel through the bush, all but the first thirty or forty are going to find it pretty slim pickings. Everybody in trail goes hungry."

He explained that while the infantry would keep an eye out for the Japs, the engineers would start enlarging Saidor's airstrip so that Air Corps P-40s and B-25s could use it to start blasting the next targets along New Guinea's coast.

After his briefing, Captain Bottcher pulled Lieutenant Irish and me aside. "As soon as we secure Saidor," he said, "you Odd

Balls will break into two squads to infiltrate through the Japanese lines.

"Dan, you and your boys will move straight south toward the hills. Jim, I want your team to proceed east along the coast.

"Your job is to spot any Jap movements and to radio the info to our headquarters here."

The orders rattled me. I was used to following Lieutenant Irish's lead, but now my men and I would be on our own. I think the captain read my fear.

"Look, men, I don't want you getting into any fights with the Japs," he said. "You are our eyes. You observe and report in at 0700, 1200 and 1900 hours. If you make contact or spot a lot of Nips, call it in immediately."

I just hoped I'd be alive after the landing.

I expected our invasion to collapse in a bloody welter against the kind of bunkers that murdered us at Buna.

Chapter 24
WHEW!!!!

I've never been so very, very happy to be so very, very wrong.

The Japs hadn't constructed a single bunker at Saidor.

What's more, they got the hell out before we even stepped onto the beach.

In fact, my boys and I didn't even have to climb down any damned cargo nets. One-by-one we settled ourselves into the LCP(R)s and then the *Sands'* crew swung those big boat davits outward. They lowered us into the choppy waters of the Bismarck Sea. From there it was a thousand-yard putt above the coral heads to the beach.

But, good Lord, was it noisy! The modern destroyers fired above us to shell the beach. Those vessels' five-inch guns go off with a wicked, ear-splitting crack that made us flinch constantly. When the ramps dropped and we stumbled ashore, we couldn't hear worth a damn. But it didn't matter. Not a Jap was present.

As our squad took a knee, letting another squad leapfrog us, Bellknap said, "You know, this is kind of a let-down."

"Bullshit!" Cajones said. "This is just fine with me. The only resistance we're getting is from mosquitos."

"The absence of rifle and machine gun fire sure makes my day," Ferraro said.

As we arrived at the airstrip, native men began venturing timidly from the jungle. Bombing and shelling had rattled them, of course, but they were smiling. In Pidgin English they said they were happy the Japs were gone. When we assured them we'd let their women alone, they began waving their families out into the open.

The landing's only casualties were the exhausted, soaked, shivering, staggering men who had spent almost two days riding in LCIs three hundred-some stormy sea miles from Goodenough Island. Those vessels were maybe half as long as our destroyer transports and much, much lighter.

Our landing was the start of a pattern. We later learned that the Air Corps and Navy created tremendous diversions, repeatedly bombing and shelling Jap installations hundreds of miles away like Madang, creating the expectation that we'd invade there. So then we'd come ashore where they had very minimal forces, meeting almost no initial opposition. Fighting would come later, after they'd trek overland to attack a well-established beachhead.

The Saidor beach itself was pitiful.

"What a dump!" Robbins said. "I was expecting golden sands with coconut trees, you know? But it's just grit and rocks."

It was difficult to cross the beach without turning an ankle on the beach stones, but at least it was narrow. We could stand in the middle of the beach and spit into the ocean on one side and the swamp on the other. In some places, long swamp oak branches extended out over the breaking waves.

# # #

Once our battalion reported the airstrip secured, Captain Bottcher sent Lieutenant Irish and me off on our own missions.

I split my squad, giving Cajones, Robbins, Miletich, Kenton and VanTuyl to Riegle, whom Captain Bottcher had just promoted to sergeant. Riegle's squad was to patrol east along the shoreline. They had binoculars so they could spot movement a good mile off in case Japs were hiking up the coast.

The rest of us struck out along a jungle path paralleling the beach roughly a quarter mile inland. At first, Bellknap took point for my gang. I kept Mendez at 6 o'clock, with Ferraro, Baker, Kraz and me being the main body.

By early afternoon, we were far enough east of Saidor that we barely heard the Japs' lone attack on the beachhead.

We learned later that a squadron of their bombers peeled off to attack the line-up of LSTs disgorging engineering equipment and supplies. The very intense antiaircraft fire from destroyers, destroyer transports and LSTs discouraged them.

Meanwhile, we sloshed through swamps, chopped through jungle and tried to wave off clouds of bugs, the hand motion that our digger friends back at Brisbane called the Aussie Salute.

But except for the screeching mynahs and parrots it was quiet. Nothing moved but big colorful butterflies and fruit bats. Not a sign of Japs. Even so, we were back in the war.

We didn't know eighteen months of fighting lay ahead . . . the last month being the worst.

Chapter 25
The First Contact

"Bleach Blonde this is Swamp Rat. Read me?" I released the walkie-talkie key.

Sergeant Riegle answered, "Loud and clear, Rat. What's up?"

"Our trail done petered out on us. And I don't like how we're separated. So halt in place. We're coming to you."

"Wilco."

It took my boys and me an exhausting hour working in relays to cut through brush tangles, bamboo thickets, saplings and, at the bottom of a deep ravine, low-hanging festoons of wait-a-minute vines. Kraz dubbed them wait-a-minutes because the vines had a way of snagging machete handles and the butts and front sights of our weapons. They always brought you to a complete and frustrating stop.

Once up out of the ravine, I was struck by the gentle twilight beauty of a shallow slope lying before us. Lovely knee-high ferns blanketed the slope.

The scenery was deceptive.

The ferns themselves hid an ankle-deep carpet of creepers that caused each of us to trip and fall at least once. And that was when we made the painful discovery that for all their soft beauty, ferns grow on stiff stalks with jagged points. They inflict lots of little punctures on hands and faces. And the bugs love supping in those little sores.

After that, all we had to do was plough through a waist-deep morass lying between us and the beach.

When I say 'morass,' I'm not just talking about muddy water. It was watery, yes. But it also was almost solid with a very stringy underwater weed. It looked as thin as spider web. You move five feet and you seemed to have fifty pounds of it wrapped around each leg. Move another three feet and you no longer can move at all. You have to stop and spend ten minutes pulling the tangle from your legs, waist, hands. It was like untangling a snarled casting reel. And then you repeat the whole maddening process.

As for the stench? Well, I wouldn't say I was used to it, but I was so preoccupied with the weed that I just didn't notice it quite so much.

We found Riegle and his boys watching the coastline to the east while comfortably hunkered behind a massive tree trunk lying across the beach.

Riegle said, "Nothing doing, Boss. If the Japs are coming, this ain't the way." He and I talked while my squad enjoyed the sea breeze and lit cigarettes to tease leaches from their legs.

"Well, they weren't anywhere along our trail, either. Trouble is, there's probably more trails further inland that we can't see. The Nips could be on those paths and we'd never know it."

"Well, yeah. So what do we do?"

"We're supposed to scout for Japs, right? But we can't spread out in a line moving through the jungle. It takes an hour to travel a hundred yards in all that fucking brush. So I want to try something different."

"What?"

"The creeks," I said. "Seems like every half mile or so, we cross a creek running due north to the coast from those mountains south of us. They flow at right angles to the Japs' line of advance. Okay, Charlie, so what say we treat the next creek as our forward line? We'll leave two guys here on the beach and the rest of us work our way upstream, dropping off a couple of guys at every trail crossing. I bet there can't be more than three or four crossings."

"Everybody's going to be soaked," Riegle said. "And these are mountain streams. Water's cold."

"Yeah, well. The rain soaks us half the time anyway. Besides, cold mountain water beats hundred-degree heat. And if we do get too cold, we can get out and warm up in nature's steam bath."

I left Eddie Baker with Riegle to watch the coast.

The rest of us proceeded south in the creek. Thank God it wasn't choked with that weed. A thin fog hanging above the cool water deepened the jungle gloom. The further inland we moved, the creek became a series of barely discernable ox-bows winding up the middle of a swamp maybe three hundred yards wide. Would have been great canoeing.

As it was, we sloshed thigh-deep ox bow to ox bow. Once I tried moving us closer to the swamp's east edges, but it meant trying to wade knee-deep in glutinous black mud.

Kraz spotted the first path, so I had him, VanTuyl and Robbins conceal themselves in some fairly dry brush where they could watch it. We dropped Kenton, Miletich and Bellknap at another crossing maybe a half mile further south. Ferraro, Mendez, Cajones and I moved perhaps a mile further when smoke tipped us off that we weren't alone.

Ferraro alerted us, claiming he smelled wood smoke. We sniffed and got nothing. A couple hundred yards further, Ferraro, a non-smoker, stopped us again. He claimed that he now smelled cigarettes. "And Sarge," he whispered, "I swear I can hear talk, too. Just can't make out the words."

With our carbines and Kraz's BAR ready, we turned across swamp toward the noise. I gave a sour grin because Ferraro the doubter, near the center of our line, had his carbine up ready to shoot the first Jap in sight.

A Jap actually did step out of the brush, but well off to our left. A cigarette dangled from the corner of his mouth and his khaki shirt was open to reveal a bony chest. He bent to pick up a couple of large sticks and caught sight of us. His narrow Japanese eyes went saucer wide and he turned to run but Mendez dropped him with a single carbine shot.

Three other Japs popped into view.

Everybody – Japs and Americans – opened fire. The big hard bark of Arisaka rifles punctuated the rattle of our carbines and the BAR's vicious high-speed rattle. Water spouts flew up around us while our bullets whipped the shoreline brush.

It was over in a flash. We suddenly had no targets.

We were just stuck there in the open, half-crouching olive drab targets feeling absolutely naked. But the Japs were gone. We arose from our crouch. Except Ferraro. He was on his back in the swamp and sinking -- caramel-colored muck slowly lapping up over his ruined face, his chin disappearing under it last.

We had to worry about Japs first.

Thanks to the clinging mud, our movement toward their position took place in very slow motion. When we finally got to solid ground, we found two dead Japs in the brush. "Well," Cajones said, "firepower beats penetration."

"Yeah," Mendez said, "and vice versa."

"What do you mean?"

"They got Ferraro."

"Oh."

We came to what looked like a little camp. In its center a dead Jap lieutenant lay at attention, formally arranged as if for burial. Next to him was a large stack of branches.

We also found a short blood trail. I followed it beyond the camp for a few yards, saw nothing and returned.

Cajones pointed to the dead officer. "We didn't nail this guy," he said. "He's been dead several hours. Swelled up enough to make his uniform sausage tight. Smells ripe, too."

"Yeah," I said, "Japs usually want to cremate their dead. I bet that's what these guys planned to do. While I call this in, you and Kraz ease down the path a ways. The main thing is to find out whether these boys were a listening post for a company or battalion, or whether they were a bunch of lost souls."

They were back in twenty minutes having seen nothing but the empty game path. "We went about a half mile," Cajones said. "It's muddy, so no telling whether the tracks are split-toe boots or split-hoof jungle deer. Anyway, we didn't see nobody. Lost souls, I guess."

While they scouted, Captain Bottcher made contact, ordering us to keep the little camp under observation through the night. "Jim, stay off that path. Burrow into the brush and lie low, eyeballing the site. If you get no action by 0600 head back here."

I sent Cajones downstream to alert our other outposts and to spend the night at the beach with Riegle and Baker.

"If the other outposts have had any contacts, have Riegle bring me up to date by walkie-talkie. And keep an eye out for Ferraro. He sank after one of the Japs got him. Try to float him down to the beach, okay? But stay alert."

We never found Ferraro.

Chapter 26
Long Range Patrolling

I had Kraz take the first watch. Big mistake. It was my first full night outside our lines and I was so goosey about it that I couldn't sleep any more than fly to the moon.

So, trying to snow everybody about what a fearless bastard I was, I pretended to sleep, trying to fantasize about making out with Suzanne. But my brain kept returning to relive our firefight, then again and again it would reprise my last sight of Ferraro going down and disappearing into the tawny muck.

It's deep in the night that your mind wanders to death. What is death? The cessation of everything? The end with a Capital T and Capital E. Or does the soul live on like the preachers say? You try to steer clear of those notions. You just hope. With a Capital H.

Naturally, by the time Kraz nudged me to take second watch, I was so sleepy that I had to stand. Lying down, I'd have dropped off in ten seconds.

Except for lizards and land crabs, it stayed quiet. As happens in the tropics, the dead Jap officer spoke to us during the night. His corpse would sigh and then give off occasional squeals and squeaks as gas escaped. Now and then, as the corpse continued to swell, it sounded as if one of his uniform seams split wider.

The stench grew so that when I prodded Mendez awake at 0300 hours we moved further from the camp site.

I promptly fell asleep. Twenty minutes later Mendez prodded me awake because I was snoring. I crammed a spare sock into my mouth, taking care of that noise, but it didn't make for the most restful slumber.

# # #

Headquarters kept us patrolling the jungle east of Saidor for five days, then sent a landing craft to bring us home.

While patrolling, we always moved very slowly and carefully, checking upstream on several other creeks. We saw some beautiful butterflies and parrots. Flying foxes, fruit bats with big spaniel eyes, hung upside down in the trees by the thousand, like so many brown leather ornaments. They often stared at us. One morning I awakened to the calm gaze of a tree kangaroo peering down from a branch ten feet above me.

But no Japs.

If any Japs were around, they didn't detect us . . . half the battle. Don't let them hear you, smell you or see you.

When the LCI returned us to the Saidor beach on Day Six we just walked straight into the surf to slosh off all the mud and jungle ooze. Then we made a bee-line to the new field hospital so the medics could work on our spongy feet. By now most of us had lost several toenails. When I started to pull off my boots, the shoe leather began coming apart at its seams.

But my feet! That puckered fish-belly white reminded me of Nana's biscuit dough. When I was a little boy she'd have me poke a finger into it. She said that if it didn't rebound immediately, it hadn't risen enough.

The macerated flesh of my feet and ankles was very slow on the rebound.

As the medics painted our new sores with some kind of stinging joy juice, we watched through the hospital's windows. The whole area was undergoing a hell of a transformation.

The engineers dug deep into their treasury of foul language as they struggled with almost bottomless mud to enlarge the airstrip. It was a case of creating a gravel base using the rocks on the beaches. Progress was better near the mouth of Saidor's little river. The engineers had driven pilings there for a large dock for PT boats while using timber bamboo to construct offices and barracks for the boats' crews. They even had thatched roofs.

Captain Bottcher and Lieutenant Irish and I got together and compared notes. The captain was happy with our work and our ability to cope with lousy field conditions. We were proud to announce that though our teams were tired and glad to be back to showers, hot chow and coffee, they had held up well physically and mentally. And they were ready for more.

"They're soldiers now," Lieutenant Irish said, "not weekend warriors."

"Yes," Bottcher said. "But now they must learn much more about scouting."

"More?"

"Yes, indeed," he said. "At first we all think of the jungle as a place of unspeakable horror. But once you get to know it, you find has its own rare beauty. Don't worry. I'm not trying to convince you. You'll discover it as time goes on that it can be beautiful. Yes, quite beautiful."

My thoughts about the jungle focused more on the fact that our patrol had only sighted five Japs while losing a promising man.

Lieutenant Irish's team, on the other hand, had moved straight south from the beachhead. He reported finding and tracking what seemed like an endless column of Japanese. He estimated at least three thousand Japs were trying to work their way west up over the jungled foothills which lay ten miles south of Saidor.

Several patrols from the task force itself clashed with Japs – either ambushing them or being ambushed. Headquarters, however, never tried to bring the bulk of enemy troops to battle. For their part, Jap patrols seemed content to screen their comrades' columns which were toiling to join the Jap garrisons further west at Madang.

As for all our artillery, we heard it on occasion. Some of the troops, men from the 163rd Infantry Regiment, said the howitzers came in very handy when Jap patrols began probing our lines west of Saidor.

Chapter 27
Learning The Job

A Japanese soldier surprised us just as we started our next move into the jungle. Apparently wandering aimlessly in the rain forest, he collapsed to his knees in front of Miletich who was the point man.

"Preeze! Preeze!" he said, trying to hold both hands up into the air. But he seemed too weak to do so.

After checking him for weapons, Miletich tried to haul the wanderer upright by his shirt collar. The tattered garment ripped from the man's scrawny torso, so Miletich brought me to meet his catch.

The guy looked so pathetic that I gave him my canteen which contained sweetened tea . . . Captain Bottcher's suggestion. He believed tea to be more refreshing for us than water, especially with caffeine and sugar to sustain our energy.

The Jap gulped from the canteen, then bowed repeatedly. In a faint voice he kept saying, "Arigato! Domo Arigato! Sank you too much."

He was too weak to walk and nobody wanted to carry him because he was spewing constant diarrhea. Bottcher wanted to interrogate any prisoner, however, so I finally hauled the Jap's arm over my shoulder and half carried him to the nearest stream where I dunked us both for sanitary reasons. He was shockingly light . . . down to eighty pounds, we learned later.

His name was Yoshi and I found quickly that his English was much better than my Japanese. He told us he was a replacement drafted from Meijo University where he had been a third-year chemistry major.

He asked, "You understand Yamato-damashii?"

"Yes. Japan's 'unconquerable spirit'."

Eyes closed as he lay on his stretcher, "I do not believe," he barked. The statement seemed to exhaust him. After a deep sigh, he whispered, "I believe science spirit. I hate foolish army. Foolish. Kill more Japanese than American guns."

"What do you mean?"

"Generals and colonels leave, take comfort girls, food. We starve."

After his own interrogation of the POW, Captain Bottcher told us the man's physical state proved General MacArthur's strategy was working. "They're suffering and dying. And now our little group is going to speed up the process."

"How do we do that?" I asked.

"We're going to patrol very aggressively.

"Now, by 'aggressively', I don't mean we're going to assault them. We're going to work harder to find supply dumps, food caches, troop concentrations. And we're going to call the Air Corps and artillery to break them up."

"Sir, how can we do that?"

"By staying quiet and out of sight. Look, boys, think of the jungle as an ocean. We know there are fish in the ocean … sharks, if you like. But they aren't lined up side-by-side in parade formation. There's a school of them here and a school of them somewhere over there. A company in one place, a battalion two miles away in another and all kinds of space … jungle and swamp … in between.

"So we're going to dive into the ocean and swim in it just as those fish do. For days and even weeks. And when we locate them and we'll call down *donner und blitzen* on them."

And so we did.

But some commander – maybe it was General Gill because, by now, half of the 32nd Division was at Saidor, or maybe it was General Kruger, Sixth Army commander – decided not to attack the main body of Japs. We and the 163rd Regiment west of Saidor let them pass as they headed on to Madang, a very big fortress base with a great harbor.

I guess it made sense. Madang is where tens of thousands of Japs surrendered on Tokyo's orders the following summer . . . after Hiroshima and Nagasaki.

# # #

For our part, we spent five water-logged weeks patrolling first south and then west of Saidor.

Captain Bottcher led us at first … both Lieutenant Irish's men and mine together. We cut into the jungle, penetrating not just toward but beyond the Japs' columns. He showed how we could patrol not just along jungle game trails, but also through the bush itself and for ever-longer periods.

"Regular infantry patrols," he said, "try to find the Jap lines, get information, and even bring in some prisoners. Our job is different – we infiltrate through to the Jap rear. We set up our own little mobile operations base where we can observe them and call in artillery or air strikes that will do the most good. We want to hit their artillery, their supply dumps and even troop concentrations. We may be able to break up Jap attacks before they ever can start."

The captain was a master at evasion. He almost always steered us clear of Jap patrols. If we had to fight he always managed to make it an ambush with us achieving surprise.

Then he returned to commanding Company A of the 127th while we started putting his lessons into practice on our own.

# # #

"This is the pattern we're going to follow, guys." Lieutenant Irish was outlining the next operation.

"Once the Saidor airstrip is fully operational, its bombers and fighters will neutralize other Jap airstrips along the coast, starting at Madang. Meanwhile, the 32nd Division will get back on its boats and seize a new beachhead someplace where the Japs are not.

"We'll build a new airstrip. Then with Air Corps' help, we'll move further west to another site that enables us to advance air power, then sea power. Eventually we'll take the next step to Formosa or maybe the Philippines."

"Yeah," Kraz asked, "but are the Japs just going to sit around with their thumbs up their butts?"

Lieutenant Irish laughed. "They're not going to be able to do much, Kraz. The jungle imprisons the Japs. They can stay in place, starving, or they can starve while trying to cut through a couple of hundred miles of jungle to attack us at one of our invasion points.

Kenton asked, "So there won't be any fighting?"

"Oh, I'm sure we'll be in combat at some point," the lieutenant said. "We'll have to fight the bastards, but on our terms.

"Guys, remember . . . starting with Bunker Hill, it's always been very costly to attack Americans on the ground of their choosing. And don't forget what the man in charge said, 'No more Bunas'."

Well, not for a while.

Chapter 28
Lowering The Boom

The lieutenant awakened me the quiet way. He pinched my nostrils shut.

The pinch didn't hurt but instantly roused me to Condition Red. I didn't even yawn because I instantly was ready to murder the guy awakening me.

Even so, I kept very quiet because, asleep or awake, I was acutely aware we were a good four miles behind Jap lines and six miles beyond the Army's Saidor beachhead.

"Japs coming," Lieutenant Irish said. "Wake everybody."

"Got it!"

I scrambled up as he tapped Sam's bare shoulder. "Youpella bilong me." Sam nodded. He and the lieutenant glided out of sight into the bamboo grove above us.

In about thirty seconds, I had everybody awake and alert. We'd been having a well-earned nap on a ledge overlooking a high-traffic jungle path. Now we knelt, ten feet apart, safeties off, muzzles up.

It was the tenth day in our patrol behind the Japanese lines, and we were tired and sore. But we all forgot it when he arrived, Mr. Moto himself, coming into sight around a bend in the trail below us.

Looking sweaty and tired, the Jap soldier swiveled his rifle side to side as he peered at the brush along both sides of the trail. He looked uphill toward us, too. But we were in deep shade behind thick undergrowth, our faces crosshatched with dark streaks of mud or shoe polish or whatever else was handy.

He walked another ten feet and swiped his face with his forearm.

Most newspaper cartoons depict Japanese soldiers as having slit eyes, coke-bottle glasses and a sneering grin over buck teeth. This Tojo had no glasses, but otherwise he was the perfect caricature. He even had that pencil-thin moustache.

The corporal who showed up behind him though was kind of a disappointment. Other than wearing a mildewed Jap uniform, he looked as ordinary as any neighbor you'd see shopping for groceries at Safeway. His eyes didn't even look particularly Asian.

The corporal said something I didn't hear. *Ten minute break, maybe.* Point Man glanced at his watch, slung his rifle and fished a cigarette from his shirt pocket. One-by-one, eight more Japs filed into sight and stopped. Next came a sergeant and a lieutenant.

The officer looked very young and he had grown a Fu Manchu moustache. Maybe he was trying to look like Emperor Ming the Merciless of the *Flash Gordon* comic strips.

He glanced back along the trail and then gave a command. His troops relaxed. Rifle butts came down onto the ground. Most of them squatted down on their haunches. The lieutenant and sergeant lit up and started speaking with each other, drawing in the dirt with the forefingers of the hands holding their smokes.

Kenton crawled over and whispered to me, "Looks like the bastards are making up a football play. You know? 'Hey, Tojo! You go long!'"

I frowned shook my head at him. "Shhhh!"

A Jap close below us heard my shush. He stopped in mid-sip from his canteen and jerked his face toward us. But just that instant a grenade exploded somewhere back out of sight along the path.

Had to be Sam or Lieutenant Irish.

The Japs all snatched up their rifles and turned that direction.

I yelled, "Fire!" All seven of us hit our triggers -- carbines and one BAR. The plunging fusillade cut them down. My shots knocked the canteen five feet from the drinker's hand and he dropped like a rag doll.

Two other Japanese came running into view, skidded to stop in their shock and died.

Ears still ringing from our fire, we heard two more grenades thump in the distance. Then came the rattle of a Tommy gun, then scattered rifle shots.

Maybe five minutes later Lieutenant Irish hissed, "Coming in!" He and Sam leaned out from the bamboo and waved at us. "Let's move! These guys were advance party for a battalion."

Mendez said, "Holy shit, man!"

The lieutenant told Sam, "Go!"

# # #

Sam looked to be all of 5-2 but was built like a miniature King Kong.

Except for a skirt made of tree bark, his midnight skin was his uniform and he was a master of the jungle. He could find and slip through gaps in the undergrowth that we couldn't even see, and he did it while hardly setting a leaf in motion.

Sam – his real name was something unpronounceable – was a native policeman consumed with hatred for Japs. Last year, Japanese troops decided his village apparently didn't qualify for membership in the benevolent East Asia Co-Prosperity Sphere.

So they burned it.

But first they raped its women.

Sam's consuming goal thereafter was to make every Jap suffer.

He made us suffer, too. Guiding us away from the enemy column, he led us at a grueling pace practically straight uphill. I thought I was in good shape, but it was very steep going mainly on hands and knees. After fifteen minutes, my thighs were on fire and I was wringing wet with sweat.

Finally, he led us atop a flat barn-sized ledge of naked granite. Everybody collapsed except for Sam, the lieutenant and Kenton, our Signals jockey.

Sam and the lieutenant crawled to peek over the rim of the promontory. Their position overlooked the forest and, on the far horizon, the blue gleam of the ocean. Sam began pointing and jabbering. Lieutenant Irish nodded, consulted his map and called in his password to the artillery.

After establishing his bona fides to the Fire Direction Center, I caught part of his artillery observer's litany. "Fire mission! Target: troop column. No danger close. Estimated range 12,600 yards, deflection 4800 to 5250 mills."

Whatever batteries got the job were out of view inside the Saidor perimeter. I joined Sam and the lieutenant as the first shell soared toward us with a loud ripping sound, bursting in a white bloom in the jungle below us. By the thousand, alarmed birds and bats soared into the air, hurting our ears with their screeching indignation.

The lieutenant glanced up at me and grinned. "Watch closely, Jim. You can see the damn shells arcing right toward us. They're 155s and the sun's just right."

Two corrections later, he demanded, “Fire for effect, mixed HE and Willy Peter. Super quick fuses.”

And he was right, you could catch sight of the shells as they came toward us out of the top of their trajectory. At first they made the bridge of my nose itch because it felt as if they’d impact right between my eyes. Fortunately for us, they were exploding in tree tops several hundred feet below us.

The jungle cloaked most of what the eight-minute shelling did to the Japs, but between those slamming detonations I thought I could hear screams. Sam was grinning.

The enemy didn’t take it lying down. Jap troops don’t. In spite of the barrage and bloody chaos down there, somebody managed to unlimber a Nambu and began chewing with it at the face of our ledge.

“All right,” Lieutenant Irish yelled. “Let’s move out before their mortars start dropping on us.”

He scrammed with the boys. My job was to bring up the rear and I waited at the woods’ edge pull for Kenton. He was yanking at his aerial to pull it down.

“Bill, for God’s sake, just leave the damned thing! Let’s go!

“Sarge, it’s our last aerial. We might need it.”

I didn’t even hear the mortar shell come in. It landed about thirty feet from Kenton, slamming him against his tree. The shrapnel slashed his back, head and neck into crimson hash accented with olive drab rags.

All I could do was yank off his dog tags for Graves Registration.

Chapter 29
Disappearing Act

Unless we left some poor dufus behind to check, we couldn't know whether the Japs were pursuing. So we took off as fast as we could, assuming at least a platoon was hot-footing it after us and.

It was the direction we went that caused the lieutenant and me to split the blanket, at least for a while.

He and Sam started leading us south, further into the hills. As soon as I could, I caught up with him and whispered, "Sir, I think we should head east."

"Screw that," he said. "For now I want to go in the direction that they least expect."

"But sir, there's plenty of cover and, besides, heading south puts them between us and …"

"Jim, I'm in command here," he snapped, "and I'm telling you we're headed south. When we're sure we've evaded them, we'll turn east and make our way to First Street."

I snarled, "But what if they get across …?"

He stopped and glared at me. "Goddammit, don't argue with your orders! We can't have a divided command. Now if you can't follow orders, proceed on your own. And if you get back alive, Sergeant, I'll court-martial your ass."

Ears burning and choking with anger, I glared back at him and shut up. He turned, signaled with his head for Sam to lead on.

As the boys passed me following in the lieutenant's wake, they gave me some puzzled looks. Mendez, who was trailing, asked, "What's up, Boss?"

"Never mind. Just keep going."

We moved south, almost running when we could, until we came to a broad savannah. It gave us the first clear view I'd ever had of New Guinea's mountain crests. Silhouetted against billowing thunderheads, they were the cruelest-looking jumble of razor-like rocks I've ever seen.

There was none of the stately undulation of the Sierra Madres or the Rockies – a procession of snowy peaks and broad valleys.

It looked to me as if the devil had taken a mighty sledge-hammer and cracked away at New Guinea's crests, leaving nothing but jagged granite outcroppings. Somebody years later told me this was the telltale sign of young mountains that hadn't had tens of millions of years to erode. Whatever the case, I'm glad that's the closest we ever got to those angular crags.

Lieutenant Irish finally changed course to the east, keeping us out of sight inside the savannah's wooded margins. From there we wound our way downslope back into jungle and swamp to an escape route that we nicknamed First Street.

Back home, I would call First Street a small creek. You've seen the sort . . . two to three feet wide with a current chuckling among moss-covered rock slabs, some of them tilting when you incautiously step on their front or back edges.

But unlike back home, Saidor's First Street ran between five-foot banks surmounted by matted brush less than an arm's length to my right and left.

The light was so poor and the foliage so dense it was impossible to see whether a Jap gunner might be lying in wait for us. Or maybe some trigger-happy GI. Or a Papuan with poison arrows nocked in his bow, or just a goofy gibbon swinging through the jungle canopy like some furry long-armed Tarzan.

In fact, we felt fairly secure because nobody else seemed to use First Street. It actually was something of a tunnel, man-sized banana leaves, palm fronds and bamboo branches meeting close overhead. Even at high noon on a cloudless day, we were in twilight.

Mendez said, "Damn but it's dark in here."

"Quit bitching," I said. "At least you can see. At night, it's black as a vulture's heart. Then you got to walk very slowly, hand-in-hand, daisy chain like. You trip headlong in these rocks and you can break anything from an ankle to your neck."

At last we came to a key landmark, what I believe is the meanest-looking tree in New Guinea. My anger at the lieutenant began to subside. I always started to relax when we came to that site.

Now, I want to point out that New Guinea has some real wild-looking flora. There are strangler figs which look like enormous wooden boa constrictors slowly choking the life out of their host trees. We often encountered something else strange … a tall, slender tree with a smooth, glistening gray bark that looked as if someone had dribbled streaks of blood down its trunk all the way from its hundred-foot top – plus other streaks of what looked like Kelly green paint.

But the meanest tree was a giant … a monstrosity looking like something out of a science fiction nightmare. I have no idea what its proper name would be, but I called it the Rasp Oak.

A lot of trees in the New Guinea jungles have some very wicked thorns, but this was something unreal. On every square foot of that massive trunk, and I'd say at least forty feet in circumference, were growths that looked like big goose bumps, almost fist-sized. And standing out in an upward curve from each of those hundreds of bumps was a wicked needle-sharp black spike about as thick as your thumb.

Kraz asked, "Hey, Sarge! How'd you like to slide down that fire pole?"

"What? And leave my balls dangling on those hooks up there? No thanks, buddy. Especially not today. Look at that!"

Today, the Rasp Oak looked more mean than usual because it had some extra special company. One of the ugliest critters in creation was sitting on a lower limb. Its pulsing throat was the only sign that it lived rather than being some disgusting carved native idol.

Imagine if you glued broken fragments of dead oak leaves to a really big toad, say, a ten-pounder. Apply them top and bottom, front, back and sides. Now plaster the critter with greenish-black New Guinea mud and then highlight the mud with pebbles, BBs and little clove-like spikes.

It just was sitting there between two tree spikes, staring at us malevolently.

"Hey, lieutenant," Bellknap called. "Do you think maybe Cap'n Bottcher includes these things in his jungle menu?"

He took one look. "I don't know, Jake. Maybe. But I'll damned well starve before I do."

He nodded to Sam, pointed to the thing and made eating motions. Sam vigorously shook his head, stuck out his tongue and made retching noises.

"Yeah, same here," Miletich said.

The squad seemed to give a collective shudder and a hearty "Yucccccch." Despite being worn-out and having very sore feet, we hurried past the creature.

The nice thing was knowing that having passed the Rasp Oak we were pretty sure of being safe back inside the Army's perimeter. All we had to worry about was an infrequent mortar round which the Japs would fire into the beachhead just for the hell of it.

From there, it was more or less a stroll to the beach. After rinsing off the worst of the mud and crud in the surf, we hurried to the headquarters tent where we'd maybe get issued some dry clothes and even pick up mail.

My feet hurt after we arrived, but I was jumping up and down because I had three letters. And the handwriting was Suzanne's.

Lieutenant Irish called me to go meet with Captain Bottcher. I held up my mail, "Aww, Dan, can't you give maybe me fifteen minutes?"

He just grinned. "Ahh, just go on and read your mail. I'll catch you up later." My lingering anger faded like drifting smoke.

# # #

When I checked in later with Lieutenant Irish he said Captain Bottcher was delighted.

"He told me that's the kind of thing we want to keep doing. Scaring the bejaysus out of them. Frustrating them. Tearing them up when possible. He said, 'They don't like the jungle any more than we do, and if we can make it hell for them, so much the better."

I apologized for questioning his order.

"Forget it, Jim, we got out of there alive. Just don't do it again, mister."

Chapter 30
Up And At 'Em

Suzanne wrote that she was enjoying her new work. She couldn't tell me what the work was or where she worked except that the new office was Good Enough. The only problem was that an Army lieutenant in her department, a man named Gergen, kept pestering her to go out with him.

> *I'm amazed the Army commissioned him because he is utterly bereft of manners. Before the Army he must have been a swaggie. That would be a tramp or a hobo in your brand of English. The man is a fair cow and I believe your word would be "louse." He has as much chance with me as he does of swimming back to San Francisco, but he was obnoxious and persisting. I finally spoke to The Badger, our boss, about him. The lieutenant no longer talks to me, but he glares constantly from across the office.*
>
> *I send you best wishes from Judith, now reunited with her Mum who has returned home thanks to contracting malaria. She will work as a sister at Fourth General where you mended. Her experiences at Port Moresby changed her, almost muted her, I would say. Being with Judith, such a cheerful soul, seemed to help, however. Silky the cat still climbs trees but has mastered the art of descent. Incidentally, a tremendous number of American women have arrived. They are WACs with Fifth Air Force. We enjoy learning each other's languages ...*

The idea of Gergen glaring at my Suzanne -- or even being able to see her while I couldn't -- had me boiling. I had no idea who The Badger was, but I was grateful that he at least had put some salt on the tail of Scumbag Gergen. A temporary solution.

I wanted the bastard gone.

After carefully folding Suzanne's letters, I joined Lieutenant Irish meeting outside the field hospital with Captain Bottcher. The captain had just led his own I&R team out of the jungle, too. The medics were swabbing iodine and other kinds of stinging stuff on festering bug bites, jungle sores and thorn gouges.

Everybody's feet were a mess again, the result of soaking too often and too long in waterlogged boots. The medics told us it would be a damn good idea to keep our feet bare, elevated and dry for a time.

No such luck, though.

We were just wrapping up with the medics when Captain Bottcher ordered us to get our gear back on and take an LCI out to an ADP – remember? Auxiliary Personnel Destroyer?

"Well, sir," I said, "does this maybe mean we're done here at Saidor?"

"Yep, Jim, I think we might have a new destination."

"Cap'n, do you think it's a place where we can keep our feet high and dry?"

He just snorted.

I asked if I could speak with him about Suzanne, the girl whom he watched teaching me chess, and about Lieutenant Gergen.

He listened attentively. I wound up by saying I'd like to be able to meet the lieutenant. "Or better yet, I'd like to get his ass up here on the line where he could practice glaring at Japs."

Captain Bottcher frowned. "I don't know, Jim. I suppose I could get you on a flight to Goodenough Island, but even if you could find their office, as a master sergeant you couldn't do anything to a lieutenant without getting into much trouble. Let me think about it."

He turned away and then stopped.

"You know, maybe there's a way we could bring him here. You say he's in Signals?"

# # #

I was just sipping my first dawn cup of coffee when we received orders to come back ashore from the *USS Dickerson*. You know how it is in the military . . . order, counter order and disorder.

It was the morning of our third day aboard the ship and I noticed nobody was bitching as we trundled our gear back down into an LCI.

Me either.

The *Dickerson* was even older and more crapped out than our first APD, the *Sands*. What's more, being aboard her during yesterday's sunny weather at four degrees south latitude was like being a turkey roasting in an oven. Trying to look nonchalant about it, one of the swab jockeys said that on sunny days, the thermometer on the bridge could register up to 120 degrees.

At least they get breeze up on the bridge.

Down in the troop spaces just below that radiating deck, the only breeze was human breath. The one group aboard the ship who had it hotter than us were sailors in the engine rooms where temps ran 150 degrees and up.

But it wasn't the high command's tender concern for our comfort that led them to order us back on shore at Saidor.

It was a high headquarters debate.

Apparently the higher-ups – maybe MacArthur, or General Krueger, or the Air Corps' General Kenney, or General Gill, who knows? – couldn't decide which outfit they would send next up the coast to invade which target. All we knew was that suddenly more of the 32nd Division's battalions were joining us in the Saidor area while the 163rd Infantry Regiment was pulling out.

So, at first, the word was that we'd stay at Saidor, tempting the Japs to assault us. With all our artillery back-up, odds were that we could devastate them.

But then came Change Number Two. They told us we would go ashore *with* the 163rd at Hollandia, not some little punk village but a substantial coastal town 450 miles further to the west in the Dutch half of New Guinea.

After that rumor had time to percolate thoroughly among us, Change Number Three emerged.

Captain Bottcher gave Lieutenant Irish briefing materials about a coconut plantation and an adjacent airfield called Tadji. That airstrip and plantation of the same name lay near a village called Aitape. And what made Aitape important was that it lay squarely between Hollandia and some Jap installation at Wewak.

"It looks like we're going to be a blocking force," Captain Bottcher said. "We're going ashore at Aitape east of Hollandia to keep the Japs at Wewak from interfering with that invasion."

"How many Japs are at Wewak?"

"It's the Eighteenth Field Army, or, at least, two divisions of it, the 20th and 41st. So, together with labor troops, we're looking at sixty thousand to ninety thousand men . . . so maybe twenty thousand to thirty thousand combat effectives."

"Jesus Christ! The 32nd is supposed to hold off three or four times its own number?"

"Settle down, Jim. It's a hundred miles from Wewak to Aitape. And those are *jungle* miles. That trek will destroy them. And we'll have lots of artillery and total air supremacy. The Japs won't have either."

# # #

That sounded nice, but as time passed, I found myself getting more and more edgy. The Japs might face a hundred-mile jungle hike, but they'd still greatly outnumber us.

And I couldn't get over my other worry about Suzanne.

I'd heard nothing from Captain Bottcher about Lieutenant Gergen. And I really doubted he'd be able to do anything. Besides, the captain had a whole damn infantry company plus General Gill's I&R program to worry about.

So I just kept stewing about whether Gergen, a coward and a bully, might end up hurting Suzanne, and me almost three hundred miles away unable to do a damned thing about it.

Chapter 31
A New Offensive

The next day, HQ announced that the 32nd Division would be called the Persecution Force. Big deal. What really stirred the troops' interest was the news that, at last, all three of our division's regiments finally would be together.

For the first time since the war started we'd face the enemy as a whole division, not just what the newspapers call "elements of X Regiment" or "Y Regimental Combat Team".

Meanwhile, the outfits invading Hollandia would be called Reckless Force. Together, both Reckless and Persecution would constitute the Alamo Force.

Cajones looked at Mendez and said, "Well to hell with that name! I heard what you Mexicans did to the boys in the Alamo. I don't want anything to do with it."

Mendez just grinned and said, "Don't worry, Gringo. I'll protect you."

"I don't know why they have to give us some stupid name," Baker said. "These headquarters twerps always try to be cute. Why don't they just call us the 32nd Division instead of that Persecution Force bullshit?"

Bellknap said, "Hell, Eddy, they've got to have something for the low-ranking officers to do. Makes them feel useful."

Captain Bottcher arrived. "Okay, now knock off your bitching and listen up!"

Now when I give an order like that to my boys, a full minute of buzz, back talk and bullshit follows.

Captain Bottcher, however, instantly got utter quiet and full attention.

"Men, we're moving soon. We'll travel by LST this time and when we land, we'll ride ashore on those tracked alligators.

"Now, we're told that the Air Corps and the Navy's carriers are blasting the hell out of every Jap airstrip within five hundred miles. The idea is to neutralize their air power, but more important to divert their Army's attention. The upshot? We're probably going to encounter very little opposition when we first land. It looks like it'll be the same as when we came ashore here at Saidor."

He unveiled a large map showing terrain very much like everything else on New Guinea's north coast, swampy and jungled coast with highlands inland and numerous streams gushing straight north to the ocean.

"Now, at first, you men working for Lieutenant Irish are going to do some scouting for us. You'll head east of our landing zone just like you did here at Saidor. But this time you're probably going to find Japs because they're likely to be moving west from Wewak to try to rescue Hollandia. Hollandia is a critically important supply center for them.

"So, if – or rather, when – you locate the Japs, you're going to fall straight back on us in A Company and First Battalion. You'll join us and fight with us. We're probably looking at a straight-up infantry fight this time around, and strictly on defense. Any questions?"

"Sir?" I asked, "Will we get replacements for Kenton and Ferraro?"

"No. We just don't have enough time to train them."

He looked directly at me and grinned.

"I did feel, however, that we were a bit understaffed with radio specialists since we lost Pvt. Kenton," he said. "So I got in touch with a friend and I'm happy to tell you now they'll be shipping a Signals officer to us from Goodenough Island."

I couldn't help smiling. "Sir, would that officer by any chance be a second lieutenant named Gergen?"

He said, "Why yes, sergeant, I believe that's his name. Do you know him?"

"Well, yes sir. He formerly was a sergeant who, for a *very* short time, was with the 128th at Buna. But the last time I saw him was at Fourth General Hospital in Melbourne. He told me he had been accepted for the officer candidate school in Brisbane."

"I see. Well, he'll be joining us from a Signal Corps office attached to Sixth Army HQ."

Mendez held up a hand and asked, "Say, sir, so do you suppose this lieutenant has been working in an air-conditioned office?" The entire squad chuckled.

"I'd be surprised if he hasn't," Lieutenant Irish said. "Personal comfort is very important in the signals business. But I'm sure that, after a time, this officer will adjust to life out here in the boondocks."

When Captain Bottcher dismissed us, I approached him.

"Sir," I said, "I'm very grateful and I just wonder how the hell you wired that?"

"Well, Jim, you remember how we managed to break through the Japs to the coast at Buna and General Eichelberger said that in return he'd help me get citizenship?"

"Right. I recall you telling me that."

"Well, he also said that if I ever needed a favor …"

"Got it, Sir. Thanks again. I owe you one."

"I'll remember that."

Chapter 32
A Touching Reunion

Second Lieutenant Gergen labored up the ramp into our LST looking whipped, face slick with sweat and breathing heavily under the weight of his duffel bag and a leather suitcase sporting a nice crop of mildew.

Like anyone thrown into a completely new situation, he was peering about nervously.

I stepped toward him, saluting smartly. "Congratulations on your commission, sir, and welcome aboard!" After being outside in brilliant sunshine, his eyes still must have been adjusting to the LST's shaded interior. He didn't make out my face at first and merely nodded.

Then he recognized me. "What are you doing here, Mays?"

"Why, sir, I'm just like you . . . a poor infantryman being shipped off to some godawful jungle to take on the Japs."

He seemed to flinch.

"Kind of like a bad dream, isn't it, sir?"

He said, "Fuck off!" and started to follow the other soldiers winding past the tie-downs that anchored the alligators to the tank deck.

I grinned. "Lieutenant Gergen! Captain Bottcher asked that for the moment you remain right here. He'll be back in just a minute and you're to report to him."

"Report to Captain Bottcher?"

"That's right, Sir. Maybe you remember him from Buna. That's where General Eichelberger got him the DSC and a direct commission – to captain, no less -- for busting through the Japs. He's the CO of Able Company, 127th infantry now, but he also wears another hat. That's where you and I come in. He's the division's top expert jungle-crawler. He runs General Gill's provisional recon team. I'm the team's senior NCO and you're our signals officer."

"Signals officer?" Gergen swallowed and looked nauseated. "Hell, I don't know that much about signals in the field. My branch is infantry."

"That's no problem, sir. We've got all the Signal Corps field manuals so you can bone up on it while we're underway."

"Great." Gergen's eyes shifted everywhere but on mine.

His main problem, it seemed to me, was the intense distaste he exhibited for jungles, swamps and combat plus a streak of yellow stretching from neck to butt.

On the third day of our abortive assault at Buna he had disappeared from his platoon, later turning up in a field hospital supposedly with malaria-related pneumonia.

And he probably did have malaria. Damn near all of us did. Most of us stayed in the line and fought through it. Then-sergeant Gergen, however, just consented to show up now and then during the second phase of that campaign and not at all during the final assault. I wasn't alone in believing he was one of those types who disappears when things heat up, an easy thing to do in such terrain.

I hadn't seen him again until I was hospitalized in Melbourne. He was in a different ward from mine so I never saw anything regarding his wounds or illness.

I was about to scare him by describing some of the behind-the-lines work we were planning. The captain showed up, however, so I saluted them and took off. As I did, I heard Gergen say, "Cap'n, I'm not sure I'm cut out for this kind of thing."

"Amen to that," I muttered. "But it beats having you pester Suzanne."

We were at anchor several days and I didn't see much of him. Lieutenant Irish, looking grim, said that Gergen had his nose in the field manuals.

Then we got underway. And our voyage this time was much calmer than our suffering in a destroyer transport. Being at sea in an LST wasn't too bad. We still had occasional squalls. But even when the wind kicked up, the ride in an LST gave me the impression of being aboard a pregnant elephant -- slow and stately, ponderous and mildly swaying. Certainly it was at least ten times more comfortable than clinging desperately to your rack in a wildly bucking destroyer transport.

As for seasickness, I felt immune to it again.

Oh sure, some of the boys became a bit green around the edges. But I don't think anybody was suffering that wretched end-of-the-world hopelessness of constant vomiting.

And the nice thing was that when it wasn't raining, we could go topside onto the main cargo deck to find some relief from the heat. You probably could have fried an egg on the deck itself, but the breeze helped a great deal.

Being out on deck during our voyage gave me several chances to see Lieutenant Gergen who often perched just outside the vessel's little wheelhouse one deck above us.

Every time we made eye contact, I gave him a big smile. I wanted him to know that in some mysterious way I had something to do with his departure from his cushy rear echelon office job.

Gergen wasn't the brightest bulb in the chandelier, but I must have rubbed it in too hard. Later on, he caused me and my boys some real problems.

# # #

"Now," Captain Bottcher said, "I've got some good news and then some news that's not so good, but it really isn't too bad, either." He was briefing Lieutenants Irish and Gergen and Sergeant Riegle and me.

"The good news is that tomorrow morning this task force will walk ashore at Aitape. We won't even need to ride the alligators. The division simply is filling in while the 163rd pulls out and heads for Hollandia.

"Things around Aitape have been very quiet. Work on expanding the Tadji Airstrip is nearly complete."

"So, Sir, what's the not-so-good news?"

"Intelligence believes that General Adachi, commander of the Japanese Eighteenth Field Army, has been ordered to deploy large detachments east from Wewak to protect Hollandia from invasion. The 32nd Infantry Division is to set up a defensive perimeter around Aitape and the Tadji airstrip. Our mission is to cover Tadji Airstrip, and to delay and defeat that Japanese deployment.

"Now as we've noted, the Eighteenth may number as many as 90,000 men. But the Aussies, bless 'em, are tying down a lot of those Japs. So we don't think Adachi can send more than 20,000 troops this way. And I remind you that it's a hundred-mile trek for them mainly through jungle and swamp. The natural attrition from hunger and disease is going to be terrific."

Lieutenant Irish said, "Okay, Sir, but Japanese soldiers have a way of being very tough, no matter what they go through." The reminder dried my throat. I heard Gergen swallow noisily.

"That's right," the captain said. "But just as at Saidor, we have artillery now – tons of it – and we now have tactical air support that's getting better all the time.

"Now that's the big picture.

"As far as you I&R people are concerned, we're going to start out just as at Saidor. Your mission will be to move out well east of our beachhead, spot the lead Jap elements when they arrive, and backpedal to the perimeter. Then they can bash their heads against *our* brick wall."

"Sir, you sure make it sound pretty easy," I said.

Lieutenant Irish turned to me. "It won't be easy. But when they're attacking the Japs have limited tactical vision. They mainly try to play tricks on our nerves . . . psychological stuff. They try to rattle you they probe for your flanks and rear.

"But look, their weapons aren't half as good as ours. They have nothing like the BAR or the Tommy Gun or the carbine. They've got the Nambu and their rifles and bayonets for those rifles.

"They can work around your flanks. Try to get in your rear. But if you maintain a solid line, they end up having to do the same old thing, a headlong bayonet charge. The banzai charge."

He paused. "It's noisy and scary. I saw it a lot in China. The screaming was just ungodly. It often worked against Chinese who were spooky and superstitious. They'd just desert and go home."

"We can't do that, of course," Riegle said. The captain and Lieutenant Irish and I laughed. Lieutenant Gergen gave a thin smile.

"Right," the lieutenant said. "The main thing," he went on, "is that you'd see forty or fifty Japs charge two hundred Chinese and defeat them. Well, we've got more firepower than Chinese troops ever dreamed of. We've got semi-automatic carbines, the BAR and M1 rifles plus submachine guns."

"That's right," the captain said. "If we keep our heads, our weapons will make the Jap Banzai charge a suicide mission.

"Oh, by the way, the word 'banzai' is just the Jap equivalent of 'hurray'."

Chapter 33
A Jungle Encounter

Thunder rolled above us and the jungle twilight deepened.

"Oh, crap," Miletich said. "Here we go again."

We were patrolling twenty miles east of Aitape. A dozen of us were moving slowly and well-spaced along the floor of a high jungle.

By 'high jungle' I mean the thick crowns of the forest giants met and intertwined two hundred feet above us. The fit of that jungle canopy was so tight that it cut out the sunlight. Down where we were, the deep gloom made for a fairly empty forest floor.

From high above in an airplane, this forest looked solid, like you actually could walk atop it. Down here though, trees were spaced well enough that you could see at least seventy-five and sometimes even a hundred yards. You still had to push through knee-deep ferns and steer around bamboo thickets and thorny brush plus occasional towers of vines massing skyward where tree tops had died, letting the sun through. This lower story of the jungle was nowhere so tight and tangled as the claustrophobic growth in the approaches to Buna.

Matching my stride off to the left, carbine in his big hands, Corporal Baker quietly hummed *Back In The Saddle Again.*

"Okay, Eddy, so where's your damn horse?"

He chuckled. "No horse, Sarge. Just a new title for an old Texas song – *Back In The Jungle Again.*"

"Oh! I get it."

Sourly, Sergeant Riegle said, "That rates half a chuckle and one har-de-har."

With a sudden roar overhead, the rain began.

We didn't feel it at first. The jungle roof caught and held the rain.

For maybe thirty seconds.

Then all those billions of canopy leaves tilted under the rain's impact and the afternoon cascade pounded down, soaking us to the skin. Heaven's waterfall cut visibility to a deep green hundred feet.

Miletich simply said, "Shit!" and we just kept moving, eyes nervously scanning right-left, left-right, looking for Japs.

I caught a quick motion. VanTuyl stopped, crouched and yanked his BAR to waist-high firing position. The rest of us stopped dead. We crouched, trying with our eyes to X-ray the rain cloaking the dim jungle ahead.

Nothing.

But then a form appeared, a dark silhouette looming from behind a tree. Rain obscured details, but he looked stout, built with broad shoulders like Mendez. Our training had us all crouch low into the undergrowth.

Dark Form moved into better view. For sure, no fuzzy-wuzzy hair. So, not a native. But no Jap soup-bowl helmet, either.

I met VanTuyl's eyes and held up a palm. Wait.

Pale blue eyes alert, he nodded.

Then the man in the rain pivoted. He waved to someone behind him and tilted a rifle upward. Now I could make out the ultra-long Jap bayonet. He motioned again and another man came into view. Another rifle. Now I could see both wore those stupid-looking khaki caps with the neck cloths.

Another minute and we sighted three more shadowy Japs. They held their rifles at the ready and faced towards us, slowly stepping sideways to space themselves out. *These guys are veterans.* One of them suddenly went rigid and snapped up his rifle to aim at us.

I yelled, "Fire!"

Ten of us fired, VanTuyl's BAR stuttering twice. The Japs disappeared. I couldn't see whether they were dead or merely had hit the dirt. Seconds later, the woods either side of our targets started winking with muzzle flashes. Maybe six or eight of them were firing back.

Bullets zipped and cracked past me as I flopped to the ground.

No good. Thanks to brush and creeper I couldn't see five feet beyond my nose.

So I boosted myself up, took a knee and aimed. I fired at every flash that appeared. As the rest of the squad fired the noise was deafening. Little bitty deadly birds zipped past. They make you flinch, but you're desperately focused on taking out whoever's making those flashes.

It seemed about a minute and the Jap shooting diminished. Then stopped. The cordite smell was strong and my heart pounded in the sudden quiet. "Anybody hit?"

Mendez said, "Nahhh."

"Lieutenant Gergen?" I yelled. "How about calling in a contact report?"

Cajones said, "Hell, Sarge, he took off when we saw that first Jap."

"Well, fuck! Did he take the radio man, too?"

"Looks like it."

I cussed again. I thought we ought to push toward the Japs, but the captain's orders at dawn were clear. "When you make contact, back off."

"Okay, boys, move back a hundred yards or so. Take it slow. Miletich and VanTuyl? Cover us until I whistle."

Japs opened fire again . . . dozens of muzzle flashes this time, in a long line. They had at least two squads in line, maybe a platoon, and were advancing. A series of larger flashes and thumps, those so-called knee mortars – little grenade launchers arcing their missiles towards us. Several small explosions cracked among us. Somebody yelped.

I bellowed, "Fire and fall back slowly. Miletich! VanTuyl! That's enough. Fall back with us!"

"Coming," Miletich yelled.

Nothing from VanTuyl and no time to check because I saw two Japs jump up and run toward our right flank while the main body was tried to pin us from the front.

"Bellknap, help me nail those bastards to the right!"

Suddenly Miletich arrived beside me, sweating and gasping for breath. He was dragging VanTuyl by the collar through brush and creepers while carrying VanTuyl's BAR in the other hand. "Sarge, I think he's dead. Didn't want to leave him behind." The Dutchman's face and chest were streaming blood. I found no pulse in his throat.

Next to us Bellknap fired a dozen spaced shots from his carbine. He hissed, "Come on, you guys! Let's clear out!"

"Right, Steve," I told Miletich. "Van's gone. We gotta scoot, so we have to leave him." I yanked off his dogtags.

Bellknap slapped a new magazine into his carbine.

A sudden wild yelling and howling stopped us. A knot of Japs bounded towards us, bayonets fixed, one waving a long, wicked-looking sword. Training on them like a set of turrets, we fired. It was my first time seeing a live target out in the open and I shot exactly how they showed us in basic . . . sight picture, half breath, squeeze trigger. I hit the first one high in the head, throwing him backward. My next shot took a Jap in the throat. He dropped his rifle, collapsed to his knees and grabbed at his wound. I shot him again in the chest. *No fair. So what? Don't care.*

Then Mendez and Baker joined us firing measured aimed shots, easing the pressure.

Later we couldn't agree whether ten or twelve Japs charged us. But they never got within twenty yards. As our bullets smacked into them, they either contorted or spun. They all tumbled, yells changing to strangled screams. With the last of them down, we began moving backward again.

"Should we check their wounded?" Cajones asked. "You know, to get prisoners?"

"Fuck 'em. Wounded Japs shoot you. Let's git."

"Hey, Sarge! Over here!" Robbins was hailing us. He and the rest of the team had taken cover in thick brush along the bank of a small stream. We raced to join them.

"Anybody see Lieutenant Gergen?"

"Yeah, I seen him take off like a scalded cat."

"Here they come again!"

Chapter 34
Banzai Time

"Spread out! Keep your spread! Space out at least five yards in case they toss more of them grenades. Or mortars, for God's sake."

The Japs charged from the front and the right, but with seven of us still healthy and firing steadily, even two dozen would have had no chance.

Soon Robbins jeered, "Hey, Tojo! Set 'em up in the next alley!"

"Quiet, damn you! Don't get them pissed off."

Kraz started inflicting some special damage on the Japs.

That big bear could throw a grenade a mile. He'd yank the pin, let the spoon fly, hold it for a three count then rear up on his knees to throw. It would explode in air, more or less in the Japs' faces.

Just after his fifth throw, a Jap marksman knocked him flat with a shot to the chest. We got compresses on the entry and exits of his wound. Meanwhile, I got very skittish about whether the Japs could overrun us. With Kraz down and two men working on him, only four of us were available to shoot now.

A second louie with two squads from A Company and a light .30 machine gun showed up. They quickly set up a firing line to our right.

"Mighty glad to see you, sir. Did Gergen send you?"

"Who? No, Cap'n Bottcher. He says for you to pull back to the company. We'll hold these bastards up for five minutes and then join you."

"Right, Sir. We're on our way."

Their machine gun and two BARs began lashing toward the Japs and we started moving back toward the perimeter.

It took most of us to carry Kraz because he was a hell of a big load, and getting him through the undergrowth was a chore because it got deeper and thicker as we worked closer to the company. The woodpecker rattle of a Nambu joined the firing behind us. They must have been aiming high.

A hollow *thunk* … an ax striking a rotten log. Bellknap pitched forward, dropping Kraz's leg.

I went to check him. Seeing the thumb-thick hole in his neck just above his collar, I just grabbed his dogtags and turned back.

When we got to the company perimeter, four native bearers helped us put Kraz on their stretcher.

As they lifted him, Miletich gripped Kraz's hand, "You're gonna be okay, buddy."

"Thanks, fellas." Kraz wiped at the blood trickling from the corner of his mouth. He looked woozy but then grinned up at me. "Sarge, I see what you meant about them 7.7 bullets. Like having Bronco Nagurski tackle you."

"Take it easy, Kraz."

As they carried him off, I figured my duty was to find Lieutenant Irish. I wanted him to know about Lieutenant Gergen. But I also wanted to just sit and catch my breath.

"Jesus, I don't believe it," Robbins said, showing me his watch, "From the time we started our little walk in the woods it's only been forty-five minutes. Feels like it took all day."

"Tell me about it," I said. "And three of us gone already."

"It ain't over yet," Baker said. "The firing is moving toward us."

"Okay, guys, get dug in."

The Japs may have starved through a hundred miles of disease-ridden jungle, but they seemed pretty sprightly to me. Maybe sheer desperation was pushing them.

We no sooner fit ourselves into line with A Company, than our rescuers, minus their lieutenant, came pushing through the brush to join us.

The Japs were right behind them.

Grabbing an extra magazine, I kept it in my left hand which cradled the carbine's fore end. It was awkward, pinching each time I fired. Shooting built a haze in front of me, but not enough to block my view of Japs. Settle that three-prong sight at belt level. Pull trigger. Dust puffs from chest. New target. Pull. Dust flies. Shift to new chest. Fire. Carbine locks open. Drop old mag. Slap in new one. Release the operating rod. Target. Fire. Blood splash this time. Look for new target.

No more targets.

I felt numb. For the moment, I marveled at having no memory of the carbine actually discharging. I knew I'd been shooting. I vaguely remember recoil. Ears ringing. Strong cordite smell. But firing? No. It just seemed part of me, like breathing or pointing a finger.

Ten minutes later they charged again and again we massacred them.

I didn't notice the little blood blisters on my left palm until later.

After that, the Japs fell back and spent the day sniping at us and probing here and there. They seemed to be searching for our flanks, because soon we were receiving fire from the west as well as the east. But we had no flanks. Company A had set up a semicircular perimeter based right on the beach.

Captain Bottcher visited our position about 1400 hours. I got up out of my hole to meet with him.

"Jim, I hear you had a bit of a skirmish this morning, correct?"

"Skirmish, sir? I guess. Seemed to me like something more than a skirmish, but I did want to mention something."

"What's that?"

"Well, first let me just ask why you sent that detachment to help us."

"I heard the firing. First a quick little burst of shooting. And then a real fire-fight started up. It got noisy and stayed noisy. I could hear Arisakas barking amid your carbine shots. Like big shepherds and a bunch of little lap dogs. Thought you could use the help."

"We did. Thank you. But, nobody came and told you about it?"

"No. Why?"

"Well, sir, our communications officer and his radio tender disappeared in this direction just as we first saw the Japs. I didn't witness this myself, but two of my men did."

He pursed his lips. "I need to talk to those two men. Their information might shed light on another matter about Lieutenant Gergen. He wants you arrested and court-martialed."

"Me? The hell you say!"

"Yes, it is true. He claims you pushed your squad into an enemy concentration against his orders."

"Sir! The bast… Sir, the lieutenant was twenty yards behind our line the entire time. He never said a word. And my orders …"

"Your orders were from me, yes? So I think his charges are, as you put it …"

"I think the word is bullshit, Sir."

He grinned. "I think you have no worry. There will be no court-martial for you. The Japs definitely are coming this way from Wewak. We're going to pull back to Aitape and Tadji airfield."

"Is there a good defense line there, Sir?"

"So, yes, it's a river. It's called the Driniumor."

Chapter 35
Getting' Out Of Dodge

Things stayed fairly quiet the rest of the afternoon. But as soon as it turned dark, the Japs started their usual nighttime tricks.

The woods began to flicker first here then there as they fired the odd machine gun bursts toward us plus a grenade now and then. They supplemented it with a few flares and lot of strange howling. Then they started lighting off long strings of firecrackers.

When the firecrackers started, Lieutenant Irish yelled, "It's just a trick. Don't shoot! They're trying to spot our machine guns."

One Jap kept yelling, "Marine, you die!" Finally, Riegle violated every order in the book and yelled back.

"Hey dumbshit, we ain't Marines! We're GIs."

"Ah, sank you too much. GI, you die! Okay?"

"You better bring some help, you slant-eyed asshole!"

As if on cue, about a company of Japs, at the time it seemed to me like a battalion, began screaming their lungs out and charged our perimeter.

"Flares," I shouted and our mortar crews obliged.

With the charging Japs silhouetted by flares, it became a very noisy suicide charge. Our machine gun and BAR tracers converged into their mass. The rest of us? Well, your carbine's sights are worthless in the dark, even with flare light. But when Japs are coming at you almost shoulder to shoulder, you just hold the weapon level, work the trigger and reload when necessary.

You can't miss.

Three machine guns and a dozen or so carbines and rifles mowed them. After ten minutes, all I could see in light of new flares was a lumpy jumble of bodies on the ground, some of them tossing back and forth in agony.

"Stupid bastards," Baker said, shaking his head. "The damn Japs are just saps."

They attacked two more times, throwing away more lives.

# # #

With daybreak, our plan was simply to march west along the coast until we got to a village about eight miles from the Aitape perimeter. We were to join the rest of First Battalion in defending the place, the idea being to bleed the enemy if he wanted to keep attacking. As part of the I&R Troop, we led the retreat, keeping our eyes open for ambushes.

Riegle spotted the first one. A Jap Nambu team with several riflemen was pinching in toward our trail, trying to cut off our retreat. He tipped off Lieutenant Irish who blind-sided the Japs with his team.

Over the next two days, the Japs encircled us twice. The second time my boys and I drew the short stick. I was to the point where I could have fallen asleep on my feet, but when I heard Japanese whispering back and forth in the brush south of us I forgot being tired.

"Quick, you guys. Follow me and be quiet."

We gingerly worked our way up a stream, arriving just as a group of Japs sloshed through it headed west. The boys and I just started firing. Four Japs went down and two others fled around a bend.

"Baker, you and Robbins! After them!"

Cajones, Mendez and I waited at the stream crossing and caught five more of them trotting up the trail practically into our arms. They were carrying a light Nambu.

We ambushed them with a three-second fusillade. Then I disabled their gun by snapping its gas tube with a blow from my carbine's butt. Baker and Robbins rejoined us about three minutes later.

"Got 'em," Baker said.

On the way back to the beach, Robbins said, "You notice some of those Japs looked a bit on the scrawny side?"

"Yeah," Mendez added, "and I'd say some of their uniforms have seen better days."

"Yeah, well, so have ours. The jungle kind of tears them up."

But if the Japs were starving, they still were aggressive as hell. We barely had time to dig in outside the village that night when they began attacking again. Our leftmost squad was near the battalion, our right was on a little creek about twenty feet wide and four feet deep … except when it was raining. Then it went to six feet deep and a hundred feet wide, flooding some of our foxholes.

This night, the Jap attack wasn't a single group charging at us. Instead, it seemed like a miles-long procession straight into our lines. After an hour of fighting, I formed a mental picture some fanatic Jap officer feeding his men to us in groups of ten. As he steered them to us, we just kept firing, knocking them flat. And rather than trying to flank us or infiltrate, he just kept delivering more upright living targets straight into our fire.

Riegle came to me once. The machine gun behind him was so loud he had to shout. "Can you believe this shit? The bodies are piled so high they have to jump over them. Kind of like one of those horses in gym class."

But the tactic eventually worked.

At dawn, Riegle reported to me again. "Hey, Jim, the Japs got a small force worked in on our left between us and battalion. They've got a machine gun with them and we're out of grenades. We can't nail them."

I fired another shot and shoved a new magazine into my carbine. "Well, I'm busy right now. Tell the boss."

"What?"

"Tell Cap'n Bottcher, for God's sake."

Eventually, the captain got on the radio to battalion which arranged for an LCM and several LCIs to come in to the beach. "Jim, the next step is for you to haul ass at high speed right down the creek. Float the wounded with you. They'll take us to Aitape."

It was bitter, abandoning positions we'd fought two days to keep. And scary. But the idea of getting away from fighting -- not to mention a ride and a rest instead of more jungle hiking -- sounded wonderful. Yet, there was a rub.

"The minute we take off, sir, they'll pile into our old positions and they'll be able to unlimber those Nambus on us."

"We'll have a surprise for them. I'll ask battalion to start dropping mortars onto your old positions. That'll keep them off your backs."

As we pulled out, the Japs did, in fact, swarm into our old positions. I was praying for the mortar mission to start, but it never did. So I cringed while making my way down the creek. I was tail-end Charlie and I felt like a living bullseye. I couldn't forget how a Nambu drilled Bellknap's neck.

Sure enough, tracers came tearing toward us. But these were crimson, American tracers from the LCM rather than the Japs' blue-white version from the land.

The U.S. machine gun bullets zipping above us were landing among the Japs in our abandoned positions. I heard some Arisaka fire behind us, but they only managed to wound Cajones. One shot knocked his helmet about fifteen feet and took off a half-inch of ear.

Once aboard our LCI, he cussed steadily as Mendez and I tied a field dressing to the right side of his head.

"Such nasty talk, Gringo! What would your mother say?"

"I don't think she'd mind. Who'd think a damned ear would bleed so much or sting so bad."

"Well, we can always shoot one of those morphine syrettes into your neck and see what happens."

"Just go stick the morphine up your ass, Mendez!"

"Boys! Boys! How you talk!"

# # #

The captain wound up in our LCI. I wanted to talk some things over with him, but it was hard to speak clearly. I felt beyond exhausted.

"Why don't you catch some shuteye?" he said.

"I'm too damn strung out. Every time I close my eyes I hear Japs screaming. I think I need a drink."

He seemed quite serene and I couldn't help wondering why. "You know, skipper, you've got three bullet holes in your fatigue shirt and two rips right along your right pant leg, there. Makes me wonder if you lead a charmed life."

He laughed. "It's too early to know."

"Oh, speaking of lives," I said, "We've got to get some more scouts. I've lost four killed and two wounded. One is okay, but the other probably will be in the hospital six or eight weeks."

"Yes," he said. "Keep your eyes open for candidates and pray for training time, and that we don't have too much more combat like we just did."

I prayed.

But I guess God was tied up that week.

Chapter 36
Plugging The Drain

"By damn, just once, just *once*, I'd like to get in one of them planes and fly way up high where it's nice and cool and dry." Robbins swept the sweat from his face as he watched an Australian P-40 climb away from Tadji airstrip, tilt sharply and swoop east in a graceful arc.

Shouting over the snarling roar of the next fighter plane as it taxied along the runway's steel matting Mendez said, "Hey, quit your belly-aching! Look straight ahead of you up there. We're headed right toward the mountains."

"Yeah, except we ain't going up *in* them where it's cool."

"Bitch, bitch, bitch! Anybody would think you ain't happy about being here. Just think how good you got it. No snow to shovel. You don't need chains on your tires. Nobody's radiator is freezing."

"Yeah," Cajones growled. "You bitch so much you give me a headache." Cajones alone among us wasn't wearing a helmet. It wouldn't fit over the grimy field dressing still tied to the side of his head.

We were passing Tadji airstrip near the end of a hike taking us to the foot of the mountain range. Here at Aitape, New Guinea's mountains pinch north fairly close to the ocean, leaving only a five-mile stretch of jungled lowland. And the Intelligence briefers told us that Jap troops from Wewak were gathering to assault across that lowland to capture our airstrip and then move on to defend Hollandia.

Captain Bottcher outlined it to us two hours earlier.

"It's our job – the 127th Infantry Regiment – to block that gap between the mountains and the sea. We can't let the Japs take the airstrip. Now our share of that gap, Company A's share, is the last thousand yards extending to the foot of the mountains. We have a hundred ninteenriflemen to defend it."

"That ain't bad," somebody said. "Works out to only about ten yards per man."

Lieutenant Irish snorted. "It's not going to be a nice flat ten yards like on a damn football field. And just remember this . . .

when your buddy gets hit, all of a sudden your share of the gap now is twenty yards, including all the Japs that are in it."

First we had to get there.

That meant the five-mile march from the beach past the airstrip to the foot of the first ridge. Then we turned east and crossed the Driniumor River. Our orders were to set up east of the river in line with the rest of the 127th and, nearer to the coast, the 128th.

Crossing the Driniumor, which we renamed The Drain, was no sweat. We were able to step dry shod along lots of rocks plus several sandbars. Where we finally had to wade, it was no more than waist deep, so our cigarettes came through dry -- well, as dry as anything can be when the humidity is bopping along near hundred percent.

Setting up a strong defense on the far side of the river was another story.

Like every other river on New Guinea's north coast, The Drain flooded whenever heavy rain came down in the mountains, meaning almost daily. But giant flash floods occurred now and then – say when six inches fell on the slopes in two hours. Those floods had washed giant tree trunks, auto-sized boulders, huge branches and mountains of silt and gravel over the banks, undermining and dropping other trees. The river's banks, therefore, were a chaotic pile of jungle trash thirty feet high in some places. And the whole area reeked of decay and rotting fish.

We started digging in about half-way through all the flood detritus, leaving a clear zone of maybe a hundred yards to the jungle's edge.

"Just thank your lucky stars you're defending this area, not attacking it," Lieutenant Irish said as he chose strongpoints for our platoon to site machine guns. "I wouldn't want the Japs' job here."

I had Mendez, Cajones and Robbins start setting up a machine gun behind a long four-foot thick tree trunk resting on a gravel mound. I picked Miletech and Baker, armed with M1s, to be their flank guards. Then I ran off to see the posting of three other guns.

These were the first defensive positions I'd ever helped set up. When I got back, the sweat was streaming as the boys shoveled up gravel and silt behind the tree to make a platform on which to mount the gun's tripod.

As we took a break to swallow down some sweetened tea, a big platoon sergeant came climbing over the flood detritus behind us. He extended his hand. "Howdy, Sarge. Name's Bryson."

"Good to see you, Bryson." I said. "What can we do for you?"

"I'm a red leg and I just want to check on where you're setting up so we can help you."

"What outfit?"

"The 129th Field Artillery battalion."

"You firing 105's?"

"Yep. Three batteries. That's twelve guns."

"Damn, only twelve artillery pieces to cover a five-mile front?"

"Don't worry. We've got a range of twelve thousand yards … almost seven miles. And, well, we've got a lot of ammo – I mean a *lot* of it." He paused. "And we have more on back order. Two LSTs coming in loaded with it."

"That's great news. But how do we contact you for support?"

"Well, the plan was to work with your commo officer. But after checking with him, we decided he doesn't have too many arrows in his quiver."

Mendez tilted his head back and laughed aloud. The rest of us grinned. "Boy, that's putting it mildly."

He grinned. "Yeah, and sometimes, he kind of disappears, too. So Lieutenant Llewellan and I are doing the artillery survey for this area and one of us will be up here in the line with phones or a radio to the fire direction center. We may even go out with some of your patrols."

"I wish we could have had some of your guns with us back at Buna."

"Me too, Sarge. That was the worst SNAFU I've seen in fifteen years in the Army."

Inspecting our half-finished set-up, he bit his lip. "Mind if I make a suggestion?"

"Sure. What's on your mind?"

"Well, look, the Japs like to get in close, right? If they do and I'm here beside you calling in artillery fire, I'll call for super quick fuses. That means the shells explode at head level in the brush, or right on the ground's surface; daisy cutters. Now when that happens, I'm gonna hunker down as low as I can get behind this big tree trunk of yours. I sure as hell am not going to be sitting up tall beside you looking *over* the log with all that shrapnel whipping the opposite direction. Get me?"

"I see your point, sergeant. So what's your suggestion?"

"Dig down behind and beneath the trunk. Make it deep enough for your tripod and gun, its crew plus ammo. Shovel away about a six-foot hole beneath that tree trunk. That way you can fire from beneath the log. It'll be like having your own bunker. The tree will intercept Jap bullets and grenades. And when we start dropping salvos there at the jungle's edge, it'll protect you from our shrapnel and blast."

I looked at the boys. "Did you hear the sergeant?"

They rolled their eyes. "More damn digging?"

"Okay, you lazy knuckleheads. Stay on break. I'll start the digging."

"Thanks, Sarge."

"Don't thank me. You'll finish it."

Later Lieutenant Irish came around to congratulate us on our bunker. "Just one thing, though. Always be ready to move … either to advance or pull back. The minute the Jap gets in close, your bunker here becomes a trap. Remember how the Aussies dealt with bunkers beside Buna's old airstrip?"

"Oh, yeah. I remember alright."

Chapter 37
The Opening Attack

In our company briefing that afternoon, Captain Bottcher looked worried. He said regiment informed him that last week, while we were fighting twenty miles to the east, a big patrol of Japs infiltrated near Aitape, crossed The Drain and set up on a ridge overlooking the airstrip.

After three days of dithering, commanders of two companies from the 128th finally got untracked and assaulted the ridge. By then, the intruders were gone.

"What that tells me," Captain Bottcher said, "is that the Japs had all the time they needed time to get to know our ground. They also had time to report it all to their command, so their generals have built it into their plans. They must know how thin we're spread."

"So when do we figure they'll attack?"

"Division G-2 said the Japs followed us pretty close in our retreat here to Aitape. They've been probing all along the line, very active patrolling, and they've probably had enough time to get a good many troops closed up from Wewak.

"General Gill is warning everybody to expect a major attack in the next day or two – night or two, actually.

"The general has asked Sixth Army for reinforcements and supposedly they're sending us two regiments -- the 124th Infantry and the 112th Cavalry. Don't know how soon they'll get here, though."

# # #

I hate it when command guestimates turn out to be right.

It was well after dark when Japanese artillery started slamming our line. That was something we hadn't expected at all.

"Incredible," Sergeant Bryson marveled. "How the hell did they wrestle artillery *and* ammo through all that jungle from Wewak?"

The Jap barrage fell well north of us, near the junction of the 127th and 128th.

Bryson clambered on all fours to the top of a leaning tree trunk. He said he was trying to spot the muzzle flashes of the Jap artillery. "No dice," he said once he came back down. "Can't spot their guns. Otherwise we'd lower the boom on them."

The cannonade to the north stopped only to be replaced by small arms fire that began as a stutter and rapidly built to a roar. "There goes the Jap infantry."

Though the attack's weight seemed north of us, Japanese machine guns began firing over us. You'd see the muzzle flash flickering back in the jungle and white glowworms would whip out to snap and crack just a few feet above our position.

Lieutenant Irish came racing past us. "Don't fire back," he shouted. "This is the Jap game. They're trying to spook you into shooting so they can see where our machine guns are. Wait 'til you've got real targets."

The noise to the north of us now intensified with flashes and a drumroll. "Our boys are getting into it," Sergeant Bryson said.

"You mean our artillery?"

"Damn right. Listen to that pounding." And there it was, a thudding bass accompaniment to the compounded rattles of machine guns and rifles. Drum fire, they called it.

Something began to stir out front of us. Remembering night training, I looked to the side and sure enough. Peripheral vision showed me motion in the darkness,

I hefted a grenade in my hand and puzzled at a *clik-clik-clik-clik* wondering whether it was a bug or some new lizard. Then a flare in the distance lighted Robbins' face, showing me his jaw moving at high speed. He was chewing gum at about three thousand RPM.

"Hey, Robbins. Are you nervous?"

"Hell no. I'm fucking terrified."

Somebody in the jungle to our front screamed a long order. I couldn't make out the word, but it had to be the Japanese equivalent of "charrrrrge" or "moooove" or something of the sort, because the next flare lighted a mass of rifle-carrying men racing at us.

Robbins pulled the trigger on the machine gun and all he got was a loud click.

He yelled, "Shit!"

As I yanked the pin from my grenade I yelled, "Goddammit, Art, you got to cock it *twice* before it can fire!" I lofted the grenade toward the Japs.

Before it exploded, Robbins had cocked the gun again and had it thundering, crimson tracers slashing into the attackers. He was firing in bursts of three and four. But for us it was like taking a beating. Machine guns are stunningly loud to the people firing and feeding them – doubly so in a confined area like the dugout beneath our log.

But if it hurt our ears, it was butchering them. Flares and the grenade's flash showed a cluster of running enemy, mouths open and yelling, bayonets high, others falling. As Robbins fired, Mendez and I were shooting with our carbines. It was hard to see clearly, but Japs were falling.

My memory's fuzzy, but I think that's when Sergeant Bryson's first 105 salvo landed. The flash silhouetted the Japs from behind. It blinded us temporarily.

But that didn't matter.

The shrapnel sliced them down like a stand of corn. Next we heard a chorus of screams.

Chapter 38
The Driniumor Battle

Before long, it became obvious that the Japs' main attack focused well to the north of us. Small arms fire roared in the distance and the artillery thumped and rumbled continuously. But the Jap command meanwhile targeted our part of the battlefield for plenty of attention. They kept us and our neighbors busy by sending squad after squad against us.

The way they did it was crazy. The Jap soldiers weren't low-crawling or making short rushes. Nor were they trying to flank us. They were just sprinting straight towards us as fast as we could shoot them.

"Those stupid, stupid bastards," Robbins screamed. "They're sacrificing their men to keep us occupied."

Lieutenant Irish scrambled into our post with two men bringing us cans of belted ammo. Over the battle noise, he yelled, "How you doin'?"

"We're still here, sir. They keep running troops at us and we keep cutting 'em down."

"It's diversionary. It keeps us from helping Battalion to the north."

"Well whether we kill them here or kill them there doesn't much matter does it?"

"Nope! You're doing great!" He slapped my shoulder. "Gotta check on the other boys. Back later."

At about 0200, a series of four blasts went off about a second apart on the ground in front of us.

"I recognize that," Robbins said. "It's a knee mortar. Got two or three guys firing grenades at us from one of those launchers as fast as they can."

Jap grenades aren't as powerful as ours, but they still have shrapnel and, like any explosive, they rattle your teeth and jar your brain. Two of the next missiles exploded fairly close to our firing slit. The blasts peppered our hands and faces with sand, pebbles and tiny grenade fragments.

"Shit! I've been hit," Robbins yelled. "It stings like hell."

"Hey, can you blink your eyes?" Mendez said.

"Yeah, why?"

"And can you pull that trigger?"

"Sure, but …"

"And I know you can talk which means you're breathing. Then you're okay. Just some razor nicks."

"Well, fuck you! It still hurts!"

I yelled, "Well, good! If you can feel it, you're still alive. So keep shooting while you're bitching. We'll check out your ugly face when things quieten down."

During a pause in the fight and after he calmed, Robbins gave us a warning.

"Sarge, in a couple of places out there, the corpses are high enough that they mask the new assaults, just like a row of sandbags. That lets 'em get a lot closer before I can see to shoot. And I think they could be setting up those knee mortars behind the bodies. Gotta do something."

While it was quiet, Mendez and I scrambled on all fours out to tear down piles of Jap corpses. I can't think of anything I'd rather do less than sneak into No Man's Land where plenty of bad guys might be lurking to kill me. But I guess they didn't want to be out there either. We ran into no living Japs . . . and no unwounded Japs.

Now it was supposed to be a simple case of dragging piled bodies off to one side, and then running back to our position, right? It was one of the lousiest chores I ever had.

For one thing, corpses literally are dead weight and hard to drag, especially when encumbered by attachments like canteens or bayonet scabbards that snag on everything. And being's how it was dark, of course, neither of us could see what we were grabbing.

But often – far too often – I found myself seizing raw, oozing meat rather than belts or sleeves or collars. And all too often, pulling one body off a pile of other bodies produced a wild scream of pure agony. Jap or no Jap, you hate doing something like that to any poor devil you can't even see. Besides, his screams might attract attention, about the last thing I wanted. I found myself praying that I'd only pull away dead men. The prayers didn't work real often.

But we had to do it.

Twice, in fact.

The second time Mendez and I scrabbled out there, light from a flare off to the north showed two Japs setting up their little knee mortar grenade launcher behind a mound of bodies. We had our carbines along, so we added those two to the Jap casualty list.

Mendez picked up the knee mortar and brought it along as we scrabbled back to cover.

"Why did you bring that damn thing? Souvenir?"

"Shit no, man. If we've got it, then they ain't shooting it at us, right?"

# # #

Lieutenant Irish showed up about 0400 with orders for the platoon to pull back and change front. He said the Japs had succeeded in breaking through Second Battalion and had managed to cross The Drain.

Our job? Company A was to pull back across the stream and set up facing north toward the Japs who seemed to be reorganizing themselves in dense jungle just west of the river.

We formed the south shoulder of the gap created by the Jap breakthrough. Battalion ordered us to hold there while the 124th Regimental Combat Team and the 112th Cavalry Regiment would counterattack the Japs from the west.

Just one problem with my little group. Our machine gun now was on strike. It was jammed so we couldn't cock or fire it.

Our little strongpoint was getting weak, being down to three wimpy carbines and two M1s.

As dawn broadened into day, Cajones and Mendez feverishly tried to repair the machine gun. Sometime during the night, a bullet struck and dented its right side plate, pinching the charging handle slot half shut.

The two men were trying to pry the slot open and swearing in frustration, when Lieutenant Llewellan and Sergeant Bryson came by doing a new survey for the artillery.

Looking over Mendez's shoulder, Bryson said, "You've got to send that gun to the armorer, third echelon, maybe. You'll never get it working without you tear it down completely and get a new side plate."

"How do you know?" Robbins asked.

"Used to be an armorer. I'd work on it, but I don't have any of the tools. Say! Lieutenant Lewellen? Do you suppose we could loan our stinger to these boys?"

The lieutenant grinned. "Don't see why not. Anson won't be happy about losing his pet, but he doesn't need it. Right now he's busy keeping our howitzers in operation."

I asked, "Sir, what in hell is a stinger?"

"It's just a .30 caliber machine gun designed for rear gunners in those SBD dive bombers. Somebody salvaged it when one of them crash-landed at Tadji. Anson fixed it up. The man can repair anything. And it fires beautifully."

"Who's this Anson?"

"Chief warrant officer, our battery's main maintenance man. You might have a problem with the stinger. It goes through ammo a lot faster than your 1919A4."

"How much faster?"

"Oh, just about twice as fast – say thirteen hundred rounds a minute instead five or six hundred. And the other nice thing is that it's several pounds lighter than your old A4."

"Hell, that's great! Will it fit on a tripod?"

"Nope. But Anson rigged it up with a bipod on the barrel jacket. Almost as good."

We drew straws and Robbins' scabbed face broke into a smile. He won the stinger.

It looked just like a slightly smaller version of our old .30. Robbins stole a long sling from a mortar crew. He figured that with the sling over his shoulder, he could carry the weapon and fire it from the hip.

Lieutenant Irish warned us. "Boy, just don't fire long bursts unless you absolutely have to. It'll overheat and start cooking off. Stick to three-round bursts."

We all practiced with the stinger and loved it.

The old gun's three-round burst had a yammering rhythm … *bap-bap-bap*. But the stinger fired so fast it sounded like a harsh *brrappp*. At first, it was almost impossible to fire bursts as short as three rounds.

We were eager to put it to use.

Chapter 39
Clogging The Drain

Battle continued north of us in the jungle west of the Driniumor for almost three weeks.

In one attack, the Japs succeeded in touching off an ammo dump at the airstrip, so that for days explosions roared and black smoke soared above the area. But the Aussie pilots still were able to fly out and rip at the Japs' jungle cover with bombs and .50 caliber strafing.

With lots of artillery help, the two fresh regiments repelled the Jap assaults toward the airstrip and slowly pushed the enemy back across The Drain.

By then, the Japs seemed stuck. They counterattacked back across the stream repeatedly. During three of these fights, their staggering losses caused the river upstream near us to rise and flood. Literally thousands of Jap corpses were clogging The Drain. Much later I read that Japan's Eighteenth Army was destroyed or, more accurately, that it destroyed itself trying to capture the Tadji airstrip.

They certainly kept attacking, especially at night. Before an assault, they would scream in English, yelling out "Medic!" or "Help me. I'm dying." Maybe they thought it would rattle us. Once we even heard some Jap screaming, "To hell with Babe Ruth" which ordinarily might have provoked a laugh.

But we were in no laughing mood. We utterly hated them because, by now, those thousands of unburied Jap bodies were putrefying in the tropic heat. We always buried our own dead comrades, but the Japs just let their dead lie there becoming putrid maggot-filled horrors.

The gagging stench went from unbelievable to impossible. We tried shifting position, moving higher on our shallow slope, but it allayed neither the stench nor the flies. We prayed for wind and storms and got torrential rain. But even that didn't help. The stench just worsened and flies swarmed in masses, even outnumbering the mosquitoes. They were so bad you literally had to wipe them from your face like beads of black sweat. And at chow time we just said forget it. Who could eat?

Smoking helped a little. Even the guys who didn't smoke learned to French inhale because it helped deaden their noses. When we ran out of cigarettes, some of us tried tying bandannas over nose and mouth. They didn't help a bit. The stench just became part of us.

Somewhere in there, the Jap command decided to change course. They must have concluded they couldn't capture our airstrip. So instead, they decided to turn south and make a run for the hills, which meant trying to attack through those of us holding the south shoulder of the gap in our lines.

The first we knew about it was a quick, hard mortar shelling. We were sitting in our holes, smoking and bitching about the flies and the smell when the shells started falling. One of their first shells landed right inside Cajones' foxhole. The big black burst spewed his entrails over much of our position.

Mendez tried to laugh it off. "Lucky bastard don't have to smell this shit any more." But he wept as he said it.

The barrage only went on for fifteen minutes or so and suddenly it seemed like a million Japs came bulling through the brush, one mass headed straight uphill for us, another veering to our left into the rest of the company's arms.

Robbins, raging about Cajones, yanked the stinger's charging handle, twice, and went to work. He screamed in syncopation with each *braaaap*. "Yeah, little bit *here*! Little bit *there*! Here! *Try this*! Have some *more*! Bastards! Shave and a haircut … *braaaap! braaap!* . . . two bits!"

The stinger jammed briefly because the belt tangled, but Mendez did a home-plate slide into Robbins' hole and helped clear the jam. The stinger was back in action.

It plowed the Japs, toppling them right, left and back. Some of them simply dropped like stones. Others clawed at their wounds and tried to crawl away. Others spasmed like rabbits hit with buckshot.

Survivors kept piling towards us, but they lagged. They showed every ounce of their fanatic courage, but their stamina and speed seemed gone. To this day I think they or their commanders were in despair over failure to seize Tadji airstrip and, as a result, were committing mass suicide.

At times, they'd stop attacking and everything became quiet. Nothing lay before us but bodies and writhing wounded. If we could have spared the ammo we'd have put them out of their misery. Then they'd attack again. They'd shell our position with mortars, killing their own wounded and some of us. Then they would charge screaming "Banzai!" We'd call in artillery and the noise seemed to build to a solid wall.

One night after hours of killing them, we just flat ran out of ammo. You fire a shot. The carbine's bolt locks back. You drop the empty magazine. And you have no more magazines to replace it. We had to fix bayonets, stand up and charge head down into the little bastards.

Robbins, virtually up to his knees in empty 30-06 casings, came leaping out of his hole with an entrenching tool and nearly chopped off a Jap's leg. The man howled as he collapsed, great gouts of blood spurting. We were fighting the old-fashioned way like in Rome or during the Crusades. I remembered to pull out my .45. For eight shots, I returned to the twentieth century. But when I tried to shove in a new magazine, some little devil hit my pistol, knocking it from my hands.

Back to hand-to-hand with cold steel and no damned shields.

At least, except for Mendez, we were bigger than them. Certainly we were stronger and better fed. Above all, we were desperate to live rather than desperate to die.

So you block a bayonet thrust or dodge a shot from one of their crappy pistols, but there's always another one coming at you. You swing your carbine like a baseball bat. The stock is sturdy and takes the impact. But they're throwing grenades which kind of equalizes things. I remember bashing a lieutenant. A Babe Ruth swing for left field seemed to crush his face. I caught a glimpse of flying teeth.

Then one of those damned grenades crushed me.

As I collapsed into darkness, I had a faint wry memory of Kraz saying something about being hit by Bronco Nagurski. Then I smiled because it seemed to quit hurting.

Chapter 40
Sent Back For Repairs

I've had a couple of surgical operations so I remember waking up from anesthesia to be a slow, foggy process.

This time I came to instantly with the sun blazing in my face. It made my head hurt. So did the roaring in my ears. When I tried moving my right arm to cover my eyes, that hurt, too. So I tried the left hand. It worked. Peering from under it, I couldn't see anything but sky and clouds and they were wheeling left to right. It scared me.

I tried asking, "Where am I?" but my mouth was too dry. It felt like friction tape. It took three tries before I could croak the words.

No answer came. But now I felt motion. I was lying on my back on something that was turning. And then I caught the smell of diesel. "Am I on another damned LST?"

Somebody said, "Jest another four foot futher down, pardner, and you will be."

"Who's that?"

"Seaman Second Fred Corliss. And I'm asteering you aboard this here LST. We gone take you boys to the Army hospital in Finschafen."

"Louder. I can't hear you. Am I injured?"

"Looks that way to me, friend. Bandages allllll over the place. But, hey, you still got both feet and both hands – eyes, too -- so I thank you gone be just fine."

"So where's this Finchwhatsits?"

"Finschafen. It's on New Guinea's coast about a day's run from here. Used to be a Jap airbase. Now it's one big-assed American hospital. The Fourth General."

"What? Can't be. Fourth General is at Melbourne. In Australia. I know. I was a patient there."

"Not now, Buddy. They done moved her lock, stock and barrel. It's all in tents and sheds now."

Now I saw him and the guide line he was pulling. I realized I was on a platform which a crane was lowering to the ship's main deck. The sailor, who guided the platform into place, looked out of focus. Everything did. But I could see well enough to tell his dungarees were grimy, though his seaman's cap was spotless and perched back from his blond greasy-looking pompadour haircut.

By damn, I wouldn't allow that hairdo in my outfit.

Looking to the side, I saw three men on stretchers beside me on the platform. I must be on a stretcher, too. With something of a jar, the platform came to a rest on the deck. A second later two sailors picked up my stretcher. "Thanks for the lift, Fred."

"S'all right, boy. I hope you make out okay."

They carried me into the shade which made things easier on my eyes but didn't help the headache. Then they put us on a big elevator down to the tank deck and, I swear, placed me at the edge of Stretcher City, USA. I'd have bet that two hundred stretchers covered the deck itself. Other wounded were stacked in four-bunk tiers lining the vessel's walls … oh, sorry, you swabbies. I should have called them bulkheads.

"Any chance of getting something to drink?"

"The nurses take care of that, buddy. Just lay back and relax."

Soon a tired-looking nurse stooped beside me, read a yellow card hanging from a string round my neck. "Well, you must be Master Sergeant Mays. How do you feel?"

"Sore and a bit fuzzy. And real thirsty. Now ma'am, I don't want to impose because I know you're swamped, but do you suppose there's any chance at all of getting a gulp of water?" (I always try to be extra polite with cops and nurses because either one can make your life hell if they take a dislike to you.)

She smiled. "The chance is arriving right now."

I heard the clank of tin dipper on galvanized bucket behind me. "Do you think you can sit up?"

When I tried, the pain across my midsection was startlingly severe. "Yoww! Can you maybe give me a hand?"

She helped me raise myself so I could slurp from the dipper again and again. I think I quaffed a quart of water, a fair amount of it dribbling down my chin and out of the corners of my mouth.

"Ahhhhh, that's wonderful. Bless you, ma'am."

She dried the water from my neck and chest and asked if I was in a lot of pain.

"A bit," I said.

She gave me two pills then smiled and moved to the next stretcher. I fell asleep.

Sometime during the night I awakened to screams.

"We being attacked?"

"Naaaaah," One of my neighbors said. "I think some joker's maybe having nightmares."

"What? I can't hear you?"

"Just shut up and go back to sleep."

Shadowy forms, nurses or medics with flashlights, found the screamer, bent over him and soon got him calmed down.

I discovered I actually could sit up now. It hurt, but the pain wasn't too bad. Sore joints and very stiff muscles, the kind of soreness you get the morning after playing a hard football game. But none of that white-fire agony of a bad ankle sprain or, say, a splintered collar bone.

It still was hard to focus my vision, but the tank deck lighting was good enough to show me two sets of stitches on my right arm. Probing gingerly with my left hand, I was pretty sure I found more stitches through the bandages on my stomach and right side. I could dimly make out two more sets of miniature railway tracks pretty much running the length of my right leg.

The self-inspection wore me out and I collapsed back onto my stretcher.

Later I awakened when the medics picked up my stretcher and carried me out through the ship's yawning bow doors. They put several of us in a truck which bounced about a half-mile past row after row of big pyramidal tents.

When they took us into our tent and lower me gently into a rack. You know the sort: Bed, steel, w/integral springs, olive drab in color, 1 ea. w/mattress and sheets, cotton, white in color.

Somebody draped a mosquito net over the bars at the foot and head of the bed. And I slept.

Chapter 41
Snooze Time

Sleep seemed to be about all I could do. I had occasional visitors, nurses and doctors. Over time, they removed most of the bandages and snipped out the stitches. I was still sore, but I didn't care. It was hard to hear anything and it was just easier to close my eyes and doze.

Two people approached me in the night, but no lift and carry, no bandage peeling, no snipping. One was a woman, I guess a nurse, and the other was a mousy-looking little captain, probably a doctor. He had a tiny flashlight that he kept flashing into my eyes. "How you feelin', Bub?"

"Like I went ten rounds with the Brown Bomber and Jersey Joe Walcott at the same time. I'm still kind of punch drunk."

"Lot of pain?"

"Just stiff and sore. The headache is better, but it won't quit. And it's hard to hear you."

"What happened to you?"

"Beats me, sir. I know we were in a big fight, but I don't really remember how it worked out."

"Well, you made it out in one piece."

"Yeah, Doc, I guess so."

He glanced at the nurse. "You're right. Concussed. But the wounds look clean. They want him in Hollandia, so . . . he needs to keep resting, but I don't think it hurts to fly him out."

"You're the doctor."

He left and she asked if I was hungry.

I told her maybe. I wasn't sure. But when she came back with scrambled eggs, toast and ham I wolfed it all down and went back to sleep.

Just after dawn she returned, this time with a new set of fatigues, socks and boots. That's when I realized that except for my dog tags and casualty card I'd been naked as a jaybird. I was kind of clumsy and uncoordinated, too, so she had to help me dress. Then she and a medic practically carried me to a three-quarter ton ambulance.

"Are they sending me back to duty?"

"No, to the airstrip. We got orders to send you to Sixth Army headquarters in Hollandia. You'll go to a field hospital there because you still need rest."

"Oh . . . okay."

I could have cared less.

I did get a bit nervous when they helped me climb the steps to board the plane. I still felt wobbly as if on stilts. And flying worried me. We went through a storm on my last C-47 flight and I was on a stretcher at the time. It seemed to bounce three or four feet in the air every time we hit an air pocket.

This time, though, the plane was a genuine airliner with plush seats just like on a Greyhound bus. Most of the other guys on the flight were officers.

Some of them gave me a snotty why-are-*you*-here sort of look, but I couldn't make out what they were saying. I just went back to snoozing.

# # #

As I eased my way down the plane's ladder, a tall lieutenant standing beside a jeep waved to me. He called, "Jim! Jim! Over here!" but the roaring in my ears kept me from hearing him at first. When I finally got the message, I marched up to him and saluted.

He looked at me quizzically as he returned the salute. "What the hell? Don't you recognize me?"

He looked familiar, but it took a minute for it to sink in that this lieutenant was my old buddy, Dan Irish, sergeant. From the Cow Palace. Frisco. And then the beach at Buna and, yeah, bringing us ammo at Aitape.

"Sorry, sir. I think my brains got a bit scrambled. Yes sir, back then you said you were a bastard sergeant. Now you're a lieutenant. Yeah, I remember."

He grinned. "Right, and still a bastard." Nodding to the driver he said, "Climb in, Jim."

He rode shotgun and I sat left rear so he could swivel and talk with me. He spoke slowly and carefully, but I found it hard to focus. The area's airstrips looked like enormous junkyards, smashed silvery Zeros and camouflaged Bettys and Vals, each with big red rising sun emblems, lined the runway shoulders. It looked like the allied fliers had caught an entire Jap air force napping. Now vines and creepers were taking over.

Other than that, Hollandia was like a beautiful resort.

We drove beside long, narrow Sentai Lake nested in a saddle behind the Cyclops Mountains which jutted two thousand feet straight up from the harbor beside its little town. Even so, compared to the rest of New Guinea, Hollandia actually was pleasant. Its altitude and strong ocean breezes made it comfortable; warm, but definitely not your damned jungle steam bath.

Lieutenant Irish pointed out that General Krueger's Sixth Army headquarters was directly across the lake from General Kenney's Fifth Air Force HQ. He said the two officers often crossed by boat to confer with each other. Meanwhile, General MacArthur had his own headquarters at Hollandia, also with a lake-front view.

Lieutenant Irish explained he was taking me to a hospital near Sixth Army HQ where I could get another week's rest. Then I'd join him and Captain Bottcher in putting the I&R Troop back together to get ready for the Philippine Invasion.

"Okay, I remember the captain. So, what's up with the troop?"

"Well, except for you and me and a couple of others, it's pretty much dead and buried. At Aitape, we got involved in the wrong kind of fight. We was shooting instead of snooping. Thank God you boys had that stinger. It helped us take out hundreds of them."

"So who won at Aitape?"

"Oh, hell, Jim, we did. They say we killed between ten thousand and fifteen thousand of them."

"Nobody counted them?"

"Because of the smell and flies, nobody wanted to get that close."

Chapter 42
Coming Back To Life

His talk about the troop and its fight confused me. It rang a few bells back inside my noggin, but the details still were sketchy and foggy. And scary. I didn't want to think about it. I didn't want to remember the stench which, somehow, still seemed to be with me. Or maybe part of me.

Lieutenant Irish and the driver dropped me off at the hospital, one of those open-air thatched-roof structures made mainly of bamboo. A medic took me to a room with two empty racks where I gratefully sank onto the mattress and promptly fell asleep. During the night I awakened because I was chilly. I actually had to pull a sheet over myself.

Sergeant Riegle dropped in next day and more pieces fell into place. I found I could trace memories of him all the way back to Frisco, too, and our voyage on the *Lurline*. I still did a lot of sleeping. And, oh yeah, all on my own I remembered we weren't supposed to call it "Frisco."

# # #

Somebody kept tugging my sleeve but I didn't want to wake up. I pawed at the nuisance to push it away.

Then she said, "Well, Judith was precisely right, Jim. You are a bloody wowser."

That voice! That *Aussie* voice! I raised my head off the pillow and found myself looking up into gorgeous green eyes. "Suzanne? *Suzanne!* It's you! You're really here? How …"

I couldn't believe it. I put my hand up to touch her hair. I stroked her cheek. Tears welled up out of her eyes. "Good Lord … you're *real*!" I sat up, grabbed her shoulders and pulled her lips to mine.

After a second she pushed herself away from me, smiling. "Jim! That's wako, but we have company." I heard chuckles and laughter. Looking around, I saw Lieutenant Irish and Captain Bottcher.

"See, Cap'n, I said he'd recover fast. Pay up."

"How did this happen?" I said. "NO! I don't give a damn how it happened. You guys, get out of here! Leave me and my girl alone for an hour or two. Or maybe a month or two."

They roared in laughter. Suzanne was giggling and weeping together. She reached over to hug me.

The captain stood up. "Come on. Let's let these lovebirds get reacquainted."

He paused at the door. With a big grin, he said, "Just be advised, Sergeant Mays, that this room is part of a hospital. At 1800 hours I'm ordering Miss Bennett back to her quarters. Otherwise patients here might riot."

Right. She wore olive drab fatigues just like the rest of us. But let me tell you, she made them look fantastic.

I said, "Oh, yes sir. We'll see to it, sir."

As he shut the door, Suzanne and I hugged again. It was the most wonderful moment of my life.

When you think about it, there's no reason that having someone else's arms around your shoulders, or her cheek against your cheek should make you feel a bit different.

But it did.

Hugging and holding Suzanne and having her hug and hold me brought me back to life. Yeah, sure, I had the old gorilla impulse to start ripping off all our clothes and doing you-know-what.

But that reaction strictly was in the background. Merely being beside her and talking with her, merely holding hands, was a miracle cure.

Suddenly I gave a damn again. For the first time in days I didn't want to curl up and sleep.

At last, I mumbled into her ear, "You being here is some kind of miracle. Some day you'll have to sit down and explain it all to me."

Suzanne lit a cigarette for each of us and spent the next hour telling how she and Captain Bottcher had run into each other at Fifth Air Force headquarters.

"He walked into our Signals office and he gave me kind of an odd look. Then he said, 'Didn't I meet you when you taught chess to…?' just as I was saying, 'Didn't I meet you at Fourth General…?'"

Then the captain asked why she wasn't in Melbourne. She explained she was one of several hundred of American and Australian women working for Fifth Air Force. Hiring them was

General Kenney's way of freeing paper-pushers and radio tenders for flight operations and aircraft maintenance.

He invited her to coffee and told her I was at the hospital in Finschhafen recovering from concussion and superficial shrapnel injuries.

As soon as he heard she worked in Signals for the Air Corps, Captain Bottcher explained that General Gill had assigned him to reestablish 32nd Division's I&R troop, most of which was now buried at Aitape. He was frustrated in trying to pull together the troop's remnants – chiefly Sergeant Riegle, Lieutenant Irish and me.

"So the captain went to G-1 to find out exactly where you blokes were. We got your orders cut, and signaled the information to Fourth General and – presto! -- here you are."

Then she turned grim.

"James, I'm frightfully glad to find you and I'm going to write to Judith about it straight away. She might like a letter from you, too.

"But it's a bit disconcerting to find you've been involved in some kind of spy doings behind enemy lines. And it was damned well daunting, Chum, to hear that you were wounded again. This won't do, not at all."

So right there we had our first fight. It turned into a real shouting match.

Trying to be polite at first, I explained that as far as I could recall, my injuries resulted not from lurking behind Jap lines where the enemy was few and far between, but from being right in front of those lines where the enemy was concentrated and could see and attack us.

It was like talking to a wall. Suzanne was a formidable debater.

"All that matters is that you were in danger," she said, "and you were wounded, for a second time I might add. And you'll bloody well be in danger again giving me no choice but to be aware of it and worry about it every damned minute of every damned day. You've done your bit! You've got malaria! You've got your heroic scars and you'll probably get some bright and shiny gongs! Isn't that enough?"

"Gongs?"

"Yes, gongs. Medals for bravery … DSC, Military Medal, the sort of thing that they pin on your chests."

"Oh, you mean fruit salad?"

"Damn you, Jim, this is not a joke!"

"You're right. So Suzanne what the hell do you expect me to do? Just quit? Then they'd send me to Ft. Leavenworth for life and one dark night."

And so it went for a good thirty minutes.

In the end, I just said, "Look, kiddo. I enlisted in the U.S. Army. It owns me body and soul until this thing is over. Nobody's getting out of it until we've ground the Japs into dust and then scattered the dust. Yeah, I got wounded, but from what they tell me, we killed tens of thousands of them. And we're going to have to keep doing that. And I think my chances are a hell of a lot better with the Bottcher Boys than in a regular line infantry company."

"Bloody fool!" She got up to stamp out of the room and I grabbed her arm. She spat, "Let me go, damn you!"

I held on. "Please don't leave like this, Suzanne!" I wrapped my arms around her. "I know this is hell for you. But, for God's sake, it's hell for everybody. As you Aussies put it, we have a job of work to do. And that's why *you're* here and not at your home in Melbourne."

She rolled her head against my shoulder and whispered, "I told you to *let go*!"

"I will … but only if you agree to walk with me holding hands."

She rolled her eyes, gave a dramatic sigh and said, "If you insist, Yank."

"I do."

As we stepped outside, she said, "This changes nothing. I still hate what you're doing."

"So do I, Suzanne! I want nothing more than to return to the nice, cool Pacific northwest where nobody shoots at you. It's quiet, beautiful country…"

An abrasive, "Knock it off, soldier!" came from behind us. We both turned to face Lieutenant Gergen. He was chewing me out for fraternizing with a female soldier. "You're violating every regulation in the book, soldier, while other men are in the jungle fighting. Next stop for you is gonna be the MPs and the stockade."

I started to laugh. "What would you know about jungle fighting, Gergen? I seem to recall that you did more jungle running."

He flushed in anger but didn't have a chance to speak because Suzanne said, "For your information, leftenant, I am a civilian not a soldier. And that this gentleman and I are holding hands is neither your duty nor your personal concern. So bugger off."

I walked her to her jeep. We kissed and hugged and she drove off.

About a minute later, two MPs arrested me. They charged me with being out of uniform . . . no cap, shirt partly untucked . . . and fraternizing with a civilian female.

Chapter 43
Recruiting In Jail

Like everything else at Hollandia, the military stockade was comfortable. They confined us, along with stacks of medical supplies, in an outbuilding adjoining the hospital. Bars apparently being unavailable for the windows, they posted a couple of surly MPs outside.

When I say "us" I am including the entire stockade population, namely me and two fellow inmates.

Herb, an Aussie army corporal, was a blue-chinned, frosty-eyed six-foot beanpole. The other, Mac, was a merchant seaman from Scotland. During his voyages, Mac must have spent some time book-pounding. He introduced himself as a living example of Hobbes' definition of mankind in a state of nature. "Ah'm puir, nasty, brutish and short."

MPs arrested Mac and Herb after they got into a brawl in Hollandia's surviving bar. U.S. Navy airstrikes and shelling destroyed most of the town to make way for invading U.S. Army troops.

The provost marshal was holding Herb for release to Aussie authorities. Mac's ship had been torpedoed so nobody knew quite what to do with him. Maybe the MPs hoped the two would solve the problem by beating each other to death.

But though when drunk they had inflicted some fairly colorful damage to each other's faces, Mac and Herb seemed to respect each other. Mac, in fact, held up his own slab-like fist and said "Ah'm tough, laddie, but yon pongo has a hell of a left jab. Loosened me teeth, he did."

The two boasted that during the fight they took out three American sailors and two MPs before finally being buried under the weight of numbers.

"Mind you," Mac added, "those bullet-heided bastards could no handle Herb and me in a stand-oop fight."

"That's no error," Herb added. "We laid a few of them out, I can tell you."

"So, Jimmy lad," Mac asked me, "why have they thrown ye in here?"

When I explained, they both shook their heads. Herb said, "If they're trying to put you away, cobber, it ought to be at least for a worthwhile offense … summat like bashing in the face of that tall MP out there."

"Aye," Mac said, with a solemn nod.

# # #

We were furious with the MPs because they wouldn't let us go see Bob Hope when the USO brought him to Hollandia. What could it have hurt for us to see Hope or Frances Langford? It's not as if we could desert or stow away aboard a ship to CONUS. As far as I was concerned, it was pure sour grapes. The MPs couldn't attend so they kept us away out of sheer spite.

I even tried to work a reasonable deal with them. "Look, fellas, you've got handcuffs. So slap those irons on us and then take us to the show with you. That way all of us can get to see Bob Hope and Frances. How about it? We'll behave and you'll be in control the whole time."

I could tell the younger MP was starting to buy the idea, but the tall one was a wet blanket. I think he was a fraidy cat who thinks an order – *any* order -- is the Eleventh Commandment from General MacArthur himself.

So we had to sit there in the hospital supply center listening to twenty thousand GI's cheering, applauding and laughing themselves silly. We could hear the band and Hope's voice reached us now and then, but that was all. It didn't matter so much to Herb and Mac. They'd never heard Hope's radio show or seen any of his movies. For me it was a bitch, like being a block from home but unable to walk in the front door.

The same evening I told my fellow inmates that my commander would probably spring me soon. The charges against me were bullshit and he needed my help with special training.

Mac examined his fingernails casually and asked, "Noo then, lad, whit sort of special trainin' might that be?"

So I gave them some background about the I&R troop. Herb, who was stretched on his bunk sat up slowly. "Well now, that sounds better than doing time in the glasshouse."

Mac, squinting his black eye, said, "And d'ye suppose your commander might have an interest in an old ghillie?"

"What's a ghillie?"

"He's a scots huntsman …"

Grinning, Herb said, "More like a poacher, you pommie barstid."

"Give over, you daft bugger! Ah'm no bluidy English but a proper highland Scot. Noo, Jimmy, ye oonderstand that a Teuchter ghillie must stalk his deer all oot in the open. The highlands dinna have much forest. So ye've got to be inveesible to the brutes. Ye cannae let them see, scent or hear ye."

"Really! That sounds exactly like our rules of dealing with the Jap."

"What rules, cobber?"

"Don't let the Japs smell you before they hear you. Don't let the Japs hear you before they see you. Don't ever let the Japs see you."

"Right-o," Herb said, leaning forward. "That's what we teach."

So we talked about their backgrounds. Herb had spent six years as a rifleman in the Aussie Defense Force, six months of it in long-range desert reconnaissance with Eighth Army in Tunisia and Egypt. In New Guinea he led a section of infantry against the Japs at Milne Bay and, later, at Buna and, after that, near Lae.

Mac grew up the son of a ghillie employed on an estate near Carlisle in Scotland. He trained with his father. In his late teens he ran away from home to become a merchant seaman.

When The Great Depression threw him back on the beach, he returned to Scotland to take up his father's trade. Once the war started, he easily found work as a merchant seaman again.

He and Herb were on the same troop ship – Herb as a passenger and Mac as a deck hand – when a Jap submarine torpedoed it off Tanamerah Bay during the Hollandia invasion. The vessel was part of an enormous task force – up to 250 warships and supply vessels – so the two were rescued readily and sent ashore when supply vessels followed the invading troops.

The Tanamerah Bay half of the Hollandia invasion was sheer snafu. The beach, all of thirty yards wide, led into a cull de sac of jungled swamp which, in turn, led to the feet of almost sheer cliffs.

"They had to evacuate the troops by boat," Herb said. "Sent 'em east around the Cyclops Mountains to Humboldt Bay where the town is. The goin' was much easier there. No swamp. And there wasn't enough Nips to put up a real fight. Any roads, they dumped us in the town."

"Aye," Mac said, "and then after a wee bit we found the bar."

"Right, and then Mac and I had a disagreement."

I was curious about the nature of their disagreement, but hesitated to bring up the subject. I feared it might lead them to renew their fight, and I didn't want to be in the middle of it.

Late that day, Captain Bottcher and Lieutenant Irish showed up. The captain presented a release form to the MPs and told me we were going for a ride to the I&R training ground.

"Sir," I asked, "do we have a full complement of men, yet?"

"It's you, me, the lieutenant and Sergeant Riegle and more than two dozen volunteers. We have quite a bit of winnowing to do."

"Well, sir, may I recommend Herb and Mac? I think they'd fit right in. It's just that they aren't Americans."

"Well, it means nothing. I'm not either, yet."

"What's this?" Herb asked.

I explained that the captain was German.

"But on our side?"

"Right."

"Weel noo," Mac said, "havin' Scots, Yanks, Aussies and Fritzes makes a fine fighting combination, don't ye think?"

Lieutenant Irish grinned. "By God, don't forget us Paddies."

Captain Bottcher sent me and the lieutenant out to the jeep. As we sat there I asked whether it would be difficult to take foreigners into the U.S. Army.

"I don't see why. Bottcher wasn't a U.S. citizen. And General Sutherland got his Aussie sweetie commissioned a captain in the US Army."

About two minutes later the captain came walking toward us, Herb and Mac in his wake. "Next stop, Sixth Army G-1. We've got to get these guys into the army. We need to get them life insurance, too."

Herb said, "Life insurance?"

"Yep," Lieutenant Irish said. "In case you get the hammer, your wife or kid or whoever you designate gets $10,000."

Chapter 44
A Return To Training

If any of us had doubts about Hamish MacIntyre and Herb Wainwright, they quickly vanished . . . especially concerning Mac who actually seemed able to vanish, literally, into any landscape.

Once we began training in the jungle and swamps off Tanamerah Bay, Herb also showed himself to be a short-spoken very professional stalwart. His lone complaint was that he would rather have a Bren gun than the BAR we issued him.

I couldn't have agreed more. But we already had three kinds of ammo: cartridges for the .30 caliber carbines, .45 APC for Tommy guns and our 1911 pistols, plus .30-06 for M1s and BARs. If we substituted Brens for the BARs, then we'd need to stock .303 ammo as well.

Herb just nodded, "Right!" and started learning the BAR.

It was Mac who surprised us. Seamen ordinarily don't have a lot of stamina, but Mac was the exception. Like Herb, he could hike for hours either in mud or soft sand. And, like Herb, he was quiet. His only complaint was that he would prefer being cold while crawling through heather in Scotland to sweltering in New Guinea's swamps and jungles.

Herb cracked a rare grin, saying that if Mac were crawling through the heather soaked by numbing highland rain, he'd bitch about how much he'd prefer the tropics.

Mac nodded. "Aye, weel, who's denying it? As a soldier, 'tis me sacred right to greet aboot conditions."

But, like Herb, he followed orders without question.

Their stoic conduct did much to stiffen some of the program's younger men.

One of our civilian tough guys turned soldier, Pfc. Charlie Wilson, obviously was repelled by the idea of creeping through swamps in a low crouch. But he just as obviously was damned if he'd balk or complain before Mac or Herb did.

And when he saw how calm Herb was when finding leaches on his legs and torso, Wilson likewise bit back any grousing.

Some of the other lads, however, gave full exercise to a soldier's need to bitch.

At first, perhaps the most worrisome was a delicate-looking Pfc. named Ballard Medlin.

Medlin claimed to come from some silk-stocking district near Boston and bragged that he even was kicked out of a prep school. Like the others, he was a volunteer. But with his prissy attitude and constant bitching I couldn't figure out why he volunteered.

Yet he did. And even though he whined like a debutante at a barn dance, he seemed to thrive.

I overheard him one afternoon. "Here we are, slithering around in this awful mud that's just as black as Satan's ass. When the mud dries, it turns to dust and settles in a nice uniform coating over your face and your food. Even the flies dislike it. Yes, and it sifts into your ears and nostrils and down your neck. And it gets in your eyes and then it mixes with your sweat and forms a black trail either side of your nose and those parentheses beside your mouth so you look like a very sick puppy."

And, "My mother, the miserable old bitch, said there'd be days like this."

But if Medlin acted like a spoiled brat, I noticed none of the other guys messed with him. In fact, I found out later that Wilson picked on him incessantly and finally made the mistake of calling Medlin by his first and last initials.

So Medlin busted Wilson in the nose, infuriating him. Try as he might, though, he never was able to land much of a punch because Medlin was a very accomplished boxer. He danced, bobbed, weaved and blocked while using his little fists to balloon Wilson's lips, black his left eye, split his left eyebrow and turn his right ear into a nice little cauliflower.

Medlin also shot expert with rifle, carbine and pistol. He didn't like machine guns, though, because they got so *filthy* and it was so much *effort* to clean them, you know. At first, Medlin was dubious about jungle-crawling and swamp-diving, but he learned to move through the mush and weeds quietly.

Corporal Jody Toomey perhaps was the best soldier of the lot. Like Mac and Herb, he kept his trap shut and focused on carrying out orders, no matter how obnoxious they might seem.

See, he was one of those guys who took the war personally. An elder brother died when the *Oklahoma* turned turtle at Pearl Harbor. The War Department telegram caused his mother to expire of a heart attack, leaving his father a desolate shell. Toomey, therefore, ached to resume killing Japs and to kill as many as possible. As he saw it, even the most trivial order was just another critical step toward that goal.

Captain Bottcher's training program was very intense and tough, eliminating nine volunteers in three days.

But at least we got some comic relief with the surprise arrival of Corporal Luis Mendez. We all thought the Japs killed him at Aitape. Instead they captured him.

Very briefly.

"You know us Mexicans. We got enough Indian blood that you might mistake us for Japs. Well, when I got the chance, I stripped off and got into a bloody torn-up uniform off a dead Jap. Then I pretended like I was wounded and couldn't talk. Well, they sure don't have much in the way of medical care. They just kind of leave you laying there, so I was able to slip away and make it back to the airstrip. But it was a bitch convincing the air corps that I wasn't a Jap. And the big hold-up was trying to find where you guys were and then getting here."

Six other volunteers made Captain Bottcher's grade for my team. I got Pfc. Barney Foster, a coal miner from West Virginia; Pfc. Norman Gilbert, a Chicago railway baggage handler; Pvt. James Hansen, a hobo from all over; Pvt. Vincenti Lysenko, a Kansas farm boy with "Rooshan" parents; Pvt. Larry Ruud, a Detroit autoworker, and Corporal Alex Tillotson, a trucker from Florida.

I had my doubts about all of them. Granted, they were physically hardened. They knew their weapons and four of them – Toomey, Foster, Lysenko and Tillotson – had been in combat.

The big question was whether they had the mental endurance to deal with behind-the-lines pressure.

For that matter, I wondered whether I had it.

In the end, most of us showed we did.

The others died trying.

Chapter 45
And More Training

Lieutenant Irish assigned me to lead the novices, Hanson, Ruud, Gilbert and Medlin, in a night infiltration problem that took us across the beach in Tanamerah Bay, through the morass and into the jungle. Our job was to keep going until we found high ground where we could observe the pretend enemy and to radio in reports about them.

The enemy, in this case, was Toomey, Foster, Lysenko and Tillotson under the leadership of Sergeant Riegle and Lieutenant Irish. And I didn't know it at the time, but Captain Bottcher decided to get involved, too, by leading Herb and Mac as kind of a roving patrol to support Lieutenant Irish's men and just generally confuse things.

We were doing all this in the nighttime shadow of the Cyclops Mountains – a cluster of two thousand-foot forested shoreline outcroppings which jutted up from the seafloor between Humboldt Bay and Tanamerah Bay.

My goal, actually my hope, was to get my team not into the Cyclops range, but inland up in the hills to the south overlooking Sentai Lake. I was breaking the rules. But what the hell? It made sense to me because that's where all the big brass's headquarters were. The problem we faced was that Lieutenant Irish strung out his boys along a line that we'd have to cross.

I sent Medlin and Hansen ahead in the swamp to scout. They returned thirty minutes later, so muddy that it was difficult to see them at all in the dark. Even though Medlin was bitching briskly, they reported finding a gap they thought we could use in flanking past what we called The Irish Line.

I'd say two of us were through the hole when Captain Bottcher's wild card patrol attacked. Their fusillade of blank ammunition shocked everybody, of course. Two of my boys and the men of the Irish Line ended up in a hand-to-hand free-for-all with all coordination lost and plans shot to hell.

I just moved ahead on my own, figuring that no matter what happened I'd get to a position overlooking the lake where I could pretend to call in air strikes and artillery fire on the bad guys.

Medlin, moving very quietly, showed up at our rendezvous point fifteen minutes later hauling someone with him.

I whispered, "Who's that?"

"Donno, but he was trying to fight me so I cold-cocked him."

Just before dawn, Captain Bottcher surprised us by announcing his presence. "Sergeant Mays, explain yourself. You and your team were supposed to hole up in the Cyclops area, yes?"

"Yeah, sir, well I figured the rules were off once we started. And I think the lake offers a better view of everything."

"Is that right? Well, I sentence you to explain it all in a written report."

"Gee, thanks, sir."

"So, who's this that Medlin dragged in?"

"I didn't want to show any lights," Medlin said, "so I haven't been able to see him in the dark, sir. But something's funny about him."

"What?"

"Well, his uniform is different."

The captain turned a pen light on the prisoner's face. You could have knocked us over with a feather.

He was a Japanese Army superior private – the equivalent of our Pfc.

He was conscious and began bowing energetically as soon as the light illuminated his features. He apparently had no means to commit suicide and seemed rather glad of it.

"Jesus, this guy had to be skulking down in the jungle for at least a month."

"More. Our invasion was five weeks ago."

"But you notice something? He doesn't look as scrawny as so many other Japs."

Chapter 46
Next Stop – The Philippines

Soon after, we learned our captive was an enterprising sneak thief who had been living off food he stole from the Army's supply dumps at Hollandia.

He spilled his guts to a Nisei interpreter, explaining that before the war he practiced theft as a Yokohama dock worker.

We of I&R grudgingly admired the man because he also had the brass to sneak into the nighttime audiences watching Hollywood movies being shown to the troops.

I suggested to Captain Bottcher that the Nip's talents might have value in our I&R troop. The captain chuckled at the joke. "But I think," he said, "considering my background as a German, the Axis Powers already have enough representation in our outfit. Besides, I don't believe this man has any knowledge of the Philippines."

At that point, we heard the brass still was debating whether to make Formosa the target of the next invasion.

Our bets were on the Philippines, though. We knew that's where General MacArthur ached to return. The Japs caught him in 1941 with his trousers at half-mast and he desperately wanted to avenge that humiliation. Besides, we all felt we owed the Japs for the Bataan Death March.

Most of us thought an invasion of the Philippines made sense because the natives probably would be much more supportive of us than Formosans. After all, many of our grandfathers had served in the Philippines at the turn of the century. And ever since, the United States had been a benign ruler, promising independence this very year.

Medlin was ready, however, to lecture us on our abysmally mistaken view of things.

"So your grandpappy fought in the Philippines. So who did he fight? The goddam Filipinos, that's who. So why the hell would they support the grandsons of men who fought and killed *their* grandfathers? Think about it! God what a bunch of dolts!"

He also stressed the point that the Philippines would be a tough fight because it consists of about seven thousand islands whereas Formosa is only one island.

"Where'd you learn all that?"

"In high school geography, you jerk."

It seemed to me he had a point. What I'd guess you'd call the main Philippine Island, Luzon, was where the capital was located and, likely, most of the Japs. But it also happened to be the northernmost big island and, therefore, closest to Japan and the easiest for the Japs to reinforce.

So it might make sense first to invade the biggest southern Island, Mindinao. But once that was conquered, we'd face invading island after island to the north. And fighting in the islands might not be like New Guinea where jungle and swamps isolated big Jap garrisons from each other.

The Philippines had lots of jungles and swamps, to be sure, not to mention some pretty nasty hill country. But the islands also had a system of highways and roads which the Army Corps of Engineers had built over four decades. So you couldn't invade one area and assume, as on New Guinea, that the Japs would be unable to reinforce it or attack it.

# # #

When we finally learned that the Army would attack the Philippines, we also heard that for once we wouldn't lead the way.

One of our regiments, the 126th was going to help with the capture of Morotai, an island that would become the staging ground and the unsinkable aircraft carrier supporting the invasion.

General Krueger was holding the rest of the 32nd Division in reserve in Hollandia. That suited me just fine. It was a beautiful area with a beautiful girl, Suzanne, working there.

I didn't get to meet with Suzanne often, but every minute was a chance to learn more about each other.

Most of my time belonged to our little outfit.

Captain Bottcher explained that once we landed, our mission would be about the same as it had been in New Guinea. We were to infiltrate, spot enemy concentrations, notify HQ and – when possible -- call down artillery and air strikes where they'd do the most good.

He had us focus heavily on artillery and air strike radio procedure because the Army and the Air Corps had reached a high level of cooperation thanks to FM radio. Moreover, by now the Air

Corps and Navy claimed that together they had destroyed the Japanese air forces.

"Occasionally the Japs do try a bombing run on us," the captain told us, "but the Air Corps reports that the Japs no longer have the strength to interfere with our air strikes or with strafing and bombing in support of infantry operations."

Well, that's what the Japs wanted us to believe.

It wasn't long afterward that we added a new Japanese word to our military lexicon: *kamikaze*.

Our first experience with the Divine Wind – actually I think Spirit Wind would be a better translation -- came in November when our convoy was just a few miles from Leyte Island where the Sixth Army now wanted us.

Chapter 47
The Gusting Divine Wind

We'd all heard the sailors' joke that LST . . . that's Navyese for Landing Ship, Tank . . . also stood for Large Slow Target.

"That was funny the first five or six times we heard it," Medlin snapped at a sailor. "But it's pretty stale by now."

But just a day later, the Japanese Air Force gave us a whole new in-depth appreciation for the term "target." In fact, the word ceased to be stale about 1030 hours Monday, November 13, 1944, when the Large Slow Target in which we were riding was part of a troop convoy about a half-day from Leyte Island.

The convoy was carrying the 32nd Infantry Division to join the battle for the Philippines.

MacArthur's invasion, started in October, had bogged down in the face of constant rain and the arrival of major Japanese Army reinforcements. Jap troop ships were able to land regiments from China because the Air Corps couldn't attack them. The reason? Torrential rain made it impossible to pave runways on Leyte Island's liquid mud.

Meanwhile, the Navy's carriers were tied up not only polishing off the cream of Japan's navy, but also in clashing with squadron after squadron of kamikazes.

We knew none of this. We were just trying to relax in the middle of the convoy's right-hand column. In fact, I was day-dreaming about sailing out on Puget Sound.

The dream took work because unlike the Seattle area it was hot as hell. We crowded out in the open on the LST's upper deck where the breeze gave us some relief. A lot of us were sitting in the battalion's jeeps, each with an awning we improvised from tent canvas. It was that or broil. I'm not kidding. Touching say, a jeep hood or a steel ladder railing.

And, as ever, heat and humidity were causing thunderheads to billow upward, getting ready to give us some shade before dropping their afternoon deluges on us.

The first inkling we had of an air attack was when a big sleek warship veered from maybe a mile distant to within a few hundred yards of our starboard side. The ship looked like a gray castle. It was half again as long as our boxy vessel, but instead of battlements and crenellations, it had tier after tier of guns.

"Damn, look at that beauty," Toomey said. "It's got more damn gun barrels than a porcupine has quills."

The ship had three two-gun turrets up in front between the bridge and the bow, and three more back toward the stern. Yet another turret squatted about three-fourths the way back on the ship's port side. Assuming that turret had a twin on the starboard side, it looked like the ship was ready to fire sixteen five-inch guns. It also had a dozen quad 40 mm mounts in gun tubs sited like sprigs of holly here and there in the superstructure.

"That baby has got a hellish lot of firepower," Toomey added.

As the ship neared us, our own vessel's skipper sounded a klaxon. Then over the PA system came the announcement, "Air raid alert! Condition Red! All troops get below decks to safety"

As men lined up to file below, Lysenko groused, "Safety my ass! Ain't no place that's safe on a damn LST."

He just leaned back in the driver's seat of our jeep. I was trying to relax in the shotgun seat. I figured he was right, that it would be no more dangerous up here in the open than any place below decks.

Lieutenant Irish seemed to feel the same. Rather than heading below, he was climbing a ladder toward the ship's little bridge. In fact, he was part of a rush. Dozens of seamen were bustling up there, too, clambering into their battle stations in the tubs of the LST's 40 mm antiaircraft guns.

Looking forward, I watched gun crews hustling into the three gun tubs perched on steel frames above the LST's bow. They busily donned helmets and life jackets, then trained their guns upward.

Just about then the warship next to us seemed to explode and catch fire as all those five-inch guns began firing, each shot an ear-splitting *Crack*. The five-inchers were pointed almost straight up and it sounded as if we were steaming along beside a giant machine gun. Meanwhile, the ship's speed whipped brownish smoke from the muzzles back along her decks, so she truly looked to be afire.

Our own ship's guns weren't firing yet.

I took my eyes off the ship and looked upward and could see nothing against the gathering clouds.

A dozen little black puffs suddenly appeared high in the sky and there, among them, was the plane . . . or most of a plane. One wing was gone, so that the remainder of the Zero began wheeling sideways down into the center of our convoy. It was about to land in the ocean when the ship -- later I learned it was the antiaircraft cruiser *USS San Juan* -- began firing again *Crack! Crack! Crack!*

This time its guns were angled much lower and pointing out to the right, muzzle flashes silhouetting the turrets. Meanwhile, she was steering even closer to us so that the racket was becoming painful. As those muzzles blasted I felt myself flinching, my head automatically ducking as if to cover my ear with my shoulder.

"Holy Mary Mother of God," Mendez yelled, "would you look at that?"

A burning plane, chunks flying off, tore past *San Juan's* bow and cartwheeled into the ocean between our column and the next. The impact with the ocean or the exploding gasoline or maybe a bomb tore the plane apart with a roar, fragments flying another few hundred yards toward the next convoy lane. Wilson and I each cheered as if we were at a football game.

But we shut up and froze in panic when Medlin screamed and pointed, "Oh shit! Look at that!"

Yet another Jap plane came into view above the LST a quarter mile ahead.

It was coming straight at us.

Chapter 48
Kamikaze Aftermath

He was on fire, approaching us in a shallow dive. He seemed to be absorbing tracers from the guns in our bow. Each six-man crew in those gun tubs must have been working like automatons because the guns fired without let-up – a gut-shaking *Thump! Thump! Thump! Thump!*

I think *San Juan* probably was firing at it too, but I really don't know. All my attention was focused on the plane's green cowling. Through the propeller's gray arc I thought I even could see the pilot's head and shoulders. Closer now. Shells visibly tearing at wings and engine.

The plane sagged to its left, its left wing tip slamming into our port bow.

The impact sounded like the dull *Whamp* of two jalopies colliding. The LST shuddered and the plane disappeared alongside, some of its gasoline tearing and exploding along our port rails. The flames were fifty feet from me but the heat from the blaze was so searing that my eyebrows sizzled. I threw up my arms to shield my face.

I looked toward our bow, to the blaze in the port gun tub. Three black scarecrows were dancing in their own funeral pyre, dancing, slapping with blackened claws at their burning clothes, contorting and screaming, tortured, trying to escape the gasoline blaze that engulfed them and their weapon. One burning gunner leaped over the bow into the sea.

"Guys! Let's go see if we can help the gunners up in the bow."

As we ran, the *San Juan* started firing again, but our attention stayed riveted on the burning gun tub. The dancers disappeared in a cloud of white foam as somebody from one of the other guns played a fire extinguisher into the blazing tub.

Gasoline was still burning by the time we got to the bow, but only in small islands of fire floating away from the bow in foam and water. The men in the gun tub looked soaked and blackened, raw flesh and blood beginning to show through the charred holes in their clothing. The quarter-inch steel of the tub's rim itself was smashed inward where the plane's wing struck. Its jagged edges had pinned the pointer in his seat on the gun's left side. He had died without joining the dance.

Another gunner gave a manic grin as I reached up a hand to help him climb down from the tub. "God damn, man, did you see how the skipper timed it just right? Just *perfect*! Did a hard right rudder so that the fucker just barely clipped us. Couldda plowed right straight down the deck and killed everybody. The damn skipper *saved* us. Deserves a medal!"

He grabbed my hand. But as he leaned forward transferring his weight, it slipped through my grip and he lost balance. He fell out of the tub, scraping past me to land on the foam-covered deck. I looked at my hand thinking foam caused me to lose my grip.

Not so.

His entire palm had slid off his broiled hand into mine. More of him and his charred clothing adhered to my shirt.

"Get back, Sergeant!" A corpsman shoved me away before I could unlock my gaze or even vomit. "We'll take care of him."

The burned gunner, lying in the foam on the deck, began shivering. But he kept praising the ship's captain. "Man, he saved us! Saved us all, didn't he?" Looking closer, I saw he wasn't grinning at all. Fire had melted half his face, stretching his mouth to the side into a hideous caricature.

He stopped yammering and started screaming.

"You're right, Sammy," the corpsman said in soothing tones. "The skipper may only be a Ninety-Day Blunder but he sure as hell knows his ship handing, don't he? Okay, Sammy, I'm giving you a little shot now. You'll feel a lot better."

He waved to two other sailors. "You boys get Sammy into this stretcher and down to sick bay pronto, okay?"

"Right, Doc."

The corpsman stood and peered at length over the rim of the gun tub. Then he said, "The others didn't make it."

I stepped away and flung the gunner's palm over the side.

"Do you think Sammy will make it?"

"Not a chance."

###

Eight other kamikazes attacked our convoy that afternoon. *San Juan* splashed at least three of them and a battleship out beyond the left wing of the convoy accounted for others.

Like the *San Juan*, when blazing away at the suicide planes with all its five-inch guns, the battlewagon looked as if it were afire.

During one attack, Mendez dug his elbow into my ribs. “Look, Sarge! Another one! God help us!”

He pointed to the Liberty ship abreast of us in the next column. A huge ball of orange fire and black smoke roiled upward from the vessel’s center island. “God, one of those bastards flew right into the midship house. I bet it took out the bridge and everybody on it. Lord, it must have fried all those poor sonsabitches.” He made the sign of the cross.

Somehow, the damaged liberty ship in the next lane never lost speed. The survivors had it keeping pace with the convoy even though its superstructure was twisted and blackened and still smoking heavily. For hours, hoses showered big arcs of water onto ship’s midships island.

Around the ocean horizon we made out three other thick pillars of black smoke.

With the possible exception of Toomey, none of us had been at all eager to join the fight on Leyte Island.

But in the wake of the Kamikaze attack, we all were very, very eager to disembark onto the island from our Large Slow Target and never to board another.

Medlin spoke for all of us. “Man, I want to be on land where you can dig a hole and take cover in it.”

“Yeah,” Lysenko said, “and then pull it in after you.”

Chapter 49
Coming Ashore At Last

The last troops of the 32nd Infantry Division stepped ashore at Pinamopoan Beach on Leyte Island November 16, three weeks after General MacArthur made his dramatic radio announcement, "I have returned."

However great those words might have made *him* feel, or even the Filipinos, what impressed all of us was the fact that he returned with four divisions of heavily armed veteran American troops. Moreover, they arrived courtesy of an enormous fleet somehow supplying us across 6,000 miles of Pacific Ocean.

MacArthur's command initially held the 32nd and one other division in reserve. Once the Leyte invasion bogged down, they brought us ashore. Our outfit filed in the rain from one of a dozen LSTs lined up along the beach. The vessels also were disgorging everything from diesel generators and gas-operated welding machines to crated Piper Cubs and deuce-and-a-half trucks.

Pfc. Wilson was first to begin bitching.

"God, it's hot here. I thought would be a little cooler than New Guinea."

Medlin sneered. "Wilson, you're a real intellectual sunrise. Why the hell would it be cooler? We're about eight degrees north of the equator as compared to New Guinea being three degrees south of it. Either way, it's in what they call the Torrid Zone."

"Well at least we have more gear here," I said. "Look over there . . . a sight that makes me drool." Crews of soldiers were towing artillery pieces off a neighboring LST. "There's a dozen 155 howitzers lined up hub to hub and beyond them under all that netting are four Long Toms."

"What's the big deal?" Wilson asked.

"The deal is that Long Tom 155 can drop a hundred-pound shell twelve or thirteen miles away. It'll be our job to call those big suckers down on the Japs."

Lieutenant Irish nodded grimly. "And there's what *really* counts," he said, pointing to a cottage-size stack of artillery shells. "Like the man said," he grinned. "No more Bunas. Now we got all the artillery we need."

Also coming ashore were tanks, though we doubted what good they'd do in knee-deep mud.

And out in the gulf beyond those off-loading LSTs were scores of other ships waiting their turns.

In the end, the Piper Cubs turned out to be a lot more valuable to our group than tanks or trucks. But, in my book, the artillery pieces outranked them all.

# # #

It took about three days for General Gill and his staff to get on track with Sixth Army. After they did, our three regiments moved forward to take over the fighting.

They were replacing their weary 24th Division counterparts along Breakneck Ridge, a stubborn range of jungled hills about two miles beyond our landing beaches.

The 24th had been waging a bitter see-saw war with the Japs along the ridge and its numerous gullies and spurs. The 24th would capture a position, but then newly arriving Jap reinforcements would push the tiring American troops back. As we crossed the beach we certainly could hear the fight and see some of the smoke rising up from those sopping woods.

Now I should point out that the 32nd -- and before it the 24th -- was only a fragment of the Leyte Operation. The operation's first thrust was to seize the island's northeast coast.

Our division's task was to drive the Nips off Breakneck Ridge for good. Then the 32nd was to turn west and drive straight across the island's waist, about fifteen virtually trackless jungled miles of razorback hills. The division's objective was to seize and hold Silad Bay on the west coast, the site of the Japs' landing beaches.

The job of the 32nd Reconnaissance Troop -- by now we called ourselves The Bottcher Boys -- was to scout the route that the division would take and, given help from the artillery, to smooth the way.

General Gill wanted us to start scouting immediately out beyond the battle lines. In a brief meeting he gave the officers and NCOs the big picture.

"Look men, our invasion here is pulling in Jap reinforcements from all over. They can't afford to lose the Philippines because that would cut their communications between Japan and the oil fields in Indonesia and Indochina. So they're sending in all the troops they can from the nearby islands: Mindoro, Mindanao, Cebu and Samar. And they're also shipping troops over from China. They've got to push us back into the sea.

"Now this island was supposed to be the center from which Fifth Air Force could dominate the entire Philippine Archipelago.

"But because of all the rain and mud from the typhoon that hit here two weeks ago, the engineers still can't build airstrips that can handle bombers and fighters. So for now the Air Corps can't stop Jap replacements from coming in. Because of that, we need you boys behind Jap lines, spotting targets so our artillery can blast the living crap out of them."

Our troop now consisted of eighty men in teams, each toting its own crank-style generator to power its radio. Each also had an artillery forward observer and at least one Filipino guide.

When I first saw the guides, they struck me as a rum-looking bunch. Most were tight-faced little guys, maybe all of 5-2. They were pretty much dressed in raggedy shorts and sandals cut from tire treads. Some wore broad fedoras, some had wide-brimmed straw hats and several had World War I dishpan helmets.

One guide looked like a mischievous teenager. But it didn't take long to learn that Jaime Aquino actually was twenty-four. He was scrawny, but his stringy legs could take him up and down those goddamn hills all day long.

Jaime joined the resistance when the Japs murdered his wife, With shared grudges, he and Corporal Toomey wound up buddies.

When we first met our guides Charlie Riegle asked, "How do we know we can trust these guys?"

Jaime's smile vanished. His partner, an older man named Domingo, seemed to swell with anger.

"Whoa! Easy! *Eeeasyyyy*." Lieutenant Irish put up a hand. "Riegle, watch your damn mouth. You remember how much most of the Papuans hated the Japs?"

"Damn right, sir."

"Well, that was because the Japs treated them like dirt. Or worse. Raped their women, stole their crops and burned their villages. That sort of thing, right?"

"Yessir."

"Well, talk to your Filipino guides and you find out the Japs treated these folks almost identically the same."

Like most Filipinos, Aquino spoke at high speed. But when on the subject of Japs, his eyes widened, his hands waved and the words tumbled out too fast to grasp. From what he said, it seemed somewhat more complicated than in New Guinea.

"When the Japs drive out MacArthur," Aquino told us, "they promise independence. Free country. But first we must join their Asian co-prosperity sphere and that make us slaves."

As he explained it, a country could reap the benefits of inclusion in the co-prosperity sphere only after paying fees, huge fees. And the Japs claimed the Philippine nation was far in arrears because, under U.S. control, it had paid nothing. The Japs, therefore, forced the population to make up the obligation through forced labor.

"Everybody from ten years to sixty, must work for Japs," Jaime said. "*Everybody!* Boys, little girls, grandmothers. We must grow the rice for them. Or cut the trees. No pay. If no work, they shoot. Like my lady Esperanza. And when harvest comes, they take. We starve. My baby son starves.

"Also they write a new constitution for us and create a government. But no election. Japs say no time for voting. Then, they demand that all children learn Japanese."

I raised my hand, "Sounds like what they did in Korea back in 1905."

Captain Bottcher pointed to me. "Exactly! And Filipinos have become skeptical about foreign languages. The islands have more than a hundred of their own languages. Some Muslim Filipinos, the Moros, speak Arabic. Well, the Spanish required that Filipino officials speak Spanish. Then we took over from the Spanish in 1899 so Filipinos wanting to do business with us had to learn English."

"Summing up. The Filipinos want the Japs out and then they want their independence, but they find us much more likeable because we never tried to enslave them."

"Si," Domingo nodded. "Americans good guys. But Pilippines still want free."

Chapter 50
Moving And Striking

Initially, the plan was to truck us south on Highway Two past the Breakneck Ridge battle lines. Unfortunately, the Japs had established a succession of three defensive lines centered on the highway. So, no go.

There was no point in trying to drive cross-country because, thanks to constant rain, trucks sank to their axles even on native two-tracks.

So we did an end run, or actually, an end plod. Led by our guides late one night, we hiked east away from the beachhead and then turned south, skirting past the battle area.

The going was rough, especially for those of us toward the rear. Every step was an ordeal of pulling one foot high out of deep sucking mud.

"No matter what the weather," Medlin groused, "bringing up the rear is a bitch. If it's dry, you get to eat everybody else's dust. If it's muddy, like now, the front guys churn it all up so us in the back sink every damn step up to our asses in it. I wish to hell we could be in a line instead of single file and then just march across those paddies. It would be muddy, but not this thigh-deep shit."

"Yeah, well, it's hard but we don't want the Nips to know we're out here behind their lines."

And because the guides took us along narrow jungle trails, it *was* muddy. And it didn't help that the monsoon rains continued in the typhoon's wake. When we came to swamps, we waded.

"It's just about what we went through around Buna," I said. "But it's still much better because at least we're not running into camouflaged bunkers."

Our initial destination was Mount Catabaran, a twelve hundred foot escarpment behind the Japs' right flank. From there, well behind the Jap front, we cut west to cross Highway Two and kept going.

Our first move was to set up a base near the north end of the Ormoc Valley, a lowland between two strips of jungled north-south hills that more or less paralleled the island's west coast. The Japs supposed had turned the valley into their main supply route.

Once we got that base established, Captain Bottcher led one patrol north into the hills which our division had to cross in driving toward the coast.

Before he and his group took off, Captain Bottcher briefed me and Lieutenant Irish on our teams' assignments.

"Dan, you and your boys head due north and then back east. You want to locate any build-ups the Japs might be preparing for our regiments. My team and I will head west doing the same thing. Meet back here in five days, yes?"

"Right. Skipper. See you soon."

"Jim, I want you and Riegle and your boys to start a large clockwise circle here in the hills south of the division's route and in the valley. Your job is the same . . . to find targets."

"Anything that's Jap, right?"

"Yes, sergeant. Anything Jap. Camps, supply depots, artillery batteries, ammo dumps, outhouses, anything that says 'Japs.' Find them and call down *donner und blitzen* upon them."

For the first time in a long time, I saluted. He looked surprised, saluted back and said, "Good luck, Jim."

"You too, sir."

I watched him stalk off through the rain.

We never saw him again.

# # #

Thanks to constant rain, conditions were horrible. But the next day I guess you'd say we had beginner's luck.

With Jaime and Mac in the lead, we were following a ridgeline when several of us caught the odor of wood smoke.

"Spread out and proceed very, very quietly."

Domingo and Lysenko scouted ahead and returned late in the afternoon to tell us that through the trees and rain they spotted an encampment well downhill from us. They reported that it looked like at least a company of infantry. Some of the Japs were squatting in front of little alcohol stoves, like our Sterno. Others were feeding small fires after slicing away soaking exterior wood from sodden sticks and branches.

Toomey looked at me expectantly, but I gave the back-away signal. We descended the opposite side of the ridge overlooking the camp. Tillotson strapped the crank generator to a sturdy tree and our FO, Second Lieutenant David Frey, tried to call the coordinates to DivArty's Fire Direction Center.

After an hour of trying to make contact, Frey snarled, "I can't believe this. Either something's wrong with our set or nobody's listening for us."

Taking a break from cranking the generator. Tillotson wiped the sweat from his forehead. "Sir, why don't we try Bottcher? See if he's receiving."

"Can't hurt," Frey said. "Start cranking."

I watched. Frey immediately got through to the captain. Within ten minutes Captain Bottcher learned someone at headquarters had given us the wrong frequency for FDC.

Once in contact, Frey got down to business.

He repeated FDC's warnings to clear the area. To do so, we climbed downhill so that the whole ridge lay between us and the Jap camp. The first round exploded five hundred yards away. The next shots exploded in tree tops fifty yards from the target and then came an explosive deluge of steel into the camp. With each explosion, I winced because it felt like a punch in the gut. With each exploding shell, the ground gave a gentle bounce beneath us.

The next day we climbed back to take a close look into the site.

Checking through my binoculars, I said, "Well, hell. It doesn't look like we did that much damage. I figured there'd at least a hundred dead Japs. But it doesn't like there's more than twenty-five or thirty. Of course, that's only a guess. All that churned-up soil and so many pieces scattered around…"

Herb asked to borrow my binoculars.

A quick peek and he said, "Don't be so bloody downcast, Jim. If you're part of a unit that just had twenty-five or thirty cobbers carked by a surprise barrage out of nowhere, you're going to be in the dumps about it. And you've no idea how many wounded they're dragging. Last night's little barrage came close to finishing them off as an organized unit. And no error."

Chapter 51
Finding Some Friends

We were slipping and sliding tree-to-tree down a steep wooded slope when Jaime startled the hell out of me. He stopped, cupped his hands either side of his mouth and yelled *Tuwi! Tuwi*!

"Are you yelling Japanese?"

"Yes, boss. I call friends. We use Jap lingo to fool Japs."

Mendez asked, "What the hell is he yelling?"

"Hard to tell with his accent, but I think it's Japanese for 'Attention!'."

Domingo nodded solemnly.

We heard a high-pitched whistle and both Filipinos grinned. "Come! Come!" they told us, and we resumed scrambling downhill.

In another hundred yards, we reached a narrow ledge which we followed to the right, coming upon a cavernous opening in the side of the hill. Three white-headed men standing out front of the cave were aiming rifles at us. When they saw Jaime they lowered the weapons and grinned. They waved us to join them and one of them called into the cave.

Out came a tiny old lady. She hugged Domingo first and then hugged and exchanged kisses with Jaime. Tears were running down her wrinkled face, but she welcomed us with a big toothless smile.

Jaime introduced her as Maria, his mother. "Very tough lady," he boasted, pointing to the scabbard hanging from her belt. "Always carry machete to kill Japs."

Scornfully, Wilson hooted, "You got to be kidding. She's so little she couldn't beat her way out of a wet paper bag."

Jaime's mom apparently got his drift. With a deadly look, she stepped in front of Wilson and whipped her machete up against the side of his neck. Wilson was startled, but went along with the act, bugging out his eyes in mock terror. She gave a quick laugh. Then she grasped his hand and, tilting the blade, used the machete to shave the hair from the back of his forearm.

Riegle chuckled. "Ye Gods," he said, "Next thing she'll skin Wilson just like a rabbit."

She laughed aloud, patting Riegle's shoulder with the flat of the blade. "Okay, Melican GI. You okay."

Riegle bobbed his head and Wilson said, "Phew. I need to sit down."

Maria waved Riegle and me into the cave with Jaime and Domingo. By candlelight, Jaime and his mom chatted briefly, apparently just catching up. Then, through him, she asked me what we were doing.

"We're looking for Japanese targets. We either can assault them ourselves or call in artillery." She nodded approvingly but wanted to know if we had approval from Gregordio, the leader of the local guerilla band.

"Who?"

The answer, complete with a three-way argument between Domingo, Jaime and his mother, seemed to take an hour. Getting exasperated, I said, "We follow General MacArthur's orders. We don't need anybody's approval."

The general's name seemed to clarify things. Maria said she believed Gregordio might cooperate and even help, but worried about exposing his group to Japanese reprisals. Either way, it would take the better part of a day to find and meet with him.

"Perhaps first we could find a target," I said, "and then ask his help."

Domingo nodded energetically and launched back into firecracker Spanish with the old lady and her son. At first they seemed dubious, but he apparently wore them down.

Finally he spoke to me. "We destroy puente enemigo . . . Japones. Jaime will ask Gregordio."

"What?"

"Eh, boss? He say maybe kill big Jap bridge. I bring Riegle and ask Gregordio for help."

"What bridge?"

"Maybe three hour walking."

"Okay," I said. "Riegle, go with Jaime to meet Gregorwhatits. Congratulations, you're now in charge of foreign relations. Medlin and Domingo and I will check out the bridge."

# # #

We took a break and I asked Domingo how much farther we had to go.

"Just over there," he said, pointing about two hundred yards to the crest of the ridge we were climbing.

"I'll believe that when I see it," Medlin said. "You know, if we only had some snow, this would be a fine ski resort."

"Are you a skier, Medlin?"

"Hell, no. If God wanted man to ski, he would have given us very long feet. And if God had wanted humans to live in these fucking hills, he would have given us wings."

"Medlin, I've never heard anybody bitch so much."

"Well, I'm just trying to keep our morale up. I mean, think about it, Sarge. Domingo here said it's a three hour walk to the bridge. Well, it feels like we had to climb up and down about twenty vertical miles to cover maybe two horizonal miles. I'd rather fly."

But once we were able to take a look at the bridge from atop the ridge, he agreed it was worth the climb. I just said, "Wow! Let's head back to the cavern."

Medlin began to object. He wanted to rest.

"Hey," I said, "if you want to stay here by yourself and watch the bridge, that's fine with me."

He came with us.

I told the squad that the bridge itself wasn't terribly impressive. "It looked mainly like bamboo construction, but it crosses a hell of a deep gulch. Maybe a hundred yards wide east to west and I bet a good hundred feet deep. It's got real steep sides, almost sheer, with what looks like a hell of a rapids at the bottom.

"When we saw it, a column of Japs was crossing. Four abreast. Probably a battalion. Anyhow, taking it out sure would slow the bastards down. They'd either have to negotiate that gulch or find some way around it."

I was certain 155 shells could destroy the span. But after Frey conferred with DivArty, he advised that the bridge was about two miles beyond the guns' extreme range. They referred us to engineers who needed more info before they could advise us on destroying the bridge with explosives.

So Domingo and I headed back to the bridge. We were half-way there when he did a sudden about face. "Stop! Japs come."

Chapter 52
Creating A Traffic Jam

We sank into the bush to wait for a ten-man Jap patrol to pass.

Instead, the Nip sergeant decided to call a break right in front of us. They lit up, sat back and relaxed. It wasn't just a Take Ten break. They just smoked and shot the breeze and, I guess, told some jokes. They laughed enough to give the impression they were gold-bricking rather than actually searching for guerrillas.

For us, it meant lying dead still, barely breathing and trying to endure the bites and suckings of ticks, chiggers and other critters dining on our skin.

"Jesus, I swear I almost can hear them slurping."

Domingo whispered, "Que?"

I just shook my head. "Never mind. Nada."

After almost an hour, thunder told us another downpour was coming. As the deluge roared down, the Japs got to their feet and moved out.

Domingo and I gave them ten minutes and resumed course. When we finally got to our observation point, more heavy traffic was on the bridge . . . infantry route-marching at a fast pace.

Though most of its structure was bamboo with rattan ties, the bridge looked substantial, standing on two piers. I thought that would simplify things, but the engineers later told us bamboo tubing can be almost as strong as structural steel.

Back at the cave after talking with the engineers, I told Herb I was about ready to say the hell with it.

"Easy, you flamin' wombat," he said. "I'd like to have a peek at the ruddy thing. I did a bit of explosives work in Libya and Egypt. I might be of some help here."

"Oh great. About the last thing I want to do is hike back there again."

Mac laughed. "Och, sergeant, can ye no stop yer greetin'? Yer getting' paid and all."

In the end, we marched back with the whole team plus Jamie's mom. She may have looked about ninety but she hiked those hills with the energy of a twenty-year-old.

# # #

It took much of the night for Herb and Mac to climb down the gully, wire TNT blocks in spirals around the piers and then to return.

Toomey and Medlin begged to work with them but Mac said a flat no. "The more bodies on yon slope, the better the chance some Nip will spot us and send us all to buggery. Tis bad enough tekking this Sassenach bastard wi' me"

"I'm an Aussie, you twit, not from Mother bloody England! And I'm the one what knows how to place the charges. So I'm goin', see?"

They were half-way through the job when Jaime arrived and twitched my elbow. "Me and Riegle we bring Gregordio. He helps. Twenty men. Two machine guns, many rifles."

"Hot damn!"

The four of us hunkered down behind the ridge crest. It took about five minutes drawing maps in the mud to outline the situation to the guerilla, an unusually big man for a Filipino and, for a Filipino, unusually smelly. But he seemed smart, giving me no arguments. He did ask when I knew General MacArthur. I said, truthfully, that the general and I once exchanged salutes at a distance of three paces.

By dawn, Gregordio had his men into position, leaving one machine gun with us. When I saw it at first light, it looked like a slab of steel with a finned barrel – nothing like any machine gun I'd ever seen. It didn't even have a charging handle. It did, however, have a very familiar pistol grip in back and a long fabric belt of ammo.

The little Filipino behind the gun seemed to know what he was doing. He was relaxed and as calm as any veteran. He licked his lips as a Jap outfit began crossing the bridge. So, what the hell?

When Herb came into our position to connect the charge wires, he took one look at the gun.

"Gawd! I don't believe my bleedin' eyes. That gun is *ancient,* cobber. Belongs in a museum. It's a bloody potato-digger! Looks in good condition but I say it's a left-over from you blokes' war with Spain back in the last century."

"It's a what?"

"Potato-digger. Just you wait 'til he fires it. You'll see, if it don't explode first."

Just as the first rows of Japs stepped off the bridge onto firm ground, Herb pushed down the plunger. The charges flashed and the center of the bridge rose slightly.

The blast noise reached us an instant later and the span shuddered and, despite the rain, fell in a cloud of its own dust, collapsing down into a huge V. The troops fell with it, the ordered column dissolving into a thrashing mass of arms, legs and rifles. They all slid into a mass splash in the water at bottom of the gulch.

The few Japs who'd crossed turned disbelieving eyes on what happened behind them. Then they fell as our machine gun plucked at them. And as the gun fired, I saw a rod sweep down beneath the barrel, cycling fore and aft fore and aft in time with the weapon's clatter. As I took a closer look, it ejected one of its empty .30-06 casings down the front of my shirt, giving my chest a good sizzle.

The gunner shifted target and began shooting into the mass now foundering at the bottom of the gulch.

"You see," Herb shouted. "That's the operating rod, and if the gun was any lower it would gouge the earth. Dig potatoes. Get it?"

I was more interested in the column of Japs west of the destroyed span. They wasted no time unslinging their rifles and began swiveling their heads, searching for targets. Meanwhile, a team set up a Nambu right at the edge of the gulch.

At that point Gregordio must have yelled "Fire!" because his other machine gun began yammering.

Mud spouts flew up around the Nambu crew. I don't think they got to fire two rounds of their own before they died. Meanwhile, troops in the roadway began falling to Gregordio's rifle fire from the jungle.

Even so, the Japs showed they were pros with more than their share of guts. Several hard-headed Jap NCOs began bellowing, sending several squads trotting toward Gregordio's firing line.

Unfortunately for them, Gregordio's riflemen were in the woods on the opposite side of the yawning gulch. The Japs on the east couldn't close with them.

They could, however, go prone, take a breath and start returning aimed fire. Further back behind them, I spotted mortar crews beginning to set up their tubes.

Time to leave.

I fired a white flare, the signal to break off the action.

At high speed, we faded back into the jungle.

# # #

Reporting by radio next day, I refused to estimate the number of Japs we killed. I claimed we created an inconvenience that could slow the arrival of Jap reinforcements and supplies.

I also had to report on two dog tags Riegle brought to me: Ruud, Lawrence; Gilbert, Norman. The Jap riflemen hadn't been wasting ammunition.

Now I had to worry that the Japs would come after us with some aggressive patrols.

Amplifying my concern, a deadly stillness seemed to creep over the jungle next day. Where we could glimpse it, the sky had a dull, brassy look and the heat and humidity seemed to double. And it doubled my worry.

But Maria shrugged. She said it was just another *dai-phung.* It took me a minute to realize she was predicting a typhoon.

Chapter 53
Life In The Deluge

In earth's tropical zones, you don't often see a comrade with quivering blue lips and chattering teeth.

So, shivering, I chuckled to myself at the sight of Charlie Wilson hugging himself as the cold rainwater dripped from the tip of his nose.

We were cowering for the second straight day in Leyte's second typhoon this month. For those of us in the jungle, it was just a constant, cold downpour with a hard, roaring wind that whipped the forest while uprooting and toppling a giant tree about every hour.

We could only huddle under our ponchos and stay put because now the draws between the ridges were racing white-water rivers.

"Dammit, Sarge," Wilson said. "You told us typhoons were supposed to be hot, just like you said the hurricanes in Florida were supposed to be. Well I got news for you. This *ain't* hot!"

I thrust my fist out from under my poncho, turned it vertically and began rotating the tip of my thumb in a tiny circle on my curved fingers.

"You see this, Wilson?"

"Yeah. What about it?"

"It's the world's smallest Victrola and it's playing that old hit favorite, *You're Breaking My Heart*."

"Go stuck it up your ass."

"Fortunately, Pfc. Wilson, I'm too cold right now to take note of your insubordination. So thank God we're cold. Otherwise, I'd kick your ass."

"You think you could take me?"

"Yeah, tough guy, and a dozen like you. Now just shut up and shiver and be glad we're not out at sea on a ship."

He glanced over my shoulder. "We got company."

I looked around to see Jaime slipping and sliding toward us. He looked excited and was making eye contact. His straw hat looked green with mildew and he was cloaked in a poncho which, as he walked, made about as much noise as the wind roaring in the trees.

He squatted down beside me. "Boss, something funny up high."

"What's that?"

Just then Toomey showed up. "Sarge, I think we got us a radio station or maybe a relay station."

"What does it look like?"

"We haven't seen it," Toomey said, "but we hear it coming downwind now and then."

"A sound like birds," Jaime said. "Very faint. But we hear 'chirp-chirp' then 'chirp-chirp-chirp' then one 'chirp' and then it keeps doing chirp noises. But it is no bird. Some Jap machine, maybe."

"Yeah, I think we're hearing code," Toomey said. "And we heard it on the wind, so it's south of us. I think we ought to check it out."

I called Mac and Herb and left Riegle in charge. The three of us and Toomey followed Jaime up the slope and into the wind. It was damn tough going thanks to the mud and the near perpendicular climb.

It's not that the footing was bad.

There just was no footing.

We pretty much had to get to the crest by grabbing branches or tree trunks and pulling ourselves upward as if we were monkeys. At the crest of our hill, the wind was an overpowering roar in the trees. But ever so faintly I could recognize the high-pitched electronic chirp with the dit-dah-dit-dah-dah rhythms of Morse code.

It was Mac who spotted the antenna, a silvery wand quivering in the wind southwest of us on the crest of the next ridge. Likewise -- God, what a set of eyes! -- Mac also spotted three Jap sentries. One was sheltering in the lee of the buttress roots of a giant mahogany. The others were huddled in their ponchos on the crest of the ridge.

At our distance they didn't look particularly alert. 'Probably freezing their asses off," I muttered.

"Aye," Mac said, "but they'd spot us easy enough. We'll have to circle or mayhap we can get up on that wee hill to the right and look doon upon them. D'ye think it's that impairtant?"

"Damn right. The Japs always have communication problems. When we break up their mail delivery, we make it worse for them."

# # #

Hours later we got to the summit of Mac's wee hill and could understand why the Japs weren't there. Its mud-slick slopes were almost impossible to climb, let alone haul a ton of transmitter and generator connections up onto that summit.

Our new vantage point showed us a camouflaged room-sized tent in a saddle which, itself, sat in the lee of a jutting promontory.

"It's a posh operation," Herb said. "The blokes pacing beneath that tent are in headquarters togs … bloody jodhpurs with gleamin' stove-pipe boots. They definitely ain't infantry subalterns. Might be staff officers and a general or two down there.

"And I count a dozen guards," he added. "To me, that says they must have at least a rifle platoon on hand, if not a company. A real flamin' hornets' nest."

"But why the hell have the gormless bastards nae sentry oop here where we are?" Mac asked.

"Lazy rear echelon buggers," Herb said.

"What I want to know is how we take out their transmitter," I said. "I figure they outnumber us by quite a bit."

"Ah say we hit them wi mortars," Mac said. "One tube up here and the other on that first ridge we came up."

"Mac, we don't have mortars."

"Oooch, I was forgettin'. Weel, the only thing then is direct assault. Machine guns and grenades. We don't survive it, but they won't either."

"Mac, I don't want to take them out that badly."

He chuckled. Then after a long pause he said, "Ah reckon Ah could do it mesel'. Wait for dark and could shift doon in there quiet as a stoat, plant a charge an' then …"

"Mac," I said. "I think you probably could, but I don't think you'd get out alive and I don't want to pay that high a price. That transmitter may be important, but it's not worth an entire Isiah MacIntyre. We'll need you down the pike. There's got to be some other way.

"Let's get back to our camp and think it over."

Chapter 54
Hitting A Prime Target

In the end, Lieutenant Frey and his buddies at DivArty found a way for the big guns to do the job.

The problem we faced was that maps of Leyte showed nothing but the words "mountainous terrain" in the area we happened to be. So it was impossible to give map coordinates to the red legs.

But working with one of their survey officers, Frey pinpointed a known hill. From that, they extrapolated the coordinates of the transmitter's ridge.

The dangerous part about it was the ranging shots. The Long Toms were shooting directly over us to hit the ridge. So I found myself praying, sincerely praying, that the typhoon's wind and rain wouldn't make a round fall short.

Either the prayer worked or the red legs were very, very careful.

The first shot was long.

Over the typhoon's roar we barely heard the noise of the shell's railway rush. It crashed in a black-and-gray fountain on the peak of the ridge we originally used to spot the tent. The wind instantly whipped away the shell's smoke. We walked the next shot to the ridge above the tent.

The next eight shots were something we didn't expect. They cracked open in mid-air above the tent, shredding it. With each burst, hundreds of invisible knives slashed the adjoining trees, caromed off exposed rock and slashed big gouts of mud into the air. A secondary explosion, likely gasoline for the generator, fireballed and quickly gave way to wind-whipped black smoke.

I asked Frey how the artillery managed the air bursts. He merely grinned and said, "It's top secret, but baby it's a treat."

The Japs at the radio relay probably never knew what hit them. The typhoon noise was so loud they may not have even heard the ranging shot detonate. It wasn't clear to me whether any hornets would remain in that shredded nest, but I wanted us entirely out of their area. So before the barrage even began, I ordered the troops to move out.

Toomey, Frey, Jaime and I had to scramble to catch up with the rest of the team.

When we found them, they were overlooking a new tempting target.

They also had become a target.

I was just about to push aside a giant banana leaf and step over a fallen log when I heard the command, *Daeshi*! Halt!

Jaime, who was perhaps twenty paces ahead of me, answered, *Ano, sumimasen.* I'm sorry.

The first voice then rattled off a phrase that was too fast for me, but I took the opportunity to peek beneath the dripping leaf. Standing there in the storm, a Jap soldier had his back to me and his rifle trained on Jaime who was doing his best to look like an innocent peasant.

I called, "Hey, buddy."

The Jap jumped and turned saying *Uma*! Roughly "Oh, God!"

Those were his last words. Swinging his machete, Jaime almost decapitated the soldier. Admiringly, Toomey said "Wow!" as the corpse, still jetting blood, collapsed with a gurgling wheeze. I had to look away.

Jaime, though, caught my eye and nodded toward the path we had been following. "Our boys have trouble. Many Japs follow." He carefully wiped his machete on the body's thigh and grinned. "Tail-end Charlie, right?"

"Right. Let's go!"

We sped along the path for another two hundred yards.

Jaime slowed and held his hand out. We crept up to see him point. A line of six Japs was kneeling, rifles up, and an officer standing behind them was starting to raise his sword.

I was frozen in place but Toomey bellowed, *Daeshi*!

It startled the officer, and Toomey blew his brains out before he could raise the sword another inch. By then I was firing aimed shots into the backs of his troops. I got two of them and Frey nailed another pair.

The last two did the unthinkable. They stood, raising their hands in surrender and pleading *Dozo! Dozo!* Please! Please!

"Surrendering," Toomey said. "How about that crap? Should I go ahead and shoot them?"

"Naah. Bring 'em along. Make 'em strip first so we know they got no weapons."

We heard a burst of shots off to the right … carbines versus Arisakas. Then I heard Riegle yelling. "Jim? Are you back there?"

"Yessir, Charlie, it's us. We saved your bacon."

He came plunging through the brush with Herb and Wilson in tow.

"Where's everybody else?"

"They'll be along directly," he said. "They're checking out two of the boys that was getting ready to ambush us while we was checking out the target up ahead."

"What target is it?"

"It's a hell of a big a supply dump. I can't read their scribbles, of course, but some of it looks like artillery ammo crates and some of it maybe could be food. Whatever it is, I recommend we get the hell out of here because all this shooting probably done woke up the neighborhood."

"Makes sense to me," Herb said. "I 'spect we wore out our welcome."

So we made tracks for the cave.

It took the better part of the afternoon to get there. And when we arrived I wished we had picked another destination.

Some Jap patrol had stumbled on it. Or maybe they followed Gregordio's people.

The three old sentinels were dead. Two had bullet wounds and the third had been beaten to a bloody pulp before some bastard beheaded him. Jaime's mother was in the cave, dead, with an empty revolver in her hand. Her razor-sharp machete was still in its scabbard. I asked Jaime if I could have it.

"You must kill one Jap for it."

I nodded.

I sent Mac, Lysenko, Medlin and Mendez out to patrol the jungle. The rest of us dug graves.

In two years of killing I thought I'd become hardened. But this was my first time to read the burial service. As I recited the beautiful opening phrases, *I am the resurrection and the life, saith the Lord; he that believeth in me, though he were dead, yet shall he live*... something inside me ripped.

Ah, Jesus...

It was a good five minutes before I could choke back the tears and go on. Thank God the men were patient.

We wanted to rest but agreed it would be crazy to stay in or near the cave since the Japs now knew about it. We hiked away and kept moving through the night. I wanted to circle back so we could check out the target again.

"I donno," Herb said. "I think those supplies might be bait for us."

"Aye, mebbe," Mac said. "But yon Japs will no be mountin' an ambush for hundred-weight artillery shells, noo will they?"

# # #

At a distance, we circled the supply dump which lay adjacent to a two-track. Since Riegle's visit two days ago, the Japs had covered the supplies with camouflage netting. Both Herb and Mac remained suspicious about going anywhere near it.

"Look ye, Mr. Master Sergeant. Ah'm verra, verra guid at disguise and camouflage. But naebody is as guid as Jap. He's got a special eye. So whit I want to recommend is that we place it on yon map, gang off aboot five mile and then call in the cannon. Foreby, if we stay here, nae doubt they'll knacker us and we nivver the wiser."

I looked at Herb and he gave a deep nod. "Sooner the better."

Chapter 55
Eluding The Enemy

Once we had covered about five miles, we took a break and Frey tried to contact DivArty.

We were well spread out, but I was close enough to see him slap his hand against a tree trunk in frustration.

"No dice again," he said, when I went over to see him. "So I'll see about reaching the captain."

The rain had stopped, but we all still were soaked. Water drops still were plopping down onto us under the jungle canopy. The air was foggy and so super-saturated that breathing felt more like gasping.

In ten minutes Frey got back to me.

"Captain Bottcher is about ready to murder somebody," he said. "So is the FDC. It looks like some asshole sent us the wrong frequency again."

I asked him to call in the fire mission. "We're going to keep moving for now," I said. "But in the next break, check back with the CO whether the same thing happened to any of the other scouting parties."

"Yessir. Something's really screwy. But I don't like doing so much radioing. Makes it easier for Jap direction-finding to pin us down."

"Yeah, well, for now we just have to keep moving."

"Oh, wonderful. I'm telling you, Sarge, I'm ready for a rest."

"Yeah. Aren't we all?"

We pushed along single file, winding among the trees and stepping gingerly through waist-deep brush along a hillside that, for once, was a fairly gentle slope. I think all of us were anticipating the rumble of artillery fire so it was a surprise instead to hear an airplane engine. It sounded like one of the Piper Cubs that had flown over us occasionally on New Guinea.

Because of the jungle canopy we couldn't see the plane, but it sounded as if it headed in the direction of our targeted supply dump.

"Maybe they're checking out our sighting," Frey said.

"That's okay with me. I wish we had fighters and bombers up there, too."

About fifteen minutes later we heard the *whuff* of a distant explosion. "That's gotta be a ranging shot," Frey said. "Direction's right." We heard one more *whuff* and then came a five-minute drumbeat of many explosions. Then came a much louder blast that, even at a distance of miles, had a distinct roar, plus a few echoes.

"Hot dog!" Frey said. "Secondary explosion. Must have been a lot of ammo in that dump."

I was starting to debate where we should head next when Mendez raised his right fist. The sign to halt.

We all crouched. None of us made a sound, but an irregular chopping reverberated through the incessant insect buzz; somebody hacking at brush with a machete.

Mac stood up and looked at me. I nodded. He crouched and headed down the slope, moving like a shadow.

When he returned his eyes were wide.

"Jap," he whispered. "Ah'm sorry to tell ye 'tis maybe a full company of the fookers. A squad is cuttin' trail maybe fifty or sixty yards below us an' the rest followin'."

"Coming this way?"

He shook his head. "Opposite direction to us. I think if we just bide, mayhap they'll pass wi'out noticing us."

The brush certainly concealed them from us, but we could hear them clearly, not only chopping but yakking with each other. The choppers moved past us, headed toward our right. The troops that followed weren't talking, but we could hear rifle butts bumping water bottles and bayonet scabbards.

Everything would have been fine if some yahoo dreamer . . . I don't know, maybe he was a flanker . . . hadn't wandered off the path to chase butterflies. The Philippine jungles have some real beauties. This joker was trying to sneak up on a giant, a black and yellow butterfly about the size of a damned blue jay back home. And when it lowered those yellow wings, they turned as blue as a jay's

So this Jap private leaned to grab the butterfly. Just one problem, though. When you're reaching out with both hands, your slung rifle tends to fall right off your shoulder. And this guy's Arisaka landed beside Pfc. Barney Foster who was crouched beneath the bush on which the butterfly chose to light.

The Jap was utterly shocked at seeing a round-eye practically beneath his nose. I guess he literally couldn't believe his eyes, because he just stood there, bent at the waist, arms out, hands cupped, mouth open. Had Foster been holding a knife, he might have been able to kill the Jap silently. But he was holding his carbine instead, so he simply tilted it up and put a bullet through the Jap's head.

Within five seconds the whole Jap company was shooting uphill towards us and we were cussing Foster as we fell flat. "Jesus, Barney, couldn't you just *disappear*?"

He gave us the finger.

None of their shots struck us. People shooting uphill almost always fire too high. But next their company commander screamed the Jap equivalent of "charrrrge!" They tried to attack by charging uphill into thick brush . . . right into a series of exploding grenades which we lofted to them.

The grenades blunted their attack and seemed to knock some sense into their CO's head. After a pause in which we could hear somebody yammering, the Jap troops began maneuvering. Staying low and moving in small fire teams, they were trying to feel out where we were and how many of us they faced.

Since there were only thirteen of us and probably more than a hundred of them, I yelled one order, "Back!" Heavy underbrush and pure caution slowed the Japs following us, but in all that tangle we couldn't make much speed either.

Herb came across a giant tangle of vines and downed trees and we all crouched into it.

"Only one hope," Mac said. "Pick off yon officers and NCOs. Maybe it'll put them in banzai fury."

"You guys hear that? Corporal Toomey? Hear that?"

"I did, and my BAR is just the gun."

"So, start picking off the bastards."

Toomey perched the rifle's bipod on a log about thirty feet from us. As enemy troops emerged into view, his BAR would bark. You could hear that .30-06 slug smack a Nip sergeant or lieutenant. It would knock him flat and his men would duck into cover.

Finally they came screaming out of the brush, charging uphill and, in three minutes of concentrated fire, we butchered them. I said, "Good. That oughta hold them for a bit."

"Right," Herb said. "Leaves us low on ammo, you know."

"Yowser. It's time to get the hell away from here. Now, Charlie? I want you to take off with everybody. Lead them back the way we came. Jody and Luis and I will stick around and play the delaying game."

"Now just hold on, Jim. I don't want…"

"Don't argue, dammit. Just get moving. Jaime and Domingo will show you the way. We'll hold off these bastards and try to confuse them and then split up. Rendezvous 1200 hours tomorrow back on the ridge above that first camp we shelled. Now, *go*!"

Once they took off, I told Mendez to head east and Toomey west. "I'll head uphill to the south. Now the idea is that we each nail two or three of the bastards and then disappear. Either find a real good hidey hole or make tracks. They won't know which way to go or which end is up. Okay?"

"Yo, boss."

Ordinarily, moving uphill with the enemy below you is just asking for a bullet. But the brush was so thick they couldn't see me.

I did get a hell of a fright, though. Perhaps twenty minutes after we split up, I found and crept into a thick bower of vines. It was the wide base of a broad curtain of foliage twining high into the jungle canopy.

Peering through a narrow gap in the vines, I saw an exotic Asian sloe eye. It was all I could see of a Jap soldier maybe ten feet away. He was looking to my right. As I carefully raised the carbine and sighted on his right temple I muttered, "Better you than me, buddy."

I pulled the trigger. He disappeared in his own pink mist.

I ducked and stayed low during the fuss as his comrades searched and fired up into the trees trying to hit the mystery sniper.

Enjoying some of your own medicine, you bastards?

Chapter 56
Escape, Flight, Evasion

"You ver' noisy, Boss."

I must have jumped three feet when he spoke, because Domingo politely covered his mouth and laughed softly. Up to that point, I'd been getting a bit proud of my ability to move quietly in the jungle.

"Damn, you scared me. 'Bout made me jump out of my skin!" He grinned, so I grinned back, patted him on the shoulder and asked, "Is Sergeant Riegle here?"

"Oh yes, boss." He pointed up the slope. "He up there with everybody."

"Is Luis here yet?"

"Yes, but no Jody."

I was about an hour late for our rendezvous, so I figured Toomey would come climbing up the ridge at any time.

Riegle and Herb were applying cigarettes to their leeches and Frye was hissing as he dabbed merthiolate on a shin ulcer. Riegle said Captain Bottcher had called in with orders for us to start circling further west to keep pace with the advancing 127th Infantry Regiment.

"He also told us that FDC is checking on why our team keeps ending up with the wrong frequency," Frey said. "We're the only ones it's happened to. So what do you think is going on?"

Oh ho! I bet it's Gergen who's been playing games. "Sir, I have no idea. I just hope they've got it straightened out. Right now I think we should making plans for our next tour of this beautiful jungle."

"Oh, that's the other thing," Riegle said. "The Cubs have been air-dropping supplies to the 127th."

"The cubs?"

"Yeah, those Piper Cub airplanes. Scout planes. Anyway, the 127th HQ is just about five miles due north in case we need to put in an order."

"Well, we sure need ammo and maybe some medical supplies. For sure some mail."

Toomey showed up an hour later. After six hours of strenuous climbing, he wasn't exactly excited to learn that we were off immediately in search of Headquarters Company of the 127th.

# # #

As I've indicated, five miles across the jungles of Philippines' razor-back ridges easily can work out to twenty miles of up-and-down foot and leg exertion.

And, in this case, I think it felt more like twenty-five miles. I mean, you're not only trying to climb up and repel down steep slopes, some of them featuring dangerous drop-offs, but there's the constant need to be alert for the nasties.

"Hey, boss, are you draggin?"

"Yep, Luis. And I'm ready for a nice long vacation."

"Just like everybody else on this stinking island."

At dusk, we circled the wagons. That was Medlin's way of describing how we slept in a circle, heads outward, feet together, with two sentries changed every hour.

Mendez shook me awake at dawn. I snarled at him because I didn't want to emerge from a sweet hide-and-seek dream with my little sisters. Their laughter was delicious and I wanted to keep hearing it.

"Sorry Sarge," Mendez said, "but I think we're right next door to headquarters. I swear I keep hearing voices."

Sure enough, through all the chatter and quarreling of flying foxes feeding in the trees above us, I could hear people speaking. "I just can't make out the words," he said, "but it don't sound like Japanese."

"No it doesn't. Well, just in case, we'll wait for sunrise. Go ahead and catch a nap and I'll take over as sentry."

"Thanks, Sarge."

As he snugged down, I listened carefully. The voices came and went. As the day brightened, the fox bats took off for home and bird life started coming awake. I didn't need to awaken the men because the jungle's alarm clocks, the mynah birds, started up.

"Goddam birds," Medlin said as he sat up rubbing his eyes. "They make sleep impossible. It's the sound of maybe fifty people scratching their fingernails down a giant blackboard."

"Yeah," Herb said. "It's almost as bad as having to listen to your snore."

"Blow it out your ass, Herb!"

"Knock it off, guys! Mendez and I suspect we're close to headquarters. We can hear people talking and they don't sound like Japs. So let's get moving.

"Riegle! Just to be on the safe side, I want you to take Foster, Medlin, Wilson, Lysenko and Herb over the crest and check it out. We'll be right behind you."

"Aww, dammit. How come we always get the short end of the stick?"

"Medlin," Riegle snarled, "for once in your damn life, shut your hole. Just think, if it *is* headquarters, you get first dibs on coffee and powdered eggs. They might even have buttered toast. Okay?

"Any more bitching? No? Medlin, you take point. Now let's move out."

They disappeared over the crest of the slope and we moved up behind them. Lysenko was tail-end Charlie, carefully checking right and left as the squad disappeared among the trees.

He moved out of sight and I said, "Okay. Our turn. Eyes open. Check the tree tops."

As we moved downhill, I could feel my mouth watering at the prospect of a steaming cup of black coffee. But then a sudden stir to our front snapped me back to the here and now.

It was Lysenko stepping back into sight with a hand raised. "They're coming back," he said. "Fast."

A minute later the rest of the team tumbled into view, took cover and whipped their weapons up, pointing them back in the direction they had come.

I trotted downslope to them. "What's going on?"

Riegle, eyes goggled, said, "It's a whole bunch of Japs having breakfast."

"They're eating?"

"Well, they were shoveling rice into their gobs with chopsticks."

"How many?"

"Maybe six or eight."

"Six or eight. And you didn't shoot?"

"No, Sarge." He swallowed. "It's kind of like we surprised each other. We both took off. They headed west."

"Did any of them follow you?"

"I don't know. Don't seem like it."

I spread the whole team out and we moved forward. Slowly. Quietly.

We found the Jap camp. It was deserted except for a half-empty rice bowl, a few chopsticks and that Jap smell . . . fish and soy sauce.

They also had fled.

"This is ridiculous," I said. "We're here to kill Japs, not play hide and seek. Next time, for Christ's sake, *shoot* the bastards! I can't believe it!" I turned on Herb. "What the hell? You're an old-timer at this."

The big Aussie actually seemed to blush. "I know, Jim. It's just crook. Saw it happen once before in Libya. Kind of like reverse mob rule. Bloody sudden surprise on both sides."

Just then Lysenko said, "Quiet! Everybody listen."

And we heard it faintly. A screechy, furious Japanese yammer. I could only make out one word for sure. *Baka*! Idiot! One other sounded something like *gomokate!* which I recalled may have meant "fool."

Mendez chuckled. "Sounds like some sergeant is chewing out the troops." Medelin started giggling. Then Wilson. Then they were all laughing, sounding a bit hysterical.

"Come on you screwballs!" I said. "Let's find headquarters."

It took us another hour of very slow, careful hiking. HQ turned out to be three mildewed tents. One tent was covering radios and the others tables with maps. The whole staff looked as muddy and bedraggled as us. They gave us coffee. For breakfast, they offered C rations. We stocked up on ammo and a medic gave us a lick and a promise for fungus and infections.

No mail.

While we were at headquarters, two cubs circled low and slow overhead, each dropping a supply package on each circuit.

"It's been a godsend," the CO said. "If they could just get the damn airstrips functioning for the heavies, they could do real resupply airdrops with parachutes from cargo planes."

I reported to the operations officer. I didn't tell him about running from the Japs or them running from us. I figured he'd find out soon enough from his own troops. You can't keep a SNAFU like that a secret.

"I wanted to let you know, sir, that we came across evidence that a small party of Japs was moving somewhere south of here. I think we might have scared them off. Looks like they're headed west. We'll keep an eye peeled for them when we head back out into the boondocks."

"Right now, sergeant," he told me, "all the Japs are headed west. We've got the little devils on the run. Let us know if you find anybody."

"Damn right, sir. Will do. I just had one question. I was trying to locate Lieutenant Gergen. He was the team's signal officer and I wanted to check a couple of things with him."

"Sorry, Sergeant, but he's gone. They sent him back to Pinamopoan Beach."

"Oh, really?"

"Yeah, supposedly he had a real bad case of nervous exhaustion."

"Oh, too bad, sir"

"Yeah," he said with a look of disgust. "For sure nobody else around here is nervous, right?"

"No, sir. Nor tired, either," I said.

I turned away thinking wistfully about sleep and maybe a chance for another sweet dream of home. Or Suzanne. Or any place other than the goddamn tropics.

Chapter 57
Fright And Flight

As we patrolled the next two days, we came across more numerous signs of Japs … two or three rotting corpses, empty ration cans, scraps of uniforms, bloody bandages, discarded broken weapons.

We also were hearing more war. Artillery was thumping to the west and the rattle of small arms often came to us on the wind. With the arrival of December, the 32nd Division definitely was pushing the Japs toward Leyte's west coast. Several other divisions were conquering Leyte, too, but the 32nd was our parent and our focus.

We were taking a break and, for maybe the fifth time that morning, I was trying with very muddy hands to scrape away the mud clinging to my carbine. It's maddening when goopy slop covers you from head down and you can't even see your boots because ten pounds of the stuff encases each foot.

Suddenly I heard Mendez say, "Guess what, men. We got only twenty shopping days until Christmas!"

Riegle looked at me. "Gee, Jim, I seem to remember saying something like that to you on a beach in New Guinea about two years ago."

"Yeah, depressing ain't it? And it wasn't long afterwards that our young leader took a bullet through the head."

"Well, at least so far we ain't run into any live enemies. And all we're hearing right now is birds."

"Yeah, so far."

Then two loud blasts slammed just ahead of us. We went flat while every bird and fruit bat within ten miles took off in a mighty spiral above us, wings rushing and snapping as they screeched in the rain for all they were worth. Then came laughter from the direction of the blasts.

"Holy shit!" Riegle whispered. "What the hell was that?"

Another pair of blasts and the bird world went insane again.

Herb crawled to me. "Relax," he said. "It's guns. Nip cannons shooting over us. They're trying to hit some flamin' target behind us. I think the gunners are laughing about all the bird panic."

With a whip-lash crash, the weapons fired again and now we could hear their shells tear over us through the air toward our rear.

Moving cautiously we eased our way through the brush to the south. Once we got off to what seemed like a safe distance, I waved to Lieutenant Frey. "Too bad we can't take out their FDC," I said. "Without that, they'd be paralyzed."

"Hell, Sergeant, Jap artillery don't have a damn FDC," Frey said. "Jap artillery is independent. Each battery has its own observers that spot the targets. That's who we've got to find."

"Doesn't their infantry call them for help?"

"Nope," Frey said. "In Jap doctrine, infantry operates on its own. Their artillery almost runs a separate war."

"Well, that's a hell of a way to do business."

"Yeah. Their interarm cooperation is for shit. I guess it worked okay for them in China where they were in fairly open terrain and the opposition was helpless. But it's a different story here. Now, with how loud the blast is, I figure these for 100 mm guns. Guns, not howitzers. Much noisier. Either way, they've got to have some yokel up in a tree or on a ridge top doing the spotting."

"Well screw him. Why don't we just call in DivArty? They can blast these guns to bits and their dumb-assed observer can go join the retreat or slit his belly if that's his druthers."

We spent the next hour low-crawling so as to put a good half-mile of distance between us and the Jap guns. I didn't want us to be anywhere near the receiving end of DivArty's 155 howitzers.

And unfortunately, some of us apparently were visible to the Japs' artillery observer. So in between directing fire, he also hailed a squad or two of riflemen who'd been detailed to guard his weapons.

Frey was calling in our target's coordinates when the Japs first started shooting toward us.

One of them was the Nipponese equivalent of Davie Crockett.

Medlin was leaning to peer around a tree. A high-pitched crack and a thud. Medlin jerked and made a sound like "*Ooof!*" His helmet fell off and he collapsed on top of it, his bitching ended forever. Perhaps thirty seconds later the sniper killed Wilson who was just standing there in shock staring down at Medlin's corpse.

We all ducked as low as we could. Then, at length, Herb spoke.

"I've got a bead on the bastard," he said. He began firing short BAR bursts at the shooter's position. "That keeps the Nip bastard's head down, right?"

"Yeah. Close but no seegar," Riegle said.

"Right, but look at Mac," Herb said.

"I can't see him."

"'Course not," Herb said. "Nobody can. But by the time I have to change another magazine, Mac will be in position to drop that oriental bushman for good."

The rush and crump of DivArty's fire mission interrupted him. From our place in the jungle, we couldn't see the shells whopping into the Jap battery, but we certainly could hear them, along with some secondary explosions.

Thanks to the shelling, the Jap infantry stopped shooting at us and we moved out smartly.

That evening I was radioing base that we were down to seven effectives plus Domingo and Jaime.

"Hey, Jim," Riegle said. "Looky here."

I glanced up to see that we actually were back up to eight effectives. Mac had just appeared out of the brush.

In addition to his own M1, he was carrying an Arisaka with an expensive-looking scope.

"Drilled the bluidy bastard," he grinned. "He gave us a fine rifle."

Chapter 58
Fight And Flight

Shortly before dawn, we got the distinct impression that the commander of the Japanese artillery battery took yesterday's attack personally.

Somebody did, anyway.

Toomey, our sentry, was on the ball. He quietly awakened us one-by-one. "We've got visitors," he whispered. "I can hear them on the trail. They're maybe a hundred yards away."

It gave us time to wake up and get set.

The Jap leader must have been a man of considerable energy and determination – a real stubborn hard-ass – to keep tracking us during the night and to get this close. But in the final analysis, he didn't seem real bright, either.

Perhaps he just didn't realize how close he and his boys were to us.

Whatever the case, he never deployed his troops into line. They approached in single file, a narrow column marching straight into the crossbar of our T.

When they were about thirty feet away, I personally welcomed them with a grenade.

The cast steel Mark II pineapple is cool and damp with condensation as you hold it in your right hand at chest level, the spoon under your palm. You do an unconscious right face so that your left side is toward the target. Yank the cotter pin. Extend your arm back to throw. Hurl the grenade as if you're Swampy Donald pitching relief in the ninth for the Yankees. As it leaves your hand, the spring-loaded hammer flips the spoon away and strikes the top of the fuse.

Snap!

In near-darkness, you may glimpse a spark or two flying off the missile. But rather than admire the fireworks, you duck. Grenade fragments can fly anywhere.

It thumps on the ground, takes a bounce and goes *Whamp!* with a quick flash.

From the chorus of screams it sounded as if fragments hit two or three Japs. Mac and Mendez also tossed grenades producing another set of shrill ululations. But command shouts quickly overcome the noise of the wounded. The Japs unlimbered their Nambu, firing uphill at us and charging pretty much single file directly at our little firing line.

Within seconds, a pile of bodies was writhing on the trail in front of us. The Nambu, flickering and sending white tracers our way, began whacking the trees around us and gouging up mud to our front.

The Japs charged us twice more.

During a pause Herb said, “Their commander is a drogo.”

“What?”

“He’s either an idiot or he’s stupid or green as grass. Made no attempt to flank us. He must have ten times our strength and he’s throwing his men away with these bloody banzai charges. If I had his strength, I’d have wiped out your little command ten minutes ago.”

“Thank you very much, Herb.”

“Quite welcome, I’m sure.”

As dawn broke, the Jap commander had his troops charge again. Looking at the bodies out front of us, I suspect we killed or wounded at least twenty of them. I also think their commander now was among the dead, because the rest of the Japs turned around and took off.

I can’t say I felt much elation, though.

As Jaime and Domingo started looting the Nip corpses, the rest of us took stock.

Mac, our priceless ghillie, was dead. A bullet had ricocheted off his carbine’s receiver and smashed through his mouth into his neck.

“He can’t have felt a thing, Herb.”

“Right. Crazy damned Scot. Don’t make it any better for us, though.”

“No. Sure as hell doesn’t.”

Foster had taken a bullet in the head and was in a coma.

We rigged a stretcher and carried him about two hours before he died.

We were down to six effectives and I had to get on the horn with Captain Bottcher.

Chapter 59
New Characters

The captain had the instant solution to our losses. By radio, he ordered us to rendezvous with Lieutenant Irish whose team was just leaving the base.

We would link my remnant to his larger remnant. Now twenty-two of us would work as one patrol comprised of two squads.

When we made our rendezvous late in the day, the lieutenant said, “Jim, I want you to lead one squad and Riegle will run the other. I’ll be in charge overall and keep Domingo with me. Lieutenant Frye will continue as artillery liaison.”

My squad divided neatly into two five-man fire teams, Herb leading one and I the other. I gave Toomey and Lysenko to Herb and kept Mendez and Jaime.

Irish assigned Pfc. Stanley Pitt and Pfc. Frank Seibert to me. Pitt was almost as short as Luis Mendez and almost equally mouthy. He and Luis quickly founded The Self-Panickers’ Club which they claimed, after the war, would work with Jimmy Durante and Mae West to restore Vaudeville to its pre-war glory.

“For sure,” Mendez said, “I don’t want to go back to fishing for a living.”

“And this guy is a real asset,” Irish said, introducing me to Corporal Frank Seibert, a tall scrawny youth. “He’s a mountain boy from one of the Carolinas. Got a real keen eye for Jap tricks, especially their spider holes. You can rely on him. Never says much, but when he does you can take it to the bank.”

Quietly Seibert said, “One thing, Sarge. I just want you knowing that I’m no kin to Major General Frank Seibert, CO of the First Calvary.”

“You mean ‘First Cavalry’?”

“No, for me it was like Mount Calvary.”

He gave me the impression that he cared neither for First Cav or its commander. No problem since we were unlikely to come into contact with either.

For selfish reasons, I liked our own new command set-up. Now somebody else would have the worry about supplies and how to keep us out of trouble. All my boys and I had to do was follow orders, move through the jungle, spot Japs, kill Japs and stay alive until we won the war sometime in 1948 or 1949.

Lieutenant Irish mandated that we continue patrolling south of the 127th line of advance. Before we moved out he gave all of us a final briefing.

"I just want you to work on being even more careful and quiet. Stealth is more important now because our advance is piling up the Japs against Leyte's west coast. It's concentrating them into a smaller and smaller area. So from now on, we'll find more Japs per acre. It'll be more and more difficult to work around them.

"So we must become quiet, watching where we step, just like Hawkeye in *Last Of The Mohicans*."

# # #

I had Seibert on point the next morning and quickly came to think of him as a twentieth-century version of Hawkeye. He knew his way around the jungle and he'd found a way to blend into shadows. In a way, his gangly build and careful movements reminded me of a praying mantis.

He'd start forward gingerly, stop in mid-step, hold that position seemingly forever, and then snap forward and, in an eyeblink, just more or less disappear.

After a minute or two you'd hear a low, laconic, "Looks clear."

Two days after joining us, he zoomed up to about ninety-eight point six on our Most Valuable Soldier Scale. I recommended that Lieutenant Irish put him in for at least a bronze star.

"Dan, I can't believe the guy. You know we were on the right flank when we came down off that rocky hill, remember?"

"Sure."

"Well, when we got down into that little valley, more of a draw, like, and you could just *smell* Jap. You know what it's like. Their food. Their crap, maybe. I don't know. But we just knew Japs had been there.

"So, anyhow, I had Seibert trailing and Mendez was on point. And Seibert suddenly says, 'Hold up. Somethin' funny.'

"We stop, and Seibert just goes walking past us, looking right and left and, I swear, he was sniffing like a dog. Anyway, he stops. 'Boys,' he says, 'we got us some spider holes.'

"I said, 'Bullshit! Where?'

"He took three steps forward and pointed his tommy gun almost straight down at the ground in front of him. 'Got one right here. I'm gonna blast him and you-all be ready because some others might just pop up.'

"So, Dan, he fires a burst right into the ground and we hear a muffled scream. And then, not fifty feet away, the lid comes off another spider hole. We're just standing there with our mouths open and Frank blasts him, too.

"So we're still standing there with our mouths open when yet another spider hole opens up maybe fifty yards further off and Seibert hits him, too.

"He drops the old magazine and shoves in a new one and says, 'See any more?'

"So I asked him, 'How the hell did you know?'

"Jap camouflage is good, *real* good,' he says. 'But I've got a secret weapon.'

"What?"

"I'm part colorblind."

"So?"

"So I can see the camouflage material but its color fools the rest of you."

But if Seibert's eyes were sharp, Mendez and Stan Pitt also made a wonderful team.

When moving through woods, all of us tend to focus on the ground and the tree trunks in the middle distance. Pitt and Mendez, however, possessed a joint tree-top radar

Pitt would be moving ahead when Mendez would go 'Ssssst' or simply click his tongue. Pitt would stop and Mendez would say "One O'clock, old buddy."

Before you'd know it, Pitt would have his rifle up, aimed and say something like, "I got Tojo's leg in sight."

Mendez would say, "Well, take the shot. Maybe he'll flinch."

Pitt would shoot, the Jap *would* flinch and Mendez would fire and next thing a fresh Jap would be hanging upside down to dry from his treetop tether.

I talked to them once about how they did it.

"I don't know, Boss. It's just feeling more than seeing, you know?"

"No, I don't know."

"It's like some kind of pattern," Pitt said.

"It's just like when you're a kid trying to find crawdads in a creek. You look at a rock and it just looks right. A crawdad has *got* to be living under that one. Well, it's like that with the trees. Some of 'em just look right for Japs."

Mendez would grin. "I know what he means, Boss. It was kind of like that in fishing. We'd see a stretch of water where gulls or pelicans would be eyeing things. So we'd put out the nets there. Well, shit Boss, as long as it works, who gives a damn?"

"Right," I said. "But I just wish I had your guys's eyes for it."

# # #

We were sitting in the dark and the rain, too wet and too cold to sleep, so we were yarning.

"Funny thing," Toomey said.

"What?"

"Well, we're pretty close to Christmas, aren't we? But…" he give a big gust of a sigh "…it's the furthest thing from my mind right now."

"That's good, Jody" Riegle said. "You don't want to think about Christmas or snow or presents or Christmas trees or that peace on earth goodwill toward men crap. Just focus on killing Japs and staying alive. As far as I'm concerned, they ain't no Christmas until I get back to Big Rapids."

"Where's Big Rapids?"

"County seat of Mecosta County, smack dab in the middle of Michigan's lower peninsula, and about a ten-minute drive from my folks' farm. Nice town, too."

"Dammit," I said, "quit dwelling on it. Right now there's no damned Mecossa…"

"No, it's Meco*sta*."

"Charlie, I don't give a rat's ass. Whatever it is doesn't matter right now. You want to get home? The only thing that counts is spotting Japs before they spot you. Keep on your toes even when you're squatting here in the mud bullshitting."

"Gee, thanks for the pep talk," Toomey said. "I really didn't need to be reminded that I'm on the fucking jungle island of Leyte.

"Right now all I care about is my feet. My goddam toenails are coming off. My boots are coming apart and the skin on my feet is so puckered from this soaking that it's rubbing right off."

"Yeah, mate. Just be glad you're not like us old timers having to walk out a flamin' malaria relapse," Herb said. "And if your feet hurt, no worries. It's a good reminder that you *have* feet. And they'll recover."

"But they hurt!"

"Right, mate, they hurt. So do mine. They hurt until Jap shoots at you. Then you either forget they hurt because you're too busy shooting back, or because you're wounded and the wound hurts more than your feet, or you don't feel nothing at all because you're bloody dead."

# # #

The talk about sore feet followed me into my sleep. Only now the pain became the fierce deep biting of cold during a rare Seattle snowstorm. Mom, Dad and I were trying to build a snowman.

I had no boots so my toes were freezing. So were my hands, but it was fun – especially when Mom and Dad started throwing snowballs at each other.

All of a sudden Mom picked me up. "Goonness me, your cheeks are bright red. Jerry, we've got to get our little man indoors."

"Yeah, Eileen. Time for some hot toddies by the Christmas tree!"

"I've got something hot for you!"

"Ooo, really? Promise?"

They were laughing and grinning at each other it was all funny and confusing . . . and warm.

They were just kids then, I guess, because I couldn't have been more than five. So it was maybe 1928 or'29?

Chapter 60
Stepping On A Tripwire

As we filed north the next morning I remembered the dream and couldn't help grinning ruefully, because my feet sure as hell still were hurting.

Then, just as Herb mentioned, Japs made me forget all about them.

We needed to cross the top of a north-facing ridge, and the approach to the base of that ridge was, for jungle country, a fairly clear east-west lane. Through the jungle about two hundred yards away, I could just make out the incline, the base of the ridge where we'd start climbing.

Seibert, who was on point, hesitated. "Boss, I don't like it. It's just too . . . well, it looks too wide open." Jaime was nodding in agreement.

I turned to Mendez and Pitt. "What do you boys think?" They stepped out into the open and looked upward. They peered back and forth like a pair of setters. "I don't know," Pitt said. "Don't see nothing."

Mendez said, "Seems okay."

Like them, I was thinking about tree-top snipers.

That's my only excuse.

"Okay, let's move out."

Seibert scowled. Then he shrugged. "Okay." He slowly led the way into the lane. Herb gave him five yards and followed. Then it was my turn. Mendez next. Pitt was tail-end and Jaime was staying behind waiting for Riegle's team to come up.

We were half-way to the base of the ridge when somebody bellowed "Duck!" an instant before an Arisaka barked from beneath a near-by tree.

Seibert went down. Herb was hit a second later. I was lucky because I dove for the dirt at the sound of the first shot. The Jap aiming at me only managed to hit my canteen. The impact was enormous. It spun me like a stupid top, landing me flat on my back. *God, I'm dead meat. Dead!*

In falling, I dropped my carbine. Disarmed and terrified, I frantically scrabbled for cover into the brush. Because of the impact and all the moisture, the canteen water soaking my hip, I feared I had been seriously wounded.

My panic eased slightly at the comforting rattle of carbines and tommy guns breaking out behind me. Riegle and his boys were charging to the rescue. Only they were too late.

We already were damn near wiped out.

What killed us was that we didn't realize -- no, it was all my fault because I didn't have the sense to heed Seibert and Jaime

What none of us realized was that we were approaching a Jap security line in a form that was entirely new to us

Picture the roots of your basic sturdy oak tree back home. Or one of those big old curbside elms; mature trees four or five feet thick with roots spreading out like big half-buried branches. Sometimes the roots are so massive they tilt sidewalk slabs upward out of place.

But here in the jungle, instead of dandelions and grass growing between those roots, there's a deep hole. With a Jap rifleman squatting down inside it.

We didn't expect them to be there first of all because none of us would dream of trying to dig a foxhole at the base of a big tree. Considering all the underground roots, it would be hellish hand-blistering hours of hard, hard work.

Besides, once you're in your hole and someone spots you, it's a death trap. You absolutely can't see anybody approaching from your flanks or rear. Likewise, if two American riflemen spot you, it's all over. One keeps your head down by peppering your position with rapid fire from a semi-automatic carbine or rifle, a weapon you don't have, while the other moves closer to shoot you or grenade you like a rat in a trap of your own construction.

But I guess that's one of the differences between us and them.

For us, a foxhole is strictly a place for protection.

For them, the holes were concealment for a line of sacrificial soldiers, a warning wire for the main body of a battalion.

Private Kumagai. Dig your hole here and shoot the first American you see.

Hai!

So Goro Takakuwa or Yoshi Yomama digs said death trap deep enough so, when squatting in it, his eyes and the rim of his helmet barely clear the edge of the hole. Not that you can see him even then, because he camouflages his position with grass or palm fronds or banana leaves.

He waits for hours or maybe even days, perhaps fearful, perhaps his posture is making his legs cramp. But his duty is to stay there and kill GIs when they come walking past him, even if he's likely to die in the process.

And he fights from that hole as long as he can, shooting and throwing grenades until someone blasts him out of there.

When ten of them conceal themselves this way along a hundred-yard stretch of jungle, as they did along our lane, it can be a hell of an ambush.

# # #

Seibert, hit right in the spine, was stone dead.

One of those 170-grain Arisaka slugs transfixed Herb's neck from the side. He rolled back and forth in agony for the thirty seconds it took him to bleed to death from his severed carotid arteries. There wasn't time for any of us to even try to do anything about it. And we probably wouldn't have been able to save him from that kind of injury anyway.

A shot in the head sent Pitt and his Vaudeville dreams to Valhalla. His buddy Mendez was almost as lucky as I was. He merely sustained a nasty burn by a bullet that grazed his chest.

It was Riegle who yelled for us to duck. He and his team were coming up behind us when he saw two of the Japs rise through their camouflage to take aim after we passed them.

He and his men attacked the Japs just as they sprang their ambush, killing them right inside their own little graves.

As Riegle helped me up minutes later, I saw my men's corpses. The sight made me wish the Japs had killed me, too.

Oh, I won't lie. I was glad not to be dead.

But the guilt for having screwed up so badly -- for giving that fatal order "…let's move out" weighed me down.

# # #

Later we found Lieutenant Irish and he brightened the day with some news. He said the regimental commander was so impressed with the work of the I&R Troop that he recommended promoting Captain Bottcher to major. Supposedly General Gill encouraged the recommendation.

If anyone deserved kudos it was the captain.

But the story didn't get me out of the dumps. I wished I could get away from the jungle and the killing. And I'd have given a leg for a letter from Suzanne.

Thanks to hills, jungle and constant rain and the absence of roads, the Army was barely able to keep us supplied with ammo and food. There was no space for mail.

Lieutenant Irish heard what had happened and asked me about it.

After sketching the ambush, I added, "Sir, I think I'd better turn in my stripes. I've been getting people killed ever since Buna. And I seem to be getting more and more of them killed as time goes on."

He turned a very cold set of eyes on me. "Bullshit, sergeant! You can't turn in your stripes. Besides, you dimwit, you're not the one killing your men. The Japs are. It's what they're trained to do. It's what they're *ordered* to do! It's what they're trying to do all the time. Now, listen, you remember me telling you that generals have to learn?"

"Yeah. You were talking about MacArthur."

"Right. Well, sergeants have to learn, too." He paused. "Okay, Jim. Now let's go over it again, detail by detail."

"Shit, sir, I don't even want to *think* about it!"

"I don't blame you. But that's how you learn. You know, Jim, this kind of shit happens every damn day in every infantry outfit. They paid the price, Jim. So for the sake of the men you'll lead in the rest of this fucking lousy war, learn from it!"

We spent the next hour going over how I got my team butchered. The lieutenant again told me to quit blaming myself.

Just before leaving, he said, "Oh, Jim, a piece of advice."

"What?"

"Try not to get to know your new people too well."

"Why?"

"Next time it won't hurt as much."

"What?"

"When they get killed, I mean."

Chapter 61
Closing In

Charlie Riegle is a witty cuss who has one of those comic faces. Wait, that's not quite right. It's just that his expressions become comic on occasions when the rest of us still are wide-eyed and quaking from a close call.

I remember the day an Arisaka bullet smacked into a palm truck about an inch from his head.

After ducking, he rolled his eyes, puckered his lips into an O and nodded his head up and down. His whole expression said, "Oh ho, dumbass, you missed. You'll be sorry now."

And for the most part, even when we were soaked and freezing during typhoons or steaming during Leyte's normal sauna days, his face held a look of wry amusement. Having a patch of gentian violet on half his mug only heightened the effect.

As he walked toward me this afternoon, though, he looked mean as a snake.

"Boss," he said, "I got a bone to pick with you."

"What?"

He looked around to make sure we were alone and then squatted down beside me. I was sitting with my back to a tree just more or less staring into the distance.

"Look, Jim," he whispered, "you got to snap out of this and right now."

"Well, for your information…"

"Ahhhh, I don't want to hear any of your woe-is-me shit! Yep, the Japs caught you with your pants down. Sheer bad luck, man. So if my team had been leading instead of yours, you'd probably be ragging *me* right now.

"But it's over. You've got to quit acting like a goddamn zombie. You've got eight new guys over there and Mendez is having to make excuses for you. Those guys are new and the last thing they need is a fuckin' noncom who acts like he don't know whether to shit or go blind."

I just stared at him.

"Come on, Jim," he pleaded. "Get off your ass and get with it. Besides, this campaign is damn near over. The Japs are retreating and that ruckus we heard this morning was more bombing. Finally!

They must have completed the airstrips because whenever the rain quits now we get air support."

I shook my head. "I don't care, Charlie. Hell, I don't feel worth a plugged nickel right now. I'd just be going through the motions."

"Buddy, I got news. You never was worth more than a plugged nickel anyway. So haul your ass up and resume going through the motions just like me. Here! Have some paperwork." He handed me our team's new roster, got up and started to walk away.

Then he turned back and grinned. "Oh, and by the way, Jim ... Merry Christmas."

"Merry Christmas, asshole."

"That's the spirit!"

# # #

When I poured over my roster, I couldn't believe one name: Carl Marx, who turned out to be a wiry little guy from Los Angeles. "Say, maybe I ought to introduce you to Captain Bottcher. You a communist by any chance?"

"Naah. Dad's a grammar school teacher and I help him in summers when he works as a carpenter."

"Well, I think the captain would get a charge out of meeting you."

Marx looked a bit nervous at the idea.

"Don't worry," I said. "The skipper is a hell of a soldier, but he's also a very nice guy who likes Lenin's work. You ever read *Das Kapital* by Marx?"

"Hell, no. My family's Republican."

# # #

After two days of training, we headed out into the jungle again.

Charlie's team led the first two days, giving my new kids a chance to adapt. They all were volunteers and had some jungle time under their belts. But they were new to the practice of 24-hour stealth.

We patrolled for three days just beyond the north end of Leyte's Ormoc valley and found nothing but abandoned camps. You might say the valley had been kind of a spillway to the coast.

It was a route for Jap troops retreating to Silad Bay, the only place they could hope to find ships to evacuate them.

But we suspected even that had become a forlorn hope. With its airstrips finally completed and in full operation, the Air Corps now seemed in control of the skies and the seas around the island.

"If these Jap bastards had any brains at all," Riegle groused, "they'd just surrender. Any Jap ships probably are resting on the bottom of the bay with sharks doing the clean-up work."

"Yeah, well, forget it," Toomey said. "Japs don't surrender. Everybody knows it's their duty to die and take as many of us with them as they can."

"I think you're right," I said, "but right now we're just not seeing any Japs. It looks like they've all taken off."

Mendez, who was out of sight on point fifty yards ahead of us, suddenly came back into view. Holding his carbine horizontally, he pumped it up and down repeatedly and then signaled for us to get in line abreast.

"Hoo boy," I said, "Looks like we got us some Nip company after all. You boys spread out. I'll go up to see what Luis found."

When I reached Mendez, he was concealing himself behind a tree. He cautioned me with a finger to his lips. I hand signaled, "What?" and he directed me to move back. He joined me a minute later.

"Luis," I whispered, "what have you got?"

"A whole bunch of Japs, at least company strength. Maybe even a thin battalion. I damn near stumbled into one of them."

"Glad you didn't. They headed north?"

"You bet. Moving fast, too. Two columns. Good march discipline. Well spread out, so I don't think an artillery strike would do much good. Not unless they bunch up at a crossing or maybe bivouac for the night."

"Okay, I'll call it in to Base. Maybe we should tail them."

Base responded immediately.

"Item Roger. Team Baker. Sighting report."

"Team Item Roger Baker, Item Roger Base. All Item Roger units are ordered to return to How Queen. Campaign is almost over."

"Say again."

"We're done. Start returning to the barn forthwith."

"Roger that. But a company strength enemy force is proceeding north through Feature Three Zero. Forced marching. Suggest shadowing."

"Wait one."

A few minutes later, Captain Bottcher got on the horn and okayed the suggestion to trail the Nips.

"Just keep a safe distance," he said. "Don't pick any fights but report any changes. When they get to the bay, just drop it and return to HQ."

So we trailed them through the day.

Unfortunately for many of our comrades at Base, we stayed at much too safe a distance.

Chapter 62
Happy New Year

The commander of the Jap column kept his troops moving at a man-killing pace. We followed about a mile behind them while in the valley. Had it not been chilly and raining, I don't think we could have kept up.

It just got tougher the next morning, the dawn of New Year's Eve day. They turned west into the hills that ringed Silad Bay. Now fog and low clouds made it hard to keep them in sight. Worse, the terrain became a hell of a challenge, especially for those of us who'd been humping the boondocks for nearly six weeks now. A diet of snakes, grubs and half-ripe fruit keeps you alive, but all of us were hungry enough to dream beautiful dreams about banqueting on C Rations.

Corporal Toomey, who was not the type to gripe, told me, "Gee, Sarge, this is real roller-coaster hiking." We were climbing steep ridge spurs, descending into draws, and then cresting sharp foothills, making it even harder to keep the Japs in view.

As it was, every now and then we came across some played-out Tojo who just couldn't go on.

One of the new men, Jameson, called back to say, "Hey, Boss, Got 'nother one over here."

The Jap, a practically skin-and-bones corporal, lay on his back, half-buried in ferns. "He tried to grab his rifle," Marx said, "but I kicked it away,"

The man's eyes were dull with resignation. I think he felt we were going to start torturing him right then and there.

"Should we just shoot him?"

"What's the point? With this weather, he'll probably die tonight."

"Okay," I said. "Give the poor bastard a swig of water and a cigarette. Maybe he speaks English."

Davidson, our medic, knelt and reached under the Jap's head, the man flinched. But when the medic lifted the man up and offered the canteen to his lips, the Jap's eyes went wide.

"Poor bastard can't believe it," Mendez said.

The Jap choked down a gulp of water and nodded. "No berieve."

"Hungry?"

He nodded again, frantically.

"Mendez, you got any of them papayas? Slice off a couple of pieces for him."

"Yeah," Davidson cautioned, "but don't give him any more than that. He's so starved he'll just throw it up again."

"Okay, men," I said, "enough bullshitting. Let's keep moving."

"What about the Jap?"

"Just leave him be. He's no danger to anybody now." I took the Arisaka, chambered a round, and shoved the weapon bore-first into the trail's mud.

"What the hell you doing?" Mendez asked.

I pulled the trigger. The weapon gave a muffled *Whump*, followed by a quick high-pitched scream as gas escaped through the bolt.

"Jesus, it could have blown up on you."

"Not an Arisaka, buddy. It's one of the world's strongest actions. But now this one's worthless. The barrel's bulged." I yanked at the bolt's plum-shaped handle. It wouldn't move. "And no one ever will be able to cock this one again. Okay? So let's move out."

Davidson waved at the Japanese. "Good luck, buddy."

The man tottered to his feet with what looked like a supreme effort.

He bowed to us. "Domo arigato!"

Chapter 63
A Chance To Rest

During a series of blinding squalls late that afternoon, we lost track of the Japanese force. Static made radio reception lousy, but we finally got back in touch with Base to let them know the Jap force was on the loose and probably approaching the bay.

"Don't worry about it," Captain Bottcher said. "Just expedite your return to regiment. We're headed back, too. First thing in the morning."

Before he signed off, he said, "Oh, and happy New Year to you and your boys, Jim."

"Many thanks, and the same to you, sir."

Fires were impossible, so through the night we shivered and tried to doze huddled under our ponchos.

"You hear that?" One of the new guys, Voorhees, still had his hearing. "Either somebody is celebrating New Year's or a fire-fight is going on. Way off north maybe."

"Yeah," Riegle said. "I think I can hear it. Mortars too. Or maybe grenades. It's a fight, not a party."

When the wind veered now and then even I heard machine guns rattling. Thumps and thuds. "Yeah. First one we've heard since yesterday. Just be glad it isn't taking place here."

"Too bad," Toomey said. "I'd like to take out some more of those devils."

"Don't worry, Jody," Mendez said. "I'm sure you'll get many more chances."

The fight seemed to go on for two hours or so and then petered out. Nothing terribly unusual for Leyte Island.

We spent most of the next day hiking cross-country to rejoin the regiment.

All the guys were pretty high-spirited about coming in from the hills, of course. But Riegle, Mendez, Toomey and I were especially excited. It would be the first real chance in six weeks to have a decent meal and we were yakking like a bunch of kids about the prospect.

"Hey, Jim," Mendez said, "can you imagine having supper, a real supper – I mean a sit-down meal at an actual table with real chairs -- without a helping of iguana or python eggs?"

"What's a chair?"

"Forget that, what about silverware and linen napkins?"

"Don't get too carried away," I said. "I'd just be happy with C Ration franks and beans and, for once, no side order of grubs. After that. I want a shower."

"A cold shower?"

"*Any* shower, buddy, and then sleep about twenty-four hours."

"Right," Toomey said, "on one of those nice soft GI issue mattresses."

When we arrived at headquarters, the welcome mat wasn't out and nobody was saying, "Happy New Year" or singing *Auld Lang Syne*. In fact, everybody from the colonel to the clerk-typists all looked utterly depressed

I asked the duty sergeant, "What the hell's the matter? This place is like a morgue."

"You ain't heard?"

"Heard what?"

"I&R Base got clobbered late last night. Several hundred Japs attacked it with knee mortars, Nambus and regular mortars. They held for a while, but then got overrun. Cap'n Steele got out with about half the troop. And he got his arm chopped by some bastard's samurai sword."

"What about Cap'n Bottcher?"

"Dead."

"You're shitting me!"

"Nope. One of the Jap mortar shells went off near him and almost tore off his leg. Steele got a tourniquet on him and the boys dragged him out. They were on the horn with the medics here trying to get help for him. But they couldn't save him.

"Sometime before dawn he bled to death."

"Christ," Riegle said. "I wonder if it was that bunch of Japs we were tailing."

"Wouldn't surprise me," I said. "I don't think sleep's going to come real easy now."

As the news spread, morale throughout the division took a deep dive.

# # #

As he painfully eased himself down from the back of our deuce-and-a-half, Vitelli looked around at the tent city.

He turned to our driver, "I can't believe how soft you bastards have it, here. Sleeping under canvas on racks. And mosquito nets. This camp is like the fucking Hilton."

The driver turned pink. "Lighten up, buddy. I got chopped pretty good on New Guinea and I'm on light duty because of malaria. And around here, light duty means a sixteen-hour day."

The trucks had returned us to Pinamopoa, the beach on Carigar Bay where we came ashore eight bloody weeks ago. I think all of us slept the entire way, even when the truck was juddering over washboard roads.

I got Vitelli off to the side.

"Look, Brad, fighting troops always look down on service troops. Supposedly, they're safe in the rear while we fight and suffer. Of course, you weren't here when Jap planes were bombing or Jap artillery was shelling them, right? And they couldn't shoot back, right?"

"Right, Sarge."

"So now you're here for some R&R. Keep your eyes open. These guys are working pretty much around the clock.

"If you watch, you'll see they look about as whipped as we do. The ones who got malaria on New Guinea still suffered relapses, just like I do. And, if you use your eyes instead of your mouth, most of these guys also have ulcerating sore from bug bites, just like we do.

"And they're working for *us*. So stop bitching. Enjoy it."

I found out later that as we scouted and the division pushed the Japs to Silad Bay, the service troops were working almost around the clock to uncrate and assemble thirty deuce-and-a-half trucks.

Meanwhile, they also were erecting and furnishing tents for us while creating mess halls, building field hospitals, repairing artillery, bringing new clothing and boots ashore…

I can't begin to list it all. But, my God, was it welcome.

The very first thing I did, even before showering, was to sit down on a real chair at an actual table with a thing called a fountain pen and a piece of white paper.

Dear Suzanne –

We just now came in from the line. Finally, some rest! I'm sitting here with a pile of your letters beside my elbow. I haven't even opened them. I just wanted you to have this note to know that I'm okay. As soon as I clean up, I'll savor all this mail from you and then I'll write to you again, and again and again.

Love

Jim

I had nine other letters to compose first. Just thinking about them was like taking mental hike in a graveyard: Medlin, Foster, Gilbert, Ruud, Hansen, Wilson, Wainwright and MacIntyre.

The same morning, headquarters announced it was giving us twenty-one days. The Word came in tandem with an order from General Krueger praising us fighting troops for "...the highest degree of gallantry, skill, tenacity and fortitude . . . under adverse conditions of weather and on exceedingly difficult terrain... a glorious page...".

As I tried to compose letters to parents and wives, none of it seemed at all glorious. Neither did the prospect of going into battle on Luzon. The Jap Army would keep fighting with its usual ferocity.

So, twenty-one days.

After that, the 32nd Division would board troop ships to rejoin the rest of Sixth Army in assaulting Luzon, the biggest of the Philippine Islands, to liberate the capital, Manilla.

Thanks to the defeat of the Jap Navy and the near destruction of the Jap air force, Sixth Army already had landed on the island's west coast.

Luzon also was the island where the Japanese defeated General MacArthur in 1941. I had the fear that, as in our early days on new Guinea, the general would revert to his former command mode that "time is of the essence" and "push through to the objectives regardless of losses."

Having heard about the January 24 loading deadline, I just decided to pretend that date didn't exist. I sat down to open my first letter from Suzanne. I had just read, "*Dear Jim...*" when Lieutenant Irish came into my tent and nudged me.

"Sorry Jim, G-2 wants us."

"Well, Christ, can't they even give me time to read my mail?"

"Sure," he grinned. "Bring it along and read it on the plane."

"The plane?"

"Yeah. They're flying us to Hollandia. They want me since I was helping to run the troop under Captain Bottcher so I thought you ought to be there to backstop me.

"Of course, if you don't want to go…"

"Hell yes I want to go . . . if Suzanne is still there."

"I bet she is. Fifth Air Force HQ still is in Hollandia."

C-47s were reserved for luxury flights for brass, so we caught a hop in a B-25 which was being sent back to Hollandia for repairs.

Chapter 64
A Short Reunion

Trying to read mail in the waist gunners' compartment of a B-25 is a pain in the ass. It reminded me a bit of riding in an antique Aussie railway passenger car.

Granted, the speed was far greater. But, still, you're sitting on a hard bench. And instead of one wide-open window emitting smoke and cinders from the locomotive, you're seated between two huge windows emitting the bellowing roar of the plane's two monster engines.

The wind almost tore the first letter from my hand, so I stowed Suzanne's packet of unopened mail in my musette bag and just sat back. I tried to enjoy the view, but from a few thousand feet the ocean is a very boring blue.

I checked out the two .50 caliber machine guns – one for each window. Their positions, on mounts just inside the windows, made me wonder how a terrified waist gunner could avoid accidentally shooting either his own plane's engines or tail surfaces.

At least I have a chance of seeing Suzanne. Maybe. If I can find her.

By the time we touched down at Hollandia and taxied to the repair hangar, I was thoroughly chilled and punchy from engine roar and wind buffeting. Clambering stiffly down through the gunners' hatch, I wondered about Step One in trying to locate Suzanne.

Lieutenant Irish, ducking under the plane after emerging from its bomb bay, said, "I'll get in touch with you about when we fly back."

"Sir, I thought I was coming with you."

"Nope. I'm going to Sixth Army G-2. You've got an important interview at Fifth Air Force."

"I do?"

"Damn right!" He grinned and pointed underneath our plane toward the hanger. I ducked to look.

Suzanne was standing in the hangar doorway waving and smiling.

Stunned, I waved back. Behind me, the lieutenant was saying something about seeing me in day or two. Already making a bee line for Suzanne, I just mumbled "Yessir!"

# # #

Suzanne disagrees. To me it was a wonderous eternity. But she says we actually only hugged for two minutes. All I recall is looking into her eyes and saying, "This was impossible."

"No," she said with a huge smile, "it's one of the miracles of modern communications. We Dit-Dahs Girls have our own little network."

"Dit-Dahs?"

"Yes, Jim." Lightly touching my chin, "we wenches in communications call ourselves The Dit-Dah Girls, after the dots and dashes in Morse code. Let's get out of here. I've got a jeep."

She drove along Lake Sentai to Fifth Air Force headquarters. Riding shotgun I absorbed all I could of her. Such a beauty – wind ruffling her short auburn hair, khaki shirt fluttering in the wind, unbuttoned just enough.

She drove us past headquarters and steered up a narrow two-track up into the hills.

Chapter 65
Wonder Paralysis

Suzanne parked on a turnout which overlooked the exotic tumbledown view to the ocean far below. I wanted to kiss her, but you can't neck in a jeep. So we got out and just leaned against the hood, arms around each other's waists.

Finally I said, "Do you suppose we could just linger here for a year or two? Just quietly, because I bet you can't tell me about what you're doing."

"No. The Badger would have to arrest me."

"So just who is this Badger fellow?"

Suzanne said The Badger, her office manager, was an aging warrant officer whom the Army had promoted to major. "He's a rather fierce old bloke and all of us in our section love him to bits. I can't tell you what we do, but it involves wireless and he's been in the business for ages. Years back he even worked with Marconi."

"Wow! He must really know his stuff."

"He says Marconi had a vile temper and that's why he's so rotten to us. He isn't, of course. But who gives a bloody rip about all that, Jim? All I know is that I worry about you. And fear for you. You've lost pounds and your face is etched with new lines. You've become too quiet."

She tilted her head to my shoulder.

That simple sweet gesture broke something inside me. I started trembling and couldn't breathe, my legs wanted to fold. I gasped, "Need to sit." I staggered to the shotgun seat, almost falling into it. Suzanne leaned over me, one hand on my arm, the other on my forehead.

"Jim, are you ill? Malaria again? Please talk to me."

I looked at her, held out my arm, "Please."

She eased onto my lap. I put my left arm behind her and leaned forward to pillow my head against her breast. I felt her kiss my hair while she cradled my head. I took in huge white gasps of air and began sobbing violently. She soothed me gently in her arms. "There, there. There, there."

After a time I was able to speak. “Sorry.”

She asked, “Sorry? What for?”

“I don’t want to talk about it. For God’s sake, I haven’t seen or done a thing for months that I’d tell to you.”

Suzanne pulled away and softly said, “Jim, look at me.”

I turned my face to her and saw the tears on her cheeks. But her gaze was steady.

“Tell me, Jim,” she commanded. “Tell me everything.”

I shook my head and looked away. “No. I can’t.”

But she was relentless. “Tell it now, Jim, or you’ll carry this burden forever. We may never say a word about it again, but today you need to let it go.”

Her calm green eyes hypnotized me. Hesitantly, I began speaking, my voice flat. Then the words came in gushes and, hating them, I looked away. When I wound down at last the sky was darkening. I looked back up at her, praying she wouldn’t hate me.

She smiled. She got up and grabbed a blanket from the back of the jeep. “Come on, Jim. Let’s watch the sunset.” She spread it on the ledge below the turnout.

We sat, hand-in-hand. As the sun disappeared behind the ridge to our west it set the clouds and the sky ablaze in brilliant colors. She turned to me. “Make love to me Jim. Right here. Now.”

She didn’t have to repeat that order

# # #

Darkness brought mosquitos and we had to dress. But still we lay there for a time, idly waving the bugs away.

“Thank you, dear Susanne, for understanding. Thank you. I’ve felt like a battery gone flat. Dead numb. You brought me back to life.”

“I’m very glad to be here with you. And for you, Jim.”

I raised myself onto one elbow, leaned over and wiped her tears from her eyes. I caressed her cheek. She seized my hand and kissed its fingers. No words.

We were silent the longest time.

I took a very deep breath. "There is one other very important thing I want to tell you."

"What, Jim? Do go on."

"You know how Shakespeare said absence makes the heart grow fonder?"

"Actually, Jim, it wasn't The Bard. It was a nineteenth century poet named Bayly." She closed her eyes and recited.

"What would not I give to wander
Where my old companions dwell?
Absence makes the heart grow fonder;
Isle of Beauty, fare thee well!"

"Okay, Suzanne. I stand corrected. But Mr. Bayly was dead wrong. Absence didn't my heart grow fonder. I'm not bit more fond of you than I was last year when they discharged me from Fourth General and sent me away from you and Judith. It's impossible to be more fond of you than I already was – or than I am this minute.

"Suzanne, I loved you then. If possible I love you even more now. Well..."

I rose to one knee. "Suzanne?" She clasped her hands to her cheeks.

"Suzanne I want to marry you. I want us to be a family. Hell, I'm doing this all wrong. I don't even have a ring to offer you. At least not right now. But Suzanne Bennett, will you please marry me? Please! Or at least just think about it? Please?"

"Oh, Jim!"

"I don't mean right now, Suzanne. It probably would be against some damn fool regulation anyway. But, sweetheart, if you feel *any*thing at all like I do . . . and I think you must . . . Well, I guess I can see why you wouldn't immediately say 'Yes.' You've already lost a fiancé. You could lose this one. I'm certainly not immortal and I know love does *not* conquer all, especially not in a goddam war. But I'm a tough soldier with a very, very strong will to survive. Especially now.

"Annnnd," I flung my arms wide, "Suzanne. The love is here inside..."

She sat up and grabbed my face.

"Oh, Jim, you bloody fool, stop babbling. Yes, I'll marry you when all of this is over, mind. I fell in love with you from the moment you said . . . I believe your exact words were 'I can honestly say I'd rather lose to you at checkers than beat anyone else.'"

I grabbed her hands and pulled her to her feet. I encircled her waist with my left arm, put my right around her shoulders, making her gasp. I slowly and gently bent her back over my right knee and gave her a long, long really wet kiss. Really long.

Then I raised us up for air.

"My God, Jim."

"No, darling. Just a master sergeant."

She gave me a broad smile. "So, where shall we live after all this?"

"Well," I grinned, "I'm used to driving on the right, but I've got no problems with Australia, either."

"What will your career be?"

"Professional gambler – a checker-player."

She guffawed. "Crikey. You're bloody mad!"

"Well! Okay. Since that idea doesn't seem to appeal, I remind you I was majoring in East Asian studies. And the reason was that one day I want to work in international trade, likely in China or Malaya or India. And Japan, too, once they get back on their feet."

"You're convinced we'll defeat them?"

"Oh, absolutely. We're crushing them. But it's going to be hard. They say the Jap navy is sunk and its air forces are done. But the soldiers? They're not about to quit."

"Dear God, Jim, do be careful, won't you?"

"Damned right, Mrs. Mays."

"Oh, 'Mrs. Mays' has quite a lovely sound, right? Er, did I give you my answer?"

"Maybe, but it would be nice to hear it again."

She pulled us together.

"Yes, Jim. I love you and the answer is yes. We shall marry."

Chapter 66
Back To The Grind

When you're trying to get a bunch of yahoos ready for combat, you're not authorized to be in love.

Captain Irish – they promoted him and gave him the Legion of Merit when we returned from Hollandia – put it to me bluntly.

"Jim, I'm happy for you and for your girl. But during work hours you've got to forget her. We've only got two weeks before we land and we need every damned minute of it which means I need fifteen-sixteen hours a day out of you."

I refused to forget Suzanne. I tucked her way back in a special mental treasury that I don't let the Army touch or enter. No, nor even combat. And there she bides, our Hope and Future. Meanwhile, I scrambled.

As one minor cog in the enormous machinery of invasion, my job was to help organize the troop by working the replacements in, getting them accepted, and getting all of us ready for the landing. The guys who'd been with us for the long haul in the Leyte bush – Mendez, Toomey and Riegle -- were worn out and had lost lots of weight. Even the new men, who'd been through the mill for only a month, had doughy feet like the rest of us.

The big question on everybody's mind was what we'd be doing and where we were going. "Cap'n, are we going to be working as the I&R Troop this time around?"

The whole world knew Sixth Army had landed four divisions on Luzon January 9. General MacArthur made sure of it with the cameras rolling as he walked through the surf doing another one of his patented Hey-I-Have-Returned productions. So it stood to reason the 32nd Division wouldn't be too far behind.

But Captain Irish cautioned us. "Jim, from General Gill on down, nobody knows for sure whether Division will even need a reconnaissance troop. Luzon isn't like Leyte. It's much more developed so there isn't so much trackless jungle. It's got a lot more roads. It's even got some mountains with pine trees and cool dry air."

He said he had talked to an old buddy at operations who didn't know for sure whether we'd land on Luzon. "He said, depending on what Six Army does, that – and I quote – 'Your little team of snoops and spooks might wind up just being an ordinary platoon with the 127th Infantry.'"

"Well, it would be a hell of a great platoon, sir. But can you give me some idea of what might happen with us?"

"I'm only guessing, but I know this much. General MacArthur wants to capture Manila as soon as we can so's we can restore the Philippines' national government. But General Kruger is dubious about attacking directly south toward Manila. It's a seventy-five mile push and he's got a lot of mountains to his rear and more of them to his left. There's lots of Japs in those hills and he'd be leaving a lot of flank wide open to Jap attacks."

"Why didn't we assault Manila directly through Manila Bay?"

"The same reason the Japs didn't. Back in '41 we controlled Bataan and Corregidor and those positions command the Bay. Now, of course, the Japs hold Bataan and Corregidor so *they* command the Bay."

"Anyway," he said, "Krueger may need the 32nd as a flank guard for Sixth Army. Or if they don't need the division there, you can tell your boys there are about two dozen other sizeable islands that we also need to take from the Japs."

I told the troops as much as the captain told me. I also warned the men to rest their feet and keep them dry.

Captain Irish chuckled when he overheard me recommend that the troops rest.

"They're not going to care about their feet *or* rest. Mark my words, for the next two weeks the boys are going be out chasing those little Filipina tootsies who'll sell them all the torp they can get their hands on."

"Torp?"

"Yep. Booze. The sailors call it 'torp' because they make booze out of the alcohol which fuels their torpedoes. The swab jockeys strain it through bread to filter out the bad stuff. The Filipinos, on the other hand, make some kind of Kickapoo joy juice by fermenting all kinds of fruit. You know -- mangos, bananas, paw-paws, coconuts. It's sickening sweet, but it'll sure get you drunk."

Mendez added, "I guess about the best thing we can do is get their boots off when they collapse."

"Oh, don't worry about their boots," Captain Irish said. "Their little Chiquitas will take care of them."

It was kind of a relief to learn that though two of our new men – Carlo Vitelli and Bob Werth – were enthusiastic about chasing tail, neither was a drinker.

Mendez also predicted that another replacement would give us no drinking problems. "Guy by the name of Eddy Curran. He took the pledge yesterday. Swore off booze permanent-like."

"He got religion?"

"Not exactly. See, he juiced it real hard and came staggering back about 0400 so stewed that he couldn't navigate to his bunk. So he collapsed by that pylon out on the parade ground where the loud speaker's mounted?"

"Yeah."

"Wellllll, at 0530 the loud speaker starts blasting *Reveille* practically in his ear. They said he screamed because it felt like somebody was shoving chisels through his skull. He suffered a monster hangover all day long. Claimed even his fingers hurt. So supposedly he went to the chaplain and vowed he'd never drink again."

"I'll bet Father O'Neill wasn't impressed."

# # #

The Word came down -- we're confined to post, no more passes, and we can't send out any mail. Then we walked up the ramp into our LST.

Once we were underway, Captain Irish briefed us.

"Two of our regiments, the 127th and 128th will land on Luzon. And, for once, we'll be accompanied by all our own field artillery battalions. We've got a four-day run – damn near a thousand miles – and we'll go ashore next Saturday, January 27.

"The 126th will be held in reserve, but I've got a feeling they'll be joining up before too long."

"Why do you say that, sir?"

"We'll need them. G-2 now says that, all told, the Japs have almost a quarter million troops on Luzon."

"Holy shit!"

"Yeah. And we hear their orders are to delay us and bleed us as much as they can. Luzon is their last line of defense before we invade Japan itself."

"What about the recon troop?"

"For now," Captain Irish said, "it's going to be folded into Able Company just like back on Aitape and The Drain. If they need us for reconnaissance, they'll split us off. Otherwise, you're ground-pounders like everybody else."

"Are you commanding A Company."

"Nope. For starters I'll be with G-2. But if they need the troop, then you're stuck with me."

"Gee, sir, that makes my day."

"Sergeant Mays, your loyalty touches me."

Chapter 67
Off The Beach Into The Fields

As our LST made its elephantine approach to the beach, Toomey said "Guys, you got to admit this is impressive as hell."

"Damn, I guess," Vitelli said. "Looks like the whole U.S. Army is coming ashore right here, and the supplies are already stacked up for us, ripe for the picking."

Curran said, "You want to steal C Rations? Help yourself. I'll pass."

Actually, it was only I Corps coming ashore – the First Cavalry Division and two of our three regiments. Better than thirty thousand soldiers were filing onto the long miles of beautiful flat beaches at Mabilao and San Fabian. The two little fishing villages were alone among many vacant miles of pristine beaches and coconut palms at the head of Lingayen Gulf.

Sixth Army, nearly a hundred thousand men, landed here virtually unopposed two weeks earlier and, meanwhile, service troops and ships brought mountains of supplies ashore. Landing on the west side of Luzon surprised the Japs who apparently believed we would invade three hundred miles away in the south, only a hop, skip and a jump from Leyte.

But because the allies now had virtual control of the air and complete control of the sea, our convoys could thread between the islands and then barrel almost eight hundred miles north to land where the Japs least expected us – in fact, exactly where they invaded in 1941. Kamikazes still were a very scary threat, but they couldn't stop a fleet of nearly five hundred ships.

By the time I Corps arrived, the supply build-up was so great that the Army was able to convoy us by truck to our assembly points fifty miles inland. Lots of Filipinos waved to us from the roadsides. The men wanted to shake hands. The girls gave us snowy smiles and batted their huge dark sloe eyes.

When we arrived at a town named San Manuel, we had to jump down and start walking. The fun was over.

Able Company, with us attached as an extra platoon, proceeded toward a little farming town named Tayug. It's the sort of between place you hardly notice when you're driving off to vacation.

Hiking five yards apart on a dirt road, we were nearing the village. Bob Werth, a cheery sort, said, "Just looks like a wide place in the road." We heard a 'pop' from the village and Werth swung around.

"Son of a bitch," he said wonderingly. He sat down abruptly at the edge of the road. "I think some Jap bastard just shot me." A medic trotted to him and started pulling open his bloody fatigue shirt.

The men in the platoon rushed to spread out into the fields on both sides of the road.

"You there," I said to the medic. "Get yourself and him down in the ditch or they'll shoot you next."

The medic looked up at me in surprise.

"I'm not kidding. Jap snipers like to shoot officers and medics. So move!"

He was shifting Werth to the ditch when we all heard the thud. The medic, now with a hole through his skull, sprawled onto the road. A red pool slowly emerged beneath him.

"*Bastards!* Werth, just get down in the damn ditch and stay there. We'll get a new medic for you pretty quick."

Pale and shaken, he said, "Okay, boss. You guys be careful."

Staying low, we pushed forward through the fields, flanking both sides of the village. Smart defenders would have backed away to find a better delaying position. But the Japs did what they were doing all over that little plain. They stayed put and fought. They were firing vigorously with a pair of light Nambus plus maybe a dozen Arisakas.

"Their shooting don't seem too accurate," Vitelli said.

Curran said, "Tell that to Werth and the medic. I'm staying low, buddy. I like being the poorest possible target."

Staying low was a real grind. Low crawling under noontime January sun at ten degrees north latitude is like toasting yourself on a pancake griddle.

"How you doing, Jameson?"

The kid looked pale, but he was game. "Well, Sarge, the temp inside this steel helmet of mine is staying just below the boiling point. What really gets me though is that I actually can hear the sweat plop down into the dust below my chin."

"You aren't complaining, are you?"

"Why hell no, Sarge! And do you know, scrambling along on elbows and knees like this, the dust rises and gives you a bath just like the sparrows take back home? Keeps parasites off. And when I breath the dust in, it coats my bronical tubes so my breathing is a lot quieter and smoother, right?"

"If you say so, Buddy."

For sure, the *wouuw* and *whiinnne* of bullets close overhead encourages you to keep on eating dust.

"Remember to keep your feet flat," Mendez yelled. "One shot can take your damn heel right off your foot."

As we crawled closer, the firing around the village seemed desultory. Arisakas barked occasionally. M1 rifles barked back. The Nambus fired a burst or two when somebody showed himself. I wished we could call in a mortar barrage, but Heavy Weapons wasn't up yet and our radios weren't cooperating.

Toomey's squad worked its way into the other side of the village. The fire fight ended with several grenade thumps and a flurry of Tommy gun fire. The brisk rattle of carbines reached a sudden crescendo – just like when they open the popcorn popper in the theater lobby. Then things went quiet.

Toomey signaled that the village was secure.

Riegle and I walked through the village. Toomey's boys were busy rifling through the Japs' billfolds and checking the officers' corpses for papers.

Toomey was standing over an American body.

"You get hurt?"

"Yeah, I lost Marx. Took one in the head when we broke in. Horst bought it, too."

"Who?"

"Horst. Pfc. John Horst. It's gonna be a lot quieter without that pair. He and Marx always were arguing about something or other."

Glancing at the Jap corpses, Riegle said, “These Japs looked to be in pretty good condition. I wonder if all of them are going to fight to the end like these did.”

“That’s the pattern we’ve seen so far,” I said. “But I think they’re going to be a lot harder to get at.”

“What do you mean?”

“Well, just look ahead there.” I pointed to the blue ridge of hills lying several miles to the north and east of us. Mid-day haze made it hard to tell much, but through my binoculars I could make out sharp, steep ridges plus long spurs angled toward us. Beyond them, just like stairsteps, were successively higher crests. The haze made them more faint. Low-lying clouds hid some of the ridges’ tops.

“You know what diggers the Japs are,” I said. “If that’s where they’ve holed up, God help us.”

“Well, shit, can’t we just leave them there to rot like we did back in New Guinea?”

“Pvt. Voorhees, I’d be all for that, but Luzon has lots of roads and it does not have solid jungle or thousands of swamps like on New Guinea or even Leyte. It would be easy for them to maneuver, to come right down out of the hills and attack.

“Besides, I bet General MacArthur doesn’t like the idea of a hundred thousand Japs just hanging around. He’s got a score to settle with them.”

“So why do we have to settle *his* score?”

“Because, wiseass, he has four stars on his collar and we don’t. Any more questions?”

Chapter 68
The Trail

In the 1880s, a Spanish priest named Juan Villa Verde began carrying the Word of God and His Holy Sacraments to the isolated people of the Cagayan Valley in northeast Luzon.

Father Juan's parish lay in the west near the shore of Lingayen Gulf. But arching between his parish and the Cagayan Valley to the east lay the steep, rugged Caraballo Mountains. To cross the mountains, the good padre had to toil up and down knife-edge ridges and intervening valleys, a punishing, scary ordeal on a foot path the people and their water buffalos cut centuries earlier; perhaps even before Jesus' birth.

But the priest used the trail so often and – well, so religiously – that the locals appended his name to it. In a sense he sanctified those slopes and precipitous hairpin curves.

In 1944 everything changed.

As the U.S. Army began annihilating enemy forces on Leyte Island, the Japanese Fourteenth Area Army started digging itself into the Caraballos. Under orders of General Tomoyuki Yamashita, they dug deeply and camouflaged their work as only the Japanese can. They created a mountain fortress against which they hoped the American Army would destroy itself, forestalling an invasion of Japan.

The only route into those hills, the Villa Verde trail, became our path to hell.

# # #

By February 2, 1945, the 127th and 128th Infantry Regiments crushed Jap resistance in the flatlands, an area the brass called the Tayug-Natividad-San Nicholas triangle. Then Second Battalion of the 127th seized Santa Maria, a town at the very foot of the Villa Verde Trail.

The 127th began advancing into the hills east of the trail and the 128th to the west. Meanwhile, the engineers ordered up bulldozers to widen the trail itself. Their mission was to create a mountain road on which service troops could truck ammo, food and water up to the fighting infantry and truck their wounded back down the trail before shock, blood loss and infection killed them.

I got my first look at the trail during an impromptu meeting with Captain Irish and Riegle just outside Santa Maria. It was a baking hot afternoon.

"Well, boys," Captain Irish said, "I'd say we've seen the last of flat terrain for a long time."

"Oh, it's flat terrain," Riegle said. "Just vertical instead of horizontal."

I gave a weak chuckle. The stony slopes and ridges rising up before us made Leyte look like a botanical garden.

We and several engineers were at the base of a grassy ridge and peering up the path that was maybe three feet wide. Over the centuries, traffic had eroded the track so that it now was sunken between brush-covered shoulders. Aside from that, it looked like a steep grade.

The engineering major turned to one of his officers. "What do you think? Maybe a six hundred foot elevation in a mile?"

"Yessir, overall at least a ten percent grade," said the other engineer, a warrant officer studying the trail through his binoculars. "But there's some areas where it's a lot steeper."

He offered the binoculars to the major. "Sir, check out that hairpin turn up there. It's just a damned switch-back ledge. It's going to be a bitch cutting it wide enough for trucks.

"Try running a dozer up that and you're going to have a collapse. The cat and its driver will roll down that slope asshole over teacup. And even if they can make those cuts, you can bet bulldozers will be one of the Japs' prime targets."

"Yep," the major said. "Even so, we've got to do it. Native bearers can't supply two combat regiments.

"Sir," Captain Irish asked the major, "what makes you think the Japs are going to let you even *try* to widen this trail?"

"Good point," the major mused. "We'll probably have to send along some..." A rushing howl interrupted him and we all hit the deck.

With an ear-splitting *Crack!* the shell exploded fifty feet away. The Jap observer must have been on his toes because the grit and dust from his first shot still was falling when he landed his second right next to us. Deafened and terrified, I jumped up and scrambled a good hundred feet, throwing myself flat behind a small rise just as a third round came screeching in. Somehow I could picture the Jap observer belly-laughing at my panicked antics.

After that third shell exploded, the screeching continued. Somebody was wounded.

A second lieutenant lying next to me was looking up the hill and speaking into a walkie-talkie. With the ringing in my ears, I hardly heard him, but it soon became obvious he was calling for artillery support.

Four white clouds burst open a half mile up into the hill. Then four more. Aerial bursts. The observer was kneeling now. As he spoke into the mouthpiece, he grinned and nodded his head. Now I heard him faintly. "That blew away some of their cover. Looks like maybe a 75 mm. Nobody's there now."

I asked, "Who you with?"

"I'm a forward observer with the 126th Field Artillery."

"Damn good job, sir. Thanks very much and I hope you stick around."

He grinned. "I aim to."

Captain Irish and Riegle stood up and dusted off their uniforms. Riegle told me, "Boy, I never seen nobody move as fast as you did."

"Can't blame him," the captain said. "Look."

He pointed to the remains of the two engineers. Flies already were gathering where the shell's shrapnel had decapitated the major and virtually severed the warrant officer's trunk. A medic already was trying to help a third soldier who was screaming more weakly now. He seemed to be slashed wide-open.

"Shit!" Riegle said. "Let's get the hell out of here. We're gonna need some more engineers."

"Right," the captain said. "Meanwhile you push your squad up the trail a ways and see whether the Japs come back to that gun. And while you're there, put a thermite grenade in the breech."

Hours later the squad reported back that the Japanese gun crew had ducked into a cave.

"We yelled at them to surrender," Riegle said, "and one of them comes crawling out. He rears up to try and throw a grenade. Voorhees nailed him so he drops it and we duck. The grenade finishes off the Jap. So then we toss a couple grenades into the cave. Heard some screaming after that."

"So, that killed them?"

"Nope, not all of them. It blew a bunch of camouflage crap away from another cave entrance and some pecker jumps up and catches us by surprise. He wounds Voorhees. So we shoot him and throw four or five grenades down his hole. Nobody else came out, so we give the thermite treatment to their gun and come back."

I asked, "How's Voorhees?"

"Pretty bad. Got him through his left arm and into his chest."

"You know," Donnelly said, "we've got to figure a way to bury those bastards alive in their holes."

"Or maybe we could do like the Marines," Mendez said. "Just burn 'em out with flame-throwers."

Donnelly said, "To hell with that. I'm not going around with a gas tank on my back. I don't want to be no ball of fire."

# # #

Thanks to their enormous shoulders and arms, bulldozer drivers look like Superman. It's the constant and intense vibration in their machines' operating levers that builds those huge muscles.

But a 7.7 Arisaka slug takes out a Charles Atlas just as easily as any 98-pound weakling.

I saw it happen that same afternoon.

One of the Engineers' Cats began grinding up the trail, contemptuously pushing aside berms thick with brush, saplings and boulders. After the vehicle cleared about five hundred yards of trail, a Jap sniper hit the driver in the thigh. The driver swore like a madman and raised the Cat's blade perhaps wanting to shield himself.

The next shot blew off the left side of his skull.

His replacement no more than climbed up onto the bloody seat than he collapsed with a round through his guts. When a medic boosted himself up on the tracks to give the driver first aid, a shot knocked him back to the ground. The driver had to roll himself off the bulldozer.

Seeing this, a master sergeant of the 114th Engineers said, "Shit!" He turned to his radio man. "Back to the drawing board. Tell HQ we need six pieces of three-eighths inch steel plate, an acetylene rig with cutting torches and an arc-welder."

A few minutes later, the radio tender said, "Sarge, they want to know why."

"Jesus!" the sergeant said. "Gimme that thing." He yanked the mike from the radio tender.

"This is Kozlanets. Who wants to know? Oh yeah? Well I'm telling you this Cat can't move another foot until it has an armored cab. One driver's dead and t'other's gut shot. Shit, no! We don't even dare to climb up to turn the goddamn thing off until there's a way to shelter the driver. So get the stuff moving. What? No, I don't care what the old man says. Tell him he can court-martial me. If we can't run this cat, some poor bastard is gonna have to hand-carry every damn bullet up that trail and it ain't gonna be me."

He flipped the mike back to the radio man.

"Another day shot to hell. They can't get any of the stuff here until late today."

He turned to me. "You know what's going to happen, don't you?"

"What?"

"The armored cab's gonna cut way down on the driver's vision. And with that big diesel going he won't be able to hear anything, either.

"So he's going to need two guides out front where he can eyeball them. And they're going to need protection from the Japs. I bet you'll have to send a whole infantry squad along with every dozer. Talk about a FUBAR!

Chapter 69
Back On The Job

General Gill decided the division would need reconnaissance services after all. That same night our G-3 called Captain Irish and our NCOs for a briefing.

"Our overriding mission," he said, "is to engage and defeat the Japanese Fourteenth Area Army, thereby keeping it off the back of General Krueger's drive to capture Manila.

"Second, as we've seen again and again from Buna to Leyte, with rare exceptions, Japanese soldiers will neither surrender nor retreat. In fact, *their* mission is to kill as many of us as possible in order to protect their home islands.

"So, since they neither surrender or retreat, we must therefore kill all of them. Sorry if this sounds cold, men, but our attack literally must be a campaign of annihilation. We have three battalions of field artillery to back us up. And we now also have very good air support."

"So your mission, just like before, will be to scout and report back. There's not going to be much subtlety about this. We're certain they've done a lot of digging and we're going to have to go straight at them and either dig them out or bury them."

"It's going to be costly."

# # #

"General, this looks to be a costly campaign. And considering that trail, we need to set up a special field surgery."

Waiting for a briefing by G-2, I couldn't help overhearing the surgeon's discussion with General Gill.

"What do you need, colonel?"

"We need to set up as close to the line as possible. The further the 32nd advances, the tougher it's going to be on the wounded, bringing them down that trail. Before long it'll be a rough ten or fifteen miles to Santa Maria. That will be a killer for some of the seriously wounded. Too much time. Too much vibration. But with early surgery for dangerous wounds, we can save a hell of a lot of lives, sir."

The general nodded. "I get your point, Colonel. But be advised the Japs will be taking potshots at your hospital whenever they can. You know what they're like. Your wounded might be getting hit a second time. And you might take casualties of your own."

"Yessir. We'll take precautions, sir, believe me."

"What precautions?"

"We'll need sandbag walls – four bags thick and six or seven feet high – all the way around each of the tents. Unless they drop mortars right through the roof, that should do the job."

"Very well, Colonel. Make it so."

The two men saluted.

# # #

I didn't realize just how tough this would be until the third night we scouted east of the trail.

My squad of the I&R Troop was nearly a mile up the trail. We were just a few hundred yards above what the troops came to call The Bowl – a quarter-mile stair-stepped set of very sharp hairpin curves.

Peering through his binoculars, Riegle said, "Look at that! That trail makes four count 'em four 180-degree turns along the side of that hill."

"Hell, that's no hill," I said. "Looks more like a damn cliff. Even a jeep will have to go slow to negotiate those turns. I bet you can just feel the crosshairs on your face or chest.

"Or your back, depending on which direction you're going."

The casualty list from an initial probe showed the Japs seemed to have The Bowl targeted by every mortar, howitzer and machine gun in Luzon. Nothing could live on The Bowl's little narrow road until the infantry destroyed every Jap position that commanded it. Yes, we had all the artillery we needed. But somebody had to be the FO – the forward observers -- for the mortars and the big guns.

And the sad sack riflemen and machine gunners had to capture the ground first before the FO could get to work with binoculars and radios.

# # #

"Okay, guys, here's how we're going to do this." Nobody wanted to meet my eyes and I really didn't want to meet theirs.

"Toomey, you and your squad file into this draw. Now what you do is find a secure spot and start examining that slope above you. Take your time. When you've got the targets spotted, call them in to the mortar section. Meanwhile, Lieutenant Aims will be your artillery liaison and FO."

"I thought his name was Michaels."

"It is, but we just figured 'Aims' would be a more fitting name for an artillery officer. Little humor there."

"Gee, Sarge, I think somebody came up with that joke ten minutes after the first cannon was fired."

"Okay, sorry. Now, once the mortars start hitting, the Japs will do like turtles and pull their heads back into their holes.

"That's when the platoon that filters in with you people and starts moving up the ridge. One thing they've got going for them -- when people shoot downhill, it may feel like they're looking down your throats, but the fact is they usually shoot high. What's more, every little bulge in that ridge creates a defilade -- dead ground. Stay low and they can't see you or hit you.

"Now pay attention to this if you don't know it already. When you're shooting *up*hill, you also tend to shoot high. So don't aim at their heads. Aim below them, right at the base of their foxholes or cave entrances. Then you'll hit their heads. Remember that!"

"Okay," Toomey said, "Let's move out!"

God, I just hope the Japs don't bring down a shower of their own mortars into Toomey's draw.

It worked better than I ever would have believed, but still was a failure.

The kids, of course, were veterans. They'd been fighting Japs, some of them at least, for nearly three years and they knew how to read the ground.

Toomey's patrol spotted several caves and he dialed in the mortars. Meanwhile, the artillery officer started blasting the crest of the ridge. The smoke and dust obscured my view of what was happening and I hoped it would be killing Japs or at least making it difficult for them to aim.

The platoon started up the ridge. The Japs started shooting.

The boys stayed low, wiggling upward rather than crawling, pulling themselves upwards with their elbows as well as legs.

One of our men raised up on his knees to throw a grenade and, somehow, got away with it. His throw wasn't quite strong enough to get the grenade inside the Japs' tunnel, but it did explode almost under the muzzle of a light Nambu.

Like lightning, he and another soldier raced up outside the hole and threw grenades back inside it.

After the explosions, one of the men crawled inside. The other, still in the open outside the cave, got hosed by a Jap in another cave a hundred yards away. Two minutes later, a Jap in the original cave pushed out the body of the American who had crawled inside. In another minute, the Jap – or a replacement -- was shooting at us from the position we thought had been cleared.

The attack bogged down, so Toomey called in more mortar fire giving the troops cover to retreat back down into the draw.

# # #

"Captain Irish," I said, "we've got to have something more powerful than grenades. We can throw them into the caves and it might kill some of them, but it doesn't kill them all. We've got to have a way to either kill them or seal them inside permanently."

"I know," he said. "We're trying to get Bangalore torpedoes but there's been a delay of some kind. Meanwhile, we asked Ordnance to fix up some satchel charges. They're also going to make up some pole charges. Something you can shove into the tunnel while your buddies are shooting to keep the Japs inside. If they're powerful enough, they can bring down ten or twenty yards of dirt. Suffocate the bastards."

"So, sir, what's a satchel charge?"

"Oh, a musette bag or a messenger bag filled with TNT blocks or plastic explosive and some kind of fuse. The idea is that you get it inside a cave and then get your ass into some kind of cover before it goes off."

"Close combat, eh?"

"Yeah, real close."

Chapter 70
The Hidey Hole

Toomey loomed toward me out of the darkness and tugged my sleeve.

He whispered, "I've got something here that's really weird."

I didn't ask but followed him up the hill. He stopped me shy of the crest.

"All the shelling up here stripped away a lot of cover."

When we got to the crest, enough starlight was available for me to make out an eight-inch log spanning a round hole maybe three feet wide. An inch-thick thick rope tied in the center of the log disappeared down the hole.

Then he said, "Listen."

Holding my head over the hole, I thought I could hear speech. But for sure a current of air from the hole was bringing me the distinctive fish-head, seaweed and soy smell of Jap.

I gripped the rope and could tell that it was dangling and, by its weight, that it must be fairly long. As I pulled it upwards a ways, I found it had thick knots spaced about eighteen inches apart. "Shit, this is just like the climbing ropes we had in high school gym. This damn rope is the ladder to climb up out of there." I let the rope drop.

We scooted away from the hole.

"So what do we do, Sarge?"

"I think it's an entry point not a fighting hole. We could drop a couple of grenades down it, but I bet it leads to a tunnel serving a machine gun position. Or maybe two or three tunnels. Grenades wouldn't touch them. We'd need a big satchel charge."

"Jesus, Sarge, if we just stumbled across this, how many do you suppose there are?"

That was the perfect question. It made me picture Buna all over again. This time, though, it wasn't coconut log bunkers, but a whole subterranean army.

"Jesus, Toomey, it's just like the Morlocks in H.G. Wells' *Time Machine*."

"What?"

"I'll tell you later. Let's get the hell out of here. We've got to read headquarters in on this."

"Hey, Sarge, what if we just wrestle that log around and drop it down the hole? That'll fuck them up for a few hours."

"We're not playing Halloween pranks, Jody. We want to *kill* the bastards. Seal them inside. We need satchel charges or Bangalore torpedoes. Maybe gasoline like Eichelberger used on the caves on Biak. We got to talk to the engineers about this."

# # #

The next day, Operations wasn't happy about our report concerning the cave.

"This doesn't tell us anything, Sergeant, except that you found a hole in the ground. So what?"

"Well, sir, I figure it's part of a cave network. That hole is only the main opening and probably for ventilation."

The officer just snorted. Basically, he made it clear they wanted us to *explore* the damned thing.

So that night, Curran, Mendez, Toomey and I worked our way back to the base of the ridge. To keep the Japs from spotting us, we spent the next day baking in a wooded ravine. Well after dark, we crawled to the ridge crest. Riegle and four of his boys tailed us to keep any roving Japs off our backs. I wanted them for our security, but I also wanted them to keep an eye peeled to see if our explosive present to the Japs produced any visible effects on the face of the ridge.

We had a bit of a problem finding the pit because the Japs had restored its camouflage, greatly changing the looks of the ridge crest. Shelling also had ripped away lots of brush and blasted the pine trees into stark skeletons.

But once we located the pit, I pulled up the climbing rope and coiled it. Then it took about two seconds to ignite the fuse and drop the double satchel charge down that black hole.

We moved a good twenty feet away because I feared something like a giant Fourth of July burst of flame.

We got no flash at all, just a deep hollow-sounding *Whump!* -- sort of like a giant cherry bomb going off inside a garbage can. It seemed to jolt the whole ridge. I found myself praying that the charge had jolted things enough to collapse the entire tunnel. I really didn't want to climb down inside it to take the Cook's Tour.

One of Riegle's runners joined us to say the blast blew smoke and debris from two sites on the ridge face. "I *knew* it," I muttered to myself, dropping the rope down the hole.

Curran said, "Ain't you gonna wait for the smoke to clear?"

"Hell, no. I want to get this done before some asshole Jap shows up with a platoon to find out what happened."

Starting to let myself down the rope, I was sorry to find the pit hadn't collapsed. *No such luck.* I tried to ignore the gunpowder-and-feces smell. At least the descent was much easier than I expected. Some Jap engineer cut toeholds in the pit's wall so that it was mainly a case of easing down the rope knot-by-knot while stepping down the wall.

About six feet down, my flashlight scared the hell out of me when it illuminated a Jap soldier half-propped, half-lying in a big niche cut out of the pit wall. He seemed to look right at me, but he didn't move a muscle. His eyes were dusty. He was dead, unmarked except for blood streams from his ears and nose.

Concussion did him in?

The second niche was another eight feet lower but nobody was in it. When I reached the floor, the footing was squishy. The flashlight showed me I was stepping into a second dead Jap . . . or maybe two or three of them. It was hard to tell. The explosion had plastered either him or them all over the place.

Nasty damned surprise for you boys.

I pointed my flashlight up the pit and waggled it. Toomey came down the rope two minutes later, with Curran close behind.

"Welcome to hell."

The sight and the reek of ripped intestines plus the chemical smell of explosives had us gagging and swallowing convulsively, trying not to vomit.

The Jap-coated room was claustrophobic because it was no more than five feet high, forcing us to stoop almost double. We discovered openings to two five-foot tunnels leading in opposite directions. One tunnel forked and each fork led to a machine gun position on the face of the ridge. Each firing position was roomy –

at least six feet from floor to ceiling. Each had a dead Jap, a bench-mounted Nambu, a cache of grenades, a few canned rations plus whole cartons of Nambu ammo strips.

The other tunnel seemed to lead further beneath the ridge to a large room with six more dead Japs plus their ammo store, water barrels, cooking gear and latrines. The odor was beyond belief. That room – which I called the barracks – had yet another tunnel which seemed to tilt down toward the opposite face of the ridge.

I was debating whether to check that tunnel, when a timid Japanese voice echoed down it. "*Neh neh!*" Hey!

I shouted back, "*Nah neh?*" What?

"We've got company," I whispered, "and I've seen enough. I don't want to get into a firefight inside a damned tunnel."

"Damn right," Curran said. "Let's get the fuck out of here."

Another Japanese voice, authoritative, bellowed something I didn't understand. An officer or NCO.

I told Toomey, "Start climbing." Then I shouted, "*Nani mo!*" Nothing!

Toomey asked, "Screw that! Why don't we just go out through their firing points. That would be a lot faster."

"Okay! Go! Go!"

As they left, I pulled the pin and rolled a grenade into the new tunnel. Then I scrambled through the barrack and blood room before the grenade exploded. The blast from the grenade shoved needles in our ears. Screams followed. But as I got out onto the face of the ridge, I could hear furious Jap shouts echoing behind us.

We shoved the Nambus into the soil muzzle-first. Nobody could shoot them without a giving them a thorough cleaning.

It took the rest of the night to evade the patrols, sneak off the ridge and get into our own lines.

# # #

Having had no sleep, I really had a short fuse next morning when some pissant little G-2 lieutenant started hassling me about the dimensions of the underground complex.

"You mean you don't know how long those tunnels are?"

"No sir," I said. "I'm just a dumb-ass EM, not a West Pointer, so I didn't have the gumption to take along a civil engineer's tape measure. I *can* tell you the vertical tunnel, the entry, was about thirty feet deep."

"And just how did you come to that conclusion, Sergeant?"

"Because, *Lieutenant*, the Japs' climbing rope had a knot every eighteen inches and there were fourteen knots, sir."

"Well, for thirty feet you'd need twenty knots."

"Nossir," Toomey chimed in. "Unless you're very, very short, *sir,* you don't need knots for the bottom four feet of the rope."

"Sergeant, you'd better start showing more respect …"

Captain Irish said, "Back off, Mister Evans. I think you ought to show a little more respect for what these men achieved. And if you actually *need* the exact dimensions of this Japanese installation, I suggest you join the next infantry company that tackles the ridge. And take a tape measure and surveyor's transit."

The lieutenant turned pink.

"And I think the real point of this," the captain added, "is not to badger our men who have established that the Japanese have created a very elaborate defensive system.

"The only question now – and fighting men will find out – is how extensive this system is. Based on what we've seen in other areas, I'd venture to say it's very complete. And the troops who man it will do their damnedest to make it work."

He paused and looked at me.

"We'd better check what explosives the engineers have come up with."

Chapter 71
The Injury List Grows

After a sound sleep and a chance to write Suzanne, I got a solid nighttime meal and then led the boys back up into the hills. We wanted to find patterns in the Jap defense. The Japs weren't everywhere, but their tunneling seemed well thought-out.

Using tunnel and cave entrances, they appeared to have every inch of the Villa Verde trail under observation and targeted with mortars, machine guns and artillery.

We found that out at Mendez's cost late in the afternoon when we topped a rise.

It was one of those razor-back hills with a crest about four feet wide. A well-worn foot path along the crest told us somebody had been busy. By well-worn, I mean that except for slabs of rock, the earthen path had no plants – not even weeds. In fact it looked like the beginning of a modest ditch, a six or eight-inch deep notch peoples' feet had cut in the crest. The Villa Verde Trail itself was clearly visible about three hundred feet downslope from us.

"Lot of foot traffic along here," Riegle said. "I'd say people been carrying a lot of supplies."

"Right. But where the hell were they taking the supplies? Take a look-see along the face of that ridge on the far side of the trail."

Riegle and I scoured the area with our binoculars. I didn't trust my vision to penetrate Jap camouflage, and long afternoon shadows didn't help. "I don't spot anything like a hole or a tunnel," Riegle said, "but I don't like it."

"Me neither. I feel like somebody has his sights on us."

I took a deep breath. "Let's just ease back down where we came from."

"Sounds good."

Grabbing branches and bracing ourselves on half-exposed boulders, one-by-one we made our way back down the very steep slope we had just climbed. In places, loose earth and rock gave way and we'd slide three or four feet before being able to stop. Mendez was tail-end Charlie.

If it was a trap, Toomey sprang it early. He lost his footing and fell, caving in a beautifully camouflaged overhang. He wound on his butt in a cave mouth that also was a machine gun position.

"I was so damned lucky," he explained later. "I landed on my ass with my Tommy gun in my hand, and the two jokers in that tunnel only had their Nambu. I think they were as startled as I was. One of them started to pick it up but I whipped around and blasted him before could do any more than touch it. The other Tojo wanted to jump me, but three .45 slugs in the chest put him flat on his back."

All of us but Mendez raced to join Toomey.

Just after the Tommy gun's blast, Mendez saw muzzle flashes erupting in the shade on the facing ridge. He yanked up his M1 and began firing at that three hundred-yard target. What he didn't realize was that a third Nambu was firing at him … firing high, luckily.

The mount for the Type 92 Nambu heavy machine gun has two locking handles. One enables the gunner to keep the gun firing at a fixed elevation while training it right and left. The other prevents training, so that the gun hits the same target no matter how long he fires.

We think the Nambu gunner who tried to shoot Mendez was a second-stringer who didn't know enough to loosen either locking handle. His bursts kept impacting the earth about two feet above and three feet behind Mendez. Mendez didn't realize it because he was busy shooting his M1 in practically the opposite direction.

So as he was trying to take out one enemy, the other was practically digging bushels of earth right behind and above him.

We screamed like mad at him and began shooting at his would-be assassin. When Mendez had to shove a new clip into his rifle's action, it dawned on him that something was wrong. A glance showed tracers bullets chewing up earth behind him.

He jumped like a paratrooper from a plane, feet first, straight out from that slope. He landed on his back five feet down the slope and began sliding toward us.

Mendez tried to use his feet and elbows to brake his descent, but his slide was so fast he looked like a dusty comet. Trying to actually stop looked about as easy as coming to a halt half-way down a ski jump.

Donnelly put the brakes on Mendez by grabbing his collar as he tore past. We all ducked into Toomey's cave and quickly discovered we had a nasty casualty on our hands. Sliding down that rocky slope ripped Mendez's shirt from his back. From waist to shoulder blades, his back looked raw – or would have, if a plaster of dirt and blood weren't adhering it. His descent also ripped most of the skin from his elbows and forearms. Bone or tendon gleamed white through the mess.

Luis was a tough kid, but the pain had him growling and hissing through clinched teeth.

We jabbed a morphine syrette into his thigh. Once it was dark, we headed toward the field hospital carrying him face down.

# # #

We didn't get Mendez to the hospital until just after dawn.

As the medics swilled the dirt and crud from Luis's back, the surgeon quietly told me our boy probably had a million-dollar injury that would get him rotated stateside for a long, long hospital stay. "I bet he'll need extensive skin grafts and he'll spend a lot of time on his stomach."

I knelt beside Mendez's stretcher so I could meet his eye. "So, Luis, it looks like you get to keep that gold tooth for now."

"Yeah, Jim," he groaned. "I guess I'll just have to find me a wife and leave it to our kids."

"Okay, so meanwhile don't be pinching the nurses. They're all officers, you know, and you could get court-martialed."

"Jim, just get out of here, will you? You're making me hurt."

"Take it easy, Buddy."

We talked some nurses into letting us have coffee and were just starting to relax in the canteen tent when all hell broke loose. Mortar shells started exploding outside the hospital. Each blast whipped the tops of the tents, and then flying dust and pebbles rattled down onto them.

A sergeant leaned into the tent. "We're hospital security. Can you give us a hand?"

"Damn right!"

We bustled out of the canteen. Thanks to the thick sandbag walls, the mortar shelling so far had done little damage other than setting off the gas tank of an ambulance parked nearby. The subsequent fire and black smoke seemed to screw up the Japs' aim, but mortar rounds kept falling near the hospital. Meanwhile two or three machine guns began peppering the area.

"Chickenshit little bastards!' Donnelly yelled. "Why the hell they attacking a hospital?"

"Because they know it pisses us off. And maybe it takes some pressure off their boys up in the hills. Maybe."

It seemed as if a platoon of Japs was maneuvering to seize the hospital. They outnumbered the security guard. But the seven of us tipped the scales. We killed a number of attackers. The Japs began retreating up the ridge from which their mortars and machine guns were firing.

We joined the security squad in climbing toward the Jap positions.

"Jesus," Toomey gasped, "you'd think after going all night without sleep we'd get a break."

"Ain't you heard?" Curran said. "Infantry don't get breaks."

We were half-way up the ridge when artillery started crashing in on the suspected Jap positions.

"Fellas," I said, "let's keep moving up for another hundred yards and we can brush up what the cannon-cockers leave."

With the artillery falling around them, the attackers apparently took cover. They certainly ceased fire, at any rate, so that we were able to move just below the ridge crest.

When the artillery stopped, we stopped, crouched just below the military crest. We could hear orders being yelled, and then a squad of rifle-bearing Nips appeared, apparently ready to attack the hospital again.

With a staccato rattle of rifle and submachine gun fire, we took them down. We then threw grenades over the crest and, the instant they exploded, charged over the top. Our assault caught two stunned squads of Nips out in the open. Our Tommy guns, BARs and semi-automatic carbines gave us every advantage. We killed the bulk of them.

We had two men wounded. As we gave them first aid, Donnelly and Curran shot the wounded Japs.

The artillery had left a mess of the Japs' mortar section.

"Okay! Back to the hospital. Donnelly? You and Curran each bring along one of those mortar base plates. I've got the third. They can't shoot worth a damn without them."

When we got back to the hospital, we found out that the Japs' indiscriminate machine gun fire had left lots of holes in the tent roofs, hitting and wounding five of the hospital's patients.

Mendez wasn't one of them.

I apologized to one of the surgeons. I had the feeling the Japs had launched the attack after trailing us as we bore Mendez to the hospital.

"Don't be crazy," he said. "This happens once or twice a week and it's always about 0630."

Chapter 72
Villa Verde Scenes

Disease casualties in New Guinea were so heavy that headquarters demanded rigid enforcement of malaria discipline.

So, despite the 99-degree temperatures and 100 per cent humidity, we noncoms forced the kids to roll down and button their sleeves. Collars buttoned to the neck. Fewer mosquito bites that way. The Army also issued 6-22 mosquito repellant. It's fierce. It repels bugs, but you don't *ever* want to get it on your lips or eyelids.

And we force the kids to take Atabrine. "You *will* take your Atabrine, young trooper. Pop that pill into your mouth. Bitter ain't it? Now chug half a canteen of water. Good! Now let me look inside! Go 'Ahhhhhhh!' Good!

"Don't worry about what Tokyo Rose said, son! Atabine don't make you impotent. When you jump in the sack back home with Betty Boop, she'll help you get it up."

# # #

It started as a fairly quiet day. Shooting was sporadic, rifle shots came to our ears through the bulldozer's growl two hundred yards away. The driver was hugging the right side of the Villa Verde trail, carving away part of the hill to widen a cart path into a truck route.

Dirt from occasional little landslides crumbled onto the Cat's right-hand tracks and onto the armored cab that protected the driver – a crude steel box with vision slits on four sides.

A machine gun burst rattled against the cab – *Pang! Pang! Pang!* – and the squad guarding the dozer fired back. Meanwhile, the guides out front of the dozer took a knee or fell flat. Once the firing stopped, they stood up and resumed using shovels to cut visual guides in the earth for the driver.

Pushing well ahead of the dozer was a platoon from the 127th doing its best to suppress Jap attacks on the Cat. When they could, they used pole charges.

A squad spotted a Jap cave, a machine gun position, and fired at it to drive the occupants back inside. Meanwhile, two gutsy kids low-crawled practically to the cave's mouth. Using a fifteen-foot bamboo pole, they pushed a satchel charge inside the cave. Then they triggered the fuse, giving themselves a few seconds to get away before the blast.

I say "gutsy" because Japs in other caves often spotted such maneuvers and fired at the explosives team. As they did so, the team's comrades tried in turn to suppress those Japs. Desultory shooting rapidly built into an intense firefight with the clatter of machine guns and crash of mortars rising into a cacophony. The racket could get so intense it got hard to think straight.

On this particular day, everything that could go wrong did.

The first explosives team took out its cave in very workmanlike fashion. Their supporting squad's rifle and BAR fire drove the Japs from the cave mouth, the team shoved the pole charge well inside, the charge exploded and transformed the cave entrance in a heap of smoking earth.

The team's next step didn't go so well, one team member taking a bullet. The explosive had done its work as planned. But as the unwounded soldier tried to help his buddy, a Jap sniper also shot him. To save the pair, the squad had to attack up-hill.

A second explosives team went to work on another cave, but this time the Japs rolled a grenade out of the cave just as the team neared it. The grenade set off the satchel charge blowing both men to bloody tatters. Minutes later, a Japanese soldier burrowed out from the collapsed first cave and began shooting uphill into the backs of infantrymen. He hit two men before the rest of the platoon killed him.

What then led to everybody's pure fury was that the bulldozer they defended began cutting around a sharp bend. Half way through the Cat's turn, the slope's shoulder beneath its outside track began collapsing. The Cat tilted and started sliding off its own roadway.

The driver should have abandoned ship immediately.

Instead, he gunned the Cat's left track, attempting to turn uphill to the right. It only seemed to speed the vehicle's downward slide as more earth gave way. Perhaps fifty feet down-hill, the dozer tilted and capsized, crushing the armored cab as if were a pasteboard box.

Immediately we heard Japs hooting and jeering.

One of the combat engineers screamed, “You bastards! We’ll be back tomorrow with another’n.”

And they were. During the night engineering troops used tons of timber bamboo to stabilize the slope. Meanwhile, they fought off a modest banzai attack by about a company of Jap troops. And the next morning a new armored Cat made it around the bend.

After the campaign, we heard General Yamashita identified bulldozers as the top priority target. That sounded odd to me at the time. But years later I read that Admiral Halsey himself rated the bulldozer just ahead of the submarine as the most important weapon in the South Pacific.

# # #

Captain Irish was on the horn with G-2 and taking notes when he suddenly said. “Give them hell, sir.” He listened for a moment, dropped the hand set and shook his head.

“What’s going on, sir?”

“Hell’s a poppin’ down there. A couple of Jap squads attacked headquarters.”

“No shit? Hell, that’s way behind our lines.”

He gave me a surly look. “Jim, we’re behind Jap lines almost all the time. Is there any law says they can’t do the same thing?”

“Guess not.”

“Yeah, you guess not.”

# # #

The damnedest things happen. One of our men, Corporal Tillotson, was having a cigarette outside a newly-captured cave when a Jap bullet smashed his knee. Unfortunately, the impact didn’t knock him out or even stun him. He instantly was hissing and swearing with the pain while the dust beneath his wound turned to red slush. We were fumbling, getting in each other’s way trying to put tourniquet around his leg.

With a rush and a cloud of dust, our medic, Corporal Shuster, slid down the slope and practically fell into our laps. “Out of the way, dammit!” He pushed two men away from Tillotson and handed me a morphine syrette. "Hit him with this, Sarge, but only after I stop the hemorrhage."

He had a tourniquet around Tillotson's thigh in about two seconds. Pulling it tight, he told me "Okay! Morphine! No, Sarge! In his *good* leg! Now you guys get him to the field hospital be…"

At that instant, a 75 mm shell ripped in and exploded in the earth maybe four feet from Shuster. The noise and flash stunned us

Now the Jap 75 usually shreds people with hundreds of razor-sharp steel shards. But this one merely knocked Shuster flat. We were all holding our breath as he sat up. He just shook his head. "Damn!"

Not a scratch. He stood up. Stumbled briefly and then took off to check another wounded man.

# # #

I heard yesterday of a team that didn't want to use pole charges because they thought getting within ten or fifteen feet of a Jap cave is damned dangerous.

Absolutely right. It is very dangerous.

So the genius leading the team had an idea based on the centuries-old siege technique of sapping toward a hostile position. You're digging a ditch toward the enemy's flank. To protect your men as they dig, you place a big wicker basket at the head of the ditch, shovel dirt into it while staying out of sight. Once it's filled, it protects you from enemy bullets as you dig further forward. Then you do the same thing with a new basket which, again, protects you as you sap further forward, and so on.

Of course wicker baskets are a bit scarce along the Villa Verde Trail, so this guy pushed a filled sandbag ahead of the team as they approached their target cave.

The innovator got a bullet through his skull and his lucky teammate crawled back to safety with two minor wounds. Too bad some NCO didn't warn them that it takes at least two sandbags to stop a modern rifle bullet. Engineers say you're better off with three.

# # #

Hysteria overcame me only one time on Luzon. In fact, it got a bunch of us all at once.

We were ducking low in a ditch because Jap fire was coming at us like so much hail. Literally. The muddy soil was jumping and quaking around us as bullets by the dozens smacked into it.

We heard the Japs screaming as they started racing our way, figuring they could overrun us. It was the perfect time for the mortar barrage we begged from Able Company's heavy weapons platoon. So the Jap banzai charge and the mortars started arriving in the same place at the same time.

Perfect.

Except that one of the mortar shells burst a few feet away, just behind a Jap soldier who had arrived at the lip of our ditch. The shrapnel tore him apart and his lower half toppled right onto Sergeant Charlie Riegle.

Riegle started pushing all that goo off his own chest and legs. Then he looked around. "Oh God!" he screamed in a falsetto voice, "Am I really hit that bad?"

It was maybe twenty minutes before any of us could stop laughing.

# # #

Japs had a well-deserved reputation for not surrendering. And wounded Japs had a well-deserved reputation for trying to kill anyone offering them first aid.

Yesterday, though, Donnelly came out of a cave with an exception. He was practically arm-in-arm with a Japanese first lieutenant. The officer smiled nervously and bowed to me. Donnelly cracked, "It ain't like him and me shower together, Sarge. The guy's got a leg wound so I've got to be his crutch for a while."

We treated Jap prisoners well because, for all their fanaticism, as captives they often were docile and quite cooperative. In fact, I formed a theory that, having survived when their duty was to die, Jap POWs underwent some sort of psychological release from their national death wish. They seemed to embrace our own hopes for a long life.

At any rate, I assigned Curran to go with Donnelly in getting the lieutenant to the medics and G-2. When the pair returned that evening, Donnelly said capturing the POW at first was scary.

"You remember Toomey and I tossed grenades into that cave? Well, afterwards, I was so pooped that I just decided to go inside and take ten out of the sun. Their caves may stink, but at least they're fairly cool.

"So I pushed the Nambu and its dead gunner aside and just took a look around. And there was our officer, flat on his back. He wasn't moving so I figured he was dead. I took off my steel pot, sat down on it and took a drink out of my canteen.

"Well, it's pretty dark but then I spot something out of the corner of my eye. Some movement or other over by the Jap. So I flick on my flashlight and turn it on him. Nothing. So I turn it off, take another drink and then I hear a breath.

"'Okay, you bastard!' I get the flashlight on him again and my .45. Now his goddam eyes are wide open. I ask him, 'Do you speak English?'

"He shakes his head. So I bend over him to take a closer look. Now he nods his head 'Yes' and holds out his hand. He wants me to give him my damn pistol, for God's sake!

"So I tell him, 'No harry-karry for you, buddy. Nossir, you're my prisoner.' So he gives kind of a gasp and turns the corners of his mouth way down. You can tell he's upset. So I ask, 'Thirsty?' and hold out my canteen to him. Ain't much in it, but he glugs down a swallow and says something like 'abrigado'. I think that's Portagee for 'thank you'. Kind of weird coming from a Jap."

I asked, "You sure he didn't say 'Arigato'?"

"Yeah, that sounds more like it."

"Well, that's Jap for 'Thanks'."

"Oh, okay. Well, then I offer him a hand up so we could walk out of the cave. As he gets up, I find out he's been lying on top of a pistol and two grenades. So I guess he could have done me in, but maybe really did want to surrender. Anyhow, I'm glad I didn't shoot him 'cause now, bringing in a POW, I get a three-day pass, right?"

"Yes, Donnelly. You can go to Manila."

"To hell with that, Sarge. I already talked to a couple guys that went there. It's blown all to hell. I'll just go over to Malibu."

"Malibu? Are you talking about Mabilao over on Lingayen Gulf?"

"Yeah, that's what I said. I remember it's a beautiful beach and where you got beaches there's broads and booze, right? I even hear USO has set up a bar."

"Donnelly, I seriously doubt the USO set up a bar. But at least you can relax away from the shooting."

# # #

Five of us snuck up on a cave early one very foggy morning and barreled in through the entrance. Our attack killed three Jap officers and we captured five others along with some radio operators.

Two Jap survivors began shouting at each other, one so angry he was spitting at his comrade. I had the boys separate them.

"Guys! I think they're blaming each other for getting captured. Keep them apart. And be sure you treat these radio operators real well. Give them cigarettes. They can be a big help to G-2."

As the guys got busy I looked around, checked the Jap maps, and it slowly dawned on me that this must be something like one of our fire direction centers. Most of the rank insignia on the prisoners and bodies bore the pale greenish-gold background that denoted the artillery. But two bodies, a lieutenant and a major, bore the red infantry insignia.

This seemed very unusual to me and we found out that it posed a problem. Namely it was that the constant pressure from the 32nd Infantry Division was forcing the Japanese command to demand cooperation between artillery and infantry. Bad luck for us.

Previously, Jap cannon-cockers and ground-pounders operated almost independently of each other. Jap artillery would select and bombard targets of their own choice and if the infantry wanted help, it could go fish. But then the Japanese infantry was so damned arrogant it preferred to attack without any help, thank you. And if everybody died in a banzai charge, well who was left to complain?

But for the moment, what interested me most was a brass spyglass mounted on a very elaborate chrome-plated tripod.

By now the weather had cleared, so I took a glance through the scope and couldn't believe how much better its images were that those of our binoculars. I focused in on a POW whom Curran was taking down the hill. The spyglass was so good I could make out beads of sweat on their faces.

The scope wasn't the antique I'd taken it to be, but a piece of very modern lens technology.

I found the carrying case, disassembled the scope and mount and took them with us. They came in very handy in the weeks ahead.

Showing it to Captain Irish, I said, "I heard the Jap lens industry was better than ours or Germany's, but I had no idea how much better. No wonder we had the impression that they were looking down our throats."

"What are you going do with it?"

"When we head up on Mount Imugan, I'm hauling it along. I think it will be a big help."

# # #

February and March were broiling hot in the Caraballos and along The Trail, but April and May brought rains every bit as heavy as in New Guinea. I'm no weatherman, but I bet we got a daily downpour of four or five inches.

That much rain on an unpaved roadway beside a steep slope and, guess what? Where you had a road now there's a creek bubbling down the middle of a gulley. All we could do was cuss. The engineers cussed, too, and meanwhile rebuilt the damned road using, I heard, something like seventy thousand sandbags and about half of Luzon's timber bamboo.

In my book, the heroes of this campaign are the ordinary riflemen who crawl up these ridges to take on Jap troops who are fighting from very strong defensive positions. But it's hard to be a hero if you don't have cartridges for your M1 or BAR, plus lots of water to drink and at least three meals a day – even if they're only C-Rations.

In the Caraballos, you get none of those things if trucks can't run on the Villa Verde Trail.

So the campaign's other heroes are the engineers who – despite snipers, artillery and mortar barrages and day after day after day of toad-drowning downpours – kept rebuilding that vital artery so the troops could fight.

# # #

Jesus told us to love our enemies, but if He'd been with us this morning, I'd ask Him to re-think that one. And He just might.

We came in from patrol about 0430 shy a man. It was pouring and our route was new, so at first we weren't too concerned that our tail-end Charlie, Corporal Dick Masters, was missing. He probably would find his way in.

The screams started maybe a half hour later. Screams from the Jap lines were nothing new. They'd often yell out things like, "Help me, Joe! I'm wounded. Oh God! Help me!" But they'd give up after ten or fifteen minutes because we never fell for it.

These screams were different.

They started something like, "Yeeeeeoww, you dirrrrty basssstards! Stop! Ahhhhhhh! God damn you!" Soon the curses and even words stopped. The voice, though, became louder…pure throat-tearing howls of unendurable agony.

"It's for real," Riegle said. "Filthy bastards are torturing some poor bastard. I bet it's Masters. They must have waylaid him in the rain."

All we could do was grind our teeth as the screams went on and on, gradually dwindling and finally, blessedly, stopping altogether.

The next morning we saw a body huddled on a slope maybe a quarter mile away. Under cover of a full company, we went out to bring in the corpse. It was Masters alright, but the only way to ID him was with his dog tags.

Japs had butchered him. They sliced between his fingers all the way back to the wrists. Both hands. They did the same to his cheeks, slicing from the corners of his mouth back to the angles of his jaws.

They'd also attended to his eyes, nose, ears and tongue.

As we brought his tatters down the slope, some Jap behind us yelled with a tittering laugh. "Hey, GI! We fix you buddy. We fix you, too. Cut up like sushi!"

Somebody in our party said, "Filthy fucking savages."

Up to that point, I was squeamish about shooting wounded Japs. I did so, but reluctantly . . . and only to protect myself and other GIs.

But after Masters, I had no hesitation. No thought. Just *Bap!* Right through the skull.

Chapter 73
Into The Mountain

"I hate this place," I said.

"Why?" Riegle asked. "It's beautiful up here. When it ain't raining, it's just like a nice cool autumn day back in Michigan."

"I'll tell you why, Charlie. Each morning I awaken here on Mount Imugan, the whisper of a cool breeze in the boughs and the sweet scent of pine needles seduces me. For just a second I'm camping again in the mountains with my folks.

"But then I get a whiff of some rotting corpse or I hear a mortar thump and it brings me fully awake. That's the start of every new day overlooking Yamashita Ridge."

I need to point out that Mount Imugan is the tallest and northernmost feature of the Caraballos. It's as if God laid down a semi-circular cluster of foothills with alternating jungles and savannas. We fought in them for two solid months, slowly driving the Japs into a zone where God stair-stepped a parallel set of even higher ridges.

Beyond those ridges lay Yamashita Ridge itself. Viewed from the Villa Verde Trail, Yamashita Ridge looks like a single massif. Yet it actually is just another set of yet higher multi-spurred scabby hills that overlook and command our positions.

Towering over the Yamashita Ridge cluster, in turn, stands Mount Imugan. They pronounce it "Ee-*moo*-gn." Most of us call it Mount Imogene,

Now, again, that mountain is not a snow-capped peak anywhere near as high as Mount Ranier in Washington or Mount Elbert in Colorado.

Nonetheless it's very steep, rugged terrain. It's naked in some places, but has many deep dips, dark woods, false crests and narrow forested ravines and other hiding places. In fact, thirty of us were able to hide in that mountain even though we shared it with a few thousand Japanese troops.

Of course we had to be on the move constantly. They knew we were somewhere on the slopes, but the never-ending attack by 32nd Division kept their attention riveted to the south. And we were doing all we could to support that constant attack.

Other than a few squad-sized parties, the Japs never found us.

Those who found us didn't live to tell about it.

It was Major Tagliarino from G-2 at Division HQ who gave us our send-off with a mission briefing.

"We're sending I&R into the mountain because, as the 127th and 128th regiments penetrate deeper into the Caraballos, G-2 needs eyes on Yamashita Ridge itself and on the Villa Verde Trail's two main passes -- Salacsac No. One and Salacsac No. Two.

"Those two choke points are at five thousand feet elevation. As the crow flies, they're about a mile and a quarter apart. Both passes and that stretch between them are just a goddamned shooting gallery for the Jap guns on The Ridge."

"Is it a straightaway, sir?"

"You wish. No. It twists and turns toward every point of the compass, but it trends more or less northwest to southeast.

"The point is this. The only way we're going to be able to seize control of that part of the trail is by infantry assault straight up those spurs into Yamashita Ridge. And the only way we're going to be able to do that is with lots and lots of air and artillery support.

"Now the reason we need your vantage point is that the passes are high enough that they're invisible from lower ridges to the south where our artillery is sited. Our guns can reach any place on The Ridge, of course, but the gunners and foreword observers can't see the targets or how close they're coming to them."

Captain Irish raised a hand. "Can't the Cubs do that kind of spotting and keep eyes on them?" He was referring to the Piper Cub observation planes that often circled over the hills like so many vultures.

"The monsoon kind of limits their flying time," the major said dryly. "Not to mention visibility.

"And even when the weather's good, they really can't fly low and slow enough to get the kind of detail we need. Nip antiaircraft fire will pick them off. Secondly, they might be able to spot a target. But they can't really linger long enough to talk the gunners onto target or to shift targets when the Japs pull a big gun out of a hole on The Ridge. Only a set of steady eyes up on the mountain can do that.

"The other thing," he went on, "is that in addition to Yamashita Ridge, there also are eighteen to twenty subsidiary hills that overlook those passes, too. Five will get you ten most of them have tunnels with troops and at least machine guns if not artillery in them.

"And between those hills, of course, are lots of draws and saddles where the Japs can set up mortars and howitzers and where they can assemble a platoon or a company for an assault."

I gulped. He was sending us way, way behind the lines for a long, long time. "So, I take it, sir, that our mission is to observe, direct artillery fire and aircraft strikes and stay out of sight."

"That's right," the major said. "And we've got all this coded, so you don't need lengthy transmissions. Check with your artillery liaison people. I understand you're clear to just call up and say, 'Flash Reptile Five Two Zero' and then send down corrections once the registration rounds land.

"The targets, the hill tops, are numbered west to east from 502 to 533 and the artillery battalions have all those coordinates zeroed in.

"Once you get up in the mountain, you might find a zone where the Cubs can drop supplies to you. But for the most part, you're going to be pretty much on your own."

"So how do we get up there, sir?"

The major gave me a flat look.

"Well, you could form up in a column of twos and just march up there in broad daylight. If it was me, though, I believe I'd try it on a real dark night. On all fours. And I'd plan on taking at least two nights. Three if you need them."

# # #

I tripped and fell with a huge splash into an abandoned foxhole on the side of the ridge we were climbing. "Well, shit. I don't think we need to worry about alerting Japs."

Captain Irish, the dripping silhouette standing above me, chuckled and nodded. "With the rain coming down this hard, I think our only real worry is getting flash flooded all the way to Lingayen Gulf."

We crawled, slipped and slid in three parties -- a five-man headquarters and radio team, plus two squads.

Thanks to patience, great caution and the rain's masking effects, we were able to make it up the mountain near dawn at the end of the second night. We were filthy, caked with mud and grit, and tired enough to sleep like hogs in a wallow.

The next morning came close to disaster, however.

I opened my eyes looking through some kind of evergreen bush and spotted two Japs about thirty feet away. They were undressed to their skivvies and doing their morning stretching dances. I got as far as muttering "Holy shi…" when an M1 barked behind me. That single shot slapped both men down.

Captain Irish gave a harsh whisper, "Hot shit! Two in one! Come on, let's get the hell out of here!"

Our little headquarters group raced deeper into the woods where we met up with Riegle's squad. Riegle wanted to question us, but the captain just gave him a come-along signal. We spent the rest of the day evading Japs and getting to know at least part of the mountain real well.

# # #

"Now Sergeant, ain't you glad you dragged that big-assed spy glass up here?"

"Lieutenant Ransome," I said, "go stick it in your ear. I admit it isn't real useful right now, but it will be."

Ransome, our forward air controller and once a Washington University classmate of mine, snorted as he peered out of our cave toward where Maleco should be. Maleco was a little village of Igorotes, the local hillbillies, just off the crest of The Ridge. It was one of our reference points in directing artillery fire and air strikes.

Unfortunately, clouds this morning cloaked the whole of our mountain and Yamashita Ridge. The only thing visible through my spyglass was a uniform dull gray. All we actually accomplished was to let Operations know we were in place, even if we were blind.

"Looks like I can take the day off," Ransome grinned. "I hope we get some clear weather so I can show you what our fly boys can do."

"Not to be an asshole, sir," I said, "but I sure hope they can do more for us than they could in Buna."

He gave me a grim nod. "That was before my time or before we even had Air Corps people on the ground. I think you'll find we do a lot better job nowadays. I hate to admit this, but we've borrowed a lot of procedures from the Marines."

Once the fog lifted, my Jap spyglass came in handy as hell.

I covered the scope's brass housing with pine branches so nobody could spot us. Then I visually scoured the ridge. I got to know the red sand bed at the crest of the western wooded spur, then moved along to a big cluster of artillery craters, then to the bare burnt tree trunks with white sand patches, bomb craters, among them.

At first, I couldn't see a living soul anywhere on that nine-mile stretch of foothill. In war, if you know what's good for you, you stay out of sight. But I made it my business to look for patterns and changes in those patterns.

The glass revealed a long wire fence beside a trail. Perhaps a quarter mile to the east of those features I saw a team of stick figures busy digging in red sand. Two men appeared to be guarding them.

"Hey lieutenant," I said. "Take a peek and check these guys out."

He peered. "Can't really tell a thing except they're piling up dirt. Looks to me like they could be civilians forced to work under guard." He surrendered the scope to me. We both made notes and then I returned to the scope.

"Hey, I've got some activity on 508. Looks like a cave to me, a big one, with some log revetments. I bet they have an artillery piece in there."

"Well, Jim, if you can't see it, you don't know, do you?"

"I don't know, Al. The more I examine it, the more I think it might be artillery.

"Here, take a look at how those revetments are stained. Could be from muzzle blast… Ho! Al, it *is* a gun! Look at that barrel. They're rolling that baby out to fire at somebody."

Lieutenant Ransome already was on the radio, calling for Panther Control.

The Japanese field piece, which I believed to be a 100 mm gun, fired four times. That apparently was the end of their mission because I then spotted a soldier running a large ramrod back and forth to clean the gun's bore.

"Here they come," Ransome said.

"Where?"

He pointed up and to the west as he spoke into the mike.

The man with the ramrod stopped and turned to look south. He scampered inside the emplacement, leaving the ramrod jutting from the gun's muzzle. He and his crewmates started rolling the weapon back into the cave.

It was a minute before I spotted the two insects in the clouds. They grew and I heard the drone of their engines. The drone changed to snarling whine. The planes, P-40s, banked to come in from the south. The first plane arrived with a roar I recognized – fire from its six .50 caliber machine guns.

The guns tore up the ground around the emplacement.

Speaking into the mike, Ransome said, "That's it, Panther One. You're right on target."

Maybe a minute later, the trailing aircraft dropped a pair of oblong cannisters which exploded in a boil of flame and black smoke that swept over the emplacement. Even at a half-mile distance, the heat registered on my cheeks and nose.

"Jesus, Al, what the hell was that?"

"Hell is the word, Buddy. It's napalm. It's jellied gasoline and fuel oil. Now watch this."

The first plane came in higher in a second run. It dropped two conventional bombs which, even at our distance, were shockingly loud and left. They transformed the artillery emplacement into a yawning pit.

"The Japs might put some more men in that hole," Ransome said. "But that particular artillery piece and its crew are done."

Chapter 74
Lowering The Boom

Captain Irish came to visit my team and he was blunt. "Men, you spend too much time dodging. They sent us up here to help the troops and we ain't helping enough.

"All of us have done enough combat time on the slopes to know exactly what the ordinary rifleman faces on Yamashita Ridge. His odds are lousy because now the division's got to get control of both passes – that whole damn shooting gallery. The Japs on Yamashita Ridge are looking right down on them and the only way to get control of the trail is to destroy those Jap positions by attacking head-on straight up-hill at them. Our guys in the 127th and 128th are attacking troops that just don't quit or retreat . . . not even when you have a gun to their heads.

"Head-on means climbing those slopes flat on your belly. You're looking for targets and hoping for a break as those white tracers snap the air just above you. Meanwhile knee mortars and regular mortars are falling all around you."

He paused and made a lot of eye contact.

"Look, they're risking everything, so we've got to help. We've got to pinpoint Japs concentrations, their tunnels and camouflaged positions. Lieutenant Ransome showed how to burn out an artillery site. Well, we've got to do a lot more of that."

# # #

We'd often spot mortar batteries when long afternoon shadows revealed muzzle flashes. So we'd radio "Rattler concentration 511. No danger close."

"Rattler" was a U.S. gun battery. The number 511 designated the hill behind which the Japanese sited their mortars. Then "81 battery with dismounted personnel," told gunners it was a battery of 81 mm mortars, usually three of those wicked tubes, each with a five-man crew.

"Add 50," told the gunners to increase their range so that the shells would pass just over the crest of Hill 511, thereby hitting near the Japs sheltering behind it. "No danger close" meant no Americans, including us, were in the line of fire.

Within five minutes – and sometimes less -- one of our artillery batteries would manage four to eight aerial bursts directly above the Nip mortars. From my vantage, I'd see the sudden cluster of bright flashes. A lot of dust and smoke would obscure the target. On breezy days, the bloody results quickly became visible.

I had no idea how the cannon-cockers managed to explode their ordnance above the Japs – it remained a top secret -- but the effects literally were slashing. One minute twenty-five men were setting up four mortars. After the barrage, I could see two or three figures moving feebly among a gory jigsaw puzzle of body fragments and punctured mortar tubes. We called it Jap hash.

Early one evening I called in a strike on a company of Jap infantry. I was able to count a hundred fifty of them standing in four ranks in a saddle between two rises. An officer, waving his sword, seemed to be haranguing them and, in response, they appeared to be shouting and pumping their weapons up and down in the air. Their words had to be *Banzai! Banzai! Banzai!* and they obviously were preparing to charge some American position.

They were much too far away for me to hear, but well within range of the 105 mm howitzers of the 126th Field Artillery.

We called for fire and the 126th saturated the saddle with ground and air bursts. I won't describe the spectacle but it delighted me.

In fact I was gushing next morning to Captain Irish about it. He frowned. "Listen, this is just a job. Don't get gleeful about it and don't let it eat you up."

"I'm not," I said, "but my attitude about Japs has changed. When Cap'n Bottcher first recruited me for this job he asked if I hated Japs. Well, I waffled about it. Told him about a Jap POW that I thought I could have been friends with. You know, I studied Japan and took a bit of the language. The subject fascinated me.

"Well after what they did to Masters, as far as I'm concerned they're vermin. For humanity's sake, we ought to wipe them out."

"Whoa, Jim, that makes you sound like taking on what the Nazis were doing to the Jews."

"That's different. Jews never did anything to anybody. But the Japs? Hell, they just seem to enjoy butchering people."

"The more I think about them," I said, "the more pessimistic I become. The 32nd Division has been fighting its way up the Villa Verde Trail for ten weeks now, and we still didn't control much more than nine or ten miles of it.

"If it takes this much time and this many casualties to gain control over a crappy little bit of hill country, I wonder how in the hell we can invade and defeat a nation of seventy million fanatics, and all of them being so willing to die for some cockamamie stuffed shirt who rides a white horse and who claims to be a god?"

Ransome was listening and he told me to drop it. "Jim, just bottle that up. We've got enough to worry about today. Just concentrate on the next cave. We take care of the future tomorrow."

Captain Irish said, "Look, I know how you feel about Masters. I saw some of that in China. But not all Japs are like that. I think the guys who did it are very bitter people. I mean, look, they *know* they're going to die. There's no hope at all for them. They've seen what napalm and white phosphorus has done to their comrades and they know that when we take them out, it's going to be hell. So they hate their fate and they sure as shit hate us for being the ones that are going to kill them and keep them from seeing their wives and children ever again. So it must drive them crazy which is why some of them do things like that."

"I don't care," I said. "Right now they scare the crap out of me. I've got a wonderful gal back in Hollandia and it looks to me like we're going to be exterminating these bastards for another five or six years. Frankly, I don't think any of us will survive."

Captain Irish glared at me. "Alright, dammit, stop being such a pussy. We have a job to do and if you do your job right, you'll survive."

When Dan Irish speaks to you that way, you shut up.

Besides, we did have a new worry.

Chapter 75
Making Progress

As the division pushed further east along the Villa Verde Trail, Captain Irish told us of a new problem. Our trucks, tanks and men now were coming into firing range of many Jap weapon emplacements which previously were out of sight behind one of the shoulders of Yamashita Ridge.

"At least the division at least has been able to bring a few tanks to bear," he said.

"They can pretty much sit out there in the open and fire on Nip positions. The Sherman does clean house when it can shoot a fifteen-pound shell into a cave at two thousand feet per second. Even so, its gun is only a 75, so it ain't powerful enough to bust a real bunker."

He explained, however, that the tank guns had neither the range nor the explosive power needed to deal with targets, particularly Jap howitzers, high up on the ridge or on Mount Imugan itself.

"And that," he explained, "is why the 126th Field Artillery is trying to move to within a couple of miles of the mountain's east shoulder. From there, they can clobber those high caves and emplacements. And with that arching trajectory, those howitzers also can drop their shells behind the ridge tops – as long as we can spot for them.

"The worry right now is whether the 126th can get their batteries into position – those damn guns weigh two and half tons apiece. And when they get them in place, then the worry is whether they can stay."

"What do you mean?"

"Their left flank will be exposed to Japs north of them, and there's no spare infantry to protect the guns. The gunners are going to have to do it themselves."

During the next two days, we watched the cannon-cockers hand-dig forty-foot circular firing platforms. Meanwhile they filled and place hundreds of sandbags around those platforms. They had to fill yet more sandbags to protect their ammo magazines from Jap shelling and mortars.

If you want to wear your old ass out, try spending a whole day filling, toting and placing sandbags. When day is done, you look about like a sand bag.

After that, often by hand, they had to haul their howitzers up the trail and then push them into position.

We did all we could to divert the Tojos' attention by sighting for the other artillery battalions and working with tanks. I swear every time a Jap stuck his nose out of his hole, we'd drive him back inside with a well-aimed shot or two. Heavy weapons companies also helped by providing mortar and machine gun support.

Lieutenant Ransome occasionally was able to call in a napalm strike, too. Unfortunately for us, the Air Corps was using most of its napalm to burn up Japs in the mountains east of Manila.

Even so, the Japs figured out what was happening. From up on the mountain, we agonized, being able to watch half the artillery boys dig in their guns while the other half repelled Jap patrols and an occasional banzai charge.

Once the 126th got its howitzers into operation, however, we could tell that they were making a hell of a difference.

For one thing, the east approaches to the mountain became permanently noisy with the drumming of cannon fire and exploding ordnance. The 126th had three batteries of four guns each and it seemed as if at least one of those batteries was firing around the clock.

Our fault, because we were keeping them busy.

It could be an hour before dawn and all we had to do was give a simple verbal code such as "Flash 521." You'd hear *whompidy whomph-whomp* and seconds later high explosives would start their crimson winking all over the crest of Hill 521.

Sometimes, all three batteries were in action for hours on end.

Aside from the almost constant bombardment noise, the howitzers of the126th were beginning to wear on the Japs. With white phosphorous, high explosives shells and air bursts hitting them day and night, Japs must have been dying in record numbers.

I don't mean to take anything from the division's other two artillery battalions. It's just that the close placement of the 126th was our main tool in scouring Japs from the eastern and southern faces of Yamashita Ridge and from Mount Imugan. It was the move that turned an impossible fight into a grinding advance toward a victory of sorts.

The Japs weren't withdrawing. But they apparently quit replacing casualties. Their attacks on the trail remained deadly as ever, but starting in May, they launched fewer, and weaker, attacks than in February, March and April.

More and more of the Villa Verde Trail was open, and the 32nd Division now pressed toward the same Cagayan Valley that Father Juan served sixty years earlier. The valley and the mountains north of it was where General Yamashita planned his last stand.

Our goal was to link up with the 25th Infantry Division – including our own 126th Regimental Combat Team – near a town called Santa Fe at the south end of the valley.

Sniping and an occasional small unit attack continued to kill and injure GIs on the trail until the war's end. But as the 32nd and 25th fought their way into the Cagayan Valley, Luzon's unbelievable downpours and consequent cave-ins caused the main interruptions on the supply line.

Meanwhile, headquarters ordered us to come down from the mountain.

Chapter 76
A Really Vulgar Brawl

Every time I've dined in an Army officers' open mess I've enjoyed chuckling at one of the service's favorite posters.

It depicts a disdainful aristocrat in 1790's uniform – tricorn hat, blue cutaway coat, gold epaulets, skin-tight white britches, silk stockings and shoes with gold buckles.

He's holding a delicate burning taper just above the fuse of tiny muzzle-loading cannon. The weapon is pointed at a grimy pile of scruffy little soldiers bashing each other with cudgels. Beneath is a legend:

Artillery lends dignity to what otherwise would be a vulgar brawl

The quotation is from Fredrick the Great. Though its wry humor might apply aptly to warfare in general, it certainly wouldn't fit the role which the 126th Field Artillery played in the last month of Villa Verde Trail combat.

The 126th may have lent some dignity to the battle, but its men had to conduct a very vulgar brawl all their own.

Evidence of the brawl was visible as we traipsed past one of the batteries during our return to headquarters.

Its guns still were firing sporadically, but the first thing we noticed was that the crews serving the guns were pretty much down to four staggering men instead of the usual eight. More telling were the tattered rows of sandbags on the north borders of its gun positions. Those sandbag walls had blocked so much fire from attackers that their outer margins now were mere sand piles with strips of burlap scattered here and there.

Too, the cannons had a mottled look thanks to dozens of silvery splotches where Jap bullets had struck the olive drab paint of wheels, breeches, trails and splinter shields.

I yelled to a platoon sergeant I'd gotten to know on New Guinea. He was perched on a row of sandbags and speaking into a field phone. The left sleeve of his shirt was missing and his bandaged arm was in a dirty sling. "Hey, Eddie, where is everybody?"

"Yo, Jim! They're either buried or in the hospital." He pointed, "Or sleeping over there." Despite the guns' slamming reports, three men were curled up asleep inside the north sandbag wall. They were lying on a virtual carpet of expended rifle brass.

Eddie yelled target corrections to a gunner supporting himself with a cane as he peered through a howitzer's scope.

"You wouldn't believe it, Jim. We've been our own infantry for three weeks now. Had to patrol constantly. They don't teach that at Camp Sill, so we learned it OJT.

"The kids would go out, get into a fight and come hightailing back and we'd swivel a gun or two around on the Japs with cannister rounds. Just sweep them away like a broom."

"Damn," I said, "I knew you've done a hell of a lot of shooting, but…"

"A lot? Hell, man, headquarters says all three batteries have fired more than 65,000 shells since we moved here. I just hope they don't want us to pull out until we've had a chance to sleep and get some new bandages. Look over there."

He pointed to a gaunt scarecrow with a field dressing on his left thigh and another concealing his left hand. Using his one hand, he slowly screwed the gold nose cap onto a shell. A wounded corporal tightened the cap. The scarecrow picked up the shell with his right hand, cradled it into his left elbow. He hobbled to the howitzer and bent to shove the shell into the gun's breech. He then wavered erect, stepped to the side, hauled on the handle to close the breech.

"Okay!" he said. He turned away as the gunner yanked the lanyard to fire the howitzer. He already was shambling back to get another shell as the gunner opened the breech, pulled out the smoking casing and tossed it over the right trail to the ground.

"He acts a little punchy," I said.

"You would too if you hadn't slept for 48 hours. We're all about to drop."

"Well where the hell are your officers?"

"Either buried or in the hospital, like I said."

"Well, we're headed to headquarters. Can I pass any word for you?"

"Yeah, tell the bastards we could use water and…"

"Yeah!" the scarecrow yelled, "and tell them to get somebody to drink it for us, too."

# # #

We got to headquarters about 2000 hours and they immediately ordered us into two deuce-and-a-halfs headed west on The Trail. Captain Irish protested. "I was in hopes of getting the boys a day or two off, maybe time for some decent food."

The G-3 captain shook his head. "Sorry, Dan, but we're in a race. We've got to link up with the 25th Division and the 126th. And night's the best time to travel The Trail."

"What's the rush?"

"The 126th overran Hill 530 this afternoon, so Imugan is now in our hands. I mean Imugan the village, not the mountain. The Japs used it as a staging center, but now Yamashita is trying to pull east to Santa Fe. So if we and the 25th Division get there first, he's got to abandon all kinds of supplies, disperse to an extent and retreat north into the Cagayan Valley and the hills on either side of it."

"And that tells me you want us scouting that area."

"As fast as you can. We've got to keep Yamashita off balance."

It wasn't my place to say a word so I stepped back out of the tent and into the rain. I said, "Shit!"

A tall skinny guy beside me in the darkness and rain said, "You can say that again." He chuckled. "I'm awful tired of the rain," he said. "But sometimes the sound of it helps me relax and think." He took a drag on his cigarette, offered it to me.

"Thanks, buddy. I've got some butts here but I lost my lighter."

"Here, take mine. I've got another in my tent."

"Thanks." I turned to take a close look at him and my jaw must have dropped. "Jesus! Sorry, sir!" I saluted.

It was General Gill looking about seventy years old. Giving a big sigh he said, "Don't worry about it. I wish we all could take a 30-day furlough. We need it. But we've got to keep kicking Yamashita's ass, so it just isn't in the cards right now."

"Yessir."

Captain Irish bustled out of the tent. "Get the men into the trucks, Sergeant."

# # #

I suspect everybody in the troop was grateful for the chance to ride after hoofing up and down Mount Imugan for better than a month. But it wasn't what you'd call a luxury ride. We felt packed in like sardines and the fit became tighter and tighter as the truck jounced over The Trail's potholes and ruts.

We were joking about our sore tailbones being a case of Villa Verde's Revenge.

But suddenly it stopped being funny.

I was in the lead truck so I heard Captain Irish and the driver both shout in alarm. The driver slammed on the brakes, jamming us all forward toward the cab. The vehicle slewed sideways and stopped. Seconds later, silhouetted by the second truck's lights in the slanting rain, Captain Irish came to the rear of the truck.

"We're stuck! Get out and form a perimeter." He ran to the other truck yelling, "Cut off your lights! Right now!"

We bundled out of the truck and I started positioning the men on both sides of the trail. In the process, I discovered the new twenty-foot roadway wash-out that caused our stop.

Captain Irish was on the radio to headquarters. "We're on the crest of the ridge just west of Salacsac Number One. It's a big washout. The trucks can't hope to cross it. So far no problems with Japs. Yeah. We'll wait for the engineers. No damn choice. Roger. Out."

Thinking to keep it light, I told him, "Well, this is another fine mess you've got us into."

He gave a bellowing laugh. "What are you going to do, Hardy, hit me with your bowler?"

Then he sobered. "Everybody dig in. Lots of Jap hold-outs with their Nambus are still up on there on Shit Ridge. When they see us at dawn all hell will break loose."

Chapter 77
Stuck Out In The Open

As the night wore on, I hoped morning would find Yamashita Ridge cloaked with clouds and fog as happened so often.

But, of course, the rain quit, the clouds sailed away and we found ourselves under sparkling clear skies. And, naturally, it only took the Japs about ten minutes to spot us and zero in on us with machine guns and mortars.

All I can say is thank God for all the mud. Mortar shells landed all around us, shredding the trucks and finally setting one of them afire, but the mud absorbed much of the shrapnel that otherwise could have slaughtered all of us.

As it was, mortar shells killed three of us and wounded five.

Captain Irish was one of the wounded, taking several pieces of steel in his upper back when one of the shells struck the front truck. We got his fatigue shirt off and tied several field dressings across his shoulder blades.

"Dammit," he groaned, "I was hoping to make it through this one without hospital time."

"Sir, will you please quit bitching? It depresses me."

"Too damned bad, sergeant. Now listen, I'll recommend they let you take over. You and Riegle know this business as well as I do and I don't think they've got any spare officers at HQ anyway."

"What about our artillery and air controllers?"

"They're officers, but they don't know dick about night operations. You two sergeants do."

He was in considerable pain, but he wanted to tell me his thoughts about the Cagayan Valley.

"Some of the old-timers told me the hills on both sides of the valley are really tough, mainly jungle in their lower reaches. But once you climb out of it, you're in Yamashita Ridge all over again.

"Matter of fact," he added, "that's where the U.S. Army defeated the Philippine Insurrection. General Funston captured Aginaldo or whatever his name way back at the turn of the century. Things pretty much quieted down after that."

He grinned.

"But Yamashita ain't gonna give up that easily."

Every few minutes, Jap bullets came hissing over or clanged into one of the trucks. We were dug in well enough that nobody was getting hit. Some of the guys, in fact, were able to doze.

That all stopped about noon when the engineers got a Cat up to us. He pushed both trucks off The Trail and, still under fire from The Ridge, backed and shoved until he filled the wash-out and carved a new road across it. With him came a Sherman tank that stood by to blast the Jap caves that had been firing at us.

By midnight, we got Captain Irish and the other wounded to a field hospital and linked up with the 126th.

And now I was the temporary commander of a reconnaissance troop, actually just a squad. It was a job I really didn't want. But then I don't think anybody wanted any of the jobs in northern Luzon because what I called the Leyte Effect seemed to be in operation.

By that I mean our constant attacks now into the Cagayan Valley and its adjoining hills were compressing the Japanese forces – at least the ones we faced – into a smaller and smaller area. For us in reconnaissance, that made it much more difficult to sneak around undetected behind their lines.

For the poor bastards in the American line infantry, it also seemed to mean more desperation and sheer savagery on the part of the Japanese. They had a tendency to attack more often.

I remember one G-2 report referring at one point to the Japs as nowadays launching "poorly executed linear attacks."

From the contemptuous viewpoint of the author – no doubt a VMI or West Point valedictorian -- I suppose you could agree those attacks were poorly executed. After all, they usually were hopeless and resulted in the deaths of almost all the attackers.

But poorly executed or not, those attacks also had a way of killing GIs.

From a half mile away, we helplessly watched such an attack late one afternoon. We spotted a party of Jap soldiers assembling in a cluster of boulders overlooking a GI patrol moving through a field. The GIs had a point man well to the front as well as two flankers. But they obviously couldn't see the Japs and we were too far away to warn them.

We called for a fire mission on the ambushers, but the FDC apparently had a stack of such requests and couldn't respond quickly enough.

Whatever the case, the Jap officer and his men waited until the point man passed. They raced out from their cover, immediately killing the point man and one flanker. The GIs in the patrol, probably all veterans, hit the deck and concentrated their fire on their assailants. In fifteen minutes it was over. The surviving GIs were wandering among thirty-some Japanese bodies, carefully shooting the wounded.

From our distance, we couldn't tell for sure, but it looked like at least five Americans were dead.

Later Riegle told me, "Well, the only victor down there was death. That fight didn't accomplish another damned thing. In fact, I don't think what we're doing has accomplished anything. The war just keeps going and going."

I thought he was exactly right. But I didn't dare say that.

We were trapping more Japs in the hills and getting people killed right and left – certainly more Japs than Americans.

But it didn't seem to me that we were one inch closer to anything like a victory. For every enemy group we shelled, another always managed to pop up, fighting like crazy. And even though the division had overrun and captured tons of Japanese supplies – and even though we occasionally could call in a napalm strike on big caches of rice -- General Yamashita's troops never seemed to lack food or ammo.

Every time we headed up into the hills above Cagayan Valley, we knew the Japs were around us in their thousands utterly determined to kill as many GIs as they could. And all I could see ahead of us was year upon year of trying to exterminate an enemy that wouldn't quit fighting.

And once we invaded Japan, there'd be no more natives like the Filipino resistance scouts to guide us in the hills or fight on our side. Instead every school boy and momma-san would ambush us. It depressed me beyond belief. I tried to be businesslike if not cheerful, but it was just an act and probably a bad one.

Previously I always was able to sit down with Captain Irish for a few minutes and blow off some steam about how we were doing or how things looked. Then he'd either give me some kind of reassurance or tell me to snap out of it and get back to work.

It always seemed to help.

But now he was in the hospital. As far as Riegle and the other kids were concerned, I was the new Cap'n Irish. That's when it hit me: the captain led us for damn near three years, absorbing the depression of all those losses, with nobody to boost *his* morale.

Talk about scary.

But when people depend on you, you soldier on trying to ignore the worries that you can't do anything about.

# # #

On June 5, we had a miracle.

Riegle came to me just as I used to come to Cap'n Irish. "I don't know," he said. "This just seems to get worse and worse. The Japs around here are thick as fleas."

I slapped him on the shoulder. "Charlie, you know what Mom used to tell me?"

"What?"

"She said it's always darkest just before the dawn."

"What the hell is that supposed to mean?"

"Well, I think it means that things are going to look up."

"Can you give me some kind of guarantee?"

"Well, hell no, but…" Just then our radio man came trotting up, a big grin on his face. "Hey, Sarge, guess what? They're pulling us back for some R and R."

Riegle stared at me. "Jim, how the hell did you work that?"

"Well, like Mom always said…"

He made a very rude noise and walked away.

For the first time in a month, I think, I managed a grin.

Chapter 78
The End Is Near

So it was a mixed miracle.

Here was the deal.

They moved us to a camp outside the town of Naguilian, a quiet little burg south of the Cagayan Valley. It was hot, humid and often rainy, but very, very comfortable in the sense nobody was shooting at us or subjecting us to mortar barrages. No sniping.

Hot, humid weather no longer was a big deal for us. Except for the few replacements that were filtering in, we were hardened, bronzed veterans of the tropics. And now we even had a chance to let our spongy feet dry out and recover some of their tone. Hell, we even were going to get two warm beers a day.

When our little reconnaissance group settled in, I gave one of the shortest talks on record.

"Guys," I said. "I've got good news. Headquarters says we're gonna be taking it easy for a bit. For now, anyway, you can just saunter around without having to look for cover. In fact, you can cultivate that civilian habit of only looking both ways when crossing streets."

They chuckled politely.

'You've got the rest of this day off. Starting tomorrow, we'll be running some security patrols." Before the groans got a good start I added, "But they'll be motor marches, not hikes. In the afternoons, we're going to play lots of baseball. And…"

Dempsy held up a hand. "Can we play football instead of baseball?"

"I don't give a rat's ass what games you play. If Special Services has a damned football and you can find some bare ground, knock yourself out. The idea is that you keep active and stay in shape, because in the mornings, we're going to be training."

"Training for what?"

"Well, that's the bad news. We're going to be training for the invasion of Kyushu."

"Where's that?"

"It's the southernmost island of Japan."

Fifteen pairs of eyes became hard as stone.

Pfc. John Sears, a replacement just back from medical leave said, "I think I'd like to put in for a transfer."

The boys gave a sour laugh, but he said, "Hey, I'm not kidding. Do you saps realize what we face? You've heard all the scuttlebutt about Iwo Jima. Real heavy casualties because of the caves, booby traps and banzai attacks.

"And you know right now the Marines and Army are in that bloodbath in Okinawa, and the kamikazes are sinking about half the Navy."

I wanted to tell him to shut up, but figured it probably would be best to talk it out. So I chimed in. "Yeah, and don't forget how the Japs murdered so many citizens in Manila. We hear they just slaughtered people right and left – all of them non-combatants."

"Yeah," Riegle went on, "and General MacArthur was playing his support games again. He wouldn't let the Air Corps bomb Jap positions in Manila. He didn't want Manila's beauty destroyed because it had been his command back in the 20's."

"Right," Bryson said. "So that left the Japs free to turn the whole place to rubble on their own."

To me it sounded like Buna all over again. God knows what kind of foibles the general would exercise when commanding the invasion of Japan.

"So we're really going to do it?" Sears asked. "We're really going to invade Japan?"

"That's the way it looks right now," I said. "Next spring."

"So, to say the very least," he replied, "our futures look short and ugly."

Chuck Hickman, a corporal also back from the hospital, chimed in. "Yeah, you could say that, asshole, but I wish you'd shut your trap. We really don't need that kind of talk esssspecialy when I need to take a good long nap."

"Don't worry," Sears said. "Your nap will be eternal."

"Keep it up," Hickman snapped, "and I'm going to whip your sorry ass!"

"Knock it off! Both of you. This kind of bullshit doesn't do anybody any good. Now I think you should know we're going to be training with some new weapons that will help us deal with these bastards. And, just so you'll know, we won't be doing this alone. At the briefing this morning, they told us they're deploying three field armies from Europe."

Sears said, "Well, if I was running the show, I say we should just blockade Japan and let them all starve or surrender."

"Great idea," Hickman said. "Why don't you tell MacArthur about it over chow tonight."

Nobody laughed because it seemed like we were looking at a thousand Yamashita Ridges for the next three or four years.

Of course, none of us at this point had heard so much as a murmur about a program called the Manhattan Project. Nor had we an inkling about two B-29s named *Enola Gay* and *Bockscar* or the targets for which their crews were training.

Chapter 79
Security Patrols

At first we got the impression that I Corps just wanted to see how much gasoline we could burn up.

We'd load up a couple of jeeps and an uncovered deuce-and-a-half, everybody with a rifle, a .50 machine gun mounted above the cab, and head out into the countryside.

We'd drive to cover the Aringay area, then to head to Caba and back home to Naguilian. Maybe the next day, we'd reverse the route and drive all the way to Bauang and back. The division's regiments were dispersed throughout that general area, but most of it was open countryside with occasional farms.

"Theoretically," G-2 told us, "there are some stray Japs in the 32nd Division area who haven't been able to link up with Yamashita way up the valley. Just keep your eyes open and your fingers on the triggers. We also hear some Japs have stolen civilian clothes so that they look to us like natives.

"The idea hasn't worked real well, though, because Filipinos hate the Japs as much as we do."

It was on our third trip that we came across Patches sitting in the middle of a roadway. Patches was the name of one of the Piper Cubs that did observation work for the 126th Field Artillery.

The pilot, who was very relieved to see us, told us the plane got the name because it literally had several hundred holes where Nambu or Arisaka bullets and even 25 mm antiaircraft guns had struck it.

The hits had punched a great many holes in the wings and fuselage, but fortunately none ever hit any of the plane's pilots or any control wires or the motor.

On this occasion, the plane was down because the motor died. And the pilot – who had been all alone in hostile country -- was trying to clean Patches' blocked fuel line while looking nervously over his shoulder.

Two of my boys – Sears, the grouse, and Art Goodwin – were shade tree mechanics in civilian life. With the aid of a few ounces of gasoline from a jerrycan, they got the line cleared and a very happy pilot soon had his raggedy-assed plane back in the air.

He took a wide swing around us and then came gliding back with his engine off. "You got company!" he yelled and pointed. "A quarter mile ahead."

He restarted the engine and circled again, picking up altitude. That's when the FDC of the 126th got on our circuit. "Green Troop this is Reptile Base. Patches reports a dismounted platoon of Japs ahead of you. Want some help?"

"Reptile Base, Green Troop always enjoys red-leg help. What do you need from us?"

"Just stand by, Patches will call it in."

About two minutes later, we heard the ripping howl of a 105 round. It exploded well to our front in a cloud of smoke and dust.

"Green Troop, be advised that our sighting round caused alarm. The bad guys are running your direction. You should see our next splash about . . . now!"

The next explosion erupted maybe fifty yards from the first. Then, I guessed, Patches told the battery to fire for effect, because six shells landed in a line maybe four hundred yards ahead of us. Then three more exploded in the air over the same target area.

"Green Troop. Reptile Bases. Patches advises you're gonna need some brooms and shovels. He also says thanks for helping him get off the ground."

"Reptile Base, Green Troop places great value in those eyes in the sky. Thanks again. Out."

Patches flew over us one last time waggling his wings and waving.

We carefully approached the would-be ambushers and were able to secure two wounded prisoners. Like their dismembered comrades, each had a thick coating of dust deposited by exploding 105mm shells. It was hard to tell, but we estimated the artillery barrage had accounted for twenty Jap soldiers. The few bodies that were intact looked badly emaciated.

Most of the rest of June was quiet. We lazed around when we could. Played baseball when it wasn't raining, and finally got some training on the new breed of Sherman tank called the Satan.

The Army and Marines had been using Satans on Saipan and Okinawa, finding that they saved a lot of American lives. The demonstration we received was every bit as impressive as the training officer had predicted. And even when we were standing behind the tank, the heat from its roaring column of fire made itself felt on our faces.

The idea of broiling Japanese soldiers might have repelled me in 1942. In June of 1945 it seemed like a damned bright idea.

What gave emphasis to that feeling was one of our patrols late in June.

The lead jeep on our motor march ran down a screaming half-naked Jap who was sprinting at the driver with a pointed bamboo spear. The corpse was almost skeletal and all of his skin seemed absolutely pebbled with insect bites. He also had numerous leg and back ulcers.

Jake Stein, our corpsman, just shook his head. "Suicide by jeep," he said. "Stupid bastard must have lurked here in the brush to ambush the first GIs to come along. With his skin that way, he must have been suffering the tortures of the damned. Glad you killed him."

Riflemen from the patrol checked the adjoining brush-lined creek. They found nothing but a hollow in the creek bank that might just accommodate a crouching man. Inside lay a few empty crayfish shells and some fish bones.

Two other patrols had minor run-ins with wandering Japs. In both cases, the enemy soldiers tried hard to kill GIs.

# # #

"It's that attitude of theirs that gets me," Riegle said. "You didn't hear any stories about German soldiers pulling that kind of crap. Krauts are damned tough, but they've got enough sense to know when they're beat. These guys, though. Jesus! Just sitting in a creek bed, damn near naked, being eaten alive by bugs and just waiting and waiting for the first GI to come along. Can you imagine what it's going to be like going against a whole population?"

I took a deep breath. "Charlie just quit worrying about Japan for now. Pretty soon here we're going to have some other fish to fry."

"What do you mean?"

"Well, it's kind of like New Guinea all over again. MacArthur just yesterday announced that the Philippines Campaign has come to an end . . . except for some quote mopping up unquote."

"Mopping up?"

"That's right."

"And let me guess. The 32nd Division is going to do the mopping up?"

"Damn, you are one smart farm boy."

"And, Jim, just where are we going to be mopping?"

"Why we're going up to the north end of the Cagayan Valley, and then we're going to climb up in them thar hills to mop up General Yamashita and his Fourteenth Area Army."

"Jim, is this for real?"

"Afraid so, Charlie."

Chapter 80
The longest Month

I wish I could say we wound up the war in a blaze of glory.

Instead, amid the carnage of Manila The High Command – by which I mean Big Doug MacArthur himself – kept up its grim, sonorous publicity-reaping campaign for the cameras and mikes.

Naturally, there also was much bloviating about all the wonders of The Commanding General's Strategy and the Victories To Come over the Japanese nation.

Meanwhile we of the 32nd Division got the scut work.

By that, I mean we started the janitorial process of "mopping up" the supposed remnants of General Yamashita's forces. To do this, during July they scattered us piecemeal all across the northern end of Luzon.

I freely admit that during our month off, the 37th Division captured a very important crossing called Bagbac. The 37th and the 33rd Division then barreled north into the Cagayan Valley while the 11th Airborne Division landed in northern Luzon and fought its way south to meet them. The three divisions along with a division of Filipino infantry pretty much occupied the whole valley.

Enemy troops still were in the valley, but they were in relatively small units isolated from each other and unable reach or even contact Yamashita's headquarters which now retreated into Luzon's mountain interior.

It was our job to get out our mops and buckets and polish off the Jap units scattered in the valley and, above all, to keep the pressure on the Japs in the mountains.

Sometime after the war, General Eichelberger wrote that he believed the term "mopping up" should be banned from the military's lexicon. He said that it implies something routine and simple whereas it is, in fact, a cruel, murderous process calling for exacting preparation and exhausting efforts. And, he noted many of the guys wielding the mops – all hoping to go home soon -- often wind up dead.

To be blunt about it, all three of our regimental headquarters ordered their subordinate commands to "patrol vigorously" and to "destroy all enemy encountered." In another war years later, they called it "search and destroy."

To us in the reconnaissance troop, "vigorous patrolling" meant stealthily looking in every nook and cranny of the countryside – every patch of jungle, every high mountain wood, every draw and gulley plus every village. For larger outfits, the Japs often made it easy because they would attack any unit that came within range.

I started the month of July with fifteen men.

By August 6, seven of us remained alive and well. We had spotted several concentrations of enemy troops over the past five weeks and the 126th Field Artillery had "neutralized them," as gunners like to put it.

Then that afternoon, a Jap machine gunner put three bullets into Art Goodwin's chest. We called the 126th for help and five 105 shells cleared out that rat's nest by flattening the little grove of trees in which it was located.

When we investigated, we found one dead Jap and his broken Nambu. Talk about overkill.

I believe it was about that same hour that Colonel Paul Tibbets and the *Enola Gay* dropped Little Boy on a mid-sized Japanese port named Hiroshima.

None of us ground-pounders heard a word about that first atomic bomb. But by August 9 when *Bockscar* dropped Fat Man on Nagasaki, the word was starting to get out. The rumor mill had it that some tens of thousands of Japanese civilians were killed in the attacks.

It was some weeks before we learned that the attacks immolated more than two hundred thousand Japanese civilians and soldiers.

These things happened long before opinion polls were fashionable, but I don't think I ever met an American soldier in the Philippines who had a moment's regret over the use of the A-Bomb. I won't say I was exactly happy about it. The scale of lives taken and damage inflicted was, to say the least, sobering.

But it was no more sobering to me than the past thirty-four months of suffering and death in the most rotten conditions imaginable. My comrades and I had a special perspective, the prospect of at least another year or two of grinding combat against the suicidal natives of the home islands.

Finally, the A-Bomb also gave me hope for the first time that I might survive the war and be able to have a life with Suzanne.

With that hope came anxiety. After those hammer blows of Hiroshima and Nagasaki, the Japs would surrender, right? That's what Riegle, Bryson, and Metz and the others kept asking me.

I was unable to give them an ounce of reassurance because the Japanese troops we encountered showed no signs of surrendering. Some of them looked as if they were starving. Others seemed quite healthy, but they weren't quitting.

We encountered squads or even platoons of Japs in which only half the men had firearms. The rest carried knives or makeshift spears and willingly died when attacking us with them.

# # #

We received orders from headquarters to come in from the field to rejoin A Company of the 127th. They needed every man they could get and our reconnaissance team now was too small to be of much use.

So the company commander put us on outpost duty.

That was on August 12. Rumor Central had it that the Japanese government was negotiating with the Allies now.

August 13 was quiet, giving rise to new hope. Same thing on August 14.

Just after dawn on August 15, one of the men on our perimeter fired a flare which illuminated a big band of Japs racing uphill toward us from the shadows below. They were fifty yards away. The instant the flare lit them up, they began screaming *Banzaaiiiii! Banzaaiiiii!* Their eyes were bulging and their mouths were wide.

Riegle opened up with the .30 and the rest of our squad started shooting and throwing grenades. *God why couldn't I have a flame-thrower tank now?* They outnumbered us, but so what?

"Easy men!" I yelled. "Aimed shots. Take your time. We'll nail them all." And if you ignored the whine of bullets coming past us, it really was easy to hit them. They weren't even trying to take cover.

Five of them actually got to our wire which is where the .45 is so marvelous. I don't care how hopped up somebody might be on sake-sustained fervor for Hirohito, a 200-grain slug knocks him on his ass – permanently – every time.

The problem, though, was that the Japs on the ridge across the way kept shooting.

Nothing was going right and I was grinding my teeth. Snipers wounded two of my men and killed a third. Rain and fog frustrated me in trying to see whether movements in the hills might presage another attack.

So when the Pfc. said, “Hey, guess what, Sarge?” I snapped at him.

“Pipe down, dammit!”

Voice rising, he said, “For Christ’s sake, Sarge! The war’s over!”

“Bullshit!”

He held out his walkie-talkie to me. “Listen to it for yourself, Sarge! Headquarters just said Japan surrendered. We’re to cease offensive action. The war’s over.”

I pointed up toward the crags and razorback ridges across from us. “Yeah? Did anybody bother to tell those bastards shooting at us?”

“Jeeze, Sarge, don’t yell at *me*! I’m only telling you what …”

Somebody behind us yelled, “*Down*!”

As I dived into the muddy slop at the bottom of my foxhole, the faint metallic chatter from the walkie-talkie continued. Four mortar shells exploded around us. The Pfc. screamed. Four more mortar rounds silenced him. Four more landed and then I lost count.

By the time it ended, pieces of Pfc. and his walkie-talkie were strewn all over me and two other guys.

Maybe Japan had surrendered.

But World War II sure as hell didn’t seem to be over.

Chapter 81
The Forever Month

The Japs just kept at it.

So did our high command. They wanted us to attack and keep attacking.

We did exactly that.

One of the officers at headquarters tried to boost our morale by comparing us to steamrollers flattening out columns of ants.

It was a bad analogy. To an ant, a steamroller is an overpowering and impenetrable force. But our men were highly penetrable. And the ants were shooting real bullets and mortars.

We all seemed to have a case of split personality. We desperately wanted to quit fighting and to survive. We *knew* we had defeated Japan. They were down for the count and if the Air Corps was to be believed, their country was nearly destroyed.

But those vicious khaki-clad sons-of-bitches didn't have the gumption to quit and we were in a snarling rage about it.

One of those youngsters made an utterly hopeless charge into my position. His weapon was a six-foot bamboo pole with a bayonet lashed to the end of it. The bayonet was just dangling because the rattan ties had come loose. The weapon probably couldn't have done much more than gouge my skin. But he was one of five attackers. Three were carrying firearms and, as he ran, a fourth slammed a hand grenade against his own helmet.

I shot him first so that he and his now-armed grenade fell together, exploding a second later. Then it was the turn of the kid with the bamboo bayonet. I had my .45 aimed right at his contorted, screaming face. He kept coming.

At ten feet, I pulled the trigger and that big bullet blasted his skull apart. His remaining comrades died in a fusillade of shots from my squad.

Looking at their bodies, we found three of them had makeshift bandages over either badly infected wounds or tropic ulcers.

"Stupid, stupid assholes! Why didn't you stop? Our medics could have treated you."

Riegle shouted, "Goddamn idiots! What was the point in attacking us?"

"Charlie," I said, "the point was *Yamato damashii* – Japan's unconquerable spirit. And it died with him."

That little banzai attack occurred late the afternoon of August 30 just hours after we received orders to hold our positions. Again they ordered us to cease all offensive operations but to remain fully locked and loaded, prepared to defend ourselves.

After the attack, Riegle sauntered over to me.

"Jim, considering that order, do you think this is really it?"

"Charlie, I sure as hell hope so. But I'm keeping my powder dry and I think it might be wise to double our guard tonight."

"Why?"

"Well, let's just say I'm superstitious. I want this to be over so goddamn bad! I *ache* for it be over. I hope to high heaven it's over. I pray that it's over. But I don't want to get killed just in the eleventh hour. So let's stay very, very alert."

"Okay, boss."

Two sleepless nights and three days later General Yamashita and his staff surrendered.

They stepped before two of our officers and two squads from I Company, First Battalion of the 128th Infantry.

The I Company boys told us Yamashita offered to shake hands but that Colonel Barlow, the division chief of staff, just stared at him.

So Yamashita stepped back, saluted and bowed. Yamashita must have felt humiliated but, like most Japs, he kept an impassive face. He even was willing to autograph some military script for some of the guys in I Company.

It's too bad General Gill wasn't there to accept Yamashita's sword. Gill and Yamashita had been negotiating a surrender by exchanging written messages, the Japs supposedly awaiting final authorization from Tokyo.

But according to the rumor mill, our CO absolutely blew his cork, went a little crazy and was hospitalized. Later they said he was sent home on leave. We never got the straight skinny, though we heard he threw things at some of his staff.

Maybe it was because of yet another needless death.

The general had sent Colonel Merle Howe, who at one time or another had commanded all three of the division's infantry regiments, to meet with Yamashita. As it was circling to land near the Japanese headquarters, the Cub's engine died and the plane crashed. The pilot was merely bruised, but the colonel was killed.

Maybe General Gill never mastered General Eichelberger's technique of rationing his emotions.

# # #

We continued our patrols for weeks after the surrender. Yamashita claimed that our artillery and bombing had wrecked his communications and he wasn't in touch with some of his units.

A few more banzai attacks occurred in the 32nd Division's area, but in the second week of September, the bulk of Japan's Fourteenth Area Army came marching out of the hills to the town of Baguio where the MPs and the Red Cross took over.

The last I heard, the Fourteenth Area Army we'd been attacking amounted to just over forty thousand troops, outnumbering us about three-to-one. That discovery only deepened my gratitude about the A-Bomb.

We of the 32nd were gone by the time Yamashita's troops came out of the hills. Both commands thought it best to keep such fervent enemies separated.

So we returned to the peaceful shores of Lingayen Gulf where the beaches occasionally were tainted by fuel oil seeping from so many vessels resting at the bottom of the South China Sea.

Did we rest?

Not on your life. We were fitting in new men to replace those of us who now had the points to rotate home. The Red Arrow Division, a third of it brand new, was headed to Japan.

The 32nd, now part of Eighth Army, was to stand by and maintain the peace while the Japanese armed forces disarmed themselves.

Chapter 82
The Victory

Charlie Riegle was headed home. I was getting aboard a Military Air Transport C-47 for a special duty assignment with Fifth Air Force in Hollandia.

Charlie and I parted with a long handshake and very few words. Next week he was due to board an LST for a long, long voyage to San Francisco, and then the long train ride back to Mecosta.

We never got a chance to see or thank Captain Irish. They'd already sent him back to a hospital in the states.

The flight to Hollandia was tough on me.

Despite the drone of the plane's engines, it was far too quiet.

I was rigid and found myself gasping over and over again.

I finally figured out that I was holding my breath because I constantly anticipated something horrible.

# # #

Suzanne and I exchanged wedding vows in Melbourne and moved to Seattle where, thanks to The Badger's recommendations, she found research work with Bell Telephone.

Relying on the GI Bill, I finished my bachelor's degree in East Asian studies and went on to get a master's in international trade. In time, thanks to Suzanne's love, patience and tenderness, my gasping anxiety and nightmares petered out.

But we never exactly settled down because I traveled so much throughout the orient.

At first I refused to go to Japan. Hatred still foamed within me. In fact, because so much of the world still was trashed, I was beginning to regret trying a career in trade.

Then one night in 1948 I was having a scotch in one of the bars at Kai Tak Airport. A big man eased onto the stool next to mine.

"Jim, just what the hell are you doing in Hong Kong?"

It was Dan Irish.

"Hey, Cap'n! What are you doing here?"

We had a long, long talk. He was working for the U.S. Army Materiel Command and was busy reclaiming everything from airplane parts, abandoned trucks, Seabee bulldozers, mortar base plates and all the other military junk from Guadalcanal to Buna and from Okinawa to Luzon.

He also worked for an offshoot of the OSS. Today it's CIA.

When I said business wasn't going well, he recommended that I visit Japan and to locate a few dozen good machine shops.

"Cap'n, I don't think I could take being around those animals."

He just grinned.n"Get to know them," he said. "They're the best goddamn workers in the world. And take my word for it, MacArthur has achieved a miracle. The Japs worship him and they actually like Americans."

I just shook my head.

"Jim, listen, we're looking at another war soon. I think it will be in China because so much fighting already is going on there. Either way, we'll need Japanese industry."

It was the best advice I ever received. I found out Japan was healing itself and embracing Americans, literally and figuratively.

When the Korean War broke out in June of 1950 I was one of the reserve infantrymen called back to the colors. CIA and the Army Materiel Command intervened.

CIA wanted a source in Japan. I don't know why. Japan already was lousy with spies from just about everywhere. The Materiel Command, on the other hand, needed a contact with Japanese machining companies that were crying for work. American industry was too busy building homes and cars.

So Japan rebuilt its own economy by reconstructing U.S. tanks, rifles and trucks for the American Eighth Army and U.N. forces in Korea.

I never accomplished anything for CIA. But trade with the orient grew like gangbusters. What started with rebuilt firearms and cheap stamped-tin toys led over time to textiles, transistors, computers, Hondas and supertankers.

Suzanne was able to retire. I had to travel constantly so we saw the world together over and over and over.

I can't say we lived happily ever after.

But we're still living.

And happy, too, except for occasional nightmares.

About the Author

J. Scott Payne began his career as a cub reporter at the Kansas City Star. He served with the Army in Korea, Vietnam and – worst of all – Washington, D.C. Subsequently, he worked as a reporter and editor for several Midwestern newspapers and magazines. He and Jane retired to a small college town in west Michigan where they enjoy the woods, the birds and the battles -- or perhaps the games – taking place between Burt, their black cat, and Bailey, their white terrier.

If you enjoyed this story . . .

Please be so kind as to give it a brief honest review
at its site in Amazon Books

Made in the USA
Middletown, DE
28 October 2020